ENTER A H
OF LOVE

The Grandeur... The Romance... The Mystery
of

# CAMBERLEIGH

"Compelling! A brooding and romantic novel...
a fine mixture of historical and suspenseful
writing. You will be enthralled!"
—*Romantic Times*

"[Handled with] elegance and wit!"
—*New York Daily News*

### AND NOW...

The Splendor... The Passion... The Turmoil
of

# *MAYFAIR*

In this dramatic sequel to *Camberleigh*, Evelyn
Grey continues the passionate story of the elegant
Serena Miles. Her glowing love. Her shining ambi-
tions. And the shadows of envy, greed and jeal-
ousy that lurk behind the stately facades of
England's grandest estates. Enter the world of...

# *MAYFAIR*

*Berkley books by Evelyn Grey*

**CAMBERLEIGH**
**MAYFAIR**

# MAYFAIR

## EVELYN GREY

BERKLEY BOOKS, NEW YORK

To Barnaby
A man of dimension who adds
dimension to my life

MAYFAIR

A Berkley Book / published by arrangement with
the author

PRINTING HISTORY
Berkley edition / April 1986

ISBN: 0-425-08733-6

# *Prologue*

I have not been myself this past week. It is understandable, I suppose, since the tenth anniversary of my arrival at Camberleigh was bound to bring back memories. But I am surprised how vivid the events of a decade ago still are in my mind. And how their recollection is still a source of sadness and pain.

How young I was when I traveled these many miles by coach to a home and a family, who, until my mother's death, were completely unknown to me. At seventeen I was well read; I had known what it was to struggle, since, after my father's tragic death, my mother and I had led a meager existence. But I had been utterly protected from the true harshnesses of life—those borne of deceit and jealousy and evil.

Had I ever known what I was to encounter, I would have gone against my mother's wishes and never undertaken that journey. But then I would have never known my grandmother or cleared my father's name or discovered Justin's love.

There are certain events in life one never forgets—moments of experience that actually become part of one's own being. The moment I saw Camberleigh Hall—was one of those events.

It stood at the end of an escarpment—a spectacular creation of towers and turrets and crenellations. The effect was overwhelming—a castle I thought that indeed must be the most majestic in all England.

1

It was at once thrilling and frightening to think that this had been my father's ancestral home. And puzzling to know what would have prompted him to leave this obvious wealth and grandeur for our small cottage on the coast.

I was tingling with excitement over the prospect of meeting my grandmother, who, until a week prior I had not even known existed. Little did I know that the contents of the sealed letter of introduction which my mother had penned before her death would be met with such shock and distress. That I had arrived believing I would be welcomed with open arms into my family and heritage and instead had found myself compromised to accepting a position governing my young nephew, Oliver, had been a turn of events I could never have imagined.

Had it not been for Jaspar, my spaniel and ever faithful companion, I do not think I could have endured those first weeks at Camberleigh. He was the only vestige that remained of the warm and loving life I had known as a child.

Considering the distrust that my grandmother exhibited towards my claims, it was not surprising how my uncle, his wife or my cousin, Clarissa, reacted to me. After all, to them I was but a hired governess—a necessity but not a welcome one.

It was Oliver who, unknowingly, helped me keep my senses those first weeks. He was so young and frail and so grateful for the smallest assist or show of affection.

Nor can I forget the supposed kindness that Thomas, Oliver's tutor, extended to me upon my arrival. I still cannot fathom how I could have been so mistaken about him. Perhaps I was too desperate for friendship to have perceived his true character. More likely, his maniacal nature could have duped anyone—and indeed did so.

I still tease Anne, Justin's sister, that she will always be my fairy godmother. She insists that the gowns she provided so that I might attend the balls at Camberleigh and Kelston Manor were to her benefit since she was eager that her designs be recognized throughout the county. I know that it was merely her generous and willful nature, but I have always been secretly pleased that her creations have since become the toast of the continent.

Anne and Richard have truly been happy together in marriage. Admittedly, I have never felt the closeness that I might towards my uncle, but I am grateful that Anne has given him some of the happiness and solace he had missed in his relationship with Maura.

Maura. Justin and I rarely speak her name. It is still almost inconceivable to me that it was by her hand that my grandfather was murdered. And by her design that my own father was blamed, so decidedly that his own mother, my grandmother, banished him forever from Camberleigh. Had it not been for my presence, the secret would have died with Maura and my father's good name and my heritage never been returned. Although the discovery and revelation of that secret almost brought about my own demise, I shall always be grateful that I was in time to save Oliver's life from his mother's madness.

Oliver never refers to his mother. At first, this troubled us all, fearing that he was repressing his true feelings about her not only in life but in death. But with time I have come to see that it is simply his own way of coping with the knowledge that Maura's twisted mind was not capable of love, even of her own son.

I have taken such joy in watching him grow from that frail sickly child who was my charge to a handsome adventurous young man, who is the adored elder brother-figure to Daphne and Alexander, our two children.

We have never told Clarissa the secret of her birthright. That she would discover that my uncle Richard is not her real father would destroy her and, I fear, her marriage, since her husband is quite as spoiled and pompous as she. By rights she has no claim to the Camberleigh estates, though neither Richard nor I would ever take such an action. And if Oliver suspects the truth, I trust that we shall never know.

The one great sadness over these past years has been that Juliette did not live to see our children born. We had only one year together after she had acknowledged me as her granddaughter. It was a happy year, one that I shall always cherish, but I see today that her mistaken blame of my father and the subsequent shock of Maura's guilt and death weighed too heavily on her already weakened heart.

Charlotte has often reminded me that she did live long enough to see her fondest wish fulfilled: my marriage to Justin. What a glorious day that was. Anne had designed the most beautiful gown of white silk, Alençon lace and seed pearls. Charlotte was so nervous she could scarcely fix my hair, but I think it was more the fact that she and her son Robbie had been invited to the wedding than because I was getting married.

I still remember now, as I walked down the aisle towards Justin, who was so manly yet regal in his finery, that I wondered how I could have ever doubted his love or mine for him. I had almost lost him to my own stubbornness and inability to forgive, a characteristic which he occasionally still reminds me to guard against.

Our life at Mayfair has been joyous. And yes, at times, tempestuous. Certainly never tranquil. I had loved this house from the first time I had seen it ten years ago. It has not the grandeur of Camberleigh, but architecturally, it is a warmer, more welcoming, home. I have not Anne's talent for botanical splendor, but with the help of the grounds people we have managed to keep the rooms filled with flowers throughout spring and summer.

Justin has made a great success of the Mayfair and Camberleigh estates. I worry that he drives himself too hard, but he will not heed my reproaches. The burden shall always be on his shoulders, I fear, for Richard simply does not have the commitment to the farms and estates that their fathers built and cultivated. Secretly I sense that Justin has hoped that Oliver might one day succeed Richard's involvement, though I think it dubious; well I know that Oliver longs to leave England and explore his own fortunes. Alexander, though the image of his father, is scarcely prepared, at five, to even commence understanding the onus of it all. His only responsibility today is caring for the filly we gave him for his birthday.

Sometimes, when I see the children playing and laughing together, I wish that we could freeze ourselves in that fraction of time forever. But I cannot spare them as my own parents could not spare me. Camberleigh was my heritage and my destiny. Mayfair is their own.

# 1

I was startled by hands which suddenly explored the nape of my neck. I did not have to turn to know that they were Justin's.

"What on earth are you doing sitting here staring out that window, Serena?" he asked as he kissed the top of my head. "You would scarcely think by the look of you that our guests will be arriving within a few hours."

I knew that Justin would not recollect the significance of the day's date, nor would he approve of my reverie, believing, as he did, that that part of our past was best left to fade to memory. I turned to him smiling.

"You fear, my lord, that I shall embarrass you by attending the ball in my riding habit?" I teased.

"Darling, you could never embarrass me. You are ravishing in whatever you wear. But I have seen the gown you intend for tonight, and I admit it is far more alluring than your habit," he replied.

I watched him as he poured tea from the silver service on the table before us. These last ten years had only served to make him more handsome, more appealing. The light sprinkling of grey about his temples added a distinguished air to the strong, tanned planes of his face. Seeing him now looking so fit, I felt foolish for my concerns of his overworking. If anything, he appeared to thrive on it. He handed me a cup of tea, watching me closely as he did.

"Am I imagining things, Serena, or are you preoccupied?" he queried.

I shook my head. "I was just thinking how pleasant it will be to have everyone here again. I had scarcely realized that it has been months since I've seen Anne or Richard and even longer for Monique and Robin."

"I am anxious to see old Cobbett again," Justin mused.

"That man!" I exclaimed. "If I recollect the last time he was here, he convinced you to import four hundred locust trees from America. I shudder to think what next venture he will be convincing you of."

Justin laughed. "That is hardly charitable of you, my dear, since I cannot think of a man who is a greater champion of yours."

I knew what he said was true. William Cobbett and I shared a respect for one another. I think he found my vocal stands on politics, farming and the like to be somewhat refreshing. It was not in 1822 considered fashionable for a young woman, particularly one of nobility, to voice her opinions on such subjects, but I had never led my life by what was deemed fashionable.

Cobbett was indeed a fascinating character. In the early part of the century he had commenced publishing *The Political Register*, where he commented on everything from the need to expand farming operations to the brutality of the punishment known as flogging, the latter treatise which landed him in Newgate Prison on a charge of libel.

It was only natural that he and Justin should become friends since both were violently opposed to taxation. Although he was a champion of the laborer, he had respect for the landed native gentry who not only intimately knew but cared well for his tenant farmers. And that certainly was an apt description of Justin.

A knock at the door interrupted my thoughts. It was Charlotte with Jaspar, who bounded by her and into my arms.

"Oh, Miss Serena, aye be apologizin' fer the little one, but he's got 'is nose out a joint, that one, since Cook won't pay him no attention."

"No bother, Charlotte," I replied, laughing as my spaniel showered me with love.

I tried to be attentive as Charlotte outlined the menu for the evening, yet my mind was not attuned to poached tile fish and roast pheasant. Our cook, though temperamental, was a genius at preparation and presentation, and thus I scarcely gave any thought to the meals at Mayfair.

Charlotte took such pride in her role as housekeeper at Mayfair. I had never regretted my decision to install her as such after Justin and I were married. There were many I know who had doubted the wisdom of my decision since Charlotte had been but an upstairs maid at Camberleigh. But no amount of experience could compensate for the loyalty she had shown me from the first. And in truth she had risen to the challenge of the task and had proven herself thoroughly capable of managing one of the largest estates in the land.

The children adore her. And I scarcely feel she would care for them better if they were her very own. I have thought of late, however, that I will have to face the fact that Charlotte is getting older and is not as able to care for two spirited children as she once was. That madcap of black curls is now grey, and though the eyes still twinkle when she smiles, there are many lines which can hardly be deemed laugh lines.

"Would ye be wanting me to bring the children to ye down 'ere?" Charlotte asked, having completed her recant of the dinner preparations.

I shook my head. "No. I am going up to the nursery now, Charlotte. I want to spend some time with the children before the guests arrive."

I rose and turned to Justin. "Will you join me, darling?"

When he responded he needed to spend some time at the stables with Robbie, I was disappointed because the children adored his frolicking with them. But he was actually very generous with his time with them, considering that the running of the Mayfair and Camberleigh estates was an all-consuming job.

I kissed him quickly and smiled inwardly as he pulled me to him turning my light show of affection into passion. If anything, our lovemaking had only intensified over the years. I was always surprised when at occasional dinner parties or luncheons how many of the women, set upon gossiping, would admit to shrinking in horror from their husband's advances. I would flush with embarrassment thinking how horrified they would be to know of the lust I held for Justin.

Sensing that he had quickened my responses, he teased, "Now, if you would invite me to the bedroom instead of the nursery I might be able to waylay my trip to the stables."

I laughed. "You are incorrigible you know."

"And you love it," he replied.

"You are correct, sir," I acknowledged. "But I hardly think it would be appropriate if our guests arrived only to find their hosts abed. So if you will unhand me, I will go to the children."

"You might not get another chance," he mused as he spun me away towards the door with a pat to my derrière.

"I will gamble that," I tossed back as I left him grinning at me in the drawing room.

I fiddled with the spray of flowers I had arranged in the entrance hall. The roses were particularly lovely this year and I was pleased that I had been able to convince Mister Rawlings, the head gardener, to cut an extra abundance for the weekend festivities.

As I climbed the staircase I looked at the portraits of Justin's parents which hung in a niche towards the top. It saddened me that they had both died before I came to Camberleigh for I am certain that we would have been very close. It was uncanny how much Justin resembled his father. The same high cheekbones, strong jaw and dark waving hair. Only his eyes, which changed color I insisted with his moods, revealed the heritage from his mother.

The children squealed with delight as I entered the nursery, less from delight of seeing me, I think, than from the opportunity to cast aside the lessons they were doing with their tutor, Master Farraday.

"I did not mean to interrupt, Jonathan," I offered, knowing that he was fastidious about privacy during his lessons.

"We had almost concluded, Lady Barkham," he replied.

Jonathan Farraday had come to us three years ago when Daphne was five. Many of our friends considered it foolish to employ a tutor for a girl at such a young age, believing that matters of embroidery were far more important than matters of the mind. But I was insistent that my daughter should be afforded the same advantages as my son. Not able to afford a tutor, my own father had commenced teaching me my letters very early and it had stood me in good stead. I doubted that Daphne would ever, as I had, have to prepare for a life of service to another, but I did not want her to grow into one of those insipid women whose only conversation would be of the latest fashions. No—I wanted my daughter to grow into a woman whose brains were a match for her beauty.

And a beauty she was going to grow to be. Justin said she was the image of me and I admit that my appearance was very similar at her age. We have the same red gold hair and fair skin and I trust that she, too, will be considered tall for a woman. Our eyes separate us. Not by size or shape—we share the open almond shape and prominent brow—but by color. Where mine tend to green, Daphne's are the color of violets; when I look into them I feel as if I am able to look into my grandmother Juliette's eyes when she was Daphne's age.

Alexander came over and sat on my lap. "Mother?" he said pulling at the gold braid on my riding costume.

"Yes, darling, what is it?"

"Daphne says that we cannot go to the ball, is that true?"

"I fear it is, my love. It shall be far too late for you to stay up and there will be no other children there. Besides, I need you both to watch over Jaspar."

"There, you see, Alex," Daphne pouted, looking very smug.

"I told you that you would not be allowed to go."

Daphne had an unfortunate habit of liking to lord over her younger brother. And until recently he had been intimidated by her imperious manner. I knew that my young daughter was going to be in for some surprises from now on in her interactions with Alexander. He had found his voice and there was a clever mind at work under those dark curls. It would not be long before Daphne would discover that she had met her match in her baby brother.

"What are you thinking, Mother?" Daphne asked.

"I was just realizing how you both have grown and wishing that I could slow the process a bit," I replied wistfully.

"Will Oliver be coming this evening?" she asked coyly.

I nodded, amused by her interest in Oliver. He was, after all, a cousin but one admittedly who doted on Daphne. And he had grown into a handsome young man.

"You mustn't trouble him while he is here, darling," I warned.

"Oliver likes to be with me," she retorted. "He has even told me so."

"Then he is stupid," Alexander quipped.

"You are the one who is stupid, Alexander Barkham," Daphne retorted.

"That is quite enough from both of you," I snapped as Alexander climbed off my lap.

"Would you like me to work with the children tomorrow, Lady Barkham?"

I turned, surprised to see Master Farraday still in the room.

"That will not be necessary," I replied. "There is to be a hunt tomorrow and I am quite certain that my husband will permit the children to watch the festivities. If you would like to attend yourself, please feel welcome."

"That is very gracious of you, Lady Barkham, but I would like to visit my sister in Sussex, if you will not be needing my services."

"Of course," I responded, thinking that the man appeared to have few friends and certainly not much life other than the training of the children.

If humorless, he was indeed a good tutor. I had been somewhat chary of him at first, but I think it was a leftover reaction to my nightmare with Thomas Masters, who had been Oliver's tutor at Camberleigh. As Justin had assured me, the chances that Master Farraday would be or do anything untoward was almost not calculable. His references were impeccable and his methods, though strict, appeared to have achieved success with both children. Daphne is very verbal and has a good ear, which should help her in the study of French. Alexander is responsive to any and all adventure stories, and I hope that as he matures that will translate into an interest in history.

"Mother, will you come and show me your gown before the ball commences?" Daphne pleaded, forcing me to realize that it was well past the time that I should have commenced dressing.

"If you promise to stay very quiet and eat all your dinner, your father and I shall look in on you for a few moments before we go down," I replied, rising to leave.

"I promise," the children responded in unison.

I suspected that Daphne, who was a somewhat finicky eater, would pawn most of her meal off on Jaspar, but I was not about to challenge her pledge. As I opened the door I saw that Jaspar was curled up waiting outside. I bent down to him, laughing.

"I should have known you would have followed me up here, little one," I said, scratching an ear. "You go inside and watch over Daphne and Alexander."

Having placed him inside and bidden a pleasant weekend to Master Farraday, I crossed the long hall to the wing where Justin and I had our suite of rooms.

Justin's father had constructed the bedroom suite with two sizable bedrooms, one for him, one for his wife with an enormous living space and library in between. There were few major changes I had made at Mayfair since our marriage save that one. I had the one bedroom opened up into the other, using the second bedroom as a library for Justin's penchant for late-night studying of his ledgers.

The central focus of our bedroom is—appropriately so— our bed, which was crafted in the Chinese manner with a pagoda-like canopy and lacquered in black and gold. The fabric hangings at the posts match the hand-painted wallpaper which we imported from China.

I was shocked to see Justin almost fully dressed as I entered the room.

"I am not that late, am I?" I asked, admiring how handsome he looked in his pantaloons and waistcoat.

"I wanted to be early," he assured me. "I am expecting a few associates and would like to spend some uninterrupted time with them."

"Oh, Justin," I chastised, "you promised to put business aside this weekend."

"Serena, these estates do not run themselves, you know."

"I understand that, but I thought that now that you had turned the overseeing of the tenants over to Robbie you would have more time."

He tugged at his cravat before the mirror. "Robbie is doing a fine job, Serena, but you have to understand that he is not born to this responsibility."

"I am surprised at you, Justin. You have always been a champion of the common man," I retorted as I commenced to remove my garments. "I would hate to have Cobbett hear you say that."

"You misunderstand me, darling. Robbie is bright and in time he may exceed even my own hopes for him. But being Charlotte's son he was not raised to have any understanding of the complexity of these affairs. He was a groom and a good one but one who would never have known his letters had not some governess taken him under her wing."

That part I had to admit was true. When I had come to Camberleigh and was forced to live under the guise of governess, it was Robbie who cared for Jaspar during the days.

I could not afford to pay him but had offered to tutor him as reciprocity. His eagerness made him an apt student and I had been delighted when Justin had suggested bringing him to Mayfair as the stablemaster. Robbie had grown up with the tenant farmers and many of their children, and it had seemed very natural when Justin took him under his wing and encouraged him to take over the day-to-day interaction with the farmers. They trusted Robbie—he was one of their own. Not that I suspected that my husband was not on good terms with them. It was only that the title and power that went with the Mayfair and Camberleigh estates proved intimidating to most.

"Justin, would you stop in to see the children before you go down?" I asked, consciously changing the subject. "I fear that I promised them and they will be devastated if you do not make an appearance, if only briefly."

He came towards me smiling. "Your wish is my command."

I was brushing my hair before the mirror and he reached down and withdrew the brush from my hand, placing a gray velvet box in its stead.

"What is this?" I asked, my eyes searching his in the mirror.

"Open it and find out," he replied, a sheepish grin spreading across his face.

I placed the box on the dressing table and unwrapped the band which sealed it. Inside lay an exquisite necklace of alternating emeralds and diamonds fashioned in a single strand with matching earrings. I stood up and threw my arms about him.

"I have no idea why I should receive such a gift today but they are exquisite. And they will be perfect with the gown I am to wear this evening."

He was pleased. "I must admit that I bribed Charlotte into telling me what your gown was to be for this affair. And as to why I am giving them to you today—it is simply because I worship you, Serena."

He responded instantly as I drew his head down, my lips

finding his. The silk robe that I wore fell open as his hands pressed the small of my back and found their way to my buttocks, pulling me up and into the swelling of his masculinity.

"There is time," I whispered, biting gently at his lower lip.

He pulled back from me. "Now, who is the one who is incorrigible?" he asked huskily.

"I cannot tempt you?"

"You can always tempt me, Serena, but this once I think I had but let my head have its way, particularly if I am to stop to see the children."

"There was a time when I could corrupt you, Lord Barkham," I chided.

"And there will be a time when you can again," he replied, pulling away and straightening his waistcoat.

I pulled my robe about me and turned back to the dressing table, where I had left my gift. "They are truly beautiful, Justin," I acknowledged. "I shall cherish them always."

Once Justin had departed I prepared for my bath. Charlotte, who could not have known we would be momentarily diverted, had drawn my bath water sometime earlier so it had lost most of its warmth by the time I slipped in. Fortunately those August days kept the air warm and the tepid water proved almost refreshing.

As I dried and began donning my petticoats I wished that for once I might abandon them, but even Justin might question my sense of decency. I picked up the gown which Charlotte had pressed and laid on the bed. Anne had commenced designing it several months before when I had told her of our plans for an end-of-the-summer gala. I had wanted something breathtaking and Anne had, true to her talent, designed an exquisite gown.

The main fabric of the gown was an ivory silk which Anne had brought back from a recent visit to Paris. The neckline was very décolleté with a simple shawl-like drop from the shoulders. The bodice was desperately tight which, of course, was the fashion, but I did wish comfort could override the mode. The skirt fell full and in tiers, each caught up with emerald green rosettes backed by an ivory puff of lace.

I turned suddenly, startled by a knock at the door.

"Who is there?"

" 'Tis only me, Miss Serena," Charlotte responded, entering sheepishly and looking about for Justin. "Aye didn't want to be disturbin' ye if the master was still 'ere.''

I shook my head. "He has gone to look in on the children. I'm pleased you are here, however, for I should never be able to get into that gown myself. There must be fifty little buttons along the back.''

I moved over to the dressing table and added a bit of rouging to my cheeks and lips. Charlotte began arranging my hair. It was hardly considered her duty, but I knew she was pleased when I insisted that only she could dress my hair properly.

"Would ye be wantin' me to weave some flowers through it?'' she asked as she gathered the heavy weight of my hair high at the back of my head, allowing a few tendrils to frame my face while the bulk cascaded down about my back.

"I think it would be too much, Charlotte,'' I replied, opening the gray velvet case containing the emerald necklace and earrings Justin had given me.

Charlotte gasped. "Oh, they be the most beautiful jewels ay've ever seen.''

"He is far too extravagant, I fear. I thought the two of you must have conspired, for they will indeed be perfect with the gown.''

"Aye swear aye knew nary 'bout them,'' Charlotte said as she placed the necklace about my neck. "That Lord Barkham be a devil, 'e is, 'cause now aye be knowin' why 'e was askin' me 'bout yer gown an' 'im not lettin' on at all.''

I donned the earrings as Charlotte fetched the dress. Stepping into it, I took a deep breath as she deftly began fastening the diminutive silk buttons. Charlotte beamed at me as I turned to the mirror to catch my reflection.

"Ye be lookin' like a queen, Miss Serena,'' Charlotte praised.

I smiled. "Then Lady Camberleigh will be pleased.'' It was, after all, Anne who had given me my first formal gown, not long after I had arrived at Camberleigh. No jewels adorned my being then. But I could not have felt more elegant if I had sported the crown jewels. Anne certainly no longer needed me to promote her designs, though I would always feel committed to singing her praises.

I jumped as I heard the strains of the orchestra from the ballroom.

"Good grief, Charlotte, I must be on my way,'' I said, grabbing my fan. "Bless you for all your help.''

"Ye be goin' an' 'avin' yerself a wonderful evening."

I stepped out into the hallway. I felt slightly flushed but I knew it was the anticipation of the evening. The side hall on this end of the house extended approximately five hundred paces, interrupted in the middle by the center hall. I had just turned to move down the center hall when I thought I heard a noise along the opposite end.

I paused for a moment, thinking that perhaps I had been mistaken, but when the sound repeated I made my way down the side hall to investigate. Such noise would not have been unusual except that this wing of Mayfair had not been used in years. Justin told me that his maternal grandmother who had lived with his family for years had used a suite of rooms until her death. We had never re-opened them since our marriage as we had more than sufficient bedrooms on the other side of the house to accommodate houseguests. It was my intention to install the children in this wing once they were a bit older.

I slowed as the sound became louder. I could not imagine that any of the maids would be cleaning down here now. With some apprehension I turned the handle on the door and, pushing it open, stepped into the room. Light from the fireplace flooded the room. Puzzled, I moved over to the bed on which lay some clothing. I picked up a men's waistcoat and then, realizing suddenly that I was obviously intruding, turned to leave the room. As I did, a voice startled my senses.

"Well, what do we have here?" the resonant voice queried.

## 2

I turned and was startled as I looked upon a bare-chested man smiling at me.

He was not as tall as Justin, but about the same age, although his thick blond hair had not begun to gray. The blueness of his eyes was evident even in this light.

"I beg your pardon, sir," I mumbled, realizing that whoever he was he was a man of breeding. "I did not know that these rooms were occupied."

He smiled at me broadly. "Please do not apologize, fair lady, you give me hope that this weekend shall prove far more pleasurable than I had dared anticipate."

I flushed, flustered by the unabashed admiration of his regard.

"I do apologize, sir," I repeated as I went to the door and fled down the hallway against his protestations and laughter.

I slowed as I reached the center hall, determined to compose myself before seeing the children. I was tempted to find Charlotte and ask why I had not been told that those rooms were to be used this weekend. It was not her fault, I was certain; more than likely she had simply assumed Justin had informed me. But I was mortified to have walked in on a half-naked man, whoever he was. Of course, his amusement at my shock at finding him there had not helped.

Peals of laughter emanated from the nursery as I approached, and upon entering, I discovered that the children had taken various articles of clothing and dressed poor Jaspar in full regalia. He bounded from the bed, tripping over Daphne's bunched-up petticoat as he did.

I knelt down to him. "Poor old friend, I suspect that you sometimes wish your mistress had never had children." I turned to Daphne. "You know, sweetheart, Jaspar is a good sport, but you musn't press him too much; he is not as young as he once was."

"You look beautiful, mother," Daphne effused, running over to touch the dress. "I do think it is the nicest gown I have ever seen, except for mine, of course."

"Yours?"

"Aunt Anne brought it for me," she replied, pulling a charming blue organza dress from a large box. "You see, I knew she wouldn't forget me."

"That was most generous of her and I hope you thanked her properly."

"If I am very quiet, might I wear the dress to the ball?" she pleaded.

"Daphne, we went over that earlier," I reminded her. "This is simply not an affair for children. But tomorrow I am certain that your father will take you to the hunt."

"No, he won't," Alexander pouted. "He said he would be ockpied."

"That's occupied," I corrected, "and I assure you he will not be too occupied."

I kissed the children after getting them to promise they would disrobe both Jaspar and themselves and get ready for bed.

Many of the guests had already gathered when I descended to the ballroom.

Before I could look about for Justin, Anne's hand was at my elbow. We embraced warmly and then she held me at arm's length, her eyes taking in the gown in full.

"You look ravishing, Serena," she praised. "You know, while most of us age you simply grow more beautiful. If I didn't love you so much, I think I'd hate you," she laughed.

"Anne, you know perfectly well that there is not a smidgeon of hate in you."

"Perhaps," she mused. "Thank God I have enough talent to create some stir, for otherwise I do think I would be jealous, if not of the way you look, then at the very least of those emeralds. Am I to assume that is an exhibition of my brother's good taste?''

"They are exquisite, aren't they?'' I noted. "Justin surprised me with them tonight. They are far too extravagant, but I obviously did not insist on their being returned.''

"Well, you are not a fool, Serena. Besides, you must humor my brother by accepting his generosities from time to time. He can afford it and I know how he treasures you.''

I smiled in acknowledgment. "You look wonderful yourself, Anne,'' I said, admiring her gown. It was fashioned of a deep rose silk taffeta, the lines much sleeker than most of the gowns of the current mode.

Anne's real genius in her designs is the ability to style specifically for each woman. Her own countenance reflects that. Pretty was a word I never connected with Anne as the strong bones and considerable height she shares with her brother are not as becoming on the female form. But her active imagination and purposeful mind are reflected in her demeanor, giving her an interesting statuesque air. Of course I am admittedly prejudiced since Anne is not only my sister-in-law but my dearest friend. Her clear mindedness has seen me through many a quandary in these past ten years. I could not be closer to her were she of my own blood.

"Promise me that you will save some time for me this weekend?'' I coaxed.

"Is anything wrong?'' she queried, a look of concern on her face.

"Nothing,'' I assured her. "It is just that I have not seen anything of you this summer and I miss our woman-to-woman talks.''

She smiled. "I agree. I love Richard dearly, but he has no time for my flights of fantasy.''

"How is he?''

"At present,'' she replied, nodding to where he stood across the room, "I trust he is rather peeved at me for leaving him in the company of Louisa Montrose.''

I giggled. Louisa Montrose, wife of Lord Montrose, was an overweight matron whose mouth, being always in motion, was her most notable characteristic. When she wasn't bantering about who knows what, she was chewing on whatever delicacies were at hand.

"Shall we rescue him?" I asked.

Anne agreed. We began wending our way through the crowd with my extending greetings to our friends. I had paused to speak to our clergyman when hands suddenly covered my eyes from behind.

"Who is it?" I asked.

"Your most fervent admirer," my mystery guest replied.

"Oliver," I exclaimed, turning about and allowing myself to be crushed by my cousin's arms.

"How did you know?"

"I would know your voice anywhere," I chided.

He shrugged.

"You cannot fool an old governess, you know," I continued, winking at him.

"What is this about Serena being a governess," a voice interrupted.

"William," I exclaimed, delighted at seeing our good friend after these many months.

He smiled broadly. "You could not keep me away, my dear. After all, it is not often that my eyes can feast on such magnificence."

"You flatter me, William, but I will not deny that it is healthy for my ego." I paused. "Oh, I am sorry," I said, realizing I had ignored Oliver, "do you know my cousin, Oliver Camberleigh?"

They shook hands. "A pleasure, sir," Oliver responded. "I have enjoyed your *Political Register* for some time now."

"Well, then, we must talk further this weekend, for as you know it is a subject close to my heart." Turning back to me, he asked, "Where is that handsome husband of yours, Serena?"

"I have been wondering that myself, William. He mentioned that he was going to be meeting with someone earlier this evening but I cannot imagine what would be detaining him."

"Conversation of the farms, no doubt. He is as great a zealot as I on this subject."

I agreed. "You will excuse me for a moment; my uncle is over there and I have not had an opportunity to welcome him."

Anne had already gone ahead and Lady Montrose was no longer in his company.

"Serena, you are looking well," he praised, embracing me warmly.

I wished that I could return the compliment. My uncle looked tired. He had aged greatly over the past few years. His once dark hair was now completely gray. There were dark circles under his eyes, and the scar, which ran jaggedly along his cheek and had always kept him from being considered a truly handsome man, seemed even more prominent with age.

"I see that Lady Montrose managed to ensnare you for awhile," I said with a wink.

"That woman is a fright," he mumbled. "If old George did away with her, I think any court in the land would call it justice."

"Richard, really," Anne admonished while peering about my shoulder.

"Well, there is my long lost brother. I thought he was going to abandon us. Who is that attractive man with him?"

I turned and flushed as I came face to face with the man I had encountered in the bedroom upstairs.

Justin stepped forward. "Philip, let me introduce you to my sister, Lady Camberleigh, and her husband Richard. Lord Taggart."

I looked down at the ground as they exchanged amenities.

"And this ravishing creature," Justin continued, placing his arm about my waist, "is my wife Serena."

If he was surprised, his only display was by a quizzical raise of his brows.

"I admired her beauty earlier this evening, but I had no idea that this vision was your wife, Justin," he said smiling at me. "You are indeed a fortunate man."

"You flatter me, Lord Taggart," I said, trying not to show that he had threatened my composure.

"On the contrary, I only speak the truth," he replied. "And if we are to become friends, I would hope that you would call me Philip."

I nodded, not wishing to be impolite, though I found myself wondering what Justin's association was with this man who positioned himself as an intimate.

Before I could ask, we were joined by another man, years senior to both Justin and Lord Taggart. The obligatory introductions made, it was obvious that Mister Jonathan Leech was at the very least well acquainted with Lord Taggart. The two could not have been more dissimilar. Whereas I had to agree with Anne that Taggart was indeed a handsome man, Mister Leech was short and well rounded. There was a pudginess in everything about him, his hands, his cheeks and, I assumed, if they were ever to be revealed, even his feet.

He wore spectacles that scarcely seemed to assist his sight since he was constantly squinting and adjusting them on the bridge of his nose.

"Charming," he effused, taking my hand. "Charming party, Lady Barkham. Charming. I am indeed honored to be here. Much cooler than London, you know, at this time of year. Beastly hot there."

I was about to ask him what he did in London when Justin abruptly excused himself, saying that there were several people to whom he had promised to introduce Lord Taggart and Mister Leech. After they had left my uncle turned to me and asked, "Who are those two, Serena?"

"You know as much as I do, Richard," I replied, "though I do wish they would not preoccupy Justin so."

"Oh, look, Serena," Anne interrupted, "Monique has just arrived."

I excused myself and wound my way through the now crowded ballroom to welcome my old friend.

We kissed, as was her country's tradition, on both cheeks.

"You cannot imagine, *chère amie*, 'ow I ave been looking forward to theez night," she gushed in her French accent as pronounced as it had been when I had met her some ten years earlier. "Let me look at you," she continued, twirling me about in front of her. *"Ravissante*, as always. You are even more beautiful as a young woman than you were as a young girl."

I laughed. "Monique, you have always been very healthy for my ego."

*"Mais c'est vrai, ma cherie, tu es vraiment ravissante."*

Fortunately my father had insisted that I become proficient in French—Monique was invariably lapsing back into her native tongue whenever she was excited.

"I have not seen Robin as yet," I noted, admiring Monique's ageless elegance. She really looked not a day older than when I had first met her. Her long silky dark hair was bound at the nape of her neck, the length of which was accentuated by the high lace collar of her emerald green chinese brocade gown. She had never remarried since her husband's death, which must now be some fifteen years prior. There had been lovers; even Justin prior to our marriage had been an ardent admirer. It amused me that if any other woman of our acquaintance had so unabashedly taken such a series of lovers she would be labeled wanton and indecent. But not Monique. She was considered by most a woman of great resourcefulness. Admittedly her wealth gave her an undeniable standing, but I had to admire the life she had made for herself on her own.

"*Chérie*," she prodded, "I do not theenk zat you have heard a word zat I have said."

"I am sorry, Monique," I apologized. "Now where was I? Oh, yes, I was asking about Robin."

"He is wiz me and, *naturellement*, Lilliane. She is probably still dressing. Zat woman, she is in love with a mirror."

"That doesn't sound like you, Monique," I replied, noting her tone. "You and Lilliane are not having a disagreement, are you?"

"No, no, no, *chérie*. Lilliane and I will never be, how you say, close, but I thank the stars each day for her. Zat woman is a genius when it comes to my Robin. He is my son, *mais il est très méchant de temps en temps.*"

Monique understood Robin well. Lilliane had made great strides in taming the attractive rogue I had met when I first came to Camberleigh. Justin thought it was her American way of frankness which had succeeded in keeping Robin in line. I would admit that I was amazed at how settled he had become in the past years. Of course, children had helped, and their twin boys were eight-year-old challenges.

"Serena, who are zos men whiz Justin?"

"The short one is a Mister Leech."

"And ze other?"

"Lord Taggart. Philip Taggart."

"*Très intéressant*, zat one," she replied, eyeing him across the room.

"Rather assumptive if you ask me."

"Hmmm," she mused. "You would not theenk one rude if I prompted Justin to introduce me?"

"Actually, I would appreciate it, Monique," I replied honestly. "I have not been able to pry him away from those two. You might be just what I need."

Monique moved off and I found myself besieged by our

many friends who had come to celebrate with us what we hoped to be an excellent year of harvest.

When it came time to dine, recognizing that Justin would not easily be pried from the entourage which now gathered about him, I approached William Cobbett, who I selfishly knew would prove a stimulating dinner companion.

I was pleased as I entered the dining room. The Venetian crystal chandeliers shimmered as the candles burned brightly above. The sprays of flowers here again were large and quite spectacular. I hoped that Anne in particular would appreciate them since so many of the roses had been planted and cultivated under her direction when she had lived at Mayfair.

As Oliver entered the dining room I nodded to him to come and join Mister Cobbett and myself at the head of the table.

"Delightful young man that cousin of yours," Cobbett acknowledged, having seen my gesture to Oliver. "Shame, he is not want to follow in his father's footsteps, for he, like Justin, is the kind of young man we need at the helm of this country."

I was slightly taken aback. "Well, William, I do not think that he has exactly abandoned that end. It may take a few years before he shares Justin's commitment, but then he is young and I doubt that even my husband was as passionate about the farms at Oliver's age."

"Perhaps I have misunderstood, Serena," he replied, holding my chair as I sat, "but I distinctly recall his telling me but an hour ago that he intended to seek to make his way in the New World."

His response troubled me, for although I knew of Oliver's passion for history and want for adventure and travel, I had never truly contemplated that he would leave the Camberleigh/Mayfair estates. Perhaps selfishly, for indeed I believed that Oliver would adjust as he grew older and assume the responsibilities of his heritage. I say selfishly for I had hoped that his involvement would help disperse some of the responsibility from Justin.

My thoughts were interrupted by Oliver, who had joined us at my left.

"Serena, you are so pale. Is there something troubling you?"

I brushed a napkin to my lips. "William has just shared with me your intentions of going to America soon."

Oliver looked pained. "I had hoped to tell you this myself."

William coughed. "Sorry, old chap, I had no intention of being the pivot of revelation this evening."

Oliver waved him off. "You simply have brought to fruition a conversation that I was destined to have with Serena this weekend, Mister Cobbett."

"Call me William," he interrupted as the first course of pike with a walnut, anchovy sauce was served.

"No, 'tis true," Oliver objected. "I have dreaded this weekend as I knew that at some juncture I would have to address Serena."

"Oh, Oliver," I chastised. "I thought that we were close enough that you would never have to think of 'addressing' me."

He pressed his hand against my arm. "You do not understand, Serena. It is because of the affection that we have shared over the years that my decision is most difficult to share with you. Do not misunderstand, I will miss Richard and Anne dreadfully, but it is you, and of course Justin, with whom I share an indelible commitment. In leaving I will leave a part of my soul behind."

I felt the tears well in my eyes and swallowed hard to prevent an embarrassing scene. The fish with its very fluid sauce stuck in my throat.

"Serena, don't," Oliver pleaded. "Of all, I need your support."

I sipped the wine which had been poured.

"Oliver, you have it," I assured quietly. "It simply is a shock to come to terms with your leaving. Believe me, I have been in a surround where I have needed support. And trust. And love. You shall always have that from me, Oliver."

William raised his glass. "To the most exquisite woman I know." With a regard to Oliver he added, "And that is not a compliment I impart lightly."

We finished the first course and I made note to compliment the cook on the delicacy of the dish.

"William, let me depart for the moment," I said, wishing a relief from the conversation. "What are you championing these days?"

"Things are not what they seem, Serena," he replied, obviously enjoying the next course of roast goose. "The prices of cows are dropping disastrously and the farmers maintain that unless we have another Napoleon we shall be doomed."

"But how can that be?" I asked. "Justin says that we are due for our most profitable year ever."

"Perhaps, but the itinerant laborers are almost destitute. Were it not for the common causes of Justin and a handful of others, there would not only be a paucity of work but of income within the land."

"Since the arrival of the children, I feel, admittedly, so bereft from an involvement in this," I responded.

"Hardly, Serena," Cobbett advised. "Of any woman I know, you are the one who has remained compassionate about the land."

"Part of that I suppose is my inheritance," I replied.

"I would counter that, my lady. I know how you involve yourself with the tenants. You have always been a champion of the common man, just as I am—which is most likely why I have such enormous regard for you."

The next course of roast lamb was being served.

"May I interrupt?" Oliver asked.

"You are not interrupting, Oliver," I replied.

"I simply want to make it clear to Mister Cobbett, William, that my zeal to travel to America does not mean that I do not have a commitment to England. Indeed, I, too, am a believer in Parliamentary reform. But I feel that there is much that I can learn from the governments in the New World."

"I respect your decision, Oliver," William retorted, then drained his glass. "Were I not sixty years of age I might follow you. Indeed, when I was eleven I left my father's small farm to see the Royal Gardens of Kew, where I temporarily obtained work. And you may not be aware of this but when I was but a year older than yourself I was in America, in Philadelphia."

"That is a surprise, William," I exclaimed. "But then I should have learned not to be surprised by your travels and accomplishments."

"May I ask why you returned to England?" Oliver queried.

William laughed. "It all had to do with *Peter Porcupine*."

I tried to recollect if that was someone I should have known. Seeing my puzzlement, he replied, "An inanimate object—specifically a monthly political paper that unfortunately prompted a libel action necessitating my return to England."

As the next course of roast stuffed goose was served Celia

Fenwick, who was seated to William's right, leaned forward to compliment the cook's fare. I knew that her intent was more to stir Oliver's notice than to discuss the evening's meal, but I also knew that her efforts would cause little reaction from my cousin.

She was a pretty enough girl, the daughter of the local vicar and his wife whose parsonage was prestigious within the county, but far too vapid for Oliver. Her father had made great strides to set a match between the two, but Oliver had no intention of settling down at present.

We completed the meal with fresh berries and little cakes with a sugary topping. I looked down at the end of the table towards Justin and raised my glass once, getting his eye. It was a signal we had designed for these few times when we dined in the great dining room, indicating that we were ready to excuse ourselves and thus our guests.

"William, Oliver," I said, pushing my chair back, "you have been delightful dinner companions but if you will excuse me I believe that Justin and I are about to commence the ball."

William rose to assist me. "You know, Serena, I am scarcely what one would call adept at these dances, but I would be honored if you would partake of a waltz with me this evening."

"You have but to ask," I replied.

Just then Justin reached my side, his arm encircling my waist. "I should have known better than to leave my wife with you, you old reprobate," he teased, winking at William.

"Were I but thirty years younger, my good friend, I would not be so subtle."

As we left the dining room Justin pulled me to him and whispered, "Do you think our guests would miss us if I ferreted you off to the bedroom for a few hours?"

"Justin," I chided "we cannot do that and you know it."

"I do not," he argued. "Frankly, if I have to listen to one more word from the vicar or Lady Montrose I think I shall scream."

"You have seemed to be far more preoccupied with Lord Taggart and Mister Leech than anyone," I replied. "Who are they?"

"Just business associates," he retorted, releasing me.

"Might I ask what kind of business?"

"Nothing that should concern you, my dear," he responded as he guided me towards the ballroom.

I was hurt by his comment. Justin usually shared everything with me and I was unaccustomed to being relegated to the position of the abiding wife.

My tone was one of annoyance when I challenged, "I should think that you would have had the courtesy to alert me that they would be attending the ball."

"Why are you being so testy about this, Serena?"

My arm stopped his gait. "Frankly I was mortified earlier this evening. I heard a noise in the east wing and went down to investigate. And upon entering one of the rooms what do I find? A man disrobed. That man was Lord Taggart."

Justin burst into gales of laughter.

"I did not find it amusing, Justin," I insisted.

"I am sorry, Serena, but I find it humorous. I am also imagining what would have happened had it been Jonathan Leech that you had happened upon. I think the poor man would have had an attack of apoplexy."

I had to admit that of the two it was probably best I had encountered Lord Taggart, though I still experienced a feeling of unease remembering how brazenly he had looked at me as he had stood there almost naked.

The orchestra commenced playing as soon as we entered the ballroom, and before I could comment Justin had placed his arm about my waist and was twirling me about the room. I relaxed as he guided me adroitly through the now milling guests. He was an expert dancer: strong and self-assured, yet sensitive enough to feel the passion of the music. Whatever anger I had felt had subsided by the time he stopped me in front of Monique, who seemed to be enjoying the company of Lord Taggart.

"I should have known that you would find our Monique, Philip," Justin said. "I compliment you on your exquisite taste."

"Ah, Justin, *toujours* you zay ze things I love to hear," she effused, reaching out her hand to caress Justin's cheek.

I felt a slight knot in my stomach. I knew that whatever passions they had shared had long ago ceased to be demonstrated, but as fond as I was of Monique I could never suppress my jealousy over that special feeling they shared.

"I must say, Justin," Philip replied "that I can easily return the compliment. With Lady Barkham at your side you are the envy of every man in the county."

I thought the compliment a bit excessive but at that moment I was truly grateful for it.

"Might I share in your bounty and ask your wife to dance with me?" he continued, "that is, if she will oblige."

"Just remember to bring her back," Justin replied gallantly.

I know that he could not have refused the request but I so wished I could excuse myself.

I was surprised at his strength as he took me in his arms since he was slighter and less muscular in appearance than Justin.

"I must apologize if I startled you earlier, Lady Barkham," he said, turning me into a waltz.

"It is I who should apologize, Lord Taggart," I insisted. "No one had informed me that those rooms were to be used this weekend."

"Well, you were a welcome surprise," he replied smiling. "My only regret is that the vision who entered my room so suddenly is promised to another. But if it must be, then I suppose I am pleased that it is Justin. He is a fine man."

"Yes, he is," I agreed. "Might I ask how you two have come to be acquainted?"

"Through business principally," he retorted.

"And what might I ask is the nature of your business?"

"I have a variety of interests, Lady Barkham. I suppose you could call me an industrialist of sorts."

That was odd, I thought to myself. Our holdings were totally, as far as I knew, in land and the farming of same. Justin had never talked about any investments in the new industrial movement. If anything, I would have supposed that he was strongly opposed to it.

"Have I tired you already, Lady Barkham?" Lord Taggart asked as the waltz came to a close.

I shook my head. "I am sorry, I fear I was simply preoccupied for the moment. Would you mind if we returned to Justin and Monique, I believe I could use a spot of refreshment."

"Of course," he agreed, leading me back to where Justin and Monique seemed to be deep in conversation.

"Your wife dances as divinely as she looks," Philip said, bowing to me slightly. "I only hope that I was not too dull a dance companion."

"Not at all," I assured. "Would I be terribly rude if I asked to dance with my husband again," I directed to Monique, "before the rest of the ladies occupy his time?"

A hand on the middle of my back startled me. "Not until I have this dance, Serena."

I turned to face Oliver.

"Possibly the only man here whom I could not refuse," I replied gaily. "Other than my husband, of course."

As he led me across the room he whispered, "Actually I just wanted to get you alone, Serena. We have not talked in far too long a time."

"I agree," I replied, accepting a glass of champagne which was passed by Thomas, our head butler.

"I truly am sorry that you had to learn of my impending departure through Cobbett. I had wanted to tell you myself," he said as we got away from the dancing throng.

"It was just a bit of a shock," I replied. "Actually it should not have been as I have long known that your soul thirsts for adventure."

"Then you approve?" he asked hopefully.

"I not only approve but I envy you the excursion."

He laughed. "That part I would not envy, Serena, from what I have heard, some of these voyages can be a little rough."

"It was not the trip that I envy," I assured him, "rather the experience. It must be quite thrilling to see what our friends and, in some cases, relatives are doing with their lives."

"You have an uncle there, do you not, Serena?"

"If he is still alive. He and my mother lost contact when my parents left Camberleigh. She knew that he had emigrated to America but that was all."

"Perhaps I could make some inquiries," Oliver encouraged.

"That would be kind of you, Oliver, but I would not hold out much hope.

"When do you intend to leave?"

"My ship sails September first."

I gasped. "But that is less than two weeks away."

He nodded. "I was able to arrange passage on what seems to be a comfortable ship and there truly did not seem any sense in delaying."

"Do Anne and Richard know?"

He smoothed his blond locks from his brow. "Yes. Actually Anne has known for some time. I do not think that I could have done it without her assistance."

Knowing Anne, I could understand. She loved Oliver as if he were her own, and when many mothers or stepmothers, given his sickliness as a child, might have proved overly doting, she had always encouraged Oliver to experience life fully.

"And your father, what is his reaction?"

"Shock, disappointment. I know that he had hoped that I would help him at Camberleigh. It is getting to be somewhat of a burden, you know."

Our eyes met. "He looks tired."

"There is no time that will be right, Serena. And actually the sooner I go perhaps the sooner I shall return."

I gave him what I hoped was an encouraging smile. "I fear there are two others who are going to be devastated."

He quickly knew to whom I referred.

"Alexander will announce that he shall go with you and Daphne will indubitably refuse to eat for a week."

"Do you want me to tell them, Serena?"

"Would you?" I was relieved that he had suggested it.

He pressed my hand. "Tomorrow, for certain. And now I best get you back to Justin, who, I see, seems to be searching frantically about for you."

Oliver led me back to Justin but not before Celia Fenwick had inveigled him into getting a glass of champagne for her.

It felt good to be back in Justin's arms dancing again. Our lives would change with Oliver's departure and I wanted the security or reassurance that the change would not have a drastic effect.

"I gather from your quietness, darling, that Oliver has told you," he said calmly.

I looked up at him. "You knew then," I exclaimed.

"I suspected. But he really only confirmed it tonight."

"And?"

"And I would rather not discuss it tonight," he replied, planting a kiss on my forehead. "Besides, Cobbett obviously feels that I am keeping you away from the guests too long since he grimaces at me every time we pass him by."

I scarcely saw Justin for the next hour. I danced with Richard and countless others before it dawned on me to look in on the children. Besides, it would not hurt me to freshen up a bit.

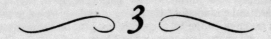

# 3

I slipped out of the ballroom and made my way up the stairs. As I approached the landing I gasped—for there stood Philip Taggart holding, unless my eyes deceived me, my own Daphne.

"What are you doing?" I demanded, my motherly protectiveness coming to the fore.

He pressed his fingers to his lips. "She's asleep. I was just going to my room for a moment when I encountered this angelic blue-gowned figure on the stairs. I knew at once who she was. She's the image of her mother. I thought it best to try and find the nursery or someone who might direct me to it since I hardly think a marble stair does well for a child's sleep."

I brushed the hair from Daphne's peaceful face. "I am sorry, Philip," I whispered in reply. "I should have known she would do something like this. She was sorely disappointed that I did not permit her to attend the ball."

"If you will guide me, I will be pleased to return her to her bedroom."

I nodded and proceeded down the hall to the nursery.

Fortunately Alexander was sleeping soundly and did not hear us enter. Jaspar seemed to sense that quiet was needed and only watched as Philip laid Daphne gently down on her bed. Philip left us and I changed Daphne from her new dress to a light nightgown. I knew that I would have to chastise her in the morning but her sleeping face, now so innocent, quelled all my anger.

I removed to my room where I adjusted my hair and added a bit more rouging to my lips. The ball would continue for several hours to be followed by a light late-night supper. It would not be obligatory for me to attend—a welcome relief since the preparation for the affair had gone on for weeks and I was tired from all the planning and fussing.

As I reached the top of the staircase I turned to see that Philip was but steps behind me.

"I assume that they are sleeping soundly," he said, offering his arm.

"Do you have children, Philip?" I asked.

"None that I know of, but perhaps that is a blessing since I have never married."

"I see," I replied. "Well, then, you have not experienced the trials and tribulations of being a parent. One really always does have to be twenty paces ahead of them."

"If I may say so, I cannot imagine that being a problem for you, Serena. You seem to manage everything brilliantly."

We reached the bottom of the stairs just as Justin appeared in the hallway.

"There you are," he hailed. "I have been looking everywhere for you, Philip."

I felt slightly offended that it had not been me that he had missed but relaxed when he put his arm about me and kissed my cheek.

"I am pleased that you two are getting to know each other," Justin continued as we moved back to the ballroom.

"Philip was helping me with Daphne, who had decided to attend the ball from the top of the staircase. The festivities proved too much for her, however, since she was fast asleep when he found her."

Justin laughed. "My daughter is just like her mother, Philip. Serena could always get herself in more trouble than any woman I have ever known."

"Justin, really," I reproached. "Do not take him seriously, Philip."

William Cobbett strode up to join us. "Well, Serena, it is now or never. These old legs are not going to keep up much longer and you did promise me a spin about the room."

We all knew that William was scarcely feeble. Only the year

prior he had commenced making rides throughout the countryside to try and talk to the people and discover what their problems were.

"I am all yours, William," I said as he guided me to the dance floor.

"William," I continued, "do you know anything about Lord Taggart?"

He shook his head. "I have just met him tonight. He does not seem to have much affinity for the land. Power and steam seem to be his passion. And you know me, Serena, I am constantly fighting these bloody industrialists."

"Then you have no idea why he and Mister Leech are meeting with Justin?" I asked.

"None. But I hope that husband of yours isn't getting involved with something. We need aristocrats like Justin to keep the farms active and prosperous."

We had but finished our dance when Robin Kelston asked for the next. We had become great friends over the years since my arrival at Camberleigh. He would oft tell Justin that the mistake of his life was not marrying me, but I knew that although he had been smitten when he had first met me that Lilliane was the right woman for him. He had ceased to gamble and, though he would always be somewhat of a rogue, had settled down greatly since becoming a father.

"You are looking smashing tonight, my love," he flattered, "but then you always do. Those emeralds must have cost Justin a pound or two. But I must say they could not be on a prettier neck."

"They are truly overwhelming, are they not?" I replied. "I hope we need not go into debt over them."

Robin laughed. "Hardly, my dear. Your husband is a genius when it comes to running these estates."

"Well, you have hardly done poorly yourself, Robin," I noted, knowing that Kelston Manor rivaled us annually at harvest time.

"True," he acknowledged. "But I do not have his insightfulness when it comes to investments. I chose to put my profits on the gaming table, he has put his in everything from tea to manufacturing. Of course, I like my pleasures too much. Justin is a driven man. I admire him but I like my port and trips to the seashore too much to compete with him."

"I do wish he would relax more, Robin," I replied honestly.

"Our life has been so idyllic these past years and I would hate to see anything happen to mar that."

Robin patted my hand as the dance ended. "You worry too much, my lovely. With you at his side, Justin can do anything."

An announcement was made that the late supper would be served shortly in the dining room. I looked about for Justin and found him in deep conversation again with Mister Leech. He smiled as I approached.

"I think, Jonathan, that I am about to be reproached for not spending enough time with my wife."

"You think correctly," I chastised. "Would you think me terribly rude, Mister Leech, if I borrowed my husband for a few moments? I have only danced with him once this evening and I want to be certain that my first and last dances are with him."

"Oh, but of course, of course, Lady Barkham," he spluttered, adjusting his spectacles. "Far be it from me to stand in the way of young love."

Justin took me in his arms, holding me closer than was fashionable, but I did not object.

"Your ball is a grand success, my love," he whispered as we twirled about the outer realm of the room.

"I had thought it was our ball," I replied, though secretly pleased.

"I simply meant to give you the credit, Serena. Certainly I had little to do with its organization."

"Thank you," I replied, our eyes meeting. "We could slip out shortly, you know," I suggested. "We would scarcely be missed."

"You temptress," he retorted, winking at me. "I would delight in nothing more, my love, but I promised Taggart that we could conclude a few matters this evening. If you are tired, why do you not retire? I shall not be too late and if you are agreeable I shall awaken you, gently I vow, when I come to bed."

"I shall be devastated if you do not."

I let Justin hold me a moment as the music stopped. I knew without question that I would wait up for him tonight. I made my excuses to our closest friends, who knew that I was not one traditionally to continue until the early morning hours. Although a late supper was expected at these affairs, I always believed that a sumptuous dinner was quite sufficient.

I smiled to myself as I wound my way up the staircase and to our rooms. The ball indeed had been a success. I was fatigued but it was a peaceful tiredness. The bedroom was very dark as I entered it. The candles had burned down and no one had thought to replace them at this late hour. The flames from the fireplace threw sufficient light, however, for me to undress by.

It was tedious removing my gown as the tiny button closings at the back kept eluding me. I breathed a sigh of relief as the layers of silk taffeta fell away from my skin. I returned the emerald necklace and earrings to their velvet case and placed it in the small compartment at the back of my dressing table where I kept the rest of my jewels. I could never understand Justin's insistence that I sequester my valuables away in such a fashion since I trusted all the members of the household explicitly. But he persisted in believing that I was too trusting and that fate is best not tempted.

The room was very warm and I opened the window in hopes of attracting a small breeze. I had never been able to convince Charlotte that there was scarcely a need to use the fireplace in the summer. She would argue, and rightly so, I suppose, that the nights in the north of England could turn unexpectedly cool and that a small fire would assure less dampness in a room.

The stars were high in the heavens over Mayfair this night and the moon was just short of being full. It was very still save for a blend of voices so distant that it sounded more like the rustle of leaves.

I moved to the bed, delighting in the sheets as my limbs began slowly to relax. I hoped Justin would not be too late as I closed my eyes to rest for a bit.

It seemed only moments later when I awoke, startled by a sound at the end of the room.

"Justin, is that you?" I called out.

He came to me, his strong taut body outlined by the dim light. He sat by me on the bed and cupping my face in his hands explored my lips with his own.

"I did not mean to startle you," he said huskily.

"What time is it?"

" 'Tis late. The sun will be up in but a few hours."

"I must have fallen asleep," I replied drowsily.

I moved back on the bed so that he might join me there. He

lay down, lifting his arm so that I might cradle in it against his chest. My fingers played with the hairs that formed an almost crosslike image against it.

"You shall never get me to sleep that way, my love," he whispered.

"Might I ask who said that sleep was my intention?" I purred in return.

Our lovemaking that night was languid and gentle. Although it was almost dawn it seemed as if we had all the time in the world. And when his final thrusts brought us to a release that seemed as though it had been timed in unison there was a joyous peace in drifting off to sleep entwined in each other's arms.

When I awoke the next morning Justin was already up and about.

"Good gracious," I gasped, pulling myself up to a sitting position, "what time is it?"

"It is past ten," he replied, striding over to me and kissing me lightly on my forehead. "Charlotte was here earlier and left our breakfast trays but I did not want to wake you. You were in such a deep sleep."

"Ah, well," I yawned, "my only consolation is that I am certain that none of the other ladies will arise before noon. Who is watching the children?"

"Oliver," he replied.

"Oh, Lord," I moaned, "when will they learn not to be such a bother to him?"

"Actually, from what Charlotte says, he volunteered. In truth I think he enjoys it."

I brushed my hair back, coiling it with my fingers. "He may have made a special effort since I told him that I would appreciate his telling the children personally about his impending departure. Oh, I am going to miss him dreadfully."

"No more than I, believe me," Justin agreed as he pulled on his boots.

He looked so handsome in his riding habit. And he sat a horse beautifully. Our stable was renowned throughout all of England and I knew that Justin looked forward to seeing his newest stallions perform in the hunt.

"Shall you be down at the stables to see us off?" he queried.

"But of course," I insisted. "I have also promised the

children that they might attend.''

"I would suspect that Anne will attend and, of course, Lilliane.''

Lilliane, Robin's wife, was a brilliant horsewoman able to compete with almost any of the gentlemen of our acquaintance. She rode very much the way she spoke, with frank assurance. I supposed it had something to do with her American upbringing.

"Darling, I am going to be leaving you for a while," Justin said as he fetched his crop. "There are a few items I must review with Robbie before this hunt commences.''

"Just be certain that you schedule the riders to be back by two as luncheon shall be served shortly thereafter.''

After Justin left I rose and bathed using one of the scented soaps which Anne had brought from a recent trip to Paris.

Although I would not ride, I decided to don my riding costume since I found it not only comfortable but pleasing to the eye. It was fashioned of a lightweight green wool, high bodiced with gold braid about the open neckline and wrists. A heavily ruffled white shirt was worn underneath. I coiled my hair high on my head affixing it with several tortoise shell combs.

The house was remarkably still as I strode out towards the nursery. The ladies had undoubtedly taken to their beds with sore feet the evening before and their husbands would wake with throbbing heads from having overindulged in port, so it was not uncommon for all to rise late after such a ball.

I heard peals of laughter as I approached the nursery. I was encouraged, for assuming that Oliver had told them about his plans, I expected Daphne at least to be dissolved in tears.

"Mama,'' Daphne cried out as I entered.

I struggled to hide my amusement. She had taken lately to using the French paternal references for Justin and myself when she wanted to appear considerably older than her eight years.

"And did you enjoy the ball?'' I asked as she came and gave me a kiss.

She looked puzzled.

"It was I, with the assist of Lord Taggart, who returned you to your room last night.''

"Oh,'' she moaned in a voice which almost asked what her punishment was to be.

"Truly, Mama," she pressed, "I did not mean to disobey you. I just dreadfully wanted to see all the gowns," adding, "yours was by far the prettiest."

"But the point is, Daphne, that you did disobey me."

Oliver cleared his throat. " 'Tis not as bad as all that now, is it, Serena? Look, there was no harm done."

It was not a wonder that the children adored him for he was ever their champion.

I knew that I should be firmer, but I had to agree it was hardly a catastrophe and I did not want to dampen their spirits for the day.

"Alexander, you seem particularly quiet," I noted, changing the subject.

"Are you feeling poorly?"

He shook his head. Oliver looked at me and rolled his eyes, which told me that he had in fact shared his plans with the children.

"Is not our Oliver's news exciting?" I ventured. "To think, a journey to America."

"Why cannot we go, too?" he pouted.

"Perhaps you shall," I offered, "when you are Oliver's age."

"Oliver said he would bring back a splendid present," Daphne gloated.

"Well, that is most generous of him," I replied, pleased that the idea of his return had taken on more importance than his departure.

I looked about the room suddenly aware that something was missing. "Where is Jaspar?"

"Charlotte told Molly to take him down to the stables," Daphne replied.

"Shall we go down and find him? The hunt should be commencing shortly."

I let the children run ahead, wishing to thank Oliver for what seemed a miraculous accomplishment. I had not looked forward to their tantrums today and whatever he had said, or however he had said it, it must have been just right since they seemed full of merriment as they skipped down the staircase.

Many of the guests were already at the stables when we arrived.

Anne waved to me and I walked over to join her. As I did Jaspar spotted me from afar and came bounding up, his brown and white body wriggling with pleasure as I leaned down to pet him.

"Good gracious," she laughed, "I have never seen such a love affair between a dog and his mistress."

"You are looking very smart today," I said, noting her hat, which sported several large ostrich plumes rising from the crown of a pleated cloche, its airy veil trailing at the back.

"I am not feeling very clever," she retorted. "Richard warned me about the champagne but I refused to listen."

"If it is of any solace I scarcely believe that you are alone."

"Oh, look, there is Lord Taggart," she commented. "I must say he is a handsome fellow. Monique seemed quite taken with him. But then most of the ladies did."

"Hush," I advised. "I believe he is heading our way."

He stopped before us, tipping his hat. "Good morning, ladies. Splendid day, is it not? Will you be riding in the hunt, Lady Barkham?"

"I leave that to my husband," I demurred.

"Monique, Lady Kelston was telling me that you are an accomplished rider, however," he challenged.

"She flatters me, I fear."

"You are far too modest, fair lady," he retorted. "Well, if you will excuse me I shall saddle up."

As soon as he was out of earshot Anne turned to me and winked, "I think you have an admirer there, Serena."

"Nonsense. He is just being polite to the hostess. He most likely thinks it would be wise if I thought well of him since he and Justin apparently have business dealings."

"Whatever it is must be fascinating for it certainly monopolized most of my brother's time last evening. Really, Serena, you are going to have to get him to go away on holiday or something. He scarcely listened to a word I said last night. Not that every word I utter merits hearing, but it is not like Justin to turn a deaf ear." It was odd that she should say that for, although I had not truly thought about it, it did now seem that Justin had been daydreaming lately. "Preoccupied" was the better word.

The riders passed their mounts before us as Robbie gave the first call on the bugle. Justin was atop Serena's Fancy, a chestnut stallion he had named for me as it had birthed on our fifth anniversary. I signaled the children to come and stand by me.

"Where is Richard?" I asked Anne.

"He was feeling poorly," she replied. "I have urged him to see the doctor but he refuses. I am worried about him, Serena. He seemed so tired when we were in France."

"Perhaps I can ask Justin to talk to him."

"That's a splendid idea," she replied, cheering slightly. "I should have thought of that months ago."

The second bugle had sounded, announcing that the foxes were loose. The hounds followed in chase. Jaspar, whose own hunting instinct was peeked, barked at the yaps and groans of his kind.

The last bugle sounded and I saw Serena's Fancy take to the lead. I was so entranced with the chase that I did not hear Monique and Lilliane come up behind us.

"Is that George Montrose I see on the gray mount?" Lilliane asked.

"I believe it is," I said, squinting against the sun.

"One hardly knows whom to feel sorrier for, George or the horse. He is an abysmal rider you know."

"He'll survive it, no doubt," Anne replied. "Just to endure further torture from his wife."

When the last rider was out of sight we retired to a small garden area set above the stables. At the center was a large stone gazebo, its domed roof a welcome protection from the heat of the day. The children ambled to a small stream below where they appeared content, pitching stones into the running waters. Anne regaled us with her adventures from their last trip to France.

"Have you traveled to London zees summer, Serena?" Monique asked.

I admitted I had not.

"I have decided to go zer next month. Eet eez too dreary for me resting *toujours* in the country. You should come with me," she encouraged.

"It is tempting," I agreed, "but I would not want to leave Justin and I doubt that he would leave Mayfair. Besides, I fear if I went to Channing Hall now I would have to spend months refurbishing it."

I stopped as I saw Robbie running back up the hill. "They are returning, Serena," he called out.

"Ah," I said, rising and adjusting my skirt, "we had best go down and welcome the victors."

Robbie grinned and went back ahead of us. He had come a long way since his days as a stable boy at Camberleigh ten years ago. He still had his long lanky frame and toothy grin which was so like his mother Charlotte's. But his once unruly red hair was now slicked neatly back and his eyes spoke of the knowledge he had gained.

I had promised Robbie while still at Camberleigh that I would help him with his letters and figures since he had always cared so well for Jaspar. I had kept my promise and he had learned his lessons well. So well in fact that Justin had not only promoted him to stable master but trusted him with the overseeing of many of the tenant farms. It had been clever of Justin, for the boy, now man, was considered a "regular" amongst the farmers. They shared with him many of the insights and problems which they would never have imparted to an outsider.

Our friends had at first been shocked by the familiarity Robbie expressed with Justin and myself, but over the years those tongues wagged less and less.

When we reached the stables it did not surprise me to find that Justin had been victorious. As had Lord Taggart. The two seemed to have enjoyed the chase and were congratulating each other on their success.

Justin dismounted and embraced me warmly, whispering in my ear as he did, "I shall claim my reward later."

As I turned to congratulate Lord Taggart I saw that his expression was one of amusement and I flushed with the thought that he had overheard Justin's murmurings. But if he had, he was not about to embarrass me, for he simply thanked me for my well wishes.

Realizing that the luncheon would commence shortly, I gathered the children and started back to the house. Monique fell in step with me.

"It eez good zat Justin was victorious today, *n'est-ce pas?*" she stated more than asked.

"Why do you say that, Monique?"

She shrugged. "*Peut-être*, I sense zat zer ees somesing which troubles him."

"What do you mean?" I pressed, surprised by her comment.

"*Malheureusement*, I can give you nothing, what you zay, specific. *Mais* I am zure there eez somesing wrong. I have

talked to him, Serena. He eez not ze Justin I know. He is restless, distant."

"I would remind you, Monique, that you and Justin have
not been close, or, shall I say, *intimate*, for years. A certain
amount of change, I trust you would agree, is healthy in any
man."

I was annoyed with myself for allowing her comments to
unnerve me. It was ridiculous of course. If there was anything
awry with Justin then I would be the first to know. We shared
everything. Unless, of course, he was ill. I suddenly recollected
Anne's conversation with me earlier. She, too, had hinted that
he seemed preoccupied. A growing anxiety stirred within me.

Monique sensed that I was troubled. "Perhaps I am wrong,
my dear," she assured, taking my hand, "you know zat I have
a tendency to dramatize."

That, I acknowledged to myself, was true. But Monique was
also a perceptive woman. I wished that I did not have to endure this luncheon before confronting my husband.

My spirits were buoyed that afternoon, for as I watched
Justin carefully I was convinced that his bronzed handsome-
ness could not disguise some serious illness. As with the evening prior he seemed to find Lord Taggart's company most
amusing for the two were again in constant conversation,
joined now by Mister Leech.

The luncheon of oysters, roast pheasant and ham was, as I
was told by my guests, quite delicious. I had seated the vicar to
my right, and though I was surely expected to be enthralled by
his regaling of plans for his new church, I could not dismiss
the feeling that his position and its perks were tantamount to
his dedication to the service of God.

Oliver blessedly rescued me after the luncheon and we discussed his planned trip to America. He would sail to Boston
Harbor where he intended to study the advances being made in
the areas of importing and exporting. William Cobbett had
promised to give him letters of introduction to old colleagues
in Philadelphia and he intended to travel to Virginia to talk at
some length with the colonists instrumental in the new laws of
governing.

When we were quite alone I grasped the opportunity to ask
him if he had noticed any change in Justin. He responded that
he had not, but perhaps that could be attributed to his preoccupation with his own life and plans.

It was dusk before the last of our guests had departed. The children who had tired from the day's activities were far less appeasable than they had been earlier about Oliver's leaving. I promised Anne that I would bring them to Camberleigh soon, she insisting that the old house needed the liveliness of youth. The Kelstons left, chattering that we truly should think of wintering in London this year. It amazed me when Justin replied that "one should always keep all their options open," but then I surmised that it was best not to flatly refuse the proposal and cause consternation at this late hour in the day.

As we waved off the blue and gold carriage which would take Robin, Lilliane and Monique back to Kelston Manor, Justin put his arm about me and drew me to him.

"Well, my love," he said, smiling down at me, "once again you have made me the envy of every man in the country."

"You were pleased then?" I teased.

"Pleased? How could I not have been? You are the perfect hostess. Beautiful, intelligent, accomplished."

We climbed the steps slowly to the entrance of the house.

"Then I was imagining that you seemed a bit out of sorts these past two days?"

"I cannot think why you would say that," he countered.

"Perhaps because you are normally so attentive I have come to expect you to be oversolicitous. The fact is, you preferred Lord Taggart's company to mine."

"You are being silly, Serena," he said, releasing my arm, "and frankly it does not become you."

"Well, if I am being silly, then Anne and Monique are ridiculous," I snapped, "for it was they who first brought it to my attention."

"I find it unfortunate that my sister has so little to occupy her thoughts that she must take to female gossip."

"Justin," I reproached, "that is not at all what she was doing. She is not a meddler and you know it. I am certain she only spoke out of concern. Besides, it was Monique who made greater issue of it."

He mumbled something which I could not decipher.

"I am going up to bed." I said, moving towards the staircase. "Will you join me? We can have Thomas serve us a light supper later in our rooms."

He shook his head. "You go on ahead, Serena. I will join you later."

There were few times in our married life that we had squabbled. Generally over small trite things. I loathed any friction between us, but I also knew that it was best not to press the issue. Justin was, in his own way, a very private man, and pressure only served at these times to aggravate him.

I looked in on the children briefly before retiring to bed with Jaspar at my heels.

Undressing, I placed my riding clothes in the back of the large armoire which Justin had imported for me from France and donned my nightdress and robe. Withdrawing the combs from my hair I let it cascade about my shoulders.

I plumped the pillows on the bed. "Come, Jaspar," I urged, motioning him to jump up beside me. "Perhaps you can give me some solace. Do you think there is something amiss with your master? Am I imagining things?"

I laughed as his ears cocked and I watched those brown eyes trying to fathom my questions.

"You are right," I said, petting him. "I must get my mind off of this."

I reached over to the night table and withdrew several sheaths of paper that William Cobbett had left for me. He knew how much I enjoyed his writings. They were never a source of pleasure, for the role of a reformer is not to entertain, but they did inform me about things that I might otherwise never be acquainted with.

His treatise on Newgate Prison was shocking. Fifteen to twenty people were housed in rooms no larger than 23 by 15. The prisons were farmed out to people for profit and the keeper charged exorbitant fees. Even poor Cobbett had to pay £ 12/12s per week when he had been sentenced to two years for libel a decade before.

With the narrow passages and lack of drainage and air, disease festered amongst the prisoners and threatened respectable citizens brought into the court. Cobbett was a champion of John Howard, the great prison reformer who was so actively trying to get the Gaol Acts passed which everyone knew would lead to the condemning of Newgate.

I had seen Newgate only once when we had been staying at Channing Hall, our house in London. I remember shuddering as the carriage had passed, looking up at the walls of windowless solid block masonry. It was difficult enough to think of the men imprisoned there but I did not know how the women endured even the briefest confinement.

It was hours later when I replaced the papers on the night-stand. Charlotte had come to see if I had wanted a late supper, noting that Justin had asked for a small repast to be brought to him in the library. I had simply taken tea, having no appetite after the unusually large luncheon.

Grown weary from reading in the dimly lit room, I did not fight as sleep overtook me. I knew it was hours later when I awoke, for the candles had burned fully down. I reached out to my left where Justin usually slept to find that Jaspar was curled up there in his stead.

Replacing the candle in the holder by the bed, I rose, drawing my robe about me, and made my way out into the hall. Although I could not imagine that he was still at work, Charlotte had said that he was in the library so it was there that I chose to look first.

I found him in the large wing chair staring into the fire. He had obviously not heard me enter, for he was startled as I stood before him.

"You should not be up at this hour, Serena," he chastised. "The house has drafts even on these summer nights."

"I am not cold," I said quietly.

He made no response.

"Justin, what is it?" I implored as I dropped on my knees before him. "Please do not shut me out. I cannot bear this worry."

He smoothed the hair back from my face, which I had buried in his lap.

"It is nothing to trouble you, Serena. It is simply something for me to decide and resolve."

"Have we grown so apart that I did not even recognize that you cannot or no longer want to share your problems with me?" I asked. "If I knew what it was, perhaps I could help, but I cannot fight without knowing what or whom I am fighting. Whatever it is could be no more dire than what I might imagine."

It was a long time before he spoke and when he did his voice was so low that I had to strain to hear.

"If I have been so preoccupied, it is not due to you—but because of you."

"I do not understand," I replied.

"The reason that Philip Taggart and Jonathan Leech came

to Mayfair this weekend was to attempt to persuade me to invest in a new venture.''

"That being?" I queried.

"As you know, Serena, we are on the verge of a new era for England. That siege with Napoleon is well past. We have benefited from the spoils of war but that is not true for everyone. Many of the farms in the South are doing poorly. Factories are springing up all about us and I am convinced that manufacturing is going to continue to grow here in the North.''

"Does that concern you?" I interrupted.

"To the contrary, it intrigues me. Our navy and marine forces are supreme in the world. Steamers are already carrying passengers between Dover and Calais and I am certain this is but a modest beginning. As we have monopolized transportation on the seas, I believe we can and will also do so on the land. The Stockton and Darlington Railway opened only last year and is already carrying goods. Imagine, Serena, roadways being laid from one end of England to another. Imagine were we able to take our harvest and transport it to other countries. Better yet, imagine transporting people. Think of the mobility we would have were we able to travel to London within one day.''

I looked up at Justin's face. I do not think I could recall when I had seen such animation in his eyes.

"Taggart and Leech," he continued, "are at the center of this new industrialism. They are convinced that within five years there will be navvies laying tracks for railways which may attain a speed of up to 35 miles per hour. George Stephenson is already at work on something he calls 'The Rocket.' ''

"Darling, forgive me," I interrupted, "but I do not see where this is all leading.''

He rubbed his chin with his hand. "Taggart wants me as an investor in a major railway endeavor that he and Jonathan have been working on. They feel certain that if they can obtain the funding they need that theirs will be the first official passenger railway in England.''

"But you are not an industrialist, Justin," I argued. "Good Lord, Cobbett would faint if he heard you talk like this.''

"I suppose he would," he replied quietly. "Cobbett is wedded to the land and for him these new fangled apparatuses will be the death of us all.''

"You say Cobbett is an agriculturist," I pursued, "but so are you. I do not know any other titled gentleman who is as passionate about these farms as you."

"It is because I am that I feel so strongly about the need to invest in this railway venture. You know what unrest there has been due to those Corn Laws and the population is growing daily, which I suspect is going to be affected even more strongly as the Irish continue to immigrate. These people are going to come to the North, Serena. And they are going to come looking for jobs. You know as I do that they are not going to find them on the land. But the railroad, that would give them work. And it would, I am certain, strengthen the country's economy. Serena, I do not want Alexander and Daphne to be left a heritage of land that has gone fallow or estates that have shrunk because their father did not perceive the mood of the country."

I ruminated about what he had said. It was difficult to grasp, for although conversation on the new industrialism was not uncommon in our household, Justin, or so I had thought, had always fought so radically on the side of the agriculturist. He had been opposed to heavy taxation of the tenants, he had fought the Speenhamland Act from pervailing the North arguing that it would destroy the common farmer or laborer, and he had opposed the hiring of farmers' wives, knowing that it was simply a ploy to keep down the wages of the men.

"You are opposed then," he said gruffly.

I shook my head. " 'Tis not opposition, Justin, it is simply such a departure from anything I had imagined would be part of our lives, but if you feel so strongly about it then I suppose you must invest."

He took a sip from the glass of port, which had until then been left untouched. "It is not as simple as that, Serena."

I toyed with a lock of my hair. "Is it that you are weary of our life, Justin? Have I become so tedious to you that you need to look to investments and work for diversion?"

"Good Lord, Serena," he retorted, "Do you not understand that this is the reason for my dilemma about this venture? It is because I so love you and the children that this decision is so torturous. Taggart needs my money—of that there is no question—but in this instance I would not be but a silent investor. I would be actively involved in every aspect

from the organization to working with government functions
for laws and clearances, even in the actual design and routes.''

"But why, pray tell, does that make it so difficult? You are
accustomed, heaven knows, to hard work."

"That is true. But I am not accustomed to being apart from
you. Do you realize that in the years that we have been married we have not been apart for more than a week at a time?"

"Why would this then be so different?"

"Because I would not only need to be in London for several
weeks but Taggart feels it mandatory that I travel to America
to work with some fellow there who seems, like Stephenson, to
have made strides in the area of rail by steam.''

"To America?" I gasped. "Goodness, it seems we are all
destined to take major journeys this year. First, Oliver and
now us."

"I do not believe you understand, Serena," he pressed. "I
said that *I* would be going. That did not include you."

"Why could I not join you?" I argued. "The children
would adore it and I am certain they would not prove a hin-
drance. I could keep up with their studies, we could even
rendezvous perhaps with Oliver.''

"Absolutely not," Justin insisted. "These passages are not
easy, Serena, I would never subject you and the children to the
rigors of such a voyage. And it is not as though I shall be on
holiday while there. It will be work—work, which I must add,
I would like to accomplish in as little time as possible so that I
might return forthwith.''

"Justin, you make me sound as though I am one of those
delicate fainting females. I would remind you that before we
met I had undertaken some arduous journeys and tasks on my
own."

His hand stroked my cheek. "I have never implied that you
were anything less than capable, Serena. But I am unwavering
on this issue. Were I to undertake this venture it must be on
my own."

"What of Oliver?" I ventured. "You trust him—could he
not be sent as your emissary?"

"I thought of that," Justin admitted. "But this is my passion, not Oliver's. Besides, I talked to Taggart and he was opposed to it.''

"Where does that lead us to then?"

"I fear at an impasse. You must know, Serena, that I would never enter into this without your approval. I cannot deny that it would be difficult on us all. And thus, I cannot gamble this without your support." He pulled me to my feet. "This is not a decision for this late hour, however. I have thought upon it for some two weeks now. I scarcely think you should be pressed for some conclusion tonight."

I would have preferred to have continued our conversation but I was admittedly exhausted. I had no idea what time it was when we finally climbed into bed. Justin pulled me into the crook of his arm and I welcomed the warmth of his body against my own. It was not long before his breathing quieted and I knew that he was asleep.

I, too, closed my eyes, wishing that sleep would come soon to me. But as weary as my limbs were, I was not able to silence my mind, which was racing with our earlier conversation. In the moonlit shadows of the night I watched my arm which crossed Justin's chest rise and fall in a steady rhythm. I could not imagine lying in this bed alone for months on end separated from the man I loved so dearly. And yet I could not fathom what Justin's reaction would be should I tell him that I could not approve of this venture. I knew that he would accept my decision, certainly he was beyond any pettiness or vindictiveness about it. But would there be resentment? I wondered. Heaven knew Justin was not a man to be confined. If I did not encourage him, would it affect our relationship? By holding him to me, would I really be driving him away?

It was dawn when, having reached my decision, I slept.

It was raining when I awoke the next morning. I lay abed listening to it pelt against the roof. It was soothing somehow.

When I finally rose and bathed I selected a pale blue muslin gown which was embroidered with yellow and green flowers. It was a very airy, feminine dress and I knew one of Justin's favorites.

It being Sunday, I knew that the children would be looking forward to spending the afternoon with us but I wanted to discuss my decision with Justin before seeing them.

I found him in the library studying what looked to be architectural plans. He smiled as I entered. "You look like a little girl in that dress."

I pushed my hair back and crossed over to him. "Charlotte

has the day off and I fear all I could do was put a brush to my hair."

"You know I like it loose about your face like that," he said as he embraced me.

"What are these plans?"

He rolled them up binding them with a ribbon. "Nothing important."

"They have to do with the railway, do they not?" I queried.

"We do not need to discuss this now, Serena," he assured me.

"But I think we do, Justin," I argued, seating myself in the chair opposite his desk. "I have slept this morning away because I could not sleep last night."

I poured two cups of tea, offering one to Justin. "I cannot feign to completely understand your seemingly sudden passion for railroads," I continued. "But it shall be for others, if they can, to thwart your enthusiasm. I shall not be the one to keep you from your dreams even if it will bring certain periods of loneliness to me and the children."

"Are you saying then that you approve of the investment?" he said eagerly.

"Approve is not the word I would use, but yes, I agree."

He jumped up so quickly that he startled me and, pulling me to my feet, spun me about. His lips found mine and his ebullience was communicated in the passion of his kiss. When at last he released me he whispered, "You shall not regret it, Serena, I promise."

"I pray not," I replied, swallowing against the lump that formed in my throat.

"There is so much to plan, Serena," he said excitedly. "I shall need to spend three, perhaps four, weeks in London before journeying to America."

"That is something I wished to discuss with you, Justin. I shall want to accompany you to London, with the children, of course. I fear I would find the winter far too dreary here without you. Monique, I know, is planning to be in London for several months and she will prove good company while you are gone. Besides, Channing Hall needs a thorough refurbishing and what better time to do it than now."

"I see I am to pay dearly for this," he said, winking at me.

"Actually I think it makes good sense. There will be far more to amuse you in London and it might well be beneficial for Daphne and Alexander. Not to mention myself. I far prefer having you at my side for as long as possible."

"When shall you be wanting to leave?" I asked.

"Would one week be too soon?"

"One week?" I gasped. "That scarcely gives me much time to prepare. Not to mention you. I scarcely think you can simply abandon Mayfair."

"I admit that part will not be simple, but I am pressing to move quickly for the timing is excellent. We have almost completed the harvest, which means that Robbie will not be excessively burdened. I shall, of course, need to ride over to Camberleigh and discuss my plans with Richard. He shall be less than pleased, I am certain, for it will mean that he shall need to be more active, certainly with the accounts."

"That worries me, Justin," I replied. "Anne spoke to me this weekend about Richard. She does not believe he is well. Indeed, she even asked if I would ask you to speak to him. You know how stubborn he can be."

"She mentioned it to me as well. I do not know what strides I can make in that area but I certainly will try."

I rose to leave. "I am going to fetch the children. If you do not object, I should like to share our news with them together. I will ask Charlotte to prepare a special luncheon for us."

I had just reached the door when I heard Justin call my name. I turned to face him.

"Thank you, Serena. Not for bowing to my wishes but for understanding. I love you dearly and cherish your empathy in this."

I closed the door behind me saying a silent prayer that I had indeed made the right decision.

We shared our plans with the children over a delicious luncheon of poached salmon, fresh beans and corn cakes. Daphne was thrilled at the prospect of residing in London and quickly extracted promises from me that I would take her to the shops and theater. It was difficult to perceive Alexander's reaction. I sensed that he was not taken with the thought of being apart from his father, but he was attempting to be stalwart at Justin's reminder that he would have to be the man of the house while he was gone.

With Jaspar in tow we wound down to the stables after our meal, where the children amused themselves riding their ponies. I was surprised at how calmly Robbie took the news but suspected that Justin had already pursued the possibility with him sometime earlier. No matter how capable I knew Robbie to be, I could not help but be concerned that Justin was overburdening the boy.

As planned, Justin departed for Camberleigh the next morning. I enlisted Charlotte's aid in helping me commence the enormous task of packing. It would be six months before we returned to Mayfair, and heavy clothing would be needed by then to brave the cold damp London winters. Charlotte was miffed with me, I knew, for my intention was not to bring her with us initially. There was adequate staff at Channing Hall, and she could use the respite.

Master Farraday, on the other hand, once assured that his position was secure, was pleased at the prospect of an interim holiday. While Justin remained in London I wanted the children to be able to spend as much time as possible with him, and their tutor, I decided, would be superfluous. I would spend time with their lessons each day, and the pause in their formal education should not prove harmful.

When Justin returned two days later, he was appreciably less enthusiastic than when he had left. Richard had agreed, but reluctantly so, to assume a more active role in the running of the estates. I suspected that Richard had driven a hard bargain with Justin. The subject of his health had been broached but was discounted by Richard as his wife's overactive imagination. If Justin was going to waver from his decision, I knew he would do so in those first hours of his return to Mayfair. With Oliver's impending departure and doubts about Richard's well-being, he felt guilty about placing additional burdens on his brother-in-law. Had I encouraged his quandary over his selfishness in the matter, there was no doubt in my mind that this venture with the railways would have been set aside forever. But I had made a decision and that commitment would remain firm.

# 4

Those final days at Mayfair were hectic. I tried to keep the disruption from the children as much as possible for I was loathe to have them sense the emotional as well as physical turmoil I was feeling. Jaspar, once having seen the valises spread throughout our rooms, shadowed me constantly. He, of course, would journey to London with us, but until he climbed into the coach he would be suspicious.

The night before we were to leave, Justin and I shared a long intimate dinner in the octagonal garden room. The air was heady with the scent of late summer roses and we were serenaded by the chirps and hoots of night's creatures. I wished that I could have shared his enthusiastic ramblings about the adventure ahead of us, but I could not help feeling that my whole life was being uprooted. It was not fear that I felt—simply uncertainty. Mayfair was a secure haven. From those days when I had first traveled to Camberleigh, I had never journeyed well into areas of the unknown.

It was a warm sun-filled day when we climbed aboard our carriage and started out for London. Charlotte had had the cook prepare baskets of food for us, which we shared midday at a fresh flowing stream beside the road. Justin preferred to ride atop the carriage with our driver to be able to oversee some of the tenant farms while the children and I played word games inside until the steady sway lulled us to sleep. We stayed

the night at a small inn midway to London. It was not highly
fashionable, but it was comfortable and the food they served
was delicious. Several other families had joined us in the large
dining hall and Daphne was quite taken with dining amongst
strangers. We set out before dawn the next morning as Justin
was eager to reach London by nightfall. The children's enthusiasm had paled a bit and keeping them amused was growing increasingly difficult. Knowing that it would be very late
before we would reach the house, we stopped at another inn
and partook of a hearty soup, roasted pork and fresh breads
in the early afternoon. Refreshed, we sang songs until by dusk
Alexander had fallen asleep across my lap while Daphne and
Jaspar slumbered soundly on the seat opposite.

Channing Hall I had always thought to be one of the most
impressive homes in all of London. Crafted of polished white
stone, its Ionic portico was raised on a terrace and flanked by
many wings fronticed by Ionic columns. The house was set
back from the street and there were heavy plantings of yews,
foxwood and juniper. The sound of the horses' hooves against
the cobblestone street stopped. I looked from the carriage window through the ornate iron fence with its heavy double gates.
Lights flickered brightly in the front hall. I hoped it was a sign
of welcome.

Justin climbed down from the carriage and lifted Alexander,
who was fast asleep, into his arms. "Here comes James," I
whispered. "Let him take Alexander and you take Daphne."

Justin nodded and handed the boy over to the stout balding
man who had managed Channing Hall for us for the past ten
years.

Jaspar jumped from the coach and I followed the entourage
up to the house. "I have taken it upon myself to set aside the
fourth floor for the children and their governess," James said
as he prepared to mount the stairs. "That will be fine, James,
thank you," I replied as I followed him up the spiraled staircase.

Daphne would be thrilled, I knew, to have her own bedroom. The rooms in the house were all of generous size,
though the entry hall, as the rest, was in need of refurbishing.
We climbed the stairs to the rooms James had designated for
the children.

"I will see to Alexander," Justin said, placing Daphne on

the bed. "James said that Cook has prepared a small supper, will you join me?" I nodded.

"Just let me freshen up a bit first, and send Mary up to the bedroom. I should like her to unpack for us tonight."

The driver brought the children's valises up and I opened Daphne's to fetch a nightdress.

She awoke as I attempted to change her clothes.

"Where are we, Mother?"

"At Channing Hall, darling. This is to be your room and Alexander is just across the hall. Our rooms are just below, should you need anything, and Mary, who you will like, is here on this floor with you, as are the other servants."

"Is this room to be all my own?" she asked as I helped her remove her clothing.

"You won't be frightened here by yourself, will you?"

"Oh, no," she assured me.

I turned back the covers. "You get a good night's sleep and I will have James show you about in the morning."

Mary was already unpacking as I reached the master bedroom.

"Oh, Lady Barkham, 'tis a pleasure it is to have ye back in London again," she effused as I entered.

"How have you been, Mary? You are indeed looking well," I replied, noting that she looked almost radiant.

"Oh, aye've been fine yer ladyship an' aye am to be married next year."

"Mary, that is wonderful news," I replied. "I am happy for you. But I hope this does not mean that we will be losing you."

She laughed. "Not unless ye'll be givin' Sidney and me notice cause we're wed."

"Sidney. You mean our Sidney?"

"Just the one. Kin ye imagine it? 'Ere we've been livin' in this house together now for eight years an' all of a sudden like 'e says te me one day, 'ow about ye an' me start courtin'. An' before you know it 'e proposed."

"He's a good man," I said sincerely as I watched Mary continue to unpack. It was good to see her so happy. She had been so forlorn when she had come to us. She must have been no more than fifteen at the time and already a widow—and nowhere to turn. Justin always said Sidney was the best driver in

London and I sensed he would be a good husband to Mary.

"Aye brought up some hot water, yer Ladyship, thinkin' that ye'd be wantin' to freshen before yer supper."

I bathed quickly and changed to a pale pink muslin gown. I uncoiled my hair and brushed it well, tying it back with a satin ribbon.

The hallway was dark and I made my way carefully down to the drawing room. I had always thought it to be one of the most graceful staircases with its curved balusters fashioned from iron patterned in repeats of scrolls and foliage. The drawing room was enormous for a city dwelling ranging some thirty-five feet wide and forty feet long. There were eight columns in the room, Corinthian in nature, which supported the half-domed ceiling. I had always thought the most appealing part of the room were the architectural panels which we had filled with paintings of noted artists. Most of the furniture was Hepplewhite fashioned from tulipwood and walnut. The pieces were almost too delicate for the size of the room, though I think it was the lack of strong colors that kept it from making the statement it should.

Justin was seated at a small round table at the end of the room which had been laid in preparation for our supper.

"I must say you look refreshed, darling, hardly as one who has been traveling for two days."

"Thank you, I feel better."

"I fear I have some rather shocking news," he said, handing me a glass of wine. I steeled myself for his words. "What has happened?"

"Castlereagh has taken his own life—he slit his throat."

"Good Lord!" I gasped. "Why? How do you know?"

"James told me. Apparently it has but happened a short time ago. I cannot imagine what drove him to it except perhaps overwork."

"Well, you were never that fond of him," I replied.

"Oh, he did well enough with our Foreign Offices, but I cannot think of what he has proved as Leader of the House of Commons."

"Who do you think will replace him?"

"Ironically, I think it shall be Canning."

"Was he not being sent to the East?"

He nodded. "But he will be needed here now as Foreign Secretary, what with Castlereagh gone."

I took a sip of wine. "I certainly have pity for the man, but I must admit I am relieved that the crisis was not an immediate one to the family." James entered with one of the serving girls and placed trays of oysters, smoked sturgeon and fresh asparagus before us. "Excuse me, Lord Barkham," he said as he removed the trays, "a Lord Taggart was here to see you earlier. He said that he would call again tomorrow morning."

"He knows of your decision then?" I asked.

"I sent him a note by post the day after you gave me your decision. I am certain the chap is as anxious to begin the plans as I."

"Shall you be working at the house?"

"Most days, I expect, though do not rely on seeing too much of me. We have an enormous amount to accomplish before I leave."

"If I am to refurbish this house, and heaven knows it needs it, I shall be at the drapery shops most of the time anyway. As Monique is in town, perhaps I might persuade her to help me."

"Would it be too tedious to ask you if we might have Taggart and Jonathan Leech here for dinner at the weekend?"

"I will simply tell Cook," I agreed. "Perhaps I shall invite Monique as well. She seemed quite taken with Philip at the ball."

"You know, I think you should consider interviewing a governess for the children, Serena. If you are to undertake redecorating this house and entertaining, you certainly cannot have them underfoot all the time."

"Oh, I love having them about," I protested. "And they shall be great solace for me when you are gone."

"Well, at least then consider bringing Charlotte to London before I leave."

"I will," I assured him, "but Mary will be of great assist in the interim."

We finished our meal with Justin being exceedingly tolerant of my ramblings about what I intended to do with the house. It was very late when we retired. I was amused that Mary had obviously instructed the chambermaid that Lord and Lady Barkham would only need one bed turned down for the night. As we had never had separate bedrooms at Mayfair, we had never made use of the adjoining room here in London. I climbed into bed first and watched Justin as he released the heavily tasseled cords which held the dark silk curtains at the sides of the bed.

"How tired are you?" he whispered as he drew me to his nakedness.

"I shall never be too tired for you," I replied, shuddering with pleasure as his hand moved gently up under my nightdress. When he finally exploded within me and turned from me, cradling his hand against my breast, which he continued to arouse with his tongue, I found myself thinking that I would be happy if another child would be formed from this union.

Justin had already risen and left when I awoke the next morning. I lay abed for a while and studied the room. There was a double armoire in one corner and near it an inlaid mahogany dressing table with its toilet mirror and stand draped in muslin. The silver-backed brushes, tortoiseshell combs and silver ringstand which lay atop had been a gift from Justin on our first anniversary. The fireplace was marble and skirted by a brass fender. The mantelshelf held a wealth of china ornaments which had long been in the Barkham family. I was very proud of the tall fire screen which I had petit-pointed myself while awaiting the birth of Alexander. The tall case clock chimed ten and I decided it was time that I arose.

I selected an apple green printed chintz gown for the day. I missed Charlotte's assistance with my hair and thought that it might indeed be wise not only for the children but for myself to bring her to London.

As I left the room I almost fell over Jaspar, who was curled up outside the door. I reached down to pet him and his tongue licked at my hand. "Let's go find your father," I persuaded and followed him as he dashed down the stairs towards the library.

I halted suddenly as I flung open the double doors. "Oh, I am sorry," I apologized as I saw Lord Taggart and Mister Leech conferring with Justin. "I had no idea that we had company."

"I fear these early meetings shall disturb your routine," Lord Taggart said, rising to greet me, "but it is important that Jonathan and I spend as much time as possible with your husband before his departure."

"We are used to rising early in the country, Lord Taggart,"

I replied. "Please be seated. And how are you today, Mister Leech?"

"Well, oh, very well, thank you, Lady Barkham," he mumbled, shuffling his portly frame over to where I stood.

"Please call me Serena," I insisted. "We are going to be seeing a good deal of each other and I think we should be on familiar terms. We also would be very pleased if you both would join us for dinner on Saturday evening. I am hoping that Lady Kelston will join us as well."

"I cannot think of anything that would please me more," Lord Taggart replied.

"Excellent. Then I shall expect you at six." Turning to Justin, I said, "I am going to take the children over to see Monique. Perhaps we shall luncheon together but I will ask Mary to prepare something for you here."

I left the library with Jaspar in tow and found the children who were happily reading some nursery stories. They were thrilled by the idea of going out and seeing Monique, whom they both adored. I instructed James to have the driver bring the carriage round to the entrance and after gathering my parasol and bag we were on our way.

The children chattered constantly, asking who lives here and who lives there.

"Where does the King live, Mother?" Alexander asked.

"At Windsor Castle," I replied. "It is a ways from here."

"Master Farraday told me that the King's wife never had a father," Daphne pronounced.

"Really, Daphne," I chastised, "you must not repeat things like that. I am surprised at your tutor—he should show more discretion."

"Is it true?" she persisted.

"Well, it is rumored as such. Caroline was not a very attractive woman and had some curious personal habits, but the poor woman is dead now and we must not dishonor the King by making reference to her. He is a man of great taste and it was an unfortunate marriage."

It did not take long to reach Broughton House, the Kelstons' London residence on Queen Anne Street. A smaller house than Channing Hall, it was designed in the late eighteenth century by Robert Adan. It was simple in design save for the Doric fluted columns which embraced the doorway. Lantern holders graced the front railings on either side.

I did not recognize the manservant who opened the door but inquired if Lady Kelston was in. He said that she was and ushered us through the large hall, the walls of which were covered with paintings done in the school of Raphael. From there we were ushered to the right into a large parlor. Monique was seated on a big chaise doing some embroidery.

"*Chérie*, what a zurprize zees ees," she effused as we entered. "So you decided to join me after all. Theez eez *magnifique*. I have just been tortured over this silly needlework, longing for some amusement and you have come to rescue me. Daphne, Alexander, come give Monique a kiss."

The children did so warmly.

"Let us go into the garden," she continued. "I shall have Jane bring us some lemonade."

We followed her to the gardens, stepping down from the house to sit on stone benches which lay between two groves of tall lime trees bordered with tubs of bays and orange trees. The children went to play on a terrace below which surrounded a large fountain.

"Now tell me, are you alone, Serena, or eez that handsome husband with you?" Monique asked as we sipped on the drinks which had been brought to us.

"There is a great deal to tell you," I commenced as I proceeded to explain at length why we had come to London and Justin's venture with the railroads.

"So zat eez what was troubling him," Monique mused. "I am certain zat you have reservations, Serena, but you have done ze right thing. You cannot hold Justin back. He eez not a man to be contained."

"I am so pleased that you will be in London, Monique. It will be dreadfully lonely for me, and if you will help me redecorate Channing Hall I would be ever so grateful. I need something to divert my mind."

"We shall commence tomorrow. I have a wonderful seamstress. By the time Justin returns he shall not recognize zat house of yours."

The afternoon passed quickly. Monique had a light luncheon served in the garden and the children played hot cockles and pig tops. I invited Monique to join us for dinner on Saturday and she accepted, seeming particularly interested when I told her that Lord Taggart would be there. We arranged for her to come to the house the next morning to commence making plans for the house.

It was late afternoon when we returned to Channing Hall. Mary took the children up to their rooms and I went to the library where I found Lord Taggart by himself.

"Your husband and Jonathan have gone out for a bit but they should return before nightfall," he said. "I hope you do not mind my being here."

"You are always welcome here, Philip," I assured him. "Is your home far from here?"

"I have a very small house in the north end. Not terribly fashionable but until now I have spent very little time in London."

"Should I assume then that you are from the country?"

He nodded. "From Cornwall."

"Really," I exclaimed, "I was raised along the coast, but I have not returned since coming north. The farming has certainly been more profitable up here but I must say that I still long for the smell and sound of the sea."

"Do you go to Brighton?" he asked.

I admitted that I had never been, though Robin and Lilliane Kelston were frequent visitors, often extolling the virtues of this seaside resort. It was very popular among the stock jobbers or so William Cobbett had told me.

"Am I interrupting your work, Philip?" I asked realizing that he had been studying some papers when I first entered.

"To the contrary, Serena. If I may say so you are much softer on my eyes than these technical drawings."

I flushed at his compliment. It was not difficult to understand Monique's attraction to him. He was handsome but he was also charming. I knew very little about him but I sensed that many of the ladies of my acquaintance with daughters of an eligible age would find him a highly suitable prospect.

"Might I ask how you came to be interested in the railway?" I asked.

"It is very simple, really. My family's farms have all been but sold off. Crops, as you know, are very poor in the South and admittedly, unlike Justin, I have never had his passion for the land. I met Jonathan quite by chance about six months ago, and though the man seems scatterbrained, when it comes to understanding the workings of iron and the technical possibilities of transportation he is a genius. The rest, I believe, you know. Your husband's name was given to me by a mutual acquaintance who suggested that he might be interested in making an investment in the project. I must say that his enthusiasm has been surprising. I had thought that he would prefer to be, shall we say, a silent partner.''

I laughed. "You do not know Justin then. He is rarely silent about anything. Particularly when money is concerned.''

"I have learned that,'' he replied.

I rose to leave. "If you wish, Philip, you and Jonathan are certainly welcome to remain for dinner. I cannot promise anything too extravagant since Cook is just getting back into the routine of having the house filled, but you are more than welcome.''

"Thank you, Serena, but I shall decline this evening. I should not want you to tire of me so soon.''

"Scarcely,'' I replied. "Well, then, I shall see you tomorrow, I expect. Would you be so kind as to tell Justin that I will be in our rooms?''

"Of course,'' he agreed. "Serena?''

"Yes, Philip.''

"I want to thank you for putting me at ease. After that faux pas I committed at Mayfair I worried that there would be a schism between us.''

"It is forgotten,'' I assured him.

I left the library and went up to the children's rooms. I read to them until their supper was brought up. Daphne beseeched me to let Jaspar remain with her for the night, which I agreed to, suspecting that she was not as comfortable as she professed about sleeping in her own room. I had returned to our bedroom and was making notations for my meeting with Monique the next day when Justin returned.

"Have Philip and Jonathan left?'' I asked.

"About a half an hour ago,'' he said as he unbuttoned his waistcoat.

"How did your day go?''

"It was interesting, though I fear that I have made some enemies.''

"Enemies?'' I queried. "Why? Of whom?''

"This railway venture is not going to be popular with everyone you know, Serena. There are many who feel that these iron monsters will literally eradicate life in the small towns. That it will literally destroy our rural counties. Not to mention those who fear that it will encourage common folk to move about and thus breed overcrowding and crime in the cities. Even the educators are against it."

"And you—do you have second thoughts on this venture, Justin?"

"I think there is some truth in what they say but I am still convinced that it is right. It will be a source of work for many who would not otherwise have it; it could bring fluidity to the land. We will be able to transport coal and even grain in a faster and more economical fashion, not to mention people. But other than the Quakers from the Midlands, I know of few groups who wholly support it."

"If you believe in it, Justin, you must not waver. I am certain we have been gossiped about before. I shall not faint, I assure you, if our popularity suffers a bit."

He smiled at me. "Philip is right."

"About what?" I asked.

"I am fortunate to have you as my wife."

I laughed. "And do not forget it, Lord Barkham, when you are those thousands of miles away from me."

"I am missing you already."

"I do wish that you did not have to go to America. Could not Philip go in your stead?"

"He insists not. He believes that my associations are stronger and will carry more credence in getting the information we need."

"Are the railways more advanced in America?"

"Far from it," he replied. "I predict that they shall be England's gift to the world."

"Well, then, what can you seek to gain over there?"

"Philip knows of some chap who has some new ideas about powering the engines. I do not think that we can afford to leave any avenue unexplored."

"When will you leave then?"

"I checked on that today. I am ticketed now for the twenty-fourth."

"But, Justin, that is only a little more than two weeks away," I exclaimed.

"We shall make it a very full two weeks, I promise."

"I assumed you would be working."

"I will, but in the evenings we might take in a concert if you like," he tempted.

"Nothing would please me more," I assured him, "but I think it best that we spend more time with the children."

Which is exactly what we did. Monique, true to her word, was in the drawing room early the next morning ready to whisk me off to the drapery shops. By the week's end I was thoroughly confused by the seeming hundreds of samples which were spread throughout the house. Justin was of no assist, assuring me that he would be delighted with whatever I selected. Monique had heard of a new cabinetmaker who specialized in sofas and chaises and I hired to him to make some twenty pieces which would accommodate the new drapery and upholstery selections. I decided to wait until Justin's departure to bring in the painters and wallpaper craftsmen as I did not want to intrude on his daily workings with Philip and Jonathan. The children and I did manage to get him out one afternoon to the marionette theatre, which even he seemed to enjoy, but for the most part his preoccupation was with his new venture.

As planned I had a small dinner party that first week back in London. Monique and Philip continued to seem to enjoy each other's company. I had no thoughts that this dalliance might lead to something more permanent. Philip was certainly too young to be considered a suitor for Monique but I knew that she was attractive to gentlemen, and he, the more I knew him, appeared charming with a clever wit, so it was that each seemed to draw satisfaction from the friendship.

When Monique reciprocated our invitation the next week, I was somewhat startled to find that Philip appeared to have an intimate knowledge of her house but I never made mention of it to her. Nor to Justin, who I knew would be amused by my naiveté.

When I paused at last from my what now seemed overzealous spending, I was staggered by the amounts that I had actually committed. I did not consider myself profligate but it had been some time since I had had to ask Justin for such vast sums of money. He did not seem the least troubled by it so I assumed that there was no need for concern. Money was not a topic which my husband and I discussed. I knew that our holdings were vast but I had never asked him the extent of our wealth. I had inherited an enormous sum upon the death of my grandmother, though I had insisted that Camberleigh go one day to Oliver. As the estates were merged by our ancestry, it was not as though I had given up all claim to it, and I knew that, withstanding what seemed some impossible schism, the house would always be welcome to me.

The children were very good during those weeks, but, admitting that Justin was right, I finally sent off a letter to Charlotte asking her join us. I also penned one to Anne telling her of my plans for the house and informing her of the date of Justin's departure. I longed for her to join me in London but as they had traveled so extensively in the past six months I doubted that they would leave Camberleigh so soon again. And, of course, with Richard needed there to oversee everything, my pleas would have fallen on deaf ears. I apologized for not having taken the time to see Clarissa but I knew that Anne would understand. Although I kept up the ruse that she was my cousin and would carry the secret of her illegitimacy with me to my death, we had not grown closer over the years.

The day before Justin was to depart we committed to spending together with the children. We rose late and took a quiet luncheon in the garden behind the house. It was a balmy day and we sat on the terrace under the shade of an oak gnarled with age. The scent of the roses in their final bloom of the season perfumed the garden.

In the afternoon we had our driver take us down to the Thames where the children sailed paper boats which Justin had made for them. I was always so proud of strolling with him in public, even though we did so infrequently it always amazed me how many gentlemen whose acquaintance he had made through business would approach to bid their respects.

We came to rest finally in a small pavilion which was situated on a knoll above the river, but still in full view so that we might watch the children.

"You have seemed most pensive today, my love," he said as I removed my bonnet.

"One can hardly blame me for that," I retorted.

"I thought, Serena, that we were not going to brood about my departure."

" 'Tis a promise I am finding very difficult to keep."

"I need you to be strong about this," he implored.

I nodded. "Believe me, I thought that I was managing my feelings. I think I simply have kept myself busy so that I would not have time to think. Now that your leaving is imminent all my resolve seems to have abandoned me."

"Admittedly, it would be awkward, but if you were to bid it I would discard this whole scheme and we could simply return to Mayfair tomorrow."

"Well, you can relax for I shall do no such thing," I assured him. "Just do not think of me too harshly if I should spill a tear or two before tomorrow."

He put his arm about me and kissed me lightly on the cheek. "I could never think harshly of you, Serena. My God, I adore you as life itself." I started to reply and he pressed his fingers against my lips.

"Serena, I have some things I want to say to you and I want you to listen well to me."

"Certainly," I replied.

"I want to insist that you do not coop yourself up at the house when I am gone. It shall be a full six months before I return and I do not want to leave here thinking that you are going to be pining away here in London. You have a life to live, Serena, and I am going to rely on you to keep some sort of continuance in our lives. The interior of the house will change but I selfishly want everything else to be familiar when I return to you and the children."

"Given good fortune nothing shall change," I assured him. "The children may have grown a bit, I might have a dalliance or two," I chided, "but otherwise all will be constant."

"You are a devil," he laughed. "But I am twenty paces ahead of you."

"How?" I asked.

"I have assigned someone to keep an eye out for you."

"And who, pray tell, is that?"

"Philip Taggart."

"Philip Taggart?" I echoed. "Why, I scarcely know the man."

"That is true, but he seemed the logical choice. We have, after all, entered into a partnership and he is unencumbered by family here in London."

"Justin," I argued, "beyond it being an imposition, I scarcely need someone to hold my hand while you are gone."

"Holding your hand was not what I had envisioned, my love. It simply is someone who will look in on you from time to time or who you might call on if you should need something."

"I think it is ridiculous," I insisted. "We have a staff full of servants, I have sent for Charlotte, Monique is in town, not to mention other friends.''

"I realize that, Serena, but pray, humor me on this point. Philip will not interfere, I am certain. He will simply be at your disposal should you need him.''

"I see," I replied with some resolve.

"You do not dislike Philip, do you?" he asked anxiously.

"Of course not," I assured him.

"Good, then it is settled."

The sky had clouded over during our conversation and a light drizzle had commenced falling. I called to the children, who came back slowly from the water's edge, Jaspar following at their heels. We walked back to the carriage and got in just before the clouds broke and torrents of rain fell from the heavens. Justin was playful with the children on the way home, amusing them with tales of his own childhood visits to London. I knew that he was simply extending the inevitable confrontation of his departure and since I was loath to deal with it myself I went happily along with his avoidance. I had been able to steel myself this past week from showing anxiety about Justin's impending trip. Having promised him my support, I did not want him to feel that I was reneging on that. In truth I was not, but inwardly I was already dreading the loneliness of the next months.

There was no question that compared to other women of my age and standing I was considered self-sufficient. But I also recognized for the first time my dependence on Justin. He was such a strong man, and although I had not planned to, I had come to rely on him in our life together.

In many ways I resented his persuading Philip Taggart to look in on me from time to time, although I had to acknowledge that a man's assistance would be welcome should I need it. The natural choice would have been Clarissa's husband, but although he was a successful stock jobber he was scarcely a sort who inspired much confidence in difficult situations. There were times when I wished that I had not been so quick to decide to remain in London for although Mayfair was somewhat remote, it was home and the familiarity of the surroundings would have given me solace. I could, of course, reverse my decision, but now that I was committed to the renovation of Channing Hall I would have to stay for at least another three months.

The rains had not subsided by the time we reached the house and I insisted that the children change their clothes before dinner. Justin and I did the same and I left him with James, who had brought the trunks out and was already laying out his clothing for the journey. Jaspar, who had followed us up to the bedroom, would not leave my side once he saw the valises and accompanied me back down to the library.

I was glad Mary had seen that a fire had been laid since the rain had given a dampness to the house. I sat on the large couch which faced the Adam fireplace and gestured to Jaspar to come and sit aside me.

"Oh, Jaspar," I said aloud as I stroked his long silky ears, "what are we going to do while Justin is gone?"

Sensing my unhappiness, he licked at my hand.

"You are a dear old friend," I continued. "There are many who are amused by my trust in you but I do not think there is anyone other than Justin that senses me better than you."

He moaned a bit as I massaged his ears. I knew that my obsession with this dog seemed an oddity to those who did not understand our special relationship. I would never believe that dogs did not have higher intelligence than we credited them for. He certainly had a vast vocabulary and responded even to my changes of facial expression. I wondered at times whether he pondered about what I was thinking as much as I did when studying him.

It was about an hour later when Mary told me that Justin and the children had gone into the dining room. I joined them there.

"I hope you do not mind, Serena," Justin said as I entered, "but I have promised the children that they might come to see me off in the morning."

I grimaced at his decision, for although I knew that Alexander, in particular, would be thrilled to see the tall ships, the actual experience of seeing their father leave us might be too painful.

"If you think it wise," I cautioned.

"Oh, please, Mother," Daphne pleaded. "Besides, Lord Taggart is to take us to the circus after Papa's ship sets sail. We all are to go."

"We are, are we?" I asked with considerable surprise. "What is this about the circus, Justin?"

"Philip will be at the port to deliver some papers to me. Actually, it was he who suggested the circus. I fear that I agreed to it, darling. I truly thought it might prove amusing for you and the children."

I knew by the children's faces that I could scarcely deny them the opportunity since it would be the first for them both. And although I would have far preferred to return to the house, I had to admit that its emptiness would pall on me quickly.

"We shall have to rise very early," I told the children.

"We will, we will," they chimed in unison.

We all ate with great relish, our appetites having been stirred by our outing. I found it hard to take my eyes off of Justin. It was as if I wanted to memorize every furrow, every plane of his face, the dark brows that hovered over his smoldering eyes.

Our dinner finished, I whisked the children off to bed and Justin and I retired as well. I changed to a filmy white gown which had a coordinated white robe. I was standing by the window looking out onto the garden below when I heard Justin come from the water closet and move to where I stood. His hands reached up and gently withdrew the tortoise combs which held my hair up.

"You know, Serena, it is the little things, like removing these combs, that I fear will be what I shall miss the most in these next months."

I turned and pressed my head against his bare chest. "Hold me very tight, Justin," I whispered.

We stood there entwined in each other's arms, not saying anything. Finally he released me from his arms, moving down to sweep me off my feet and carried me over to our bed. He gently removed my robe and his own, then, kneeling over me, began caressing me so lightly that I shuddered under his touch.

"Are you cold?" he whispered.

"Just responsive," I replied.

He leaned his elbow across my chest, resting his head on it, and looked down at me.

"You know what I should like to do when I return?"

I shook my head.

"I should love to have another child."

"Would you really?" I asked.

"Why, are you surprised?"

"You have not hinted anything of the sort."

"Frankly, I have not thought of it until recently."

"That is ironic," I said.

"Why?"

"Because I, too, have been wishing that we might have another child," I admitted.

He smiled. "Well, that should give us something to look forward to then upon my return."

"I do wish that were not so far away," I pouted.

"As do I," he replied kissing my brow. "But it shall pass swiftly, I am certain."

He did not wait for my reply but covered my mouth with his own, pressing me back into the softness of the pillows. He seemed, as I did, to want to savor our lovemaking this night, knowing that we would not experience each other again for many months to come. When he finally did enter me I was moist and welcomed him, urging him deeper and deeper within me. He lifted me to him and we watched each's pleasure reflected in the other's eyes as our need for release drove us into a flight of mutual frenzy. I knew by his hardness that he was ready to let his passion flow within me, but his thrusts continued until he knew that our bodies had reached their gratification together.

I had no thought of the morrow as I fell asleep in Justin's arms. The intensity of our sharing was of the moment.

# 5

Justin kissed me awake in the morning.

"I hate to get you up so early, darling," he whispered, "but I must if you and the children are to see my ship sail."

"Of course," I replied reaching hurriedly for my robe.

"Mary was here and the children are dressing. She will attend to their breakfasts in their rooms."

"And what of Jaspar?"

"He is with them. He will have to remain here today, however."

I laughed. "Somehow I do not think that he would be a welcome addition at the circus."

I bathed and dressed quickly, selecting a walking dress of a printed pale green and lavender silk with an overdress of lavender that parted at the bodice and front face of the skirt to reveal the print beneath. The sleeves, ruffled at the elbow, also sported the print beneath with an additional ruffle of white framing the shoulder drape. My bonnet was full and fashioned of the same fabrics, tying under the chin with a broad lavender bow. I slipped into my leather slippers and went in search of Justin, who had instructed the servants to bring the trunks down to the great hall.

"Oh, Mama, you look elegant," Daphne squealed as she watched me descend the center staircase. "Does she not?" she continued, poking at her brother for a response.

Alexander looked up at me with those eyes that so mirrored

Justin's and I knew that tears welled behind them. I came down to where he stood and kneeling down to his height whispered, "I do know how you feel, dearest, but we must help each other this day. I should not like your father to leave us looking unhappy. He must carry away pictures of us with broad smiles on our faces."

I knew he was not convinced but nodded to me in agreement.

"I should like you to take a wrap, Daphne," I insisted. "It can be quite brisk at water's edge this time of year."

I moved to the dining room where Justin was just finishing his breakfast. "You do not mind my not waiting for you, do you, darling? 'Tis just that I want to be certain that all the baggage is properly loaded onto the carriage."

"Of course not," I assured him. "I am not terribly hungry anyway. I think I shall just have a spot of tea and sweet biscuits."

"You look lovely," he said, his eyes admiring my costume. "That color is particularly fetching on you." He kissed me lightly and then left the room.

I squeezed my eyes together, my fingers digging at my palms. I did not know that I could get through this day. I had never fancied myself as a very good actress and I was desperately afraid that Justin should see through my ebullience and to the desolation behind it. I quickly abandoned the biscuit as it stuck hazardously in my throat. I drank the tea and went out to see how everything was progressing. I almost tripped over Jaspar as I reentered the great hall.

"Goodness little one, you must be beside yourself with all this activity," I said. "You are going to stay here with Mary today and we shall return to you later."

"That is better," I said turning to Daphne, who had donned a light wool cape, "Oh, Mary, I forgot to tell you, do not plan on us for luncheon today. We shall be going to the circus after seeing Lord Barkham off."

"T'will be a full day for you, me lady, should I set a place for Lord Taggart for dinner?"

"Heavens no, Mary," I said. "I am quite certain that he shall have had his fill after our long day. Not being a family man, I would assume that he should find the experience exhausting."

Justin who had just come in the front door laughed. "Quite

to the contrary, my love. He most probably will see that the fruits of married life can be quite delicious. It is time Philip settled down and I cannot think of a better encouragement than my wife and children.''

Turning to me, he continued, ''Are you ready, Serena? I hate to press you but I fear I must if I am to get my papers of passage from Philip and board the ship.''

Mary handed me my wrap and I shooed the children out to the carriage, leaving behind a woe-begone Jaspar, who refused to acknowledge my departure.

It was a glorious day, the early sun having already baked off the puddled accumulations of the day before. Justin kept the children occupied by pointing out various houses in the squares which belonged to various lords and barons with whom he was acquainted. Our London existence was truly more Justin's abode since we had only traveled as husband and wife to Channing Hall five times within the ten years of our marriage. I, having been raised in the country, had not a great penchant for city living, and as the journey was neither a swift nor relatively pleasant one from our northern home of Mayfair, I had invariably left those trips of necessity to Justin. Now that I was facing several months alone in the city save for Monique and Clarissa, I wished that I had joined my husband more often on these jaunts to the city.

It was fascinating to listen to Justin, who appeared not only to know who lived in many of these houses on the squares but the men who had designed and built them.

The ports of England were exciting to view. The British navy was one of the most, if not the most, powerful in the world. I had had little exposure to it since my childhood days outside of Cornwall, but it was because of those early days and my fantasies of those sailing ships that I was ever excited about the sight of them again. The exchange of passengers was, of course, not a recent development, but I knew or sensed a relatively unexplored area. In that way I knew or understood Justin's excitement about the prospect of railway development. It had never excited me to think about the transportation of tea or grain on these massive clippers, but the thought of its permitting men and women to be moved from what seemed an unmovable station in life and then transported to other lands and perhaps other lives was thrilling to me.

As the carriage moved along the cobblestones lining the port of call Justin called out suddenly, "There it is, up ahead, the *Torrance*."

I looked ahead to the clipper Justin was pointing to.

"Look at that hull, Alexander," he enthused. "Look at its sleekness."

I moved forward on my seat and peered out the window. What he said was true. The gracefulness of the rising bows seemed to beckon it to the wind. It carried an enormous spread of canvas, starting with three head sails which included a flying jib.

"You see the foremast and main mast, Alexander?" Justin asked. "Look how well they are fitted with topsails, top gallants."

"Justin," I chided, "how is Alexander to know to what you refer? He has never seen these ships before."

"Have you not studied some designs with Master Farraday?" he asked.

"Yes, Father, but only of the *Royal George*."

"Oh, now there was a ship," Justin beamed. "It mounted one hundred guns. Under Admiral Hawke it was to have been key in the defeat of the French at Bell-Isle in 1761."

"Was that Admiral Nelson's ship, Father?" Alexander asked.

"No, but one that he has commanded," he replied.

The carriage drew to a stop before the vessel Justin would sail to the New World.

"There is Lord Taggart," Daphne cried.

Justin jumped out and Philip ran to approach him. Jonathan Leech, who followed close behind, seemed to be puffing a bit from the run.

"Well, old chap, this is the big day," I heard Philip say as he embraced Justin.

"Sometimes I wonder how you have worked it out, my friend," Justin chided. "I am setting sail on what I admit is a beauteous clipper but I am leaving in trust to you what I must say is a far more bounteous situation," and with that he escorted myself and the children from the coach.

Philip came forward to greet me. "It is indeed a pleasure to see you again, Serena, though I doubt that you are as eager as I to see Justin set sail today."

I smiled at his perception of my feelings of the moment. "I

must acknowledge that although this is an exciting day for you and Jonathan and Justin, it is far less so for me."

Philip made a small bow to me. "I admire your spirit, even though perhaps veiled, Serena," he replied. "I know that this decision was a great sacrifice on your part."

"Are we truly to go to the circus later?" Daphne asked.

"But of course," he assured. "After all, we cannot allow your father to have all the adventures."

He withdrew an enormous leather portfolio from his pocket. "These are for you, Justin," he said, handing them over. "Your right of passage, your letters of introduction, all that you will need to guide you safely through these waters."

There seemed such a finality as I watched Justin take the leather case to his own hands.

"Have all the bags been loaded up?" he asked the driver, who with the assist of one of the men on the docks had delivered all the trunks on board ship.

" 'Tis all aboard, Lord Barkham," he replied.

Turning to Philip and Jonathan, who hovered nearby, he requested a moment of privacy between our family before he boarded. Jonathan, who seemed terribly embarrassed by our request, scurried off like a frightened rabbit. Philip ambled after him.

Justin motioned myself and the children to him. I noticed that Daphne stood silently apart but Alexander welcomed the cradling of Justin's arm.

"You know, you both are going to have to take great care of your mother in my absence," he admonished. "I want you to be very good, very strong for her. I would not want to return and hear that there had been bickering between you or that you had not obeyed your mother. Just because I shall be absent from you for a time does not mean that you shall have the right to misbehave. You should be hard pressed to explain any misdeeds to me upon my return. Remember, you are Barkhams, and as such you have responsibilities. Our fathers, your mothers and mine struggled to build what we have today. You must always honor that. Be proud of that. Do you hear what I have said, Alexander?"

I watched as my young son clung to his father, saying far more by action than by words.

"And you, Daphne, have you comprehended my words?"

I watched them discerning each other at a distance and then suddenly she broke loose from her stance and ran to him, throwing herself full force against him.

"You will come back to us, won't you, Father?" she pleaded.

"Of course, my lovely," he reassured. "You do not think that I could possibly not return to see you blossom to the magnificent young woman I know that you shall be, do you?"

"Do you truly believe that I shall be magnificent, Father?" she beseeched.

"You have only to look at your mother to know the answer to that, my sweet."

He put the two children aside and moved purposefully over to me. If ever I thought my heart would break it was at that moment. Why is it, I thought, as he strode towards me, that it is at that moment of threat or separation that one fully realizes the depth of one's love for another? I did not need this moment to realize mine for Justin; yet suddenly there was this desperate need for my husband, my love, to know the depth of my caring.

He reached me and silently removed my bonnet, letting my hair which I had simply pushed up under it fall about my shoulders. I stretched my arms out to welcome him.

He cupped my face in his hands. "You know you scarcely look any different than that first day I saw you on the steps of Camberleigh."

"You flatter me, my lord," I replied, trying to keep my voice even.

"No, I truly do not, Serena," he reassured.

"Do you know what a joy it is for me to see you today, to hold you like this and know that I have only fallen deeper and deeper in love with you since that day?"

"And I you, my love," I responded.

"If for any reason I were not to return from this voyage, I want you to know that you have made me the happiest man on earth."

"I beg you not to talk of that, Justin," I pleaded.

He caressed my face. "Trust me, Serena, I have full intention of returning to you. But I simply want you to know the extent of the happiness you have given me. It shall give me strength and great solace on this voyage. And in turn I hope that you feel but a part of what I do.''

I put my arms about him and held him to me.

"You are my life, Justin," I whispered. "Where you go, my heart shall always travel with you."

"Promise me that you shall not shutter yourself away during this interim."

I nodded. "But do not ask me not to miss you, not to long for you—for that should be an impossibility."

His mouth found mine and I knew that we tasted the salt of each other's tears. When finally he pushed me away, I managed a forced but weak smile.

"There is my girl," he said, pinching my cheek. Philip approached and tapped him on the shoulder. "It is time, my friend."

Justin knelt beside the children, who had now gathered about us, and pulled them to him with such a fervor that I thought that they would bruise from the action. He made no move back towards me, of which I was almost glad, for I felt at that moment that if he were to be in my arms again I would indeed never let him go. Instead he grasped both of my hands and we stood almost transfixed, studying each other.

"I love you, Serena," he whispered hoarsely, clasping my hands.

"Go safely, my love," I responded, clinging almost desperately to those strong fingers which entwined mine.

It was Philip who parted us, drawing Justin from behind. I realized later that I stood with my arms outstretched until Justin had boarded the ship. It was Philip's hand that took my own and lowered it, making me realize that I had stood transfixed for some time.

"Do not worry, Serena," he counseled.

It was moments before I realized that I was gripping his hand with a fierceness that surprised even myself.

I watched Justin move away from me and up the gangplank to the ship that was to sail him those thousands of miles away from me.

"Look, Mama, our father is fully aboard," Daphne exuded. "Do you see him waving?"

I raised my glance, searching the flailing hands which outstretched from the ship.

"Where do you see him?" I asked.

"There, Mama, there—upon the bow," Daphne answered.

My eyes roved the deck of the ship until with certainty they fixed on Justin.

I grasped Philip's hand. "Let us run along that sector," I pleaded.

His hand grasped mine firmly and we ran alongside the ship, the children chasing after us.

I could not help think how small he looked aboard the ship. Justin, who always loomed larger than life in my mind, was now so dwarfed by the massiveness of the ship.

A woman in front of where we had stationed ourselves was weeping loudly and it did not help me to check my own emotions. There had been so many things I had wanted to say to Justin before he departed, but the time had slipped away so quickly.

"Oh, Mama, the boat is moving," Daphne squealed.

"I cannot see him anymore, can you, Philip?" I asked, squinting into the morning sun.

"No, I still see him, Serena, but he has been squeezed back by another group. Wait, there he is—you can see he is waving his hat."

"I cannot see, Mother," Alexander cried.

Philip let go of my hand and swung Alexander up on his back so that the boy could look over his shoulders. I pointed to where Justin stood.

"I do see him now."

I took Daphne's hand and we all watched until the ship had moved well out of port.

"Your back must be broken, Philip," I said as he lowered Alexander to the ground. "He is much heavier than he looks."

"Alexander is being a baby, Mother" Daphne said, pointing at Alexander, whose face was wet with tears.

I gave Daphne a harsh look and knelt down to Alexander, who was looking as lost as I felt.

"Come and give your mother a hug," I said, taking him into my arms. I held him until I felt the silent sobs come to rest; then standing, I turned to Philip. "I think we should go to the circus now."

Philip tried to keep up a lighthearted banter in the carriage, which fortunately the children responded to. I did not feel as though I were functioning totally. Everything seemed a bit vague to me and I found it difficult to raise any enthusiasm about anything.

I must admit, however, that the moment we entered the Amphitheatre all our spirits seemed to rise. Philip arranged for us to be seated on the first tier, which placed us next to the ring and within good view of the stage.

"Who is that man?" Daphne asked, pointing to the lavishly dressed man who had entered the center ring and was being flanked by a clown who burlesqued on horseback.

"He is the ringmaster," Philip answered. "You must pay close attention to him for he shall call out all the sets."

I quickly found myself entranced as I watched spectacles of horses thundering about the ring and gaily attired ladies jumping through paper-covered hoops. There were, of course, the tumblers who cavorted about, displaying their body agility, slack rope vaulting on full swing and tricks on chairs and ladders.

In the intermission the stage came alive with tableaus which featured an opera singer, a comic dance, then concluded with a hornpipe.

We all agreed that the most spectacular event, however, was the conclusion, where seemingly endless numbers of men piled upon each other, creating images said to represent the Egyptian pyramids.

The clowns came back into the ring, then waved about to the audience, which had now commenced to disperse.

"You were terribly kind to spend this time with us, Philip," I said as we proceeded to follow the crowds leaving the Amphiteater.

"Frankly, Serena," he said, moving close to me, "if the truth be known I've enjoyed it thoroughly. And I hope you are not going to insist on it being brought to an end for I had planned that we would perhaps go to Vauxhall Gardens for some refreshment. I am certain the children would not object to a light luncheon, certainly not to a tall glass of lemonade. That is, unless you have something terribly pressing at home."

"Frankly, I have nothing except perhaps examining more swatches for the upper rooms, but I have looked at so many these past weeks that I am quite dizzy from the experience. But what of *you*—you must have endless amounts of work to do."

"Only to meet with Jonathan later this afternoon."

"He appears to be a pleasant sort," I said as Philip lifted

Alexander and Daphne down to the walkway.

He laughed. "You are very kind, dear lady."

I looked up puzzled by his comment.

"Oh, do not misunderstand, Jonathan is really quite an affable fellow, but as you must have noticed he does seem rather cloddy at times."

"But I was given to believe—I mean, Justin told me he thought him to be quite brilliant."

"Brilliance has nothing to do with it, dear lady. *That* he most certainly is, but what I refer to is more his social graces. He is, shall we say, scarcely to the manner born."

I bristled at his remark for if there were anything that I loathed it was pompousness or snobbishness of the titled classes.

Sensing my displeasure, he quickly changed the subject, calling to the driver of our carriage and informing him to proceed to Vauxhall. I was somewhat tenuous about adventuring there: although it had once been a popular recreation place I knew that its reputation had dwindled in the past years. But Philip seemed fully confident and since I did not imagine that he would have taken us to a place which was considered dangerous in any way, I let myself be carried along with the children's enthusiasm.

I had always found London to be a city of such enormous contrasts and I continued to do so now as the carriage moved throughout the streets. On the one side there were the elegant squares as with Eaton or, more importantly, Belgrave. And on the other, areas where only hovels could be found and disease festered. It was the children who were the most pathetic and helpless of victims. Along one end of the Thames they were called mudlarks. Dull witted by birth (certainly, I supposed, largely from incest), they had come to be known as such from their habit of squelching through the mud and refuse along the riverbanks to gather what small rewards they could—bits of coal, wood, metal, bones—all which would be sorted and sold.

The reformers, our dear friend Cobbett amongst them, maintained that many—even children as young as six—wound up wards of the prison. It was said that few objected, for although the likes of Newgate were indeed unwelcome, it was a better life in some instances than what they found at home.

"You seem so pensive, Serena," Philip said, intruding on my thoughts.

"I am sorry, Philip, I did not mean to be rude. It is simply that the enormity of the poverty here is so secreted from our day-to-day lives. I suppose I feel a bit guilty for the riches that we have."

"Ah, but you must not," he cautioned. "After all, it is men like Justin who are going to bring greatness to this country of ours. And with those advancements there shall be a far greater wealth—one that can be shared with the masses."

"Do you really believe that, Philip," I pressed.

"I would scarcely be so involved in this if I did not."

I pondered that for the moment. I truly knew very little about Philip. The more I knew him, the more I understood why Monique found him a charming companion—for he was indeed that. But I scarcely envisioned him as an altruist. He was hardly in this venture for humanitarian reasons. Money? Perhaps. He was a man, I had observed, of expensive tastes.

"There is Vauxhall up ahead," he said, turning my sights to the gardens and pavilions we had just entered.

The carriage came to a stop before the largest of the structures. I could scarcely contain the children who were fascinated by the throngs of people strolling about. There was a band of violinists whose music kept the pace gay and lively. The children scrambled out of the carriage and Philip helped me alight. We had no longer started towards the pavilion than a chapman approached Philip peddling toy parachutes. I was shocked as he bought one and handed it to Alexander, who was immediately pleased by the gift.

"You should not have done that, Philip," I admonished.

"Oh, it is but a small token, Serena," he argued.

"I know, but Justin and I have taken great pains not to spoil the children."

"And they are delightful," he said. "You can be extraordinarily proud of them both."

Philip escorted us to a table where he ordered lemonade and hot sticky buns for us to share. With Alexander eager to play with his new parachute and Daphne pining to join several girls of her age who were playing Queen Anne, I excused them from the table, extracting a promise that they would not venture far.

"You really should eat a few of these biscuits, Serena, they are delicious," Philip said, offering them to me.

I shook my head. "I simply do not seem to have an appetite."

"You are not worrying about Justin, are you?"

I admitted that I was. "I cannot seem to help it, Philip. I realize that you have known us but a short time, but I am certain you can perceive that ours has not merely been a marriage of convenience."

"I envy him that," he replied, regarding me thoughtfully.

I looked up at him, aware of a strange longing in his voice. "I hope that you shall find someone one day then who shall make you as happy as Justin has made me."

He laughed. "Unless you have a twin I fear that I shall be destined to bachelorhood."

I blushed and sipped on my lemonade. The children's laughter diverted my attention and I turned to watch their play. They appeared to be enjoying their games for which I was relieved. Philip's insistence on the afternoon's activities had been justified by simply seeing how happy they appeared. It had been a far better solution than returning to the house where my own brooding would indubitably have affected them negatively.

I looked up startled, realizing that Philip had been addressing me. He reached over and took my hand. "Are you feeling unwell, Serena?"

"No, no, I am fine, Philip," I insisted, withdrawing my hand quickly. "I was simply watching the children and realizing how much I appreciate your efforts this afternoon."

"Good, then I shall assume it has helped."

"It has," I assured him. "But would you think me terribly rude if I asked you to take us back to Channing Hall shortly?" I had not realized how much these past days had proved so stressful.

"Of course," he agreed, calling over a waiter to pay the bill. The children were less than pleased to be rousted from their frolicking but Philip thankfully took charge and was firm with them; they seemed to respond to his combined authority and jocularity.

I do not remember the carriage ride return to Channing Hall, for, much to my embarrassment, I fell asleep almost immediately after we commenced our return trip.

I was again so grateful to Philip, who had somehow managed to keep the children not only quiet but entertained on our journey home. He assured me that he had enjoyed it but I sensed that it had tired him as well; after Mary had removed the children to their rooms, I offered him a brandy in the drawing room. I was admittedly taken aback slightly when he accepted so readily, but having offered I could scarcely withdraw my invitation.

"Might I propose a small glass for you, Serena?" he asked, having poured his own.

"Would I shock you if I said yes?" I replied.

"I doubt that you could shock me, Serena."

"I did not mean it that way," I assured him. "But do you realize that it is but six o'clock?"

He laughed. "You sound like Monique. Ah, Monique," he sighed as he strode to where I sat and handed me the brandy glass.

"Why do you say that?" I asked quickly.

"What did I say?" he countered, sitting in the chair opposite mine.

"I suppose it is what you did not say," I retorted. "It was your intonation more than anything."

"I see," he said, regarding me.

I took a sip of brandy. "You know, Philip, you must excuse me."

"Why?"

"For I have by naive intent asked you a very personal question."

"I must surmise that you refer to the relationship between Monique and myself."

"What I intended to say was that Monique is perhaps the only woman I know who feels completely unabashed about many of these things we women are so careful to be correct about."

"Perhaps she should be more so," he replied quietly.

I looked up at him. He had lit a pipe, which surprised me for I was accustomed to being asked first whether or not it were offensive to me. Justin rarely smoked; when he did it was mostly with his male compatriots, and usually not in the company of women.

"I have offended you," he said quickly as if reading my mind.

I shook my head. "But you are used to Monique and I fear I fall far short of her hostessing."

He drew on his pipe, the smoke rings growing larger as they dispersed towards me. "You could never fall short of Monique, Serena."

I commenced to object and he put his hand up to silence me.

"Believe me, I have a great deal of appreciation of Monique," he assured me. "She is a remarkable woman, and even though I consider her son quite a wimp, I find her to be, shall we say, refreshing."

"I caution you, Philip, that Robin and I are close friends."

"If you will forgive me, I have heard that you were paramours."

"Scarcely," I argued quickly.

"Well, then, his taste is worse than I had imagined."

I bristled at his comment for although it was common knowledge to some that Robin had had an interest in me at some point a decade prior, ours could hardly have been called an affair of any sort.

"You know, Philip, I scarcely know from whence your information has come, but I think that I should set certain things to right." Without allowing him to interfere I proceeded. "Robin and I met when I had come to Camberleigh."

He rose to pour another brandy saying, "Ah, the famous rags to riches story."

"Do not mock me," I snapped at him angrily.

He returned to his seat, assuring me that he was not. "Serena, I would never have known but I admit that I have asked Monique about you and—you know Monique. If anything she is a straightforward woman."

"Yes, she is," I agreed, disturbed slightly by the thought that I had been the topic of conversation at some juncture between Philip and Monique.

"And so then you know," I continued, "that Robin and I are—and have always been—just friends."

"Yes," he acknowledged, "and I also know that Monique wishes that you were her daughter-in-law."

I took a swallow of brandy. "Then you do not know Monique as well as I think. I would have been a disaster for Robin. Lilliane and I are not terribly close, but she has been a marvelous influence on him. She is strong, even willful, which is exactly what my dear friend needs."

"You are very kind, Serena," he replied. "Frankly I find her to be brash and egotistical, and I think Monique is insightful enough to see her that way."

I wanted to reply but remained silent.

"I have offended you," he continued.

"Not offended. I would simply say that your observations are quite different from Justin's and my own. Oh, I admit that the two women shall never be confidantes, but I really do believe that Monique appreciates the direction that Lilliane has given her son."

He sighed. "You refer no doubt to his frequenting of Brooks."

"In part," I acknowledged, realizing that Robin's reputation for frequenting the gaming houses at the cost of losing small fortunes was public knowledge. "But beyond the fact that Lilliane has managed to curtail his gambling, I feel quite certain that she has provided a stabilizing force that he needed without being too confining. I sense that much of Robin's earlier *trouble,* shall we call it, came from the lack of a father figure while he was growing up. You know, his father died when he was quite young," I added.

"And Monique inherited all that money," he mused.

"Well, you scarcely think she married him for his money?" I challenged.

"You are serious, are you not?" he retorted, an expression of genuine surprise playing across his face.

"Monique loved him dearly," I pursued. "She was devastated after his death. Left not only alone but somewhat of a stranger to this country. I think she is to be greatly admired for what she has managed to achieve."

I sat back in my chair slightly taken aback at my own vehemence, blushing as I looked up to see Philip smiling broadly at me.

"I have amused you," I said.

"Far from it," he assured me. "But I must say that if I ever am in need of a champion, I hope I should have you on my side. You defend as a mother hen protects her brood."

"She is a friend," I said firmly. "And yes, if I feel it necessary, I do defend my friends."

"Then again I say to you that I hope that we shall be friends."

"I can see no reason why not, Philip."

He swallowed the brandy remaining in the glass and rose. "I am going to leave you now for I want to be certain that I shall be invited back."

"Of course you shall," I assured him, "but I must add that I shall not press you into staying this evening. I am tired, Philip, but I should thank you for that—I actually believe that I shall sleep soundly tonight."

"You must, Serena," he counseled. "You certainly cannot sit here pining for Justin for eight months or so. It would not be healthy for you or the children."

"You sound like Justin now," I replied.

"Well, I am not Justin, but I hope that you know you can rely on me in his absence."

"I appreciate that, Philip, truly I do, but you must not concern yourself with me. For one thing I shall have quite enough to keep me busy with this house."

"Well, you cannot absorb yourself with that twenty-four hours a day, Serena."

I laughed as we moved towards the front hall. "Obviously you have never had children, Philip. They alone can occupy a major percentage of your day."

"I am certain that they can but you must allow yourself some time for yourself, Serena," he countered.

I shook my head. "Spending time with the children is scarcely penury."

"I did not say that," he argued. "Only that there are so many amusements that one can partake of in this city and you should not deprive London of your great beauty and charm."

"You are very kind, Philip," I said, extending my hand.

"Only truthful," he replied, drawing it to his lips.

I was startled and embarrassed by his gesture but remained silent.

"Might I call on you again tomorrow, Serena?" he asked.

"Oh, I must learn to be self-sufficient."

"Well, then, humor me," he teased. "Give pity on this poor lonely bachelor and allow me to call if only for my own solace and pleasure."

"You have wily ways, do you know that, Philip Taggart?" I laughed.

"I have been revealed," he retorted, striking a mock shocked pose.

I opened the door. "Good night, Philip."

"You would thrust me out on the street in such a fashion, dear lady?"

"I would and will," I assured him, taking his hand and leading him to the door.

I pressed him through it, he feigning protestation and I, though insistent, dramatizing my own gestures as well.

"I shall return," he teased bowing grandly to me.

"Good night, Philip," I repeated as I closed the door on a facial expression as forlorn as one of the clowns who had paraded before us earlier in the amphitheater.

I smiled to myself as I leaned wearily against the door. He was really a very nice man. Opinionated but amusing—and indeed charming. I began to see how he could have so quickly convinced Justin that this investment was not only sound but vastly important.

I waited for several moments until I heard the sound of the carriage move off into the early evening and then climbed the stairs to our room. Hearing no noise from the upper floors I assumed that Mary had seen to the children. I hoped that they, too, were overly fatigued so that they would fall quickly to slumber. I had no appetite and certainly the thought of eating alone tonight had no appeal for me. That perhaps would be one of the things that I would miss most about Justin's absence. Our dinners together were always our special times. The children were abed by then and we always kept a minimal serving staff so that we might revel in some privacy. Justin said that he was always amazed at how much we seemed able to talk about. I was never surprised for I had experienced that kind of relationship from childhood when my parents would talk incessantly over what was always a modest meal. I never had tired of it and in later years I realized that almost through some unseen force had I absorbed and learned a great deal from those family dinners.

I removed my clothes methodically, placing them carefully in the armoire at the end of the room. I was particularly critical of my appearance as I uncoiled my hair and brushed away the tangles. At first glance I was convinced that I had aged overnight, but a more rational part of me told me that it was simply a lack of luster about my eyes and mouth. I scrubbed myself, suddenly realizing that it was neither exhaustion nor aging which had given a dark cast to my visage but an emptiness that had been borne from the departure of my beloved Justin.

I was pleased that Charlotte would be arriving the next day. She always had a way of setting me to right. I was fond of Mary and she certainly was capable with the children, but it was Charlotte on whom I relied—perhaps because from the first we had shared so much together. There was no way that I could compare her to my mother for certainly my own mother by comparison had had a genteel upbringing. But, I knew that, akin to my mother, she was indelibly committed to me—to nursing me, protecting me—countering with me when she thought I was diverging from my proper path. And thus, though a servant, she had become a familial figure in my life.

The bed felt cool and empty. I stretched my arm across almost expectantly, deeply wanting to believe that I would encounter the warm hardness of my husband's body. I clutched at a pillow which fell against my arm, drawing it to me as a poor second. My hand pummeled the pillow as I fought the realization of my need. I had not been challenged in such a fashion since our marriage. We had been apart, of course, for times but always with the realization that it was just a day or an evening or a weekend, but never weeks, months on end. I wanted to believe that I was stronger than this, but I lay there pushing and pulling the pillow closer to me, feeling more vulnerable than I had ever felt in my life.

I had promised Justin that I would be strong. But as I lay in the bed with that stretch of space between us, I knew that somehow I would have to come to terms with the fact that the space was truly one of miles and not feet.

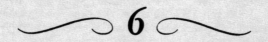

# 6

I do not know when I fell asleep. I know that I awoke several times in the night feeling frightened and lonely and mostly terribly sad. When I rose the next morning it was to the sound of torrential rains accompanied by thunder. I bathed and dressed quickly, wishing to reach the children as quickly as possible. From the time Daphne had been an infant she had been terrified of storms, and I knew that Mary's best assurances would not suffice her.

My instincts had been correct for as I reached the third floor I heard Daphne's screams as another clap resounded throughout the house.

"Darling," I said, going quickly to her and taking her in my arms, "you must not let that frighten you so. We are quite safe here."

"When will it stop?" she asked, holding me tightly.

"T'wont be long, I am certain," I reassured.

"What are we going to do today, Mother?" Alexander asked.

"I truly had not thought much about it," I admitted. "What would you like to do?"

Alexander shrugged and I racked my mind for something inventive to offer as an inducement.

"Lord Taggart said he would take us to the marionette theater," Daphne interrupted.

"That was very kind of him," I replied, "but you must not expect that you can monopolize Philip's time. He is a very busy man and we should be grateful that he shared himself with us yesterday."

"He was only trying to keep us from missing Father," Alexander chimed in thoughtfully.

I turned to him, amazed at the perspicacity of this small child. He was always so quiet—this boy who physically at least so resembled my dear, dear husband, yet ever full of surprises. His insights were always far beyond his years.

"It did help us a bit, though, did it not?" I asked.

Their silence was my answer. "I see it was wonderful while it lasted but that was only temporary. Well, I can scarcely disagree. I feel a bit blue myself this morning. But I do have one piece of news that will excite you, I think."

"Have you heard from Papa?" Daphne asked eagerly.

"Do not be silly, Daphne," Alexander chided. "It will be months before we receive the post from him."

"Guess who is arriving today?" I tantalized.

"Aunt Anne," Daphne guessed.

"No, 'tis Charlotte," I admitted.

Alexander let out a large sigh.

"You sound relieved," I said.

"I thought for a moment it was going to be Master Farraday."

"You know, Alexander, simply because we are residing in London while your father is away does not mean that I shall allow you to neglect your studies."

"But who is there to teach us?" Daphne asked.

"Why, myself, of course," I replied.

Daphne climbed down from my lap, relaxed by the subsiding of the noise of the storm. "Well, I shall far prefer you to Master Farraday," she confided.

"That is only because Mother shall not be so harsh with you on your tables," Alexander teased.

"Ah, do not be so certain," I assured him. "No one but your mother, except, of course, your father will ever love you as much but I shall also be your harshest critic. After all, I want my children to be prepared for life, and knowledge is perhaps the greatest gift that we can give you."

"When is Charlotte arriving?" Mary asked as she coaxed Daphne into a dress.

"Later today, I should expect," I replied, sensing that Mary's nose was a bit out of joint by my having sent for Charlotte. "You know, Mary," I continued, "we have spent so little time here in London that I had not realized the extent of the work involved here. You do such an exquisite job of maintaining this house, but with the addition of myself and the children, it truly is far too much for you to handle. Particularly with all these renovations that I have planned."

If Mary's feathers had been ruffled they seemed suddenly becalmed.

"Aye will o' course appreciate the assistance," she insisted, "as long as ye know 'tis not necessary. But then should ye be planning many large dinner parties t'will o' course be beneficial to 'ave Charlotte 'ere to oversee the children. Aye'm certain that she would be quite overwhelmed by the demands o' the city."

I smiled to myself, knowing that Charlotte would hardly be overwhelmed by London entertaining. Not that I planned to do any. But Mary would be shaken if she were made aware of the scope of Charlotte's responsibilities at Mayfair. The last thing I needed was to set up a rivalry of sorts between two women that I trusted as valuable housekeepers.

"Things, of course, will not be as busy as when my husband was here," I ventured, "but I appreciate your willingness, Mary, and certainly it gives me great ease knowing I can call upon you for those important occasions within the next few months."

As quickly as I said it, I regretted it for I knew that Mary would now pressure me to social commitments which I had neither the need nor desire to pursue. Justin and I had discussed this before he left for he had been greatly concerned that I would shutter myself off from our friends and society. I had assured him that I would not, but admittedly I had not been truthful. Justin perceived me as such a capable and independent woman and I was loathe to shatter his image. Certainly I had my own mind, but he was not aware of how much I relied on his presence. At this moment I hated myself for it. I thought of Monique, who had been forced by circumstance to build an existence for herself. Most women would not have been as successful. For I realized that most women, like myself, come to rely entirely on their mate. For the first time in my married life I found myself becoming angry. Frustrated was a better word. Suddenly I was aware of how much of my life revolved around my husband. While he was with me it had always seemed so natural. But now, parted from him, I was experiencing great anxiety and a reticence that I knew had not been a part of my being before we had married.

I was drawn out of my reverie by Daphne, who was pulling at my sleeve.

"Mother, you are not listening."

"I am sorry, darling—what were you saying?"

"Only that I should like to take a carriage ride throughout the city today."

"Well, perhaps that can be arranged," I replied. "And then when you return you can most likely greet Charlotte. Let me go and see if I might arrange it with James. But only for a tour about the city."

"We might visit Aunt Anne's shop," Daphne ventured.

"You will not alight from the carriage, my sweet," I replied. "Perhaps in another ten years I shall allow you to venture on your own but today it is impossible."

"Oh, Mother, you insist that I am such a child when I truly am all grown up."

I looked at this beautiful child who was my daughter and wondered if I had challenged my own mother when I was her age. In truth, upon reflection, I remembered that I, too, had been as self-possessed as she and as wantonly convinced that I had a maturity far beyond my years. Certainly, I had been far simpler for my mother for, despite my precociousness, my opportunities had been limited by our environment and finances.

"You can plead all you wish Daphne, but as long as you are a minor and I am about, I shall confine you as I see fit."

"I wish Oliver were here for he would say that you are being quite silly, Mother."

"Perhaps," I admitted, "but he is not and therefore you have to deal with me."

"Even Father would say you are being too severe," she pursued.

I stood up suddenly. "You know your father is not here and he is not going to be here for a good while and you are going to have to respect what I say. You may not like it but until he returns my word is sacrosanct."

"I told you everything would change," Daphne pouted, addressing her brother.

"Nothing need change, Daphne," I assured her, "unless you want it to."

I looked at her and felt strong pangs as I saw tears well in her eyes. As much as Alexander was a miniature of his father, she was, though I rarely admitted it, a replica of myself. She, too, missed Justin desperately and in her own harsh anger was being more truthful than I was to myself.

I rose, realizing that I was hungry. "I am going to descend and have some breakfast in the drawing room. You are both free to join me should you wish. Otherwise, I will talk to the driver and see if we might plan a brief ride for the afternoon, given, of course, that the weather improves."

When the children made no move to follow, I called to Jaspar, who sprang happily to my side and bounded down the stairs ahead of me. One of the maids had anticipated me and had placed some coffee and hot biscuits out on a tray. I was surprised to find a sealed envelope with my name on it tucked at the side of the tray. I opened it and immediately recognized Monique's hand. It was an invitation to come for dinner the following evening. I smiled, knowing that she had no doubt orchestrated this evening to coax me out of the house. She was a good friend and I did not want to hurt her, but I truly wished that people would understand that my better way of dealing with Justin's absence was to withdraw into myself.

"Oh, Jaspar, you're such a good companion," I said as he nuzzled me, forcing the invitation to drop from my hand. "You know I adore your Aunt Monique, but I would far prefer to just stay here tomorrow and cuddle close to you and the children."

A light knock at the drawing room door interrupted me and Mary entered, closing the door behind her.

"Excuse me, Lady Barkham, but Mister Leech has come to call."

"At this hour?" I replied.

She nodded. "He knows that you did not expect him but he did seem quite insistent and brought the most beautiful bouquet of flowers—I could scarcely turn him away."

"That is all right, Mary," I assured her. "It is hardly as if I am too busy to see him."

I laughed as he entered for Jaspar bounded up to him barking a greeting. I thought Jonathan would die of fright.

"Jaspar," I shouted, "behave yourself. Do come in, Jonathan, he will not hurt you. He is just exuberant, perhaps, from missing his romps in the country."

"Oh, it was good of you to see me, Lady Barkham," he spluttered.

"Serena," I corrected.

"Ah, yes, yes," he agreed, thrusting the flowers at me. "Just a small token, I thought it might brighten the day."

"They are lovely," I said, accepting the huge bouquet. "Mary, would you find a nice vase for these? I think they would be delightful in the foyer."

"I hope I am not intruding, Lady—I mean, Serena," Jonathan said, eyeing Jaspar warily.

"Not at all," I assured. "Come sit and tell me how things are progressing."

As he plunked down beside me I noticed that Jonathan's waistcoat was scarcely of a contemporary cut. And his shoes, though polished, were highly worn. I rather suspected that although Jonathan Leech seemed too absentminded to pay much attention to his countenance, in truth his finances, or the lack of them, was the bigger influence.

"So you must tell me about what you are doing," I pursued.

"Well, I have been working on some ideas I have for powering the engine. Not vastly interesting to you, I am certain."

"Ah, but you are wrong, Jonathan," I assured. "I may not understand all that you tell me, but when my husband is as involved as he is in this, I feel that I should have some comprehension of the railways."

It was as though the heavens had opened suddenly. Jonathan commenced describing things that I admittedly knew little about and by the time he finished I felt that I knew even less. But I was charmed by his enthusiasm and listened attentively while he shared his knowledge with me.

"Now you see," I said, pouring some coffee for him which a maid had refreshed, "now at least I will not be completely befuddled when I hear you or Philip talk about this."

He smiled adjusting his spectacles nervously. "I fear I have gone on at too great a length but you are most gracious." As he leaned to replace his cup on the tray he knelt down to pick up the invitation which had earlier fallen to the floor.

"I am quite looking forward to tomorrow," he said, handing the manila invitation to me.

"You will enjoy it immensely, Jonathan," I assured him. "Monique has a wonderful home and she is a fabulous hostess."

"I assumed that I would be seeing you there, Serena."

"Jonathan, I must admit that I have mixed feelings. As a matter of fact I was just thinking about it when you arrived. I do not want to put a damper on things but frankly I am not terribly responsive to the thought of venturing out quite yet."

"Oh, of course," Jonathan replied, getting to his feet. "I really must be going."

"Please do not leave on my account," I assured.

"No, no, I must go."

"You were very kind to call, Jonathan," I assured him, extending my hand. "You must feel free to come by from time to time. It has been pleasant as well as educational."

Jonathan tugged at his waistcoat, risen above his full belly which was pressing insistently against the buttons. "If I can do anything, you will call on me, will you not?" he asked, embarrassed by his overture.

"Of course, and do know that I appreciate it."

He left as abruptly as he had arrived. As much as I had dreaded the intrusion it had left my spirits buoyed. I had liked this jolly, preoccupied, bespectacled man from the first, and I knew, given his innate shyness, what an effort this visit had been. He was deliciously bright and hopelessly ill at ease, but I liked him and knew he would come to be a good friend.

Jonathan had not been gone but five minutes when the children raced into the drawing room. Alexander raced up to me, thrusting before me a picture he had drawn.

"Do you like it?" he asked.

I moved it back from my face, trying desperately to decipher what it was.

"It is charming," I ventured.

"Mama has absolutely no idea what it is," Daphne threatened.

"Of course I do," I replied, taking an educated guess. "It is of Jaspar."

"You see," Alexander denounced. "She does know."

I called Jaspar over and showed him the drawing. "I think it a good resemblance, do you not agree?"

He wagged his tail faithfully, simply pleased by being included in our conversation.

"Who was that who just left?" Daphne asked.

"Mister Leech," I replied.

"Was Philip with him?" she pursued.

"No. He came alone. And brought us the most beautiful flowers. I expect they are in the foyer by now."

"Why did he bring you flowers?"

"I expect, simply to give us cheer," I replied. "It was very thoughtful of him."

"Have you talked to James about our carriage ride?" Daphne asked.

"I scarcely have had time," I replied. "Besides, the rain is still heavy and you would not be able to see anything from the carriage in this downpour."

I looked up as Mary entered the drawing room again. "Excuse me, Lady Barkham, but I fear that you have another caller."

I sighed. "Who is it this time?"

"Lord Taggart."

Daphne squealed with glee. "Oh, send him in, Mary," she squealed.

"Daphne, please," I countered. "It is hardly your place to welcome visitors to this house."

"Oh, do not be so crotchety, Mama," she chastised, smoothing her dress.

Before I had had a chance to respond Philip strode into the drawing room.

"Hello, Philip," Daphne said curtsying.

"You look enchanting, dear Daphne," he said, crossing to take her hand.

"I did not expect you," I said honestly. "But then it must be the day for everyone to call. Jonathan left but moments ago."

"What was he doing here?" he asked abruptly.

"Simply a social call," I replied. "He was terribly sweet. He brought a wonderful bouquet of flowers. You might have seen them when you came in."

"You embarrass me," he replied.

"Why?" I asked.

"Because I have come empty-handed."

"You certainly have no reason to be a bearer of gifts when you come here, Philip," I assured him.

"Actually it was such a dreary day that I thought you might

enjoy going out to the theatre."

"Oh, could we, Mama?" Daphne pleaded.

"Daphne, please," I insisted.

Philip waved me off. "No, that is fine," he assured me. "Of course I meant that we would all go together."

I must admit that I was intimidated by the children's enthusiasm. I had had no intention of venturing out but I realized that I was trying to impose my own will on them. Philip was smiling at me, sensing I knew my own dilemma.

"I think you are outvoted, Serena," Philip advised.

"I suppose I am," I admitted.

"Wonderful, then. I shall be back to call on you at two. There will be an afternoon performance and then we shall all dine at the Excelsior."

I shook my head. "It is enough that I have been coerced into the theatre but I shall not be influenced further. No, I will insist that you return and have dinner with us here. It shall be simple, I assure you."

"Why not let me take you to one of London's more fashionable establishments?" he pursued.

"For one thing, Charlotte is arriving today and I want to be here to greet her."

"That is your housekeeper at Mayfair, if I am not mistaken," he replied.

I nodded.

"Well, if those are your terms for accepting my invitation to the theatre, then I agree."

"Then it is settled."

Daphne jumped for joy and Jaspar barked at her sudden spontaneity. "Come, Alexander, I shall have to find something to wear for this afternoon."

The children departed, leaving Philip alone with me.

"You are persuasive, Philip," I acknowledged. "But you know you must not spoil us so. The children are going to have to adjust to their father's absence, not to mention their own new life in the city. And if you are always entertaining them, they can scarcely adjust to what is going to be a somewhat tedious existence."

"I do not know why you insist on hibernating here, Serena. London can really be quite amusing. And it would be a pity to deny your friends the experience of your beauty and charm."

"You flatter me, Philip, but I would scarcely say that I am

hibernating. If I should wish to be reclusive during Justin's absence, it is truly my own business."

Alerted by the stress in my voice, Philip quickly changed the subject.

"I stand corrected," he said as he rose. "For now I shall leave you to whatever it was I interrupted. But I shall return at two."

Philip departed and I sought out the children, who had already changed for their outing and were devouring a small luncheon which Mary had kindly arranged. I felt terribly tired suddenly and went to my room to lie down. Jaspar, who had been with the children, dogged my steps and curled up beside the chaise, where I stretched out.

I chastised myself for feeling so weary for I had certainly done nothing strenuous. But Justin's departure was, I knew, affecting me emotionally. I wished that I could simply close my eyes and awaken six months hence when my husband would return.

To a certain extent Philip was right, I would be very happy to remain in the house over the winter. What had he accused me of? Hibernating—that was it. Well, bears did it, why couldn't I? I did not really have to ask myself that question for I also knew that they were fiercely protective of their cubs, as I was of Daphne and Alexander. And it would not be healthy, I knew, to restrict them so. I was so pleased that Charlotte was arriving today for she would help me to put some perspective on my confusions. She would also prove of great assist in taking the children in hand. Mary was very capable but she lacked Charlotte's firm but gentle manner. And her maturity.

I went to the small writing desk in the room and sat down to compose what I had earlier intended to be an apology note to Monique. In its stead I penned my note of acceptance. I had not changed my attitude but Monique was a dear friend and I was loath to insult her. Moreover, Philip had managed to intimidate me slightly and I did not wish to be the topic of speculation tomorrow night. T'was better to attend.

After making sure that my acceptance would be delivered to Monique that afternoon, I returned to change my clothes. I selected a moss green two-piece gown with pale blue piping around the collar, cuffs and hem. I had only worn the dress once before, but Justin had said the color was becoming and I loved the matching bonnet with its particularly light crown.

The children were waiting down in the parlor. I started to chastise Daphne, who had changed into a dress that was far too festive for an afternoon outing, but stopped myself realizing it was but a small accommodation on my part if it gave her such pleasure.

Philip arrived on the dot of two and we set off shortly thereafter in his carriage. The play we were to see was a comedic farce put on by a traveling troupe whose reputation was well known throughout the continent. It was light and amusing—I feared, far over the heads of the children but they were so enthralled by the theatre itself, the musicians and the fashionable people milling about that they scarcely noted the play's content.

I had to admit that I enjoyed the afternoon. Philip was most solicitous and I actually found myself laughing aloud during various scenes. Only one episode threatened to mar our afternoon. When we were leaving the theatre I suddenly heard my name being called and turned to face Lady Bellmore, a woman who had been a frequent visitor to Camberleigh when I had first journeyed there a decade ago. She was a pompous overstuffed matron and I knew that she would misinterpret Philip's presence at my side.

I cared hardly what she thought, but she was a dreadful gossip, and though I had nothing to hide, I did not want to be the subject of a bored dowager's high tea.

Philip had not helped the situation for he had appeared to be particularly attentive when she arrived. I was certain that he was not even aware that he had slipped his arm into my own. To have shrugged him off would have made more of a stir than was necessary. It was a small incident after all, one which I would no doubt have forgotten by morning.

I held firm about returning to Channing Hall after the performance. And I was pleased that I had for Charlotte had already arrived.

We embraced warmly; Alexander and Jaspar were so thrilled to see her that they almost toppled her petite frame.

"Oh, Miss Serena, aye be so happy to see ye," she bubbled giving me that winning toothy smile of hers.

I hugged her again. "You do not know how I have been looking forward to your arrival. Have you been shown to your room?"

"Aye, Mary 'as takin good care 'o me. Haven't unpacked

as yet but then aye only brought a few things."

I had been so preoccupied with Charlotte's arrival that I overlooked Philip, who was lagging behind trying to avoid Jaspar, who was sniffing at his heels.

"Philip, do come in and join us," I gestured. "Charlotte, you know Lord Taggart."

"Aye," she said curtsying. " 'Tis a pleasure to see ye again, sir."

I ushered her over to the couch. "Now tell me everything. How is Mayfair and Robbie, how is he?"

"Everythin' is fine as far as aye kin see. 'Course e'en if it wasn't, Robbie wouldn't be tellin 'is mum. T'aint the same without ye and the master, though. Cook is on the rampage."

"Why, for heavens sake?" I asked.

"Oh, aye asked 'er to fill some baskets fer one 'o the tenants an' she got all uppity."

"Goodness," I laughed. "She should be regarding this as a vacation."

I looked up in response to a knock at the door. It was James, offering us some refreshments.

"Would you care for some tea, Philip?" I asked. Then noting his grimace, I offered, "Or perhaps something stronger?"

"A glass of port would be lovely," he replied.

"You are planning to join us for dinner, are you not?"

"If the invitation is still extended," he replied.

"Of course, James, please inform Cook that we shall dine in the dining room and there should be plans for Lord Taggart, Charlotte, the children and myself."

"Oh, aye couldn't, Miss Serena," Charlotte protested.

"Nonsense, it shall be a relaxed family evening."

"I feel particularly flattered to be included," Philip added.

"Mary's nose shall be a bit out of joint, I fear, but I shall make it up to her at another time."

Charlotte took my hands in her own. "Now tell me," she asked when the children were out of earshot, " 'ave ye been terribly lonely since the master left?"

"Oh, I have had my moments," I admitted, "but thanks to Lord Taggart I have rarely had much time to think. He has even persuaded me to attend a party tomorrow evening that Lady Kelston is hostessing."

"Well, aye be thankin' ye, Lord Taggart, for lookin' after my Serena 'ere."

"Do not thank me, Charlotte. Quite frankly it has been my pleasure," he said accepting the port that James offered him. "Here's to you, Serena. I must say I am delighted that you have decided to venture out to Monique's."

We chatted quite amiably for the next hour. I sensed that Philip was bored with our chitchat but seemed content to simply have been included for dinner.

Cook had prepared a delicious meal of roast mutton of lamb with new potatoes and fresh greens. By dessert's end both children were almost sound asleep. I asked Charlotte if she would mind putting the children to bed, which she did willingly, assuring me that she was too tired from her trip.

My spirits had been so buoyed by her presence that I suggested to Philip that he might like a brandy before departing. He accepted readily.

"It was refreshing to hear you laugh today, Serena," Philip noted as he sipped his drink.

"I suppose I have you to thank for that," I replied. "It really has been very generous of you to spend so much time with me and the children, but I feel very guilty about it."

"Good Lord, why?" he exclaimed.

"Because it must be taking you away from your own interests and pursuits, not to mention your work."

"Oh, I work at odd hours," he replied.

"You must. I suppose I am just used to Justin's nonstop patterns. Even before this railroad project I had to beg him to give up time to spend with me and the children."

"If you were my wife, I fear I would never get anything accomplished—I would be so bewitched by you."

I blushed. "You should be paying these compliments to a woman who might become your bride."

He smiled. "Well, if Justin is carried off by one of those savage tribes they have over in the New World, do give thought that I would be waiting in the wings."

"Philip, that is a perfectly dreadful thing to say," I retorted, my voice quavering at the threatening thought.

Philip rose and placed his hand lightly on my shoulder. "Now I have upset you, 'tis the last thing I wanted. You must know that I only said that in jest."

I nodded. "It is silly of me, I simply do not have my emotions in check these days. And it is such a long journey with so many unknowns . . ." Philip squeezed my shoulder. "He will be fine, I assure you." He swallowed the remainder of his brandy. "I am going to leave you now, Serena."

"Of course," I replied, rising to show him to the door.

"I hope you will permit me to escort you to Monique's party tomorrow evening."

"That will not be necessary, Philip," I assured him. "Sidney can drive me."

"Nonsense, I insist," he argued "Why drag poor Sidney out unnecessarily?"

"Well, if you insist."

"Good. I shall be here at six o'clock."

The children were already bedded down and as I heard no movement from Charlotte's room I, too, retired happily.

I had to admit that the day had proved far more pleasurable than I had assumed. Philip really was very kind and the children seemed to respond well to him. It amused me in ways that we should become friends, considering our initial encounter. He never referred to that episode again, sensing perhaps that the recollection would still cause me great embarrassment. Perhaps one day years from now we might be able to laugh but there was still too much tension between us.

## 7

The next day I rose much later than I had planned but refreshed by a good night's sleep. Charlotte had the children well in hand and I determined to get back into my redecorating with great fervor. Jaspar followed me throughout the house as I went from room to room dragging about the various swatches I had collected.

The drawing room, I decided, needed the most immediate attention. The carpets were slightly worn, and though the furnishings were far from threadbare, they had seen better days. It was a room that needed brightening and I opted for a pale yellow striped wallpaper. The chairs would be done in moss green and I decided a wonderful floral chintz would be suitable as draperies. I made a mental note to ask Monique where I might find a handmade needlepoint rug large enough to accommodate this room. I also noted that the lamps, which were principally French figural, would be disastrous with the new scheme and determined to have some made to make a lighter statement.

It was midafternoon when I finally laid the fabrics and plans aside. Over tea and crumpets I set about my penning my first letter to Justin since his departure. He had begged me not to write, insisting that my letters would scarcely catch up with him, but I felt by writing that I was able to share the thoughts I normally would in person.

I had almost completed the letter when Charlotte peeked her head into the drawing room.

"Aye sorry to be intrudin' on ye, Miss Serena, but it seems ye should be gettin' dressed if yer to be goin' to Lady Kelston's this evening."

"Goodness, I had not even noticed how late it had grown," I replied, catching sight of the mantel clock.

"Would ye like me to be helpin' with yer hair?"

"Oh, would you, Charlotte? I have been at a loss since we have arrived in London. I simply do not have your touch."

She grinned. I knew that she was pleased that I had not forgotten her prowess in this area.

"The children be fine," she said as if reading my mind. "That Daphne is such a tease but Master Alexander, he's beginnin' to hold his own."

I nodded. "I have noticed the same thing. It won't be long, I believe, until my daughter is no longer going to be able to lord over her younger brother."

"He grows more like 'is father every day," Charlotte noted.

She followed me up the stairs to our bedchamber and I stood before the armoire debating which gown would be appropriate for the evening. I had just about settled on an icy blue taffeta heavily rushed about the neck and sleeves when I caught Charlotte shaking her head in protest.

"You do not like this dress?" I asked, surprised.

"Oh, no, 'tis a lovely gown but if t'were me aye'd chose the black one there."

I replaced the blue and pulled out a black silk faille which was heavily beaded in black jet beads about its low-cut bodice. Ostrich feathers which had been dyed black adorned the base of the skirt and fringed the cap-length sleeves. It was a dress that Anne had designed and I loved it, but it seemed a bit too dramatic for a woman on her own.

"You do not think this is perhaps not a bit too outré, seeing that Justin will not be accompanying me?"

"Nonsense," Charlotte chided. "Lord Barkham would want ye to be lookin' yer best and that dress becomes ye so."

I was not convinced that it was the proper selection but I abandoned my hesitation and commenced changing. It was less than an hour later when I had finished my toilet and Charlotte was putting the finishing touches to my hair, allowing it to fall softly at the sides and drawing up the weight of it in back with a clip. I pulled one tendril about the front of my neck.

"Do you think it could use a necklace, Charlotte?"

"Aye do. That lovely necklace Lord Barkham be givin' ye should be just right."

"It is in that small case in the lower left drawer," I gestured.

Charlotte helped me place it about my neck and I reflected on my appearance. I was pleased but I wished that it was Justin who would be seeing me this evening.

I was surprised by a knock at the door. It was Sidney. "Aye beg yer pardon, yer ladyship, but Lord Taggart has arrived."

"Thank you, Sidney. Would you show him into the drawing room and tell him that I shall be down shortly? I want to say goodnight to the children."

I accepted the wrap Charlotte insisted I take, thanked her for her assistance and went to find the children.

From the dishes on the floor I knew instantly that Jaspar had shared more of the evening's repast than he should have. But before I could chastise the children they had both run to embrace me.

"Careful," I laughed. "It took Charlotte almost an hour to put me together."

"You look beautiful," Daphne cooed. "Does she not, Alexander?"

He nodded. "Are you going by yourself?"

I shook my head. "Philip is going to escort me."

"He is handsome, do you not think, Mama?" Daphne mused.

"I suppose he is, though I fear that I am partial to your father's looks," I replied.

"Well, I think that some day I shall marry someone who looks like Philip."

"You will undoubtedly change your mind a dozen times or more before that time. I only hope that you will find someone as wonderful as your father. Now, I want the two of you to pay heed to Charlotte and get to bed early this evening. I want to do some lessons with you in the morning and I want you both to be alert."

Daphne moaned. "Must we?"

"Yes, but I will permit you to keep Jaspar up here tonight."

I kissed them both, gave Jaspar's ears a quick rub and turned to descend the stairs. I found Philip in the drawing room. I had to admit that my daughter had good taste, for he did indeed look handsome in a deep gray waistcoat and striped britches.

He rose as I entered. I extended my hand in welcome but he

startled me by drawing it to his lips. "You look like an exqui-site, exotic bird in that dress."

I laughed. "It is probably all the feathers. You look very handsome yourself," I continued. "Perhaps Monique shall have some eligible young lady at the soiree who will capture your heart this evening."

Philip scowled. "I hope she has the good sense not to bother."

I knew better than to press the issue so I gathered my wrap and suggested that we get underway.

We chatted gaily en route to Monique's. I told him about my plans for the house. Perhaps he was simply being polite but he expressed interest in my new selections. I was surprised, for although Justin was always attentive to my dress he rarely involved himself in the decorations of the house.

The Kelston house was ablaze with light when we arrived. From the number of carriages I assumed that Monique had turned what was to be a small gathering into a sizeable party.

The butler had no sooner opened the door for us when Monique came flying to greet us.

"Philip," she cooed, her French accent noticeable, "eet was so amicable of you to escort my dear Serena."

"Ah, but it is my pleasure," he replied, helping me with my wrap.

"You look smashing tonight, Monique," I said, admiring her gown fashioned of a chinese red silk.

She smiled. "One of Anne's *naturellement*. But I theenk she saves her truly remarkable creations for you, my dear. Ah, and well she should, since you gave her zat face and figure to work with." She turned back to Philip. "Darling, would you mind if I spoke with Serena *en privée pour un moment*?"

He looked surprised but moved off to join the other guests in the dining room.

Monique put her arm through mine. "I wanted to warn you, I am so sorry zees all happened."

"For goodness sake, Monique, what is wrong?" I asked, trying to read her expression.

"Do not be too angered with me, *mon amie*. Zere was nothing I could do. She called on me theez morning and she could see zat I was to have a soiree, I simply had to include her."

I rubbed the back of my neck. "It is Clarissa, is it not?"
Monique nodded.

It was odd to think of Clarissa now. It had been over five years since I had seen my cousin. It had not really been difficult to avoid each other since shortly after my own marriage Clarissa had met a young financier during her season in London and they had married shortly thereafter. The few visits that they had made to Camberleigh to visit Richard, her father, and Anne never included dropping in on Justin and myself. The jealousy, at times even hatred, that Clarissa had expressed towards me when we were eighteen had softened, I hoped over the years, but I had never been willing to trust it to chance. Partially, I suppose, I was also being protective of Daphne. Clarissa and Harold had had one child, a girl who was the image of Clarissa's own porcelain-like beauty. Perhaps it was because she was the image of her mother that I feared that she might also share Clarissa's stony heart.

We had all kept the promise that we had made to one another back at Camberleigh a decade ago. No one other than Justin, Anne, Richard and myself knew that Richard was not really Clarissa's father. It would have served no purpose. She would never have married well and certainly she would have been excluded from parties such as this one.

"Serena, Serena, say somezing," Monique pleaded.

"I am sorry, Monique, it just is that it has been such a long time since the two of us were together, but it is hardly the end of the world and I see no reason why the two of us cannot be civil. After all, we are both mothers now, that should give us some common ground."

"Bless you for being so understanding," Monique sighed in relief.

I took her hand. "Come let us face the dragon together. Does she know I am expected?"

Monique nodded. "I theenk she is wearing every jewel zat Harold ever gave her zo the whole lot cannot compare to your necklace."

We moved forward into the drawing room and spotted Clarissa immediately. She looked a confection in a frothy pink gown. I was disappointed to see that it was Philip with whom she was fluttering her lashes.

I extended my hand as I reached her, assuring us both any embarrassment from an unnatural embrace. "Clarissa, you look wonderfully well," I said.

She took my hand, her eyes sweeping my countenance from head to toe. "As do you, cousin," she replied. "Justin's absence seems to be agreeing with you."

Philip, not cognizant of the barb, broke in, "Cousins? You mean you two are related?"

I nodded. "Our fathers were brothers."

"Were?" he queried.

"Mine is deceased."

"I see," Philip replied thoughtfully. "Serena, might I fetch you some refreshment?"

"That would be lovely," I conceded.

"Hurry back, Philip dear," Clarissa cooed.

"You sound as though you are old friends," I noted.

"Not so old, quite recent really," she replied.

"I do not see Harold about," I said scanning the room for sight of her foppish husband.

"Oh, he has taken to his bed," she replied.

"Nothing serious, I hope."

"Just a cold, but Harold seems always to be sickly these days."

"And Constance?"

"My daughter is exquisite and so clever. And your children?"

"They are well, they miss their father, of course."

"Ah, yes, Philip was just telling me about Justin's exploits. Goodness, I am surprised that you let your husband out of your sight for that length of time, although after ten years the fascination does pale, does it not, cousin?"

"I would not know," I replied.

"Wouldn't you?" she purred, looking in Philip's direction.

"No, I wouldn't," I replied firmly. "You see, Lord Taggart is Justin's business associate."

"Business associate?" Clarissa gasped.

"Yes, they are involved in a project with the railroads. Justin is financing the operation and that man who just entered talking to Monique is also involved."

Clarissa commenced laughing.

"Might I ask what is so amusing, Clarissa?"

Just then Philip returned and handed me a glass of wine.

"I have obviously missed something amusing," Philip said questioningly.

"Obviously, so have I," I added.

Clarissa, still laughing, shook her head. "No, it is nothing, nothing at all."

"Would you both excuse me for a moment?" I said, picking

up my skirts. "I should like to greet Jonathan Leech."

"Let me come with you," Philip insisted.

"No, no. You stay with Clarissa," I assured him.

Jonathan and I greeted each other warmly and chatted gaily about generally innocuous subjects. I couldn't help but be surprised to see that Philip and Clarissa seemed to be deep in conversation when we were called to dinner. If they were friends, however, it certainly was no business of mine.

When they entered the dining room Jonathan and I were already seated and surrounded by Monique and an older couple called the Fitzhughs, who had been mutual friends for years. One thing was still disturbing me from my earlier conversation with Jonathan. He had said that he and Philip had not worked together since Justin's departure. I did not feign to understand what each of them was working on, but it did seem odd to me that they did not consult from time to time. I sensed that my suspicions were correct that Philip perhaps was not paying enough attention to his work since he had assumed the role of my guardian since Justin's departure.

The dinner was delicious and everyone appeared to be in a festive mood. Even Clarissa's presence did not dissipate my own enjoyment of the evening. I was pleased that I had made the effort and Monique was most enthusiastic about my plans for the house, promising to come by within the next few days to help with my selections.

I was surprised but pleased when, after we had retired to the drawing room for coffee, Philip sat down next to me, whispering if I would mind if we left a bit early. It had been pleasant, but without Justin I had no desire to challenge the hour of the evening, particularly with the children at home.

"Not departing so early, are you, cousin dear?" Clarissa cooed as Philip went to collect my wrap.

"I really must," I replied.

"Yes, I suppose you must, but then one can scarcely blame you—though I do suggest that you consider some discretion, my dear."

"There is no need, Clarissa, when there is nothing going on."

She smiled. "Oh, and do come to visit one day with those two children of yours."

I left without a response. Monique apologized profusely but I assured her again that it was not of major concern.

I was somewhat curious about how Philip and Clarissa had

come to know one another. Most likely through Harold, but I was loath to seem as though I was prying and I certainly did not want my queries to get back to Clarissa. Philip was very silent on the trip back to Channing Hall and I was embarrassed to find that I had drifted off to sleep. When I awoke it was to find that I had fallen against Philip, who was supporting me with his arm.

"I am so sorry," I said, righting myself quickly.

"Do not be," he assured me. "You were very tired and I have good shoulders to lean on. I must admit that the scent of your hair was one of the loveliest things my nose has ever been in contact with."

I felt myself blush. "Ah, we are home. Obviously none too soon."

Philip escorted me into the house, which Sidney had left well lighted for my return.

"Will you be all right?" he asked, helping me remove my cloak.

"Perfectly," I replied. "And I do appreciate your chivalry."

"Might I call again within the next few days?"

"Perhaps later in the week, Philip. I shall be preoccupied with this decorating for a few days. Or at least I *should* be if I am to complete this project by Justin's return."

Once Philip had departed I climbed up to the third floor to look in on the children, who fortunately were resting peacefully. I quickly hushed Jaspar, who ran towards me yelping with joy, then took him down the stairs with me.

Charlotte had kindly laid out my nightgown and robe and my bed was turned down. I undressed quickly and permitted Jaspar to come atop the bed and curl up against the pillows where Justin's head had lain with mine but weeks before.

It was Charlotte who woke me the next morning.

"Aye was gettin' worried about ye, aye was," she said as she put a tray of scones with fruits and tea down on a side table.

"What time is it?" I asked.

" 'Tis after ten, it is."

"Why, Jaspar, you old sleepyhead," I said, ruffling his ears. "At Mayfair I cannot keep him quiet after eight o'clock."

" 'E knows the sniffs and smells there better, methinks,"

Charlotte said as she hung my gown back in the armoire.

"I have to agree with him," I replied.

"Why not go back to the country, Miss Serena. Ye can't be as happy here an' t'would be far better for the children."

"Have they expressed discontent?" I asked.

"Oh, I think Miss Daphne likes the high society, makes the little one feel grown up, but our Alexander, aye not be thinkin' 'e's too happy."

"I am certain he misses his father," I said, splashing on my face some of the bath water Charlotte had brought. "Frankly I am not certain that it was such a good idea to come to London. I was so determined not to be separated from Justin but I did not give much thought to what it would be like after his departure."

"We kin be havin' Sidney take us right back if ye want," Charlotte offered.

I shook my head. "Now that I have made this commitment I am going to stick to it. Besides I am knee-deep in fabrics and changes for the house. I would just as soon see them completed. After Justin's return I hope that he will want to return to Mayfair as quickly as I."

"Seems to me ye'd be better off at home," Charlotte mused as I sat down to let her fix my hair.

"Well, this is our home, too, you know, Charlotte."

She took the heavy weight of my hair and coiled it at the nape of my neck.

"Ye know aye was just lookin' fer `yer necklace. It t'weren't in the box where ye been keepin' it."

My hand flew to my throat. "Good Lord," I gasped, rummaging quickly about the dressing table. I jumped up and ran over to the bed, pulling at the covers and shaking the pillows.

"You know I do not remember taking it off."

Charlotte joined my frenzy and began searching under the bed. "T'ain't here, Miss Serena," she said, having searched the floor.

"What am I to do?" I moaned.

"Aye'll be gettin Mary and Sidney an' the maids to lookin' fer it right away. 'Tis bound to turn up."

I agreed and quickly set about getting dressed. Jaspar was staring longingly at the scones and so I was careful to split one with him. I downed my tea so quickly that it scalded my tongue. I knew that I would not rest until the necklace was recovered. It was terribly valuable, but more than its monetary worth was its personal value to me. I would be desolate if it were lost.

Leaving to go downstairs, Jaspar at my heels, I could hear Charlotte giving instructions to the maids to tear the house apart in search of the necklace. After letting Jaspar out into the rear courtyard I went to the drawing room where Mary was in search.

As I entered she threw up her hands and shook her head.

"Aye hope Charlotte's 'avin' more luck than aye am, Lady Barkham."

"The only other possibility that I can think of is that I lost the necklace at Lady Kelston's or perhaps in Lord Taggart's carriage, though I do not recollect feeling it fall from my neck."

When after an hour later our searches proved futile, I penned notes to both Philip and Monique to ask if they perchance had found the necklace. Once Sidney had set off to deliver my queries I went in search of the children. Charlotte had cajoled them into searching along with the rest but all that seemed to be accomplished was that the house was thrown into turmoil.

"I do not know why Mother thinks her necklace is up here," I heard Daphne say as I reached her room.

"Because I looked in on you both when I returned last night." I held my arms open to her. "Come give your mother a kiss."

She embraced me and I went over and tousled Alexander's head, which was halfway under the rug.

"I want you both to gather your books and come downstairs. It has been too long since we tended to your studies."

Almost in unison they pleaded, "Must we?" but quickly knew that I was going to be unwavering in my demands.

"Since it is a pleasant day I thought we might spend it in the garden," I said as they gathered their books. "Jaspar is there now and on your way tell Cook that we shall plan to have luncheon there as well."

After they had gone I turned to Charlotte.

She shook her head. "Unless Mary be turnin' somethin' up down below, aye fear the necklace be lost, Miss Serena."

I sank down on a small side chair. "I simply cannot believe that it is gone, Charlotte. You shall see, within the hour,

I suspect, that Lady Kelston shall be at my doorstep, necklace in hand, chastising me for being so careless."

"Aye hope yer right, miss. Better te look on the bright side, aye say."

"That settles it," I said, rising and straightening my dress, "the necklace simply must be safe and if I am not to have backward children I best commence with their lessons."

The children were not in a mood for letters or recitation but I persisted, partially to keep my mind off the necklace and partially to insure that when we did return to Mayfair I should not be chastised by Master Farraday for allowing their minds to grow delinquent.

Cook had prepared a festive luncheon with their favorite cherry cobbler for dessert and that provided a welcome respite from the studies.

Our afternoon readings did not pass smoothly for Daphne, who was infinitely curious but also a master of subject change, and interrupted constantly with questions of how the party went, what the women wore and who had attended.

I was startled a bit later when Daphne inquired of Clarissa since I had consciously left her out of the guest list.

"Why would you ask about Clarissa, dear?" I asked trying to conceal my surprise since they had met only once and that was when Daphne was only three.

"Well, she is my cousin, is she not?"

"Of sorts," I replied slowly.

She looked puzzled. "If Oliver is my cousin, then since she is Oliver's sister she is my cousin as well."

I had known that these deductions would finally take place but I suppose I had hoped that it would not be for some years to come.

"If you put it that way, then, yes, she is your cousin," I replied quietly.

"And she has a daughter, about my age," she pursued.

I nodded. "Her name is Constance."

"Might we invite them over some afternoon?" she pleaded eagerly.

I turned and poured a cup of tea.

"Mother?"

"Yes, dear."

"Well, might we?"

I lowered my eyes, loathing the lies I would have to give my own daughter. "I suspect that they are indeed most occupied, Daphne. You know London is their principal residence and I suspect that their days are just as filled as ours are at Mayfair."

"You might inquire," she pursued.

"We have enough to keep us occupied," I insisted.

"You have Philip and I am stuck with Alexander," she retorted.

"Why, Daphne, what a terrible thing to say," I replied. "Firstly, I do not *have* Philip, as you suggested; he is merely a friend and business associate of your father's who has been kind enough to make himself available in your father's absence. And Alexander is your brother and you should consider yourself fortunate. I should have dearly loved to have had a brother who was so generous and, I must add, tolerant at your age."

Alexander smiled, obviously vindicated by my retort.

"Well, I still do not know why you will not invite Constance to come and play," she retorted angrily, throwing her notebook to the ground.

Before I could rebuke her, Philip's voice intruded on the scene. "What is this I have overheard—all work and no play, why, Serena, I never have thought of you as a slave driver."

"Oh, hello, Philip," I said awkwardly, confused that his arrival had not been announced.

"Forgive me for barging in, but Charlotte said to come ahead. Seems as though the household is topsy-turvy in search of that necklace of yours."

"Then you received my note?" I said hopefully.

He nodded. "I did, but I fear I am not the bearer of good news. I searched my coach immediately but found nothing."

"Oh, dear," I moaned. "Do you perchance remember if I were still wearing it when we returned last evening?"

"I fear I do not. If you recall we were both tired and I took my leave quickly."

"I must only hope then that it slipped off somehow at Monique's. She has not responded as yet."

"You must be worried to death about it. I admired it on you when we were at Mayfair. It is a very valuable piece, I know."

I nodded. "But it was also a very special gift. It was the last thing that Justin gave me. I know it is silly of me but if it truly were to be lost I would think of it as some sort of bad omen."

Philip laughed. "Nonsense. You women are highly imaginative, I must say. If it is lost, then it simply must be replaced —which I am certain is one of the first things your husband will do upon his return."

I thought it rather magnanimous on Philip's part to be so free with Justin's money, if only conversationally, but then I realized that I was upset and perhaps indeed not reacting rationally.

There was a momentary lull in the conversation and suddenly Daphne piped up, "Lord Taggart, do you not think it is cruel of my mother not to invite my cousin Constance over to play with me?"

"Daphne, really," I chided, "that is none of Philip's— Lord Taggart's concern."

He looked at me for a moment with a trace of amusement.

"Now let us see—Constance is Clarissa's daughter, is she not?"

Daphne nodded eagerly. "Do you know her?"

"We have met once or twice. A pretty little girl, very like her mother. About your age, I should suspect."

I cringed at the words "very like her mother."

"Well, I suppose you two would get on. It could not hurt, now could it, Serena?" he pursued.

I felt trapped. The last thing I wanted was to socialize with Clarissa, yet my resistance did seem foolish given that we were cousins. And I certainly could hardly broach a conversation explaining why I kept a determined distance between us.

"I suppose not," I murmured. "Perhaps someday in the future."

"Ah," Philip said, "perhaps we might make a party of it— that is, if I might be invited. Clarissa, and of course Harold, are old friends."

"Oh, wonderful," Daphne exclaimed, clapping her hands.

As if suddenly sensing that Alexander had been ignored, Philip asked, "I assume you shall be there, too, Alexander. I'll need some help with all these women."

Alexander shrugged. "I expect," he said quietly.

Sensing the boy was not about to enter into the conversation, Philip added, "Well, I suppose I must be going. I wish I could have brought you better news, Serena, which would have meant bringing you the necklace, but I fear I was not destined to be the hero."

I rose. "I appreciate your coming, Philip, I hope it was not too much of an inconvenience."

"I would have had it no other way."

"Do not forget about my party," Daphne called out.

"Oh, I shan't," he insisted.

I grimaced but kept my eyes lowered, hopeful that neither would notice.

"Might I hope that you will join me for dinner," he asked, "night after next?"

"I think not," I replied. "It is very kind of you, but what with the children underfoot and my plans for the house, I believe I shall have my hands full."

He paused for a moment, his hand smoothing his brow. "You know, Serena, I know of an excellent governess, actually she has worked for my sister, but she shan't be needing her shortly as her children are now grown and it would seem a marvelous opportunity for you both. I have no doubt that you would like her, and though I know your loyalty to your Charlotte she can scarcely cope with two small children."

"It is odd that you should say that for Justin, too, felt that we should employ a governess. The children had a nanny, of course, when they were younger, but Charlotte has since been so wonderful with them that I am loathe to bring in anyone else."

"Do think about it," he encouraged.

"I will," I promised, "but please do not make any overtures to the girl until I have given it consideration."

"Done," he assured me, then paused for a moment.

I looked up at him questioningly. "Is there something else?"

His eyes bore into mine. "You should wear green more often," he winked. "You look ravishing," and with that he turned on his heels, leaving me quite dumbfounded over his forwardness.

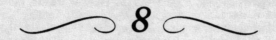

# 8

Philip Taggart continued to be somewhat of an enigma to me. Though I had certainly come to know him better over these past months, I still felt that I knew only the surface of this man. He was attractive, I had to admit; certainly he was appealing to women of my acquaintance. Of course, flattery goes far with some women. There were times, like now, that I puzzled if Philip wondered how far it would go with me. And then other times when I deemed his motive nonsensical—for surely he would not make improper advances to the wife of his business partner, particularly his financial partner. Yet there was always—what was it?—innuendo. Was I being silly or had I thought it odd that Philip had had his arm about me in the carriage last evening. A sensible woman would judge that he was being gallant in supporting my head when I had drifted off to sleep.

"This is nonsense," I murmured to myself.

"What is, Mama?" Daphne asked.

"Nothing," I assured her. "I was thinking aloud."

Realizing that the afternoon had almost passed, I told the children that they might return to their rooms. Jaspar, who had spent most of the time curled in a mossy patch under a large tree overhang, followed quickly on my heels. I returned to the drawing room where I had last left the swatches of fabric and set about finalizing and numbering my selections. When by evening I still had had no word from Monique I began to feel anxious. I had almost determined to have Sidney drive me over to her house when he announced that she had arrived at Channing Hall.

She swept into the drawing room and almost fell over Jaspar, who was sprawled by the door.

"Serena, darling, I know zat you must be frantic, but we searched everywhere *et rien du tout*, zere is nothing," she cried, wringing her hands.

The color must have left my face for she hurried over to me and insisted that I sit down.

Tears welled in my eyes and it was moments before I found my voice.

"I simply cannot believe that it is lost," I cried.

"You know, darling, I am certain zat you were wearing it when you left. I would have noticed. We searched everywhere, even on the stairs. I thought perhaps on ze way to ze carriage—*mais rien*. Have you talked to Philip? Perhaps somewhere in his coach. Eet was dark."

I shook my head. "Philip was here earlier. He, too, found nothing. And we have taken this house apart."

"What am I to do, Monique?" I begged, wishing for some solution.

"Ze only zing I could zink of is zat you have one made—*qu'est-ce que c'est le mot?*"

"A duplicate?" I gasped.

"*Exactement*. Zat way Justin would never know."

I shook my head. "I could never do that, Monique. If Justin ever found out he would be furious."

"And you do not think he will be anyway?"

My heart sank. I knew he would be angry. He disliked careless people and insisted that those blessed with wealth respect what it afforded them. On the other hand he would certainly know it was not purposeful. Initially it would be a shock but I would be forgiven.

I shook my head. "No, I will tell him the truth when he returns."

Monique threw up her hands. "*Alors*, zen zer ees nothing zat I can do."

I stood up. "I want to splash some cold water on my face, but might I persuade you to stay to dinner? The children will be in their rooms and it would give me an opportunity to show you some of the selections I have made."

She laughed. "I was hoping zat you might invite me. Zat house of mine, *c'est triste* when one eez alone."

I left to freshen up and inform the Cook that there would be another for dinner. When I returned, Monique had spread the bolts and swatches throughout the room. Fortunately she agreed with my selections for I scarcely wanted to commence again with that particular room. We ate in the dining room, which seemed a bit ridiculous since its size dwarfed the two of us but it gave us an opportunity to talk about furnishing changes. Indeed, we became so ensconced in the various plans that we paid no heed to time and thus it was very late when Monique's driver, who had come to check on her departure, startled us with the realization that the evening had come to a close.

I peeked in on the children before retiring, taking Jaspar back to my room. He adored Alexander and Daphne but he had always been my dog, and it was to me that he gave final allegiance. I did not fall to sleep easily for the mystery of the lost necklace still preyed heavily on my mind. More than anything I could not shake the sense that it was an omen of ill tidings to come. Philip had scoffed at my premonition but I was not a brooding character. It was when I did not trust my instincts that I usually faltered.

The next week passed swiftly. The days were spent giving the children their lessons and finalizing plans for the house. Craftsmen—furniture builders, restorers, seamstresses—streamed through Channing Hall on a regular basis. It seemed I had no privacy anyway, so on those occasions when Philip or Monique came to call, I rather welcomed a change of pace. The house was in such disarray that there was not the slightest possibility of my considering any entertainment. I did manage, quite by chance, to invite them both to dine with me one evening. Philip had come to call and Monique had arrived shortly thereafter, and since each seemed determined to outstay the other there was little I could do but implore the Cook at the last minute to expand the meal.

Whatever had or was transpiring between those two I knew not and had the good sense not to ask. On the surface the fascination seemed mostly held by Monique, who was far too wise to be flirtatious but managed a provocative smile from time to time. I wished that on that particular evening Philip had not been as flattering towards me as he had. I swore that he knew that it made me uncomfortable but I also wondered whether he did not do it purposefully to annoy Monique.

One afternoon, several weeks after that evening, Monique had come to call and of a sudden said to me, "You know, Serena, I should not encourage Philip unless you intend to experience ze whole of it."

I nearly dropped the bolt of fabric I was carrying.

"What on earth do you mean, Monique?"

"I know zees man. We see him differently, you and I."

I bristled. "Well, I do not know how you see him, Monique, but I see him as exactly what he is. My husband's business partner. That Justin assigned him to look in on myself and the children in his absence was not my doing. But frankly he has been helpful. He is always bringing the children some new book or game and I have come to enjoy his friendship," I finished, putting emphasis on my last word.

"Zat may well be," Monique pursued, "*mais* he ees a man and you are a very beautiful woman. Do not tell me zat you do not see ze way he looks at you. He desires you, Serena. And Philip, I know, ees a man who gets what he wants."

I did not know why I was shocked for Monique always had a directness that was discerning. I paused, wondering if what she said might possibly be true. He had never made any untoward advances, at least none that I could actually specify as such, and yet I had had that nagging sense that there was more there than what I was perceiving.

It was on that day that I determined the best way to discourage any shred of romantic notion he might be entertaining was to avoid seeing him. That was not as simple as it seemed, for although he did not call daily, he was by no means an infrequent visitor, and because of his relationship with Justin I did not want to create an awkward situation.

I decided that I must have a conspirator and chose Charlotte. I did not go into lengthy details, only to say that I was finding Lord Taggart's visits to have grown excessive and I would appreciate her informing Sidney that I was to be out during the next several weeks were he to call.

And thus a new pattern was set—one which displeased Daphne since she seemed so flattered by Philip's attention and delighted with his showering of trinkets. Oddly it was Alexander who appeared almost relieved. He never said anything but I had sensed the first week after Justin had sailed that his initial enthusiasm over Philip had paled.

The evenings were the lonely part of the day for me. Since it was then that my thoughts were filled with Justin, I chose that time to write my daily letter to him. I tried to sound cheerful but I knew that he would sense the depths to which I was missing him. After I would simply pen a line or two about the house and children, I had little of consequence to report.

Fall had passed and winter was coming hard upon us. Robbie sent word that all was well at Mayfair. The crop had been a good one as predicted and the tenants' larders would be full during the cold, arduous months ahead.

The house was commencing to take on a new look. I was continually amazed by what a mere change of paint and paper could accomplish. I was able to stave off Daphne's notions of a party that would include Clarissa and her daughter by promising that we would redo her room and allowing her to choose both the fabrics and furnishings on her own. Fortunately, even at her tender age she had a good eye, for once having given her the right of selection I would have been hard pressed to go back on my word.

Philip appeared to have accepted my avoidance politely if not agreeably. After several weeks of keeping up the ruse that I was not at home when he called, he had sent a note inviting the children and me to go to the theater with him one Saturday afternoon. I had written back, noting his graciousness but pleading that until the efforts with the house were completed I would not be able to venture out.

Thus, it was to my particular surprise, when on a dreary rain-swept day in late November I heard Sidney arguing vociferously with a man who sounded just like Philip.

I was up in the children's room, and quickly exited, scurrying to the second floor landing.

"I insist, Lord Taggart, that Lady Barkham does not wish to be disturbed!" I heard Sidney exclaim.

Then there seemed to be a slight scuffle. "Take your hands off me," Philip cried out and with that I ran to the head of the stairs. I reached it just in time to see Philip wrench himself free from Sidney's grasp.

"Damnation," he shouted, "this is not a social call, you imbecile, we are here to tell Lady Barkham that her husband is dead."

A pain stabbed through my body—a pain so searing that I lost my senses. Later they told me that they had heard me scream and the next thing anyone knew I was hurtling down the stairs.

It was Charlotte's face that I saw first when I had regained consciousness. She was explaining that I had been very lucky, just a nasty bump on my head and a slight sprain to my ankle.

I looked about puzzled to find myself in my own room. "How did I get here?" I asked.

"Lord Taggart carried ye," she replied, her eyes searching my face.

Our eyes met and in that second I remembered the words that had sent me into that oblivion.

"Oh, no," I moaned. I freed myself to sit up. "Philip—where is he? I must see him."

"He an' Mr. Leech are downstairs. But aye be thinkin' ye should rest for a while."

"No," I insisted. "I want to see them both right away."

She nodded. "Aye'll send them. If ye be needin' me aye'll be with the children."

It seemed a lifetime before there was a knock at the door and I bade them to enter.

They came to stand before me and I motioned for them to sit down.

I looked directly at Philip, gripping the bed clothes beneath me. "I want you to tell me that what I thought I heard you say before I fell is not so."

Philip cleared his throat. "I wish that I could, Serena, but I fear I cannot. I would have done anything to have had you not hear of it in that manner, but your man was insistent and I—I fear I became overwrought."

"Jonathan, what have you to say about this?" I asked calmly.

"Only that I am so very sorry, Lady Barkham, Serena," he spluttered, his eyes filling with tears. "Lord Barkham was a fine man. A fine man. It is only in these past months before his departure that I had come to know him—a man of better character did not exist."

I paused. "Please do not refer to my husband in the past tense, Jonathan," I insisted.

Philip shook his head. "Serena, please, I know it is not easy but you must hear me out. It happened some time back.

Because they were at sea, the news has been delayed in reaching us. There was an outbreak of cholera. It could not be stopped. Over half of the ship's passengers and crew were felled by it. Justin was among them. He, like the rest, was buried at sea."

"No!" I shouted, pounding my fist against the bed. "My husband is not dead. He cannot be. I would have sensed it, known it somehow. If you say that he is dead, then give me proof."

"He was traveling under an assumed name, Serena, mostly to protect our venture. There is no question. This name was given on the roster of those who had succumbed. We had agreed that if anything were to happen to him the news should come to me first."

I looked at Jonathan, who was dabbing the moisture from his face with a large handkerchief.

"Do you corroborate this story, Jonathan?" I asked.

He nodded.

"Then I shall ask you both to leave me now," I said quietly.

"Is there not something that I—we might do, Serena? Anything, you have only to ask." Philip questioned.

I shook my head. "I should simply like to be alone."

I was not even aware of their leaving. Charlotte returned to my room with a cup of tea, which I refused.

"The doctor be leavin' this sleepin' draught fer ye, why don' ye be takin' it?" she pressed.

"No," I insisted. "I must see the children."

"Oh, don' be goin' an' thinkin' about that now, Miss Serena, there'll be time enough for that. Ye not yerself right now. T'will only be more disturbin' to them to see ye like this."

"They have to be told."

I was not willing to listen to her protests. It was as though if I did not tell them right at that very moment I would not be able to.

She brought them to me and I motioned for both of them to come sit beside me on the bed. Even Jaspar struggled up for this family conference. It is odd, for when I was done I could not have repeated or recalled even one word I had said. Both children wept uncontrollably and I marveled at how easily their grief was revealed. Even Charlotte was sobbing. It was only I who remained dry-eyed. I felt as though I were in a trance of sorts. It was as if I were invisible and watching a tableau unfold before me. I do not know how long this went on, only that some hours later Charlotte was prying each child from out beneath my arms. Both had spent their emotions so fully that they had drifted easily off to sleep. Charlotte assured me that she would return shortly.

When she did, she brought with her a tray, insisting that I eat something. As with the tea I refused. The very thought of food was repugnant to me. There was an angry voice within me shouting, "I do not want food, by God. I want my husband," yet no words actually passed my lips.

Charlotte sat with me, pleaded with me, even cradled me in her arms, but although I was aware of her attempts to rouse some reaction from me, I simply did not seem to be able to break through this wall which surrounded me. Finally seeing that her efforts for the moment were to be in vain, she set about undressing me. I was like a doll in her arms. She was gentle with me, murmuring encouragement, words of solace, but I could not reach out to her from whatever depths I had sunk to.

When she left I felt a great sense of relief. Now there was no one who was attempting to penetrate my world save Jaspar, who nudged at my chin. I kept telling myself that this was all just a bad dream. I had had a fall, perhaps I was delirious. That could happen, I knew. People who had suffered an injury could be in a sleeplike state for days. And when they finally awoke, none of what they had dreamed or imagined had ever happened.

I dug my nails into the small of my palm. This was no dream. I was awake. The horror of this day was very real. They were telling me that my Justin was gone. They didn't know that was like telling me my own life had ended. None of it meant anything without Justin.

I stretched my hand across the space next to me on the bed. Once a man had lain there who had given reason to my days and nights. Now there was only emptiness.

I had been right. The lost necklace had in fact proved to be a warning. A gift that had been a celebration of our life together was lost to me—as was now my husband.

How many hours had passed before that invisible wall began to crumble, I do not know. But when it did disappear so did the numbness, replaced instead by the pain. I felt as though I were suffering, and then I heard myself screaming, calling out for my life, my love.

Within moments there were arms about me, Charlotte's holding me to her as the sobs racked my body.

"Oh, Charlotte," I moaned, "what am I going to do? Not Justin, not my Justin."

"There, let it go, Miss Serena, 'tis better if ye let that grief out 'o ye. 'Tis like a poison inside ye, ye must let it out."

When the tears subsided I asked Charlotte if she might bring me the sleeping draught the doctor had left. My head was pounding due in part to the fall, no doubt, but I wanted something to pull me blissfully away again. I wanted not to think.

After I had taken it, washing it down with tea that had grown stony cold, I lay back against the pillows feeling too spent to move. Charlotte brought me a compress for my head. I urged her to get some sleep but she insisted on staying with me until I had drifted off.

I had no idea what time I awoke the next day since the draperies were drawn fully closed. I could hear the rain on the roof and an occasional clap of thunder penetrated the eerie silence. Someone had obviously entered my room earlier in the day for Jaspar was not about and the trays from the evening before had been replaced by fresh ones.

I closed my eyes again, prayerful that the effects of the sleeping draught had not fully passed. But when I longed for nothingness it was Justin's face I saw. He seemed so far away. He was calling to me but I couldn't hear him.

"I cannot hear you," I murmured.

There was only silence.

I opened my eyes. I knew that I had to get up but my body felt leaden. I winced in pain as I turned the ankle I had hurt in the fall.

Persisting, I threw back the covers and limped towards the water closet. A fresh basin had been left and I splashed the lukewarm water on my face. My eyes felt puffy, which I confirmed when I sat down before my dressing table. My hair was in disarray and there was a small bruise to the side of my temple. I picked up a brush and gingerly began to smooth the tangles.

It was thus that Charlotte found me as she entered with an enormous tray of food. She put it down and quickly came over and took the brush from my hand.

Our eyes met in the mirror. "An' 'ow ye be this mornin', Miss Serena?"

"I suppose that everyone is going to say that I must accept this. But I cannot; no, better said: I *will* not. It simply cannot be, Charlotte," I pleaded.

"Aye would do anything to be able te bear the pain fer ye an' ye be knowin' 'ow much aye loved yer husband meself. But these things we must accept, Serena. 'Tis the Lord's will. He giveth and he taketh away."

"But why Justin? He had so much to give, so much to live for."

"If only I could be answerin' that, but ye know I cannot."

"How are the children?"

"They be sad and confused. Ye know it's hard on the little ones. But they be looked after by Lady Kelston and Lord Taggart."

"What do you mean?"

"Lady Kelston, she was 'ere before aye was up this mornin'. Moved right in she did, said ye weren't to be bothered. Then Lord Taggart arrived. He is downstairs as well."

"I know they mean well, but I want them to leave."

"Ye cannot ask that, Serena. Ye must know many people will want te be payin' their respects. An' ye be needin' friends these days. T'will be a comfort fer ye."

"There is nothing that will comfort me, Charlotte, save the safe return of my husband. You have known me for years. Do not insult me by suggesting that I can abandon thought of the man who was my life," I cried.

Charlotte folded my hair into a coil.

"Aye would never be suggestin' that, Serena. But what aye be tryin' te tell ye is that ye must fight this thing. Do not be lettin' it take ye down."

When she had done pinning my hair, Charlotte helped me dress and eased me over to a chaise. I could walk, though in a somewhat gingerly fashion. Charlotte started to bring the tray of food and I waved her off. "I truly cannot eat a bite, but I will ask if you would send Lady Kelston up."

It was only moments later that there was a knock at the door.

"Come in," I called out.

Monique approached me silently. She sat at the edge of the chaise and our arms entwined about each other. And this time it was Monique who cried. Cried for the man whom she had been closer to than her own son. Cried for the man who had been her lover. Cried for the man who had been my husband.

When we finally pulled apart she drew a chair close to me.

"You know, Serena, ze one image which I zee in my mind since Philipe brought me ze word of zees tragedy ees ze day when I first met you. You remember?"

I nodded. I remembered it well, though it was some ten years ago. There was to be a ball at Kelston Manor and Anne had contrived to have me invited.

"Ah, my Robin was zo enchanté avec toi. *Mais*, when I saw Justin look at you I knew. Eet was as though you two were made for each other. You were zo young, zo beautiful, zo full of pride—zo much pride. I knew then zat Justin—he was going to have a fight to capture you. Zere ees nothing zat one can say at thees time. I know, for when I lost my own husband, I was—how you say—devastated. But ze one thing zat kept me strong through zat time was zat I knew my Henry had loved me. You have zat, too, for Justin loved you, he adored you."

I nodded, "I know that, Monique, but I do not think I can bear not to ever hear him tell me that again."

"You must." She squeezed my hand. "I know, oh, I know, Serena, but the pain will soften in time. And for ze children you must go on."

"How do they seem to you?"

"*Triste*, mais zat eez only *naturelle*."

I suddenly thought of Anne, Justin's sister—she of course must be told. Anne, my dearest friend. She, too, would be devastated by the news. They had always been so close. The news would fall heavily on Richard as well. It was Justin who had assumed the burden of running the estates during the past years. Richard had neither the interest nor, I suspected, the health to oversee both Mayfair and Camberleigh.

"What are you thinking, *mon amie?*"

I rubbed my forehead. "That Anne and Richard must be told. It will be a great shock for them both."

"Zat has been taken care of. Philipe dispatched a driver with word of ze news last night. He has taken charge of everything. You are fortunate, Serena. When Henry died I had no one."

"I suppose that I should see him."

"Yes, you should. I do not know what happened between ze two of you. I hope it was nothing zat I said, *mais* I know zat Philipe has been worried about not seeing you these past weeks."

I waved her off. "It hardly seems important now. You may send him up when you leave."

"Would you like to come, with ze children, of course, and stay with me for a few weeks? Ze house, eet eez zo empty and eet would do us all good, I zink."

I shook my head. "I want to stay here, Monique."

"*Mais, sûrement*, you will at least return to Mayfair?"

"No, not now. I do not believe I could bear to be there without Justin. It would be too painful."

Monique rose. "*Alors*, we can talk of this another time. I shall fetch *Philipe* for you."

We embraced, and when she left I felt a great sigh of relief. I knew I had to see Philip and, of course, the children, but all I truly wanted was to go back to bed and let sleep overtake me.

Philip brought with him a note from Jonathan Leech explaining that Jonathan was so upset himself that he did not think that he should come.

"Monique has told me how much you have done to help—I do thank you, Philip."

"You need not be so formal with me, Serena. I have only done what I have unfortunately had to do." He reached over and took my hand. "I am not going to stay. Monique has made me promise not to tire you. But I shall return tomorrow."

I slowly withdrew my hand. "There is no need for that," I insisted.

He smiled and put a finger to my lips. "I will not hear of it. I shall return in the morning. Meanwhile, if there is anything you need, you have only to send your man to alert me."

Charlotte brought the children and Jaspar to me after the house was quiet. I longed to have them with me, but I did not seem to offer any comfort to them. A strange thing also happened to me when I looked at Alexander. The tears that I thought had been fully spent the night before welled within me all over again. Looking at him was like looking at a miniature of Justin. That same strong jaw, the dark waving hair and those curiously intense, dark eyes. He was a painful reminder of the man I should never see or touch again. It should have cheered me, I suppose, to have this child the image of the man I had loved so dearly. Instead, it was a painful reminder of all that I had lost.

Cook sent dinner for us all up to my room. I picked at the food for the children's sake but even the look of it was repugnant to me. Charlotte, I knew, did not approve of my not eating but this particular evening she did not press me. The staff was very kind and sent notes of commiseration up to me, which I shared with the children. Sidney's father had been with the Barkhams, too, and there was a deep sense of loss here, I knew. The one who would take it closest to heart, though, was Charlotte's Robbie. Justin had been almost a father figure to him. He had trained him, given him his time and respect and finally allowed him to shoulder much of the responsibility of the running of Mayfair.

Charlotte retired the children early. Jaspar refused to leave my side and actually I was grateful for his company. It felt good to get back into bed, its large feathered softness a protective haven of sorts. Only one candle burned on the night table beside the bed. I watched the strange shadows its flickering light displayed throughout the room. Justin and I had often done our lovemaking in just such a light. How my body ached for him. Had he thought of me in those final hours? I wondered. Had he missed me with even an ounce of the deep loss that I was feeling now? I prayed that he had not suffered. I had always hoped that it would be I who would precede Justin in death. Not that I had ever given it much thought. I knew, of course, that life was transitory but I had always thought of Justin and me growing old together, delighting in our children and our children's children. I thought of my own mother. She, too, had lost the man she had fought so hard for—my father—at a young age. It had killed her. I wondered if my own fate would repeat hers.

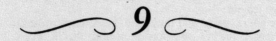

# 9

I slept fitfully that night. I awoke several times to find myself drenched in my body's wet heat. I knew that I should arise and change my gown but I had not the energy. When I awoke the next morning Charlotte stood over me, a hand on my forehead.

"Aye knew the minute aye be seein' ye. Ye poor thing, ye be filled with fever."

She left and returned with one of the maids who helped her change the bedclothes and the gown I was wearing. I sipped reluctantly at the tea she offered me but refused any nourishment. Charlotte placed cold cloths about my head.

"Ye be stayin' right to bed, ye will," Charlotte insisted, pulling the covers up about my neck.

"I must see the children," I protested.

"Time enough for that. Aye'll be takin' care of them. When ye be stronger aye'll bring them in. Ye'll be up by tomorrow, aye promise ye."

Despite Charlotte's encouragement, after two days I still seemed to be too drained to rouse myself, even though the fever had subsided. Charlotte brought the children to me for a spell each day. It was painful to see the fearful looks in their eyes, and nothing I said seemed to dispel it. Jaspar was unerring in his faithfulness, leaving my side only at the persistence of Charlotte or Mary. Philip, I was told, called daily, bringing small gifts, which he probably thought might amuse me. I was

scarcely prepared to receive him in my bedroom and I was
scarcely prepared to leave its confines. Monique, too, was
there each day. I marveled at how much she could find to talk
about. When she brought swatches that she had generously
collected for the dining room, I tried to exhibit some enthusiasm, but what had seemed effortless the week before now only
seemed tedious.

The hours passed and thus the days. A letter arrived from
Sir Henry, Justin's solicitor, explaining that it would be
weeks, perhaps months, before his affairs could be settled. It
imported that I was not to be burdened by financial concerns,
also extending, of course, his deep regrets over my husband's
untimely death. I suppose that I should have been relieved to
have been released for the moment from monetary concerns,
but for some reason it only angered me and it was Charlotte
who found me that afternoon tearing up the letter and tossing
it angrily on the floor.

She had finished picking up most of the pieces when she
asked if she might speak with me for a moment.

"Of course," I assured her. "But please, no further lectures
on my habits of late," I begged, seeing the seriousness of her
regard.

"Miss Serena," she commenced, "aye be knowin' ye now
fer 'ow long—ten, eleven years?"

"Eleven," I acknowledged.

"Aye remember when ye first came to Camberleigh. Ye was
young an' frightened but ye also had another thing. Ye be
knowin' what that was?"

I shook my head.

"Ye had courage. Now aye know 'tis not fer me to be
judgin' ye. An' aye know ye feelin' right now like yer world
'as come to an end. But aye can't let ye be sittin' around,
mopin' like ye be day after day. Yer Justin wouldn't 'a been
wantin' it, and it not be healthy fer ye. Look at ye—fadin'
away to nothin'. Ye lost the bloom in yer cheeks."

"What I have lost, Charlotte," I cried out, "is not the
bloom in my cheeks, 'tis the bloom in my heart."

"Aye know," she said quietly, taking my hand. "But ye has
to try. Ye has the courage to, aye know. But ye must try. If
only fer the children."

I shrugged. "What do you suggest I do?"

"Go back to Mayfair. 'Tis yer home, 'tis home for the little ones. You'll be findin' yer strength again there."

"I cannot, Charlotte," I insisted. "Justin lives in every part of that house. I cannot be haunted by memories. At least here there is a certain numbness. We spent so little time here during our married life that the house does not echo with his presence. It is bad enough that my mind and heart are filled with him. If it were to be the house, too, I do not think that I could bear it."

She shook her head. "Ye be wrong, Miss Serena. Ye 'ave the courage to face the memories. In time they'll be givin' ye peace."

"I simply cannot return there, Charlotte," I implored.

She sighed deeply and released my hand. "Then do as Lady Camberleigh has requested," she said, handing me an envelope.

I unfolded the note, which I instantly recognized as being penned by Anne. It was addressed to Charlotte, begging her to urge the children and myself to come to stay with Richard and her.

Dear Anne, it was like her to reach out and be protective of me, even in her own grief.

"There be no one ye is closer to, Serena," Charlotte said quietly. "Ye two need each other now. And t'would be good for the little ones. 'Tis not right their bein' cooped up 'ere with their grief."

I knew in my heart that Charlotte was right. The children had always loved Camberleigh. I dearly wished that Oliver would be there but they were fond of Anne and the country would not confine them as Channing Hall had done.

Charlotte looked at me hopefully.

I nodded.

"Tell Sidney that we will leave in the morning, that is, if you think that you and Mary can pack the baggage by then."

Charlotte rose and patted my hand. "Ye be doin' the right thing. Ye'll see."

I was not as certain as she—except the children's enthusiasm made it seem as though we were moving in the right direction. I tried to help Charlotte but found that I was far weaker than I had known. When Monique called later that day, she, too, championed my decision. I had hoped that Philip also would call. This was the first day that he had missed in over a week and I wanted to thank him for his attentiveness these past months. I had given no thought to what might happen to the railroad project, I would let Richard and the solicitor handle that. When by evening there was no word from him, I thus set about writing a note to him. I regretted that I would not have an opportunity to thank him personally. He had been such a part of our lives these past months that it seemed insufficient to communicate my appreciation in a letter, but it would have to suffice—for once having made the decision to travel to Camberleigh there was no turning back.

How everything was accomplished in those short hours I shall never know, but it was less than eighteen hours later that I found myself bundled into our carriage beside the children, Charlotte and Jaspar, with Sidney at the helm. It was not a happy trip. The weather was inclement and the children, though eager to visit Camberleigh, were fidgety. We stopped several times for refreshment. My appetite had still not returned but I was conscious of trying to provide diversion for the children. The first evening we stopped at an inn that I knew from the past. The second night we were forced to go a pace further than we had planned as the weather had drawn travelers into shelter earlier than usual.

It was late in the afternoon on the third day of our journey that we began our approach to Camberleigh. I felt a tightening in my throat as the long drive leading to the castle unfolded before my eyes. I recalled that day so many years ago when I had been a young girl traveling to this strange house. But then I had come to discover my heritage, a family that I had heretofore not known existed. I had come with a sense of promise then. Now I felt only loss.

As we approached the massiveness of Camberleigh, with its stony crenellations hidden by the darkness of the day, I hoped that Anne would not find our visit too much of an imposition. I had made the decision so quickly that there had been no time to notify Richard and her of our impending arrival.

I had to restrain the children and Jaspar from leaping out of the coach once it had come to a stop; the rain, which had been only a drizzle, was now pelting angrily against the cobblestone drive.

"Ye stay put, Lady Barkham," Sidney called out as he ran up the front steps to the house.

I could not see who had opened the door, though I assumed that it was Simon the head butler. Within moments several men had joined Sidney and had come out to fetch us, porting umbrellas for shelter. The children went on ahead and I called to Jaspar, who, once having realized where he was, was scampering about, barking his greetings.

"Jaspar," I urged, "come along now."

"Aye'll be gettin' the dog, Lady Barkham," Sidney assured me, "ye go on in now."

"Take him to the kitchens," I shouted, clasping desperately at the folds of the skirt of my traveling suit, now fully sodden. "And dry him off."

Charlotte had gone ahead of me with the children so I was the last to reach the front door. Hands quickly removed my cloak and withdrew the umbrella.

I took off my bonnet and shook out my hair. I looked up just in time to see Anne scurrying down the stairs to greet us. She nearly knocked me over with the ferocity of her embrace.

"Good Lord, you are drenched through," she exclaimed. "Molly," she said, turning to the upstairs maid whom I had known for years, "take Lady Barkham to her room. And Simon, you show Charlotte and the children where they shall be. Tell Cook that I want hot broth up in their rooms immediately."

"Anne, I—," I started to say.

She silenced me. "Hush, we have forever to talk, but I would never forgive myself if any of you became ill."

"Miss Serena, she just be gettin' over the last fever," Charlotte offered.

"I am just fine," I insisted.

Anne left me and embraced the children. "Now, you go with Charlotte, and tomorrow we shall all have a lovely day. Simon, see that the children and Charlotte have dinner brought to their rooms. Serena, shall you wish to dine with Richard and myself or are you too weary?"

"If you do not mind, Anne, I should prefer to stay in my room tonight."

"Of course, now go along all of you."

The eyes in the portraits of my ancestors seemed to watch me as Molly led me up the long staircase. I followed her down the hall. I paused at the door of the room that Justin and I always shared when we visited Camberleigh. It was our room really— Anne had even decorated it especially for us.

Molly turned back to see why I had not followed her. She

approached me slowly. "Lady Camberleigh thought ye might be more comfortable in yer grandmother's old room," she said, motioning down the hall.

"Ah," I said, thinking that it was so like Anne to have thought that I would rest better apart from a space that held so many memories.

I followed her, pausing as she entered and lit the candles which illuminated the violet-colored softness of the room.

"Aye be right back with a few of yer gowns," Molly said, "an' to be settin' the fire fer ye."

"I fear that the bags are most likely round by the servants' entrance."

"No worry," she assured me, "ye be havin' some things in ye and Lord Barkham's room."

I heard her emit a small gasp. "Oh, Lady Barkham, aye didn't mean, aye mean aye wasn't thinkin', aye be so sorry."

"You did nothing wrong, Molly," I assured her.

I removed the jacket of my suit and fought with the fastenings on the skirt, which proved difficult due to the wetness. Molly was back within moments and while I changed into a dressing gown and robe she set about starting the fire. I sipped at the hot broth that was sent up but all I truly wanted was to get in bed. I was bone tired, physically and emotionally, and I knew that what I needed most was sleep.

Molly turned the bed down and I climbed in. "Might you do me one favor?" I asked. "Would you see that Jaspar is brought to me? I suspect he is in the kitchen and by now he must be frantic about where the children and I have gone to."

When she finally returned with him I had finally warmed and was luxuriating in the quiet of the house. Jaspar, too, was now dry and I guessed as weary as I; cradling him close to me, I prayed that sleep would come quickly.

The respite of sleep had almost overtaken me when I heard the door open.

"Serena, Serena dear, are you awake?"

I recognized Anne's voice. It was cruel of me, but I remained silent. I simply did not feel that I could bear facing her tonight. I had not the energy for the emotional wrenching that I knew our shared grief would bring to the surface.

It was Molly who awakened me the following morning bringing my wash basin. I looked about for Jaspar, who was nowhere to be seen.

"Molly," I asked. "Have you seen my spaniel this morning?"

"Oh'n to be sure aye 'ave, Lady Barkham. Charlotte fetched 'im early this mornin' an' 'e an' the children 'ave been playin' in the garden. Made a ruckus in the kitchen, 'e did, ye know 'ow Cook is about that little dog."

I nodded. From that day over a decade ago when we had arrived at Camberleigh, Jaspar and the Cook had had a warring relationship. Actually, I thought that much of it was high drama staged for all our benefits but nonetheless it was an incurable love-hate relationship.

"Goodness, what time is it then?" I asked Molly, aware that it must be later than I thought.

"Oh, 'tis almost noon," she replied. "Lady Camberleigh said ye was to sleep as long as ye could. She and the Master be waiting fer ye downstairs for yer luncheon."

She drew back the heavy mauve velvet curtains around the windows and sunshine poured into the room.

"Oh, 'tis a beautiful day, it is."

I bathed quickly and selected one of the gowns to wear, which Molly was commencing to unpack from my trunks. As I buttoned it I realized how loosely it hung on me.

"Would ye be wantin' me to do your hair?" Molly asked. "Aye don't be 'avin' Charlotte's knack but I kin fix it a bit."

I thanked her and just asked her to coil it about the nape of the neck.

Minutes later I was making my way downstairs to find Anne and Richard. I moved to the library where I heard voices.

"Might I interrupt?" I asked as I passed through the massive oak doors.

"Serena, darling," Anne cried as she rose and ran toward me.

We embraced and then she held me at a distance. "Come, let me look at you," she said, her eyes roving my frame.

"Just what I thought," she concluded, looking at me disapprovingly.

"And that is?" I queried.

"I must admit that I inveigled information out of Charlotte. She tells me that you have not been eating and that is quite evident." She took my hand drawing me over by the fireplace to where my uncle sat. "But we shall change that, will we not, Richard?" she said firmly.

My uncle rose and held his arms out for me. "This is such a difficult time for us all," he said. "I am so pleased that you agreed to join us here."

"I could not face returning to Mayfair," I replied as I withdrew from his embrace and sat next to Anne, who was pouring a cup of tea for me.

"The children are fine," she assured me. "I hope you do not mind, but since the weather was so pleasant I thought it would do them good to be outside. Alexander in particular looks so pale."

"Does he?" I mused. "I fear I have not noticed as well as I should these past few weeks."

"Darling, I am not chastising you. I am only anxious that we have the three of you looking and feeling fit once again."

I nodded.

There seemed a deathly silence in the room, which was mercifully interrupted by the butler who announced that luncheon was served.

I knew that I should have responded more heartily to the glazed breast of baby chicken, fresh squash and roasted potatoes which were presented before me, but food continued to have a negative impact on me.

Seeing that I was only picking at my plate, Anne asked if I might like the Cook to prepare something special.

"No, no," I argued, "I just do not seem to have much appetite since . . ." my voice broke off.

"Since Justin's death," Anne said firmly.

I looked over at her, shocked at the acceptance in her voice. Anne's eyes filled with tears. "Serena, believe me, the loss has been greater for me than any that I have known before, even that of our parents. You know how close my brother and I were. But I have been fortunate to have Richard here with me to help me shoulder this loss. And he is right, we all must accept it. As difficult as it seems, we must go on with our lives."

My eyes studied this woman whose facial contours reflected her character—strong and even.

"You mean well, I know, Anne, both of you," I said, turning to my uncle, "but I must tell you that when I had news of Justin's death it was as though life stopped for me."

"And what of the children?" Anne implored.

"What of them?" I said wearily. "Their lives shall never be the same again, certainly you see that as well as I."

"What I see is that they have lost their father. But Serena, they have not lost their mother as well."

"Anne is right," Richard joined in. "They need you now more than ever."

"And they shall have me," I replied, "as long as I am alive."

"Forgive me for saying this, Serena," he continued, "but as you are now, you can hardly be of assist to them. They need the mother they have come to know and love: the beautiful Lady Camberleigh—the woman who is the toast of this continent. They have seen you cry, Serena. Now they want to hear you laugh."

I threw my napkin down on the table. "Laugh, did you say? My husband is dead and you want to hear me laugh?"

I pushed the chair out behind me. "Excuse me, please," I cried out and ran from the room. I heard Anne get up to follow me, but Richard must have stopped her for when I reached the second floor landing there was no one in pursuit.

When I reached my grandmother's room I flung myself down on the bed, pounding angrily at it. "Oh, Grandmother," I moaned to a ghost in my past, "why Justin, why something so cruel as this?"

If I had expected to hear a voice answering me there was none.

Charlotte brought the children and Jaspar to me later in the day. I was particularly watchful of Alexander and had to agree that his paleness did not appear healthy.

Daphne was full of chatter, particularly about the new pony in the stables.

"Uncle Richard said I might ride him tomorrow," she enthused. "Would you come with me?"

I shook my head. "Perhaps another day."

Taking the cue that I was tiring quickly, Charlotte suggested that they return to the nursery and leave me to rest.

I asked for a tray in my room that night. I did not want a schism between Anne or Richard and myself, and it seemed while all our nerves were on edge that it was best for us to go our separate ways.

And so passed the next few days. I kept to my room, happiest when sleep relieved the pain of each hour's passing. The children visited me in the afternoon. Both, I sensed, had been lectured to be quiet around me for each treated me gingerly.

Charlotte was unforgiving when she saw that the mealtime trays remained essentially untouched. I was surprised that neither Anne nor Richard made any attempt to visit with me, though I supposed that they were offended by my outburst at luncheon days earlier.

It was on the morning of our fifth day at Camberleigh that I was awakened with such a start that I was left breathless. I struggled up against the pillows only to see Anne across the room flinging open the draperies. She moved from there to the armoire and after a moment of sorting through my gowns withdrew a deep red velvet one. "Here, put this on," she said, thrusting it at me.

I winced for red had always been a favorite color of Justin's.

"Why?" I beseeched her.

"Because we are going out, you and I."

I pulled the covers up around me. "Oh, I could not, Anne, truly."

"You not only can but you will. Now come, get out of that bed and get dressed or I shall pull your bedding from under you."

"Please, Anne," I begged.

"Serena, this is my house and you shall do as I say while you are a guest in it," she said, her dark brows taking on a determined stance above her eyes.

I was not up for an argument and I almost mechanically rose and dressed.

"Brush your hair," she said. "It looks a fright."

I pulled the brush through my long coppery tresses and as best I could pulled it back into a tight coil.

She handed me a woolen cloak. "Here take this, there is a strong chill in the air."

I followed her almost blindly as she progressed down the hall. She stopped in front of the room that Justin and I had called our own. Opening the door, she reached out for my hand.

"Why are you doing this, Anne?" I asked.

"You will see," she replied, grasping me and pulling me into the room.

She led me over to the heavily carved full tester which dominated the entire wall of the room. "Now I want you to look, look around you."

My eyes somewhat warily roamed the room. There was a large dresser which had been Justin's, his silver-headed comb and brush atop of it right where he had left it. A book of poems that he particularly liked lay on the nightstand beside the bed. It was all there just as I remembered it.

"Am I supposed to be seeing something other than feeling that this is some kind of cruel ruse, Anne?"

She did not answer but instead led me to the dressing table. "Sit down, Serena."

I did as she bid, wondering why my dearest friend was doing this to me.

I looked ahead of me into the mirror beyond.

"That is it, Serena. Now what do you see?"

I looked at the face in the mirror. I knew that it was my own but it suddenly seemed unrecognizable to me. I could not think when my hair had last been washed. Its usual shimmer had long since gone. There were dark deep circles under my eyes which looked far larger than usual for the flesh that had once surrounded them was pale and taut. My lips looked raw from biting them—a habit, I supposed, which had been undertaken since Justin's death.

I stirred as Anne sat down beside me. Our eyes met in the mirror. "It is Justin that is lost to us, Serena," she whispered. "I could not bear to lose you, too. We need you, darling, especially the children. But if you continue this way you shall be as lost to us as Justin is."

As I sat there looking at our reflections in the mirror a solitary tear rolled down my cheek. "Can you ever forgive me?" I murmured.

Anne put her arm around me, pressing me to her. "Dear Serena, there is nothing to forgive."

We held each other for a very long time while she resolutely put her arms about my shoulders pushing me back. "I said we were going out and we are. 'Tis not far and I have something to show you."

As we left the room I stopped Anne as she started to close the door.

"Would you mind terribly if we left it open?" I asked.

"Of course not," she replied and I knew that she understood that I was not ready to shut Justin, or at least his memory, out of my life.

I followed her down the hall and staircase out to the front

courtyard. I quickly realized that her path was going to lead us down towards the stables. She led me through the stalls almost to the very end. There I found a chestnut foal, its only marking a diamond-shaped white crest between its eyes.

"Is it?" I asked excitedly.

"The very same," she replied, obviously pleased with my response. " 'Tis only weeks old."

I opened the gate and slowly went in. Instead of being frightened, the foal nuzzled readily against me. This foal was sired by Medallion, Justin's favorite horse. There had been a bond between those two, man and animal. It was prophetic, I thought, that his foal should come into being so near the time that we had lost Justin.

I moved out and closed the gate. "Would you mind terribly if one day soon he be brought to Mayfair?" I asked. "I would like Alexander to have him."

"You do not think that I had any other thought in mind, did you?"

It was from there that we walked, through the meadow, down by the arbor and rose gardens bedded down for the winter months. We talked as we went, mostly about Justin.

When she reminded me of how my strong, capable husband had become a blundering, nervous creature when I commenced birthing Daphne, I laughed. It startled me to hear laughter echoing from myself again, but it felt good. There was a relief to it that my many tears had not accomplished. When we finally returned to the house I went in search of the children. I found them with Charlotte in the nursery.

There was a clarity about me now and it frightened me to see how tenuous they had actually become with me. Anne had been right. By destroying myself I had also been destroying the part of Justin that remained.

I took a chair and called for both of them to come to me. It was shocking to see them look to Charlotte for approval, but then I suppose I had brought that upon myself.

Sensing that something was brewing, Charlotte asked, "Ye be wantin' me to leave ya for a bit, Miss Serena?"

"No, please stay," I begged, "this pertains to you as well."

"I have told your Aunt Anne, and I want you both to know that I apologize to you both. And to Charlotte. Your father's death was an enormous shock to me and of course it was to you, but I was so preoccupied with my own grief that I could not cope with yours. I was wrong. Terribly wrong. And I ask you to forgive me. For the last thing I would ever want to do is to hurt any of you."

"We know that, Mama," Daphne said, putting her arm about me and giving me a kiss.

"Does that mean that you will not be sad anymore?" Alexander queried.

I shook my head. "There shall always be a sadness in not having your father with us. But what we must do is remember all the love and happiness he brought us."

"Thank the Lord," Charlotte murmured, "aye been prayin' for this hour to come."

"Now," I said resolutely, "I have made a decision."

Both children looked at me expectantly.

"We are going to return to Mayfair tomorrow. That is, if you want to."

"Oh, yes," they replied gleefully.

I stood up. "Good, then it is settled. Tomorrow we are going home."

I took luncheon with the children and spent the afternoon playing games and talking as we had not done in weeks—in truth, not since we had left Mayfair.

That evening at dinner I told Anne and Richard of my decision to return home.

"Oh, dear, I was afraid of that," Anne moaned.

"Coming here was the right thing, Anne, but so is returning to Mayfair. I cannot let Robbie shoulder the responsibility alone any longer."

Richard rubbed at the scar along his cheek, which he tended to do when he was thoughtful or perturbed.

"I must say I concur with your decision, Serena. Not that you are not welcome here—of course you are, in many ways you know this is your home. However, I think for the children, it is best now for them to be in their own surroundings. But on the matter of Robbie handling the estates, surely you must see that that is quite out of the question now."

"But why?" I pressed. "He has done well with Justin these past years."

Richard took a sip of red wine. "That is just the point. Justin was at the helm. Surely you know that even I have all but stepped out of the picture these past years. I cannot feign that I ever had Justin's ambition to see these farms be as successful as he had made them, but atop that I am not as young as I once was. I have, I fear, neither the inclination nor the health to resume that responsibility.''

I was surprised that my uncle had been so candid about his physical being, and as I looked at Anne I saw her eyes willing me not to press the matter.

"Richard, you misunderstand me," I argued. "I have given great thought to it this afternoon and the solution appears simple. I shall assume Justin's role, with Robbie, of course, to guide me.''

"You?" Richard blurted out.

"Why not?"

"You have no experience," he replied. "My dear, I would be the last to insult your intelligence, but Serena, this is a man's work. You saw how Justin slaved. If it was not worrying about drought or diseased crop or the tenants it was the books. It is a monumental task.''

"I am aware of that," I said firmly. "But I shall have nothing but time on my hands now, and I am certain that I can learn. Besides, frankly I see no other alternative. Do you?''

He stared at the now empty plate before him. "Frankly no, except of course—''

I stopped him. "If you are about to suggest that we divide the estates and I sell my half, please do not even think it. Mayfair was Justin's heritage and it shall be our children's to follow. No, I am determined. At least say you will support my giving it a try, Richard.''

He remained silent.

"Give me six months. If by then I do not have matters under control, then of course we shall have to discuss some other arrangement.''

"That is not too much to ask, Richard," Anne interceded. "After all, you have not opposed my own foray into business.''

"Designing of gowns, my love, is quite afield from managing one of the largest estates in the country," Richard grumbled. "But since I cannot step in, I do not see how I can refuse you your intentions.''

Anne sighed. "Well, I certainly am pleased that that is settled.''

"There is one other thing, Serena.''

I turned my attention to him.

"This rascal railroad thing Justin got involved with. I told him not to get into that. 'Oh it was going to revolutionize the nation,' he said. 'Good for us all.' Well, it killed him, did it not?"

"Richard, please," Anne rebuked.

"You cannot stop me from having my opinion, dear. It is no secret. I thought Justin a damnable fool to get involved. Particularly with that Taggart chap."

"Philip has been very kind, Richard," I assured him. "For someone who was a relative stranger to us months ago, he has truly become a valued friend—to me and the children."

"That does not change my question. What do you intend to do about it?"

"I truly have not given any thought to it. Justin's primary involvement from my knowledge was as an investment. You are correct—he was dedicated to the concept of railroads throughout England, but it was he who put up the money. I suppose Sir Henry shall apprise me what is to be done there."

"Just do not be foolish," Richard concluded.

I was relieved when the dinner came to an end for the day had proved an exhausting one for me. My loss of appetite had weakened me greatly and I knew that I would have to pace myself until I could gain weight and with it a sense of well-being.

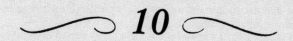

# 10

We commenced our journey back to Mayfair midmorning the following day. I had almost succumbed at the last to Anne's pleas to remain at Camberleigh until I was stronger, but the children were so ebullient at the thought of the return that I kept with my plan of the day prior.

The weather was crisp and clear as the carriage began the trip which took a little over two hours on a fair day. There was something terribly soothing about watching the sheep graze amongst the meadows and fields. My own childhood had been spent in the South, and though I often missed the sand and smell of the sea I was ever appreciative of the lushness of these lands. Justin had been wise years ago to have invested in new machinery for the plowing and tilling of the vast areas which comprised the estate. Crops had been good, the tenants had prospered and Mayfair had long overtaken Kelston Manor in its position within the county. I prayed that I would find the strength and the intelligence with Robbie's guidance to make my promise good to Richard.

"Look, Mother, we are almost home," Daphne cried as we started the yew-lined approach to the house.

"Yes, darling, I know, but sit still or you shall have poor Charlotte bruised with all your clamoring about."

When the carriage finally came to rest in the circular courtyard, Sidney could not climb down fast enough to let the children and Jaspar out.

"Now, do not go running off," I called in caution as they bounded from the carriage. Since we had been at Channing Hall I had forgotten how exuberant they could be, I admitted to Charlotte.

As Sidney helped me down she replied, "Aye but it does my heart good to see them like this again. Been too sweet with one another 'o late for me taste. T'weren't normal, if ye be knowin' what I mean."

I laughed for I knew she was right. They teased each other unmercifully. Daphne was really the protagonist but it was such a pattern between them that when it ceased one sensed it was a lull before the storm.

The great double doors flung open and suddenly Giles was on the steps, obviously shaken by our unannounced arrival. I waved to him and he descended the steps painfully slowly.

"Welcome home, Lady Barkham," he said as he reached me. "We had not expected you so soon after, I mean . . ."

I put my hand out and took his in mine. "I know, Giles. I regret that we did not send word but there was not time."

"I speak for us all, Lady Barkham, when I tell you that each one of us—well, we are simply devastated by this tragedy. The master, 'e was well loved. 'Tis a great loss."

"Thank you, Giles," I said appreciatively. "You and Lord Barkham had been together for many years. I know that he valued your work and your friendship." Then turning to Charlotte, I said, "Perhaps you had best round up the children and Jaspar and get them settled in the nursery. Giles, if you would inform Cook that we have returned and ask her to prepare some small luncheon. I shall take mine in my room. Oh, and Charlotte, when you see Robbie would you tell him that I should like to see him in my room?"

"Soon as the young ones be settled," she replied.

Resolved that everyone had been dispatched to their various tasks, I proceeded up the steps to Mayfair. There was a lump in my throat but I steeled myself against releasing the tears that pressed to fall. There was a mustiness about the house which I quickly attributed to the servants since I knew that when we were not about they tended to stay to their quarters. Hopefully the weather would continue to be pleasant and I could air the house over the next few days.

I found our room completely unchanged, but that no longer surprised me for I had experienced repeatedly over the past weeks how nothing surfacely changed in the face of death. Within moments of entering the room, Sarah, one of the upstairs maids, arrived and nervously commenced changing the bed linens. I had an urge to stop her for I knew that they had likely not been changed since the last time that Justin and I had lain together in this house. It was silly, I supposed, but I knew his scent would still be there, able to bring him back to me if only for a moment. Since I could hardly explain my abhoration to Sarah, I set about changing from my traveling suit to a pale blue wool dress. It hung so shabbily about my shoulders and waist that I was forced to borrow a sash from another gown so that I would not trip from its dropped length. When the luncheon tray arrived I made a conscious effort to eat everything that was placed before me. I had grown appallingly thin and I was going to need my strength if I was indeed to assume the running of the estates. I had eaten as much as I was going to when there came a knock at the door. It was Robbie.

I put my arms out to him and he came quickly to me, kneeling before me. When I released him and motioned to him to sit beside me, he did so pushing back the red locks which insisted on falling about his face.

"T'was a black day fer me when aye be hearin' the news, Miss Serena," he said quietly. "Me mum told me aye was not to go on talkin' about it at ye but aye could not 'a come 'ere an' keep silent. Lord Barkham, well 'e was like a father to me, 'e was. T'would that aye could 'a given myself instead o' 'im, aye would, an' that be the truth.''

I studied Robbie. I was so used to see him grinning that toothy smile, his dark eyes flashing like Charlotte's, that I was surprised at how mature his regard was when seriousness overtook it.

I shook my head. "Justin would not have wanted that," I assured him. "But I am grateful for your sentiment. Would you like a spot of tea? Sarah is about some place and she can fetch it."

He shook his head. "Me mum said that ye is goin' to step into the master's boots an' be runnin' this place."

I was sorry that Charlotte had broken the news to him for I should have preferred to break it differently, but then there was no easy way to get into it.

I was amused by the thought of stepping into my husband's shoes for they were indeed twice the size of my own. I

wondered if the running of Mayfair was also twice what I
could manage.

"Robbie, I have thought about it and frankly I see no other
way. You have my complete trust but you cannot bear the
burden alone. We both know Richard has become less and less
involved over the years and frankly he does not look well.
That leaves myself. I do not pretend to know anything of how
these estates are managed but if you are willing to help me I
know that I can learn."

"Aye be ready to help ye, Miss Serena, ye know that but
there's a plenty that aye not be knowin', too. Oh, workin' with
the tenants an' keeping the machines goin' and the like, aye
kin do. But t'was the master who be the one who knew 'ow to
put it all together. It was 'e who did all the books. Aye know
ye taught me my numbers but other 'an the simple things 'tis
foreign to me."

"Well, fortunately I have always been good with figures. I
cannot promise that I can make sense of those books but I can
at least give it a try. That is, if you will help."

"Ye 'ave me word," he agreed.

We agreed to meet the next morning in the library. I promised to have all Justin's books and ledgers brought down and
he in turn said that he would arrange to have Medallion's foal
brought back to Mayfair as a surprise for Alexander. I spent
the remainder of the day with the children, who seemed relieved if not pleased at my new determination. That evening,
realizing that the moments that I might spend with them would
be meager over the next few months, I penned a letter to
Master Farraday, explaining the death of my husband and
begging him to return posthaste to resume his tutelage of the
children. I hoped that he had not traveled from his sister's
home, since then it might be months before I was in contact
with him and I did not want the children to fall behind in their
studies.

When my evening tray arrived, I decided that someone must
have informed Cook of my weight reduction for the plate
was brimming with sausages and kidneys and small potatoes.
Henceforth, I decided that we should take our meals in the
small dining room. We all had to eat and it would afford me
some time with the children each day.

Sleep did not come easily to me that night. My body ached
with loneliness at the cold empty space beside me. I yearned

not so much for our lovemaking but for those moments of tenderness that followed when, cradled in Justin's arms, he gently stroking my hair, I would drift into a peaceful reverie.

The next morning I rose and dressed quickly, looking in on the children who, I noted almost happily, were bickering. Jaspar, who had remained with them since our return, bounded to my heels, his brown eyes imploring me to take him with me.

"I assure you," I said scratching his ears, "you are bound to have a more amusing day right here. On the other hand, perhaps you can give me a clue or two about those ledgers."

Robbie was already in the library arranging the books into some sort of order.

"You must think me daft," I said, overwhelmed by the number of volumes which surrounded him, "but I had no way of knowing which we would need so I gave instructions to have them all brought down."

"Aye would not want to be worryin' ye straight out, Miss Serena, but aye fear we be needin' all 'o them."

After he had arranged everything in five enormous stacks he said, "Now this one, this be on the taxes. This one on the rents. The end one there be the tally 'o crops. These two aye cannot make hide nor hair out of."

I looked skeptically at the stacks. "Which one do you think I should commence with?"

He laughed. "The one aye cannot figure."

And so we spent the day poring over the first of the ledgers, breaking only for luncheon and dinner. By day's end I was thoroughly exhausted and even more depressed. Early on, it had become clear to me that Justin had his own system for everything. I should not have been surprised for he had never been one to follow traditional modes. What made it nigh impossible was that although I seemed able to reconcile the figures I could not decipher his abbreviations. Thus I was hard pressed to know what the figures stood for. Robbie, too, was frustrated for, just as he had forewarned, he had had little exposure to these ledgers and thus was as puzzled as I was to their origins and purpose.

After the first week of this routine that we had set for ourselves, I called a halt to it. Not only had we made pitiful progress but I was conscious that Robbie was torn between his obligation to me and the regular duties which he had been forced to let lag these past seven days.

We—or I should say—I decided upon a new arrangement. We would meet one afternoon a week and I would share with him what I had gleaned. It was during the ensuing weeks that I came to have such an enormous respect for the volumes of details my husband had been able to balance single-handedly. I cringed when I thought of all those times I had chastised him for working so hard. I now knew that he had done it largely out of necessity. Just the balancing of the household budget was a monumental task. We had always maintained a large staff. Mayfair was an enormous manor and it took dozens in help to maintain it. But I was shocked when I reviewed the monthly outlay. Not that it was out of proportion with the number of servants, or the amount of food consumed— simply, I had never related it in pounds. The money that I had in a secret cache that Justin kept in the anteroom to our bedroom would fast be dispensed, I could quickly see, and I made a mental note to contact the solicitor as soon as possible to see when I might expect additional funds.

The days were arduous for me and yet I almost reveled in my exhaustion for it gave me little chance to wallow in my grief. The children tried to be understanding, but they simply did not have enough to keep them occupied. I made a valiant effort to keep up appearances with them, not admitting to my fatigue or frustration in front of them. The one main diversion occurred for them the day that Medallion's colt arrived. Robbie alerted me that it had come and I broke from my routine and scurried the children down to the stables. It was love at first sight between Alexander and this young colt.

"What shall you name him?" I asked as he stood before the horse, his eyes bright with wonder.

He paused a long time. "Justin. I think I shall name him Justin after Father."

Tears filled my eyes. "He would like that, I am certain, Alexander. Justin, it shall be."

Daphne turned to her brother and spat out, "Well, I think it is a stupid name for a horse," and she ran sobbing from the stable.

Alexander looked up at me perplexed. "Daphne did not mean that," I assured him. "She is simply upset. You will learn, Alexander, as you grow older that women react strangely to things at times. She is simply not over grieving for your father. None of us are. Try to understand."

"I do," he said quickly.

We walked hand in hand back up to the house. I could have kissed Anne for on returning there I found that she had sent a large box which was marked for Daphne; upon examining its contents I discovered that she had sent several new dresses. Alexander and I took them up to her and within moments her vanity overtook her mood and she was flouncing about the room pretending, as was her favorite want, to be a grand lady.

It seemed to me that days passed into nights and nights into days during those weeks. There were no callers at Mayfair save the post which had been dispatched from London. I was overwhelmed at the letters of condolence, many from people we scarcely knew. I did not share them with the children, determining that it would serve only as yet another reminder of their recent loss. Instead, I tied them up carefully and put them aside. Each letter in its own way was a tribute to their father and one day I would pass them on to them when I felt it important that his memory be kept alive.

By the end of the first month I was fighting with an inner voice that was telling me that the task of managing the affairs of the estates was much too arduous for one alone. Charlotte was ever reprimanding me for not eating enough, not resting enough, not taking better care of my appearance. I assured her that it was not purposeful. The energy that I put into my work seemed to undo the efforts I was making to regain my original appearance and strength.

One thing had given me small encouragement during those days. I received a letter from Sir Henry informing me that he would travel to Mayfair within the ensuing weeks and review with me all the details of my husband's estate.

It was on a Thursday afternoon in December when Giles told me that I had a visitor. Lord Taggart was in the drawing room.

"Lord Taggart!" I exclaimed. "What on earth is he doing here?"

"He apologized for arriving unannounced, Lady Barkham, but he says he has business of an urgent nature."

"Of course," I said, realizing that it must have to do with the railroad venture.

"Show him in here please, Giles."

I knew that I scarcely looked the role to receive visitors, but since I could not leave the library without being viewed from the drawing room there was little opportunity to escape upstairs to change. I smoothed the folds of my heavy wool gown and tucked a strand of hair back that had fallen. At least I had let Charlotte do my hair this morning; clean and hanging in soft folds about my face, I knew it diminished only somewhat my wan appearance.

He strode in looking very fit. His blond hair had been clipped shorter than I was accustomed to seeing it and it flattered his already fine features.

"Philip," I said, "I am surprised, but pleasantly so."

He took my hand which I had extended and kissed it.

"You are lovely as usual, Serena."

I laughed. "It is good to hear you say that even if it is only a half-truth. Everyone tells me I am far too thin and pale but then when I see myself in the mirror I have to admit that they are right. Come," I said, withdrawing my hand. "Sit by me and tell me what brings you here."

"First off—you, of course. I tried so often to see you and then to find that you had left London—frankly I was gravely disappointed."

"You received my note, did you not?"

"Yes, of course, but I thought that we had become better friends—you and I—than for you to leave without seeing me."

"I wanted to, Philip," I assured him, "but you did not call that particular day and the decision was made quickly. Frankly I was in no state to be particularly rational at that point."

"I have scarcely been able to forgive myself for your hearing the news the way you did. I was overwrought myself. I know what a shock it must have been for you. But you are improved now, I trust," he questioned.

I sighed. "It was not your fault, Philip. Please do not chastise yourself. But tell me about you—how are Jonathan and Monique, of course?"

"Jonathan is well, he sends his regards. I must admit that I have not seen a great deal of Monique since you left."

"Oh?"

"Let me just say that our paths have not crossed."

I was curious but decided not to pry.

"And the railroad venture?"

"Ah," he said, "that is what I have come to see you about."

"There is no trouble, I hope."

His fingers played thoughtfully at the corners of his mouth.

"That should largely depend on you, Serena. I truly wish that I could postpone this conversation for the last thing you need now are external pressures but I have no choice than to speak of it now."

"Goodness, now you have piqued my curiosity."

"Justin was a remarkable man, Serena, but then I need not tell you that. But I think what I liked best about him was his foresight—that, and that he was a bit of a gambler. Did he by any chance discuss with you the terms of our agreement?" I shook my head.

"To be slightly indelicate, you have no idea, then, of the sum that your husband was to invest?"

"No, I do not, Philip."

"Well, let me tell you it was substantial."

He uttered a sum that momentarily took my breath away.

"I must admit that I knew that Justin was committed to the project, though I had no idea of how fully."

Philip cleared his throat. "When I said earlier, Serena, that this project now depends on you, what I meant was that as Justin's rightful heir the decision of whether to proceed or not now rests in your hands."

"But I do not understand, Philip. If Justin made the commitment, then right or wrong, I suppose it must stand."

"There is the matter of money, Serena. Justin advanced funds to get us started before he sailed but that was only a fraction of what is needed. You see, the rest was to come upon his return. Unfortunately that cannot be, unless of course you stand by his pledge. Then, of course everything would proceed as planned."

I was grateful that Giles arrived with some tea for I needed time to take stock of the situation. Though I knew I was not frivolous I found myself wishing that we had not the wealth we did. The burdens of these financial matters, I realized, rested on me now that Justin was gone and I found it difficult to cope with the decisions that were being demanded of me.

Philip leaned forward to take his tea. "If you need a few days, perhaps a week, to reach a decision, I am certain we can delay for a spell."

I shook my head. "No, Philip. Frankly if I ponder it too long it shall only serve to confuse me. Besides," I continued, gesturing to the ledgers about me, "there is another task here, that of managing the estates that I have undertaken and, believe me, that needs my full concentration."

Philip laughed. "You cannot mean to say that you are going to attempt to assume Justin's role in all of this."

I was irritated by his attitude. "I most certainly do," I snapped in retort.

"Serena, forgive me. I in no way intended ridicule. I am simply amazed, that is all."

I shrugged. "Well, if it is any consolation, you are not the only one, Philip. Anyway, we are diverging from the reason for your journey here. You were right earlier when you said that my husband had vision. I would never have thought it for he was such a dedicated agriculturist but he was nearly obsessed by the prospect of these new iron engines. I can almost see him now saying to me, 'Watch, Serena, these railroads are going to make England greater than she has ever been.' It was a passion with him, not one I admit that I readily share but then perhaps I am more the skeptic."

"Then you shall terminate the project," Philip said, his brows furrowed. "I am not surprised, but I trust you will understand my disappointment."

"I did not say that. What I said was that I do not share Justin's passion about the project. But that does not mean that I am correct. He had good instincts and frankly I think he would want me to proceed with it. So in answer to your question, yes, Philip, you shall have the money."

He looked at me incredulous at my response. "You really mean it Serena? You are willing to continue the project?"

"I am. In fact I am expecting my husband's solicitor to arrive here shortly and I shall instruct him at that time to transfer the funds to wherever you designate."

"I certainly would not want to add undue pressure but in the essence of time, Serena, why do you not write him some small note which I might take back to London with me? That way he can draw up the papers and arrange for the transfer before he arrives."

"If you wish," I replied.

I rose. "Now that that is settled, I must tell Cook that there shall be another for dinner this evening."

He waved me off. "That is most kind of you, Serena, but I must refuse. I shall leave shortly and travel most of the night. It is imperative that I get back to London as quickly as possible."

"Surely you can at least stay for dinner," I insisted.

"Another time," he refused. "Given your generosity I am loath to ask you for a further indulgence, Serena, but it is central I fear to the continuance of this venture."

"Perhaps you should tell me, then," I replied, sitting down again.

"As you know, most of the routes that we have designed were to be initially centered in the North."

I nodded.

"Upon Justin's return he was to have come back to Mayfair and he had kindly extended the invitation for me to come here as well. In essence, until the first tracks were laid, Mayfair was to be the base of our operations."

I sensed what he was about to ask. "And you now want to use Mayfair as your base of operations, as you call it?"

"I realize that it is a tremendous imposition, Serena, but it would prove very difficult for me to find quarters that would be as suitable within the area."

"Then of course you shall stay," I said, hesitating only for a moment, "though I do not know where you shall put all your machines or whatever it is you are working with."

He laughed. "We are scarcely going to build the railroad on top of Mayfair. Serena, I promise you there shall be no steam engines born here except on paper."

We spent the next hour making pleasantries. He asked after the children and I explained that they were well, though with too much time to fritter away. I had still not had a reply from Master Farraday, but I said that I hoped to by week's end. Philip appeared anxious to leave, and though I once again extended my hospitality for the evening, he refused. It was only when he had risen to depart that I thought suddenly of Jonathan Leech.

"You know it never occurred to me, Philip, but I expect that you meant that Jonathan would be joining you as well."

"That will not be necessary," he replied slowly. "You see,

his part truly functions best working in London."

"I am surprised, Philip. I thought that Jonathan was, let us say, the architect behind this railroad venture."

"Really, trust me, Serena, he is best off in London."

I accepted that he knew best. And in truth, though I was enormously fond of Jonathan, one less person under foot was better to my liking.

Philip took my hand and kissed it. "To say thank you seems so inadequate, Serena, but I do thank you. I am grateful for your generosity but I must admit that I am impressed most by your courage."

I flushed slightly not from his words of appreciation but the glance that went with it.

"When shall I expect you then, Philip?"

He released my hand and rubbed his chin. "Within the week I should guess, unless that is inconvenient for you?"

"So soon? Not that it is a problem, I just did not expect that you would commence so quickly."

He smiled. "I have never been known to waste time, Serena."

As I had been married to a man of like nature I did not argue. Philip departed and I joined the children in the dining room. It had been an oddly eventful day and they were most curious who our visitor had been. When she learned that it had been Philip, Daphne was furious with me for not allowing her to see him. I explained that it was purely business and that he was eager to return to London.

"Besides," I said, "you shall see him soon enough for he is to return here within the week. He shall be staying with us for a while."

"You mean he shall be living here at Mayfair?" Alexander asked, his eyes wide with astonishment.

I explained that Philip was going to continue with their father's plans for the railroad and would be staying with us until the initial steps could be completed.

"How long is that?" Alexander asked.

"You know I never thought to query him," I mused, "but you are pleased, are you not? You like Philip."

"I think he is ever so handsome," Daphne replied.

"And you, Alexander, what do you think?"

He shrugged.

"Well, even if he is not to be your best friend, do try to be pleasant with him while he is here. Rightly or wrongly I have made this commitment and it would be very difficult to go back on my word.''

I lay in bed that night praying that I indeed had made the right decision. Monique would not think favorably on it for she persisted, I suspected, in the belief that Philip saw me as more than the wife of his business partner. I could not deny that her suggestion had me uneasy but time had passed, and if Philip had once harbored any notions of the sort I was convinced that he had bandoned them. Ours was a financial arrangement. What he conducted in his personal life or whom he conducted it with was of no concern of mine.

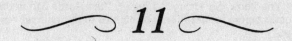

# 11

I worked feverishly over the next few days studying some additional papers that I had found of Justin's that helped to clarify his expectations on the sale of the fall harvest. So absorbed had I become in reconciling the ledgers that I had completely forgotten about the approaching holidays until Charlotte reminded me. Christmas has always been such a happy time at Mayfair and I was painfully aware that this year I was going to have to make a special effort for the children. I wrote to Anne and Richard imploring them to come and stay for a spell. As it was hopeless to think of my going to London to make any purchases, I prepared a small list and engaged Charlotte to do the best she could with it at the shop in the nearest town.

It was but two days after Philip departed that the solicitor arrived. Sir Henry Waltham had been with the Barkham family for years. He was a tall gentleman with steely eyes and a rather grim countenance which was softened only by a smile that he fortunately displayed fairly frequently.

"Lady Barkham," he said as he was shown into the drawing room. "I came sooner than I expected for I was most disturbed by my visit with Lord Taggart. And naturally I wanted to see you right off."

"But how could you have seen Philip, I mean Lord Taggart? He only just left Mayfair."

He scratched at the side of his head. "That is odd for he

163

made no mention of his intention to come to Mayfair."

I did not mention that I also found it odd—for Philip, unless I had misunderstood, had not told me that he had visited with Sir Henry.

"Might I ask what you discussed while he was here?"

"You know, Sir Henry," I began, "that Justin had in the months before his death been committed to this railroad venture."

"I do," he nodded.

"Well, since I am his rightful heir, the decision whether to proceed or not is now mine, is it not?"

"It is."

"Lord Taggart came here to determine whether or not I would sanction it—which of course means whether I would stand behind it financially."

"And your response?"

"I told him that I would."

Sir Henry coughed and withdrew a handkerchief that he rubbed furiously at his nose. "I apologize, some damnable allergy of mine. Lady Barkham, did he mention to you the sums involved?"

"They are substantial, I know."

"Of course I knew that Justin, Lord Barkham, was committed to the project," Sir Henry replied. "As a matter of fact we advanced a fairly large sum to it just prior to his departure for America. But I must confess to you I had no idea of the amount of the total commitment. I was frankly shocked."

"I sense that you disapprove, Sir Henry."

He shook his head. "I am only here as a consultant. In truth I am the purveyor of your wishes, Lady Barkham. The money is yours to do with as you wish. I have brought papers here to show you exactly what you have inherited. You are a woman of great wealth, Lady Barkham. But I must forewarn you that should you commit to this railroad venture you should tie up a sizable portion of your assets. That sum could be put at great risk."

"If Justin was ready to make the gamble, then I feel that I should be as well, Sir Henry. They were his wishes, and though I loathe being put in the position of making such an enormous decision, I feel that I must follow the path he had set. He obviously set great store in Philip, Lord Taggart, and

Jonathan Leech. I truly believe that this is what Justin would have wanted.''

"Then I shall accommodate it," he said, rising. "And now I am off to Camberleigh to discuss a few matters with your uncle."

"I am pleased then that you did not make the journey just for me. It is an arduous one, I know. But then if Justin's dreams about the railways come to pass perhaps it shall be less so in the future.''

We said our goodbyes after Sir Henry assured me that I should be receiving funds henceforth on a regular basis.

The pattern of my days resumed after Sir Henry's departure. I felt that whether or not I had made the right decision about the railroad venture at least I had made a decision. Justin had trusted that it was a wise investment and I had to do the same. The ledgers were commencing to make some sense to me and I knew that I had made more progress this week than I had in all the past.

It was exactly one week before Christmas when Philip returned. I had just put the children to bed and, feeling a bit restless, I had gone back down to the library to find a book to read. Jaspar followed wearily at my heels. It was a particularly cold night. Winter was full upon us and I could see a tracing of white flakes falling outside the window.

The knock at the door, which I heard through the silence of the night, startled me. I rose, not knowing whether Giles had already retired, but I heard him open the door.

"Lord Taggart," he exclaimed.

I moved out into the hallway. Philip was there, shaking the melting flakes from his head.

"You must forgive me for arriving so late, Serena, but the weather delayed us dreadfully. I would have paused at an inn but the closest one was filled.''

"Nonsense—of course you should have come," I said, noting for the first time the young woman who stood behind him. My eyes must have reflected my surprise for Philip quickly drew the woman forward.

"Serena, this is Amelie. Amelie Wythe. Amelie, Lady Barkham.''

I was shocked that Philip would have taken it upon himself to bring this young woman into my home but my sense of propriety kept me from confronting the issue at that moment. I took the hand that she extended.

"Why do you not come into the library, both of you?" I said as I noticed that Amelie was regarding me tenuously.

They removed their cloaks and followed me into the library. "Help yourself to some brandy, Philip," I said, motioning to the decanter set. "It would not hurt you to have some as well, Miss Wythe, it will help take the chill off."

"Will you join us, Serena?" Philip asked.

"No, thank you, Philip," I replied, watching Amelie as she took the glass from him.

"I should like to propose a toast," Philip said, "to the continuance of our railroad venture and to Amelie, who I hope shall be an answer to your prayers as the new governess at Mayfair."

I was glad that I had not accepted the drink for I think it would have spluttered from my mouth.

"Before you say anything, Serena, let me explain. You will recall that I told you that my sister had a governess who was going to need to find a suitable new post?"

I nodded.

"Well, that governess is Miss Wythe. Forgive my assumptiveness, Serena, but with your tutor absent you cannot possibly manage the children on your own and Charlotte, to whom I know you are terribly loyal, is after all your housekeeper."

"The children adore her," I said quickly. "No offense to you, Miss Wythe."

"Well, when you told me that you were intending to take over the management of Mayfair, well it was then that I thought that Amelie would be just the answer. I hope that I have not presumed too much."

I resented being put in such an awkward position. I was sensitive about saying anything which might embarrass Miss Wythe for my own days as a governess, though long past, were not forgotten. I looked over to her and she met my gaze. She was really quite a striking-looking woman. Her dark brown hair, clustered atop her head, accentuated her swanlike neck. Her eyes were of a distinct almond shape and her skin, which had an unusual olive cast, hinted at tracings of foreign blood.

"You were with Lord Taggart's sister for what length of time, Miss Wythe?"

"Almost six years," she replied softly.

I was surprised for she looked no older than twenty.

"How many children were under your supervision, Miss Wythe?"

Before she could answer Philip said, "Two. She has two, like you, Serena, a boy and a girl, though they are much older than Daphne and Alexander."

"I see. Miss Wythe, I hope that you understand my hesitation. Quite frankly it is something that my late husband and I discussed but I was simply not prepared. The hour is late and I am certain that you are weary after your journey. We can resume discussion of this in the morning."

She looked enormously relieved.

"I shall ask Giles to have one of the maids ready your rooms."

"That is most generous of you, Lady Barkham," she said sweetly.

I bid them both goodnight and left to search out Giles, who had already dispatched a maid to arrange the rooms.

When Jaspar and I had finally bedded down I ruminated on the situation presented. Although I was certain that Philip had only intended to be helpful by bringing Miss Wythe to Mayfair, I could not help but slightly resent his assumptiveness. Momentarily I wondered whether my being magnanimous about Philip's staying at Mayfair had been wise. I resented what felt like an invasion of my privacy. It was foolish, of course, and I knew that much of it was due to the fact that I had been so solitary over these past few months. But I did not like feeling trapped. If I turned Miss Wythe out without any prospects, I would not feel very charitable. I knew not whether she had a family to turn to, and with the holidays approaching it was not likely that she would gain employment until after the new year. On the other hand I was not about to hire her simply because she had been dropped in my lap. I decided that I would let the children decide. If they liked her I would hire her at least for a trial period.

I rose early the next morning. The snow had abated and Mayfair's parklike grounds were covered with a glistening blanket of white. I selected a black wool dress with a high collar and slim tight sleeves for the day. When I looked at myself in the mirror I decided that the severity of the gown only seemed to accentuate my weight loss and I released my hair from its coil and let it fall freely about my shoulders.

Charlotte arrived just as I had finished dressing.

"Aye hear we've a new governess afoot," she said coolly.

"Who told you that?" I asked, annoyed that the servants were obviously gossiping.

"Miss Wythe 'erself. Was up bright an' early, walkin' around 'ere like she owned the place."

"And she told you that she was the new governess?" I asked, appalled at the young woman's nerve.

She nodded.

I proceeded to explain to her that Philip had placed me in an awkward situation by literally foisting her upon me. "I have not formally engaged her, however, and I am appalled that she would have concluded otherwise."

"Might aye be askin' ye why ye do not think aye kin be handlin' the children?"

"Oh, Charlotte," I pleaded, realizing that the possibility of a new governess had hurt her, "you know me better than that. There is no one whom I trust more with the children than you. But I cannot ask you to oversee the household, the staff and the children as well. When we were in London it was another thing, for Mary was there and you did not have the worry of Channing Hall, but now that we are back at Mayfair it seems clear to me that extra help is needed. I am not certain that Miss Wythe is our answer but I think perhaps temporarily we can form some arrangement. That is, of course, unless the children do not respond favorably to her."

"Seems high and mighty, she does, te me if ye be askin' me," she offered.

"That may just be an attitude to cover her nervousness," I replied.

She shrugged.

" 'Ave ye been seein' 'er references?"

"No," I said, surprised that she should ask. "I did not frankly even think of it since she worked until recently for Lord Taggart's sister."

"Oh," Charlotte murmured.

"Where was Miss Wythe when you saw her last?"

"In the breakfast room talkin' te Lord Taggart."

"My, everyone is up early today," I mused. "I would have thought they would not be about for hours. Might I ask a favor of you, Charlotte?"

"Ye 'ave only te ask."

"I would like the children to meet Miss Wythe. But I should like to speak with her first. Would you bring them downstairs in about a half hour?"

"Consider it done," Charlotte replied.

When I went downstairs I found that Giles had a letter for me, which I quickly saw was in Anne's hand. Barring any problems with the weather, they would be arriving the next day. I was delighted, for the more people about this Christmas the better it would be for the children.

Traditionally Christmas Eve we shared with the servants. Robbie and Justin would always fetch a large tree, usually a spruce from the woodlands, and the entire household would gather about to trim the tree. One member of the staff would fashion a new ornament each year and present it to us that evening.

I made a mental note to ask Robbie to take the children with him this year to select the tree.

When I entered the small dining room I felt that I had intruded somehow on an argument between Philip and Miss Wythe.

Philip looked up at me awkwardly. "Good morning, Serena," he said, rising quickly.

"Please excuse my raised voice of a moment ago but I fear that I was chastising Amelie—Miss Wythe—for being too assumptive about her engagement as the governess for Mayfair."

"I see," I replied, motioning him to sit down.

"Well, then, we both have the same thing on our minds," I said, looking at the plate of eggs and fresh ham that was placed before me.

"Miss Wythe, I did not appreciate your telling Charlotte that you had been employed as the new governess for Mayfair. First off, I distinctly suggested that we discuss it in the morning. Furthermore, Charlotte has been with us since my husband and I were married. She is a marvel with the children and the topic of replacing her in that role, quite frankly, is a sensitive one."

"Naturally," Miss Wythe said.

"To the idea of engaging someone new I have already given some consideration. Charlotte is not a young woman and her responsibilities as housekeeper keep her days full. The children are growing and they are active. A younger woman, I think, would find it easier to cope."

"I would certainly like to be given the opportunity, Lady Barkham," Miss Wythe said quickly.

"That decision I have determined to leave to the children. Charlotte will be bringing them down shortly and I shall leave you to get acquainted with each other. I am, of course, prejudiced but I think you will find them to be agreeable children. They are intelligent, and although they at times need certain reprimand, I would in no case call them undisciplined."

She nodded. "Lord Taggart has told me that they are delightful."

I smiled. "Lord Taggart was very kind to us all following my husband's departure. My daughter in particular, I believe, has been flattered by his attentions."

When Charlotte brought the children down moments later, they were surprised and, I sensed, pleased to see Philip. I introduced them to Miss Wythe, whom Daphne regarded somewhat suspiciously.

"Children," I said, "I shall want to spend the morning with Philip, Lord Taggart, for as you know he shall be staying with us while he works on the railroad venture that he and your father were involved with. I should like you to take Miss Wythe up to the nursery. Charlotte, perhaps you would accompany them, and then I would like you to return to the library and help me review the plans for our Christmas festivities."

Amelie followed Charlotte and the children, leaving Philip and me to ourselves.

"I would be amazed if the children do not take to her," he offered. "My sister had been very pleased with her performance, and she is highly critical."

"You know, Philip, I am surprised, given that it is the holiday season, that you are not spending it with your family. Not that we are not pleased to have you here, of course—'tis only that I think of this as a family time."

"There is only my sister, Serena, and her husband and I are not, shall we say, on the best of terms. It seems a more reasonable thing for me to keep my distance."

"Actually I am pleased that you shall be with us, Philip," I said.

His eyebrows cocked in obvious surprise. "It is very pleasing to me to hear you say that, Serena.''

I flushed, embarrassed that he might have misinterpreted my comment.

"What I mean is that this shall be our first Christmas without Justin and for the children's sake I think it will help having friends milling about.''

He leaned forward and studied me carefully. "Are you certain that it is only for the children, Serena?''

He was correct, of course. I too was happy for any small diversion to ease the emptiness that gnawed at me daily.

"My uncle and his wife shall be arriving tomorrow,'' I continued.

"You are avoiding my question, Serena,'' he persisted.

"I truly do not think that it is any of your business how I am feeling, Philip,'' I snapped.

He leaned back in his chair. "Ah, but I should like to make it my business, Serena.''

I could feel my cheeks grow hot with flush.

He laughed. "I do believe you are blushing, Serena.''

"I should like to remind you, Philip, that ours is a business relationship.''

"I did not know that I had implied otherwise, Serena, although you must know that I am not immune to a natural response to you. You are beautiful and intelligent. An almost irresistible combination in a woman. As I have said to you before, your husband was a very fortunate man.''

I was angry with myself for having retorted in such a fashion. I had interpreted his comment as an advance when it appeared that he had only intended friendship. I could hardly condemn the man for flattery—flattery which, admittedly, I heard little of these days.

"Philip,'' I said, hoping to change the subject, "I have asked Giles to arrange to have the end of the west wing opened for you. You should find that you should be able to work there quite undisturbed.''

He smiled, his eyes teasing mine. "I do believe that is where we first met, was it not?''

I shivered at the remembrance of coming upon his nakedness the night of the ball. Intentionally or not, this man had a way of unnerving me.

I lowered my eyes. "I shall know better next time to

knock," I said, trying to keep my voice evenly modulated.

"The rooms should do very nicely, Serena, it was kind of you to arrange it."

"Please understand that you are certainly to feel free to have full use of the house, I simply thought that you might wish some privacy."

Philip put his napkin down and rose. "If you will excuse me, Serena, I believe that I shall get started now."

"Of course. Luncheon shall be served here at noon. We take dinner in the formal dining room at six. Should you wish some other refreshment you have only to ask Charlotte."

I retired to the library where I quickly enveloped myself again with the ledgers. When Charlotte arrived I inquired after Miss Wythe and the children. She indicated, less than enthusiastically, that they were seemingly compatible. It would take some time, I knew, before Charlotte would come to accept the arrangement, but she was a reasonable woman and I knew that the initial impact would pass. We discussed the plans for Christmas including preparing menus for our holiday feasts. I found myself doing it rather perfunctorily for I was steeling myself from allowing my real emotions to dominate. I used to tell Justin that I thought he was actually the real child in the family when it came to Christmas. He loved the holidays; it always transformed his normally serious self into an elfin-like character.

"Ye be thinkin' about the master, be ye not?" Charlotte asked.

I nodded. "I am sorry, Charlotte, I did not mean to drift off. I am trying not to."

"Ye shouldn't be hidin' yer feelings, Serena," Charlotte advised. " 'Tis only right that ye be thinkin' about the master."

My eyes filled with tears. "Oh, Charlotte, it just does not seem to ease. I miss him dreadfully. I am trying, truly I am, but I do not seem to be able to get a full hold on myself."

She came and put her arms about me. "Ye be doin' fine, just fine, Serena. Ye bein' too 'ard on yerself. Give it time."

At noon we all met for luncheon. Amelie seemed to have fully won the children over. Whether she did it cognizantly or not she had quickly deemed that the way to reach Daphne was seeming to treat her as an equal. Alexander, who was not a boy to force oneself upon, she dealt with quietly, giving him space to force his own opinions. I was impressed at how adroitly she handled them both.

Philip was in particularly good humor and the sadness that I had felt earlier in the morning was, in part, replaced by pleasure at the children's laughter. After luncheon I asked Amelie to join me in the library. I motioned for her to sit down.

"You seem to have made an immediate conquest of the children," I commented, noting that her gown was fashioned of a particularly fine fabric.

A small smile played about her lips. "Then might I assume that you intend to engage me?"

"I do," I replied.

We discussed the terms of our agreement.

"Will that be satisfactory, Miss Wythe?"

"Very, Lady Barkham."

"Then I see no reason why you cannot commence immediately. I would ask, Miss Wythe, that you try to be as cooperative as possible with Charlotte. She is a dear but I am certain you can understand that things might be a bit awkward, shall we say, for the first few weeks."

"I shall be as accommodating as possible," she replied.

"There is one other thing. The children's tutor, Master Farraday, we sent on holiday when we moved to London. I have sent for him but I have no idea whether he remained with his sister or not. It may be several weeks more until I can come in contact with him. Might you be able to assume some of the children's studies until he returns? I certainly do not expect you to replace him, 'tis only that I am painfully aware that they have fallen far behind. Even if you were only to help them with their readings and letters it would be of enormous assist to me."

"I am hardly a tutor, Lady Barkham," she cautioned, "but I should be pleased to assist in whatever way I can."

"Thank you, Miss Wythe," I replied sincerely. "It relieves a great burden from my mind. Now I shall ask Charlotte to have your room changed so that you might be closer to the nursery."

I did not think she looked pleased at the prospect, but although the children were growing daily, it seemed, my protective instinct demanded that Daphne and in particular Alexander have someone close by.

The next day and a half passed quickly. The house was far from quiet with the servants giving the house last-minute polishing touches. The smells emanating from the kitchen were enticing. I dispatched Robbie, who took Miss Wythe, Jaspar and the children with him to fell the largest tree that they could find. He took me at my word, returning with a deep blue spruce that was a good fourteen feet in height and seemed nearly that in breadth.

By the time Anne and Richard arrived Mayfair was festooned with Christmas spirit. We had hung two enormous wreaths on the entry door and garlands graced the mantels of each fireplace on the first floor.

Charlotte had convinced me that I should make a special effort with my appearance for the occasion. She had washed my hair, which, when dried by the warmth of the fire, fell in heavy waves about my shoulders. I selected an emerald green velvet dress with a square-cut neckline and an inset of ecru satin and lace about the bodice. Charlotte had quickly stitched two double pleats on each side of the waist since although I had managed to gain a few pounds, my clothing still did not fit me properly.

When I studied my reflection in the mirror my hand went automatically to my throat. The necklace that Justin had given me would have been the finishing touch. But then it was gone and so was Justin. Charlotte brought me a strand of pearls that had belonged to my grandmother. I nodded as she clasped them about my neck.

"Do tell Amelie, Miss Wythe, Charlotte, to have Daphne don one of the new gowns that Anne sent over. She would be terribly disappointed, I fear, if Daphne did not wear one this evening."

Charlotte agreed and I ventured downstairs. Philip was in the drawing room. He rose as I entered. "You look lovely, Serena," he flattered.

"Thank you," I demured, noticing that he too had made an extra effort in his dress.

"Lord Camberleigh and his wife have arrived. They asked me to tell you that they would join us momentarily."

"I did not hear them arrive but I am relieved that they were able to make the journey." I went to the window and looked out onto the drive. "It has commenced snowing again."

"If those clouds are any indication, we are going to be in for a major storm."

"Even more reason that I am relieved that Anne and Richard have arrived," I replied.

"I do wish you had forewarned them that I would be at Mayfair, Serena."

I turned to face Philip, who had a distinct look of annoyance on his face.

"Well, I am sorry, Philip, but as you well know I have not seen them since I was last at Camberleigh. Your plans to come here were made, you must admit, quite swiftly."

"Well, it proved an awkward situation, their simply encountering me here. It is just that I do not want to make anyone uncomfortable, particularly during the holidays."

"I cannot fathom why it would have been. You have met them both before."

"Whether you realized it or not, your uncle did not take kindly to me."

"I am quite certain that is your imagination, Philip," I rebuked. "Richard is a bit remote at times, which can lead you to misinterpret his demeanor."

"You are being, if you would forgive me, Serena, a bit naive. Your uncle is hardly a champion of the prospect of railroads in this country. He would like to see chaps like me carted off to the West Indies."

I thought for a moment about what Philip had said. I could not deny that there was truth in it but I scarcely thought that that was reason enough for a serious schism between the two. Perhaps it had been foolish of me not to alert Anne and Richard. I hoped that if what he said was true it would not serve to mar the holidays.

Before I could respond, Anne and Richard entered the drawing room. I could not help but notice that my uncle studiously avoided Philip as he strode over to greet me.

"How are you, my dear?"

"Still far too thin for my taste," Anne said as she pulled me from my uncle into a tight embrace. "But far improved from the last I saw you."

"I think she looks quite ravishing," Philip offered.

Anne looked about in surprise. "I fear you misunderstood my comment, Lord Taggart. Serena, we can all see, is a great beauty, but my brother's death affected her greatly, as you must be aware.''

I gave Anne a squeeze, teasing, "My sister-in-law is simply concerned that her gowns are going to look less than stylish.''

"And rightly I should,'' she retorted playfully. "You could positively ruin my reputation. Those gowns of mine are meant to be worn, not hung. Now, where are my niece and nephew, did Daphne like the dresses? Oh, wait till you see the new ones I have brought,'' she babbled on.

"They shall be down shortly,'' I replied, leading her over to where Philip and Richard now sat.

Richard cleared his throat. "What brings you to Mayfair, Lord Taggart?''

"Thanks to Lady Barkham's generosity, I shall be living here for a spell,'' Philip replied.

My uncle fell completely silent but he needed not say anything for the shock registered on his face said more than words.

"Philip,'' I said, trying to keep my tone light, "I think that needs to be explained. I have offered Philip quarters here until the railway project is fully underway.''

"You do not mean to tell me that you are going to let him proceed with that nonsense, do you?''

"Richard, please lower your voice,'' Anne chided. "Lord Taggart, you must forgive my husband but it is no secret that he did not share Justin's enthusiasm for this project.''

"You need not speak for me, Anne,'' Richard snapped, rubbing his hand brusquely against the scar on his face. "I apologize if I was shouting, Serena, but I am appalled that you would consider this. You know how I felt about Justin but this hare-brained investment in these railroads was a mistake. And as your uncle I can only advise you as such.''

I was too stunned by his outburst to respond.

"Lord Camberleigh,'' Philip interjected. "I think I might point out that it is Lady Barkham's money and therefore her decision.''

"With your studious coercion, no doubt,'' my uncle retorted.

"Richard, that is not fair,'' I said, regaining my voice, "the decision was solely my own. And quite frankly I am insulted, as I am certain Philip is, at your insinuation. Pioneering the railroads was Justin's dream and I intend to see it through.''

Anne, who sat next to me, patted my hand. "Darling, I think it is a very noble thought but do you really think that is what Justin would have wanted? I am doubtful. My brother was a gambler but he was also practical and I am certain that he would not have wanted to burden you emotionally or financially."

"First off, I am surprised that you both appear so shocked since Sir Henry, I know, was to visit briefly with you after he visited here." I stole a look at Philip, whose calm assurance seemed suddenly shaken. "I would have thought that he would have imparted my intentions to you."

"Sir Henry is very discreet, my dear," Richard offered. "Though I must admit in this case I wish he had not been."

I was about to continue but just then Amelie arrived with the children. They sprang enthusiastically forward to greet Richard and Anne.

"Daphne, you look wonderful," Anne enthused, admiring her as she pirouetted in her red velvet dress.

Richard agreed. "And you, Alexander, how is your young colt?"

"He is quite well, sir," Alexander replied, shaking Richard's hand. "I have named him Justin."

My uncle looked momentarily surprised but said only, "Well, it is a fine name and a fitting memory."

I turned to Miss Wythe, who had hung back by the door. "Do join us, Miss Wythe. I should like you to meet my sister-in-law and uncle. Lord and Lady Camberleigh. Miss Wythe is our new governess."

"You have been a busy bee, Serena," Anne mused, extending her hand to Miss Wythe. "As their aunt I am prejudiced of course, but I must say you are fortunate to have found this household, Miss Wythe. I know no two more delightful children, not to mention their mother."

"I quite agree," Amelie replied.

"Have you seen Charlotte?" I asked.

She nodded. "Yes, Lady Barkham, she is gathering the staff for the festivities."

I hoped that they would arrive soon for I did not want to continue our prior conversation in front of Miss Wythe or the children.

Sensing my uneasiness, Anne complimented Miss Wythe on her gown. It was very simple but its cut highlighted the length of her neck, which gave her almost an appearance of aristocracy.

It was only minutes later that Charlotte entered, the staff behind her. I rose to greet them. The faces were so familiar to me since most of the servants had been with Justin and I throughout our married life; many in fact had tended to Mayfair when his own family had resided here.

"Where is Robbie?" I asked, noting his absence.

" 'E an' the stable boys are fixin' to bring in the tree. Jaspar be with 'im," Charlotte replied.

"Well, everyone must gather about and have some celebration punch," I said, motioning to the wassail bowl filled with Cook's traditional mixture which had a light lacing of rum. A twinge of sadness spread over me as I thought of the punch. Justin would each year make the Christmas toast, take a sip, then demand that extra rum be added. Cook annually feigned disapproval but we were always amused that it was she who traditionally imbibed more than anyone.

When the cups had been filled I realized that all eyes had turned to me. A lump formed in my throat. It had not occurred to me that it would fall to me to say the words that commenced the evening of cheer.

My uncle was at my side and I felt his hand on my elbow. "Do you want me to do it, Serena?" he whispered.

I shook my head. "It is my place, Richard."

A hush drew over the room as I stepped forward. I had a few moments to regain my composure for just then Robbie flung open the doors and the stately spruce was brought into the room standing on a pedestal fashioned from raw hardwood. As murmurs of appreciation resounded throughout the room Jaspar came bounding to me, barking his greeting.

"It is a glorious tree, Robbie," Anne enthused. "You have outdone yourself this year."

Robbie grinned as the tree was safely anchored. "Aye cannot be takin' all the credit, Lady Camberleigh; t'was Alexander there who spotted it first."

"I helped, too," Daphne pouted.

"I am certain that you did," Anne assured her.

Suddenly realizing that there was a toast left unsaid, the room quieted again.

"This is the tenth year that we have celebrated together in this house," I began slowly. "We are all aware that there is something, someone, missing this year. My beloved husband and the father of my two dear children, Justin, cannot be with us. But seeing you all gathered here like this, I know that his memory lives within us all. Justin, Lord Barkham, is not lost to us. Mayfair with all your help shall continue to maintain its position within this great land of ours and with Lord Taggart's guidance my husband's dream of railways shall likewise flourish." I raised my glass. "I bid health and peace to you all."

The room was deathly still. Had I put a toll on the evening, I wondered, by my remembrance of Justin?

Robbie stepped forward, extending a small package wrapped in tissue.

"We be wantin' ye to know, Miss Serena, that we loved the master, we did. T'was me turn te be makin' the ornament fer ye but this year t'were alot of us who had a feelin' bout what it should be. So 'ere 'tis. 'Tis not as fine as aye should 'a liked but ye'll be gettin' the idea."

I took the package from Robbie and called the children over to see what was inside. There in the folds lay what I knew to be a miniature railroad engine.

"Oh, Robbie, everyone, it is beautiful," I said marveling at its intricacy all fashioned in wood. "But how did you possibly design it?"

He motioned to Philip. "Lord Taggart gave me a drawin' when 'e was 'ere last."

I threw a grateful look to Philip, who seemed pleased by the acknowledgment.

I handed the ornament to Alexander. "Would you hang it on the tree for us, please?"

Daphne began to protest but quieted as I whispered to her that she had had the privilege the year prior.

Alexander, though tall for his age, struggled to get it on a higher limb. It was Philip who came forward and, hoisting him above his shoulders, allowed the child to place it where it could be seen by all.

"Here, here," came the shouts with a round of applause.

The silence had been broken and everyone set about pulling the old ornaments from the boxes. Some of the younger maids had strung a berry garland that they deftly wound about the tree.

Philip brought me another cup of punch, and as he helped

me add a few ornaments he whispered, "This punch needs more rum."

I looked up at him and he winked, unconscious, I knew, of the significance of what he had said.

I smiled back. "The way to remedy that is to tell Giles. He has a cache held aside for just such an occasion."

He nodded and I saw him move over to Giles. Philip did look particularly handsome this evening in his gray waistcoat. I could not help but notice that Miss Wythe seemed to think so as well. This was not the first time that I had seen her watching him, positioning herself so that she might be closer to him. If Philip were aware of it he did not acknowledge it. Of course one might assume that she was simply a governess not likely to be noticed by one out of her station, but since it was in the same mode that I had met Justin I did not think her admiration totally fanciful.

When the tree was complete I passed out the Christmas envelopes to each of the staff. I had given them each a stipend that was larger than what Justin had awarded the year prior. We had had a good crop harvest; moreover, each had continued with great loyalty since Justin's death and I wanted to reward what I deemed their faith in me and in Mayfair.

I particularly watched Robbie as he opened his envelope. I knew that it was likely more money than he had ever had in his hands at one time. He walked over to me and murmured, "Aye do not know what te be sayin' to ye, Miss Serena, except aye thank ye with all me heart."

I kissed him lightly on the cheek. "It was well earned, Robbie. Justin would have done nothing less."

Philip, I noticed, had been watching me closely as I doled out the envelopes. "Are you not being a bit magnanimous, my dear?"

"Perhaps," I mused, "but I scarcely think it is any of your business."

"Unfortunately for me it is not. Your solicitor must have given you good news."

"I wanted to ask you about that, Philip," I replied. "How was it that you did not mention having seen Sir Henry in London?"

"You are right Serena, I should have told you."

"Well, there must have been some reason that you paid him a call."

"I simply wanted frankly to get a sense of whether continuance of this plan was feasible. You do not think that I could even have broached the subject with you of continuing this project had I thought that it would prove financially too demanding. As eager as I am to see this project completed never would I do so if I believed that it would have proved too great a burden."

I was puzzled, for as discreet as Sir Henry was I could not believe that he would have imparted any information about our personal finances to Philip.

Philip studied me. "I am sorry if it troubled you Serena, my intent had been to spare you concern."

"I scarcely said that I was worried, Philip," I rebuked. "I simply found it odd that you had not mentioned your meeting."

Before I could continue Daphne came up to me and announced that Cook had asked her to tell me that dinner was ready. Everyone was hungry and needed little convincing to move to the dining room, where savory smells of roast goose, hot chestnuts, squash and fresh onions filled the room.

Richard, who was to my right, said grace, and everyone partook happily of the holiday feast.

Anne, who was to my left, leaned forward and in a low tone said, "This is not the place, I know, Serena, but I should like to talk to you privately after dinner."

"Of course," I assured her, puzzled by the seeming urgency in her voice.

The evening progressed nicely. I was most grateful to Philip, who seemed able to put aside the earlier unpleasantries and was amusing the children with tales of his childhood Christmases. Richard had lapsed back into his brooding mood and was silent through most of the meal, but Anne and I chattered easily. She had had news of Monique, who was apparently bored with London and planning to leave for France at the first of the year. I found it odd that Philip seemingly had had no news of same. Apparently he had been more out of touch with Monique than he had indicated.

After a dessert of plum pudding, brandied pears and sweet cakes the staff retired. Amelie saw the children off to bed, Richard had a private word with Robbie and also excused himself. Thus it was that Philip and Anne and I came together in the library.

"Might I fix you ladies a brandy?" Philip offered as he poured one for himself.

"Not for me, thank you," I refused.

As he turned and strode toward us Anne spoke up. "Philip, would you think me terribly rude if I asked you to leave Serena and I alone for a spell? There are a few things that I should like to discuss with her privately."

Philip did not respond but instead seemed to defer the answer to me by looking at me questioningly.

I shrugged. "You know women, Philip. I doubt that whatever we have to say would amuse you and I so rarely have an opportunity to visit with my sister-in-law."

Philip looked displeased but promptly excused himself for the evening, though I sensed that he would have preferred to remain in our company.

"I hope you did not mind, Serena," Anne said quickly, "but I sense that I should scarcely have any time with you alone unless one is blunt with that man."

"What do you mean?"

She reached up and reworked a comb that was holding up her dark hair. "Well, he follows you about like Jaspar, my dear."

I laughed. "I think that is a bit of an exaggeration, Anne. The man is living in this house. I could scarcely not invite him to join our holiday celebrations."

"Serena, that is the point," Anne argued. "What is that man doing living in this house?"

"We went over that earlier," I sighed. "I know that Richard does not approve of this railroad venture but I expected that you would understand that it is very important to me to see this commitment through."

Anne shook her head. "Darling, I know what you are trying to do but I wish you would see the folly of it all. The railroad matter aside, you simply cannot permit this Philip Taggart to move in here and take over this place. I am not suggesting anything, not that it would be my affair, but for appearances alone his presence here is an embarrassment."

I was totally shocked by Anne's outburst. "Quite to the contrary, Anne. I think you *are* suggesting something," I choked out. "How could you, knowing how I felt about Justin?" The tears now were flowing freely.

Anne came to me quickly and put her arms about me. "Oh,

Serena, please do not cry. The last thing I want to do is upset you. I know how difficult this holiday period is for you.''

"Then why are you saying what you are?" I pleaded.

"Because I do not want you to be hurt, Serena."

I accepted the handkerchief she gave me and wiped away the tears, trying to regain my composure. "The way to assure that, Anne, is to give me your support. Philip is here on business, nothing more. If you feel that his living here while he conducts his business is indiscreet then I am sorry. It did not occur to me that anyone would jump to conclusions, particularly you. Now that I have offered Mayfair to him as his base of operations I can scarcely go back on my word. Nor frankly do I intend to. Philip has been a good friend to me and I owe him a great deal for his kindness to me over the past months.''

Anne pulled away from me and stood by the fireplace, her fingers tracing the dentil moulding.

"I am certain that he has been helpful to you, Serena, but do you not think that perhaps he has been overly attentive?"

"Why would you say that, Anne?"

"Sometimes it takes another to see things as they really are," she mused. "And if I am to believe Monique's letter, she is quite convinced that Lord Taggart has designs on you and I do not mean in a business sense."

"We are friends," I insisted, somewhat hesitantly troubled by the memory of Philip's subtle advances. "You know that Monique exaggerates."

"I gather that the two, shall we say, had an involvement of sorts?"

I shrugged, not wishing to share my own suspicions.

"One thing that Monique wrote I found disturbing."

"What was that?"

"In reference to Philip she simply concluded by saying that appearances can be deceptive."

"I would prefer not to comment, but I think you should know, Anne, that Monique was quite taken with Philip, or so it seemed. I am not certain that he returned her affections."

"Well, after all, she is years his senior," Anne admitted. "In any event, Serena, it is not Monique that I am concerned about."

"I see no reason to continue this, Anne. The last thing I want is for any schism to come between us, but I must tell you, and you may tell Richard, that I am not going to be dissuaded from this project or from allowing Philip to remain here until it is completed.''

"I just hope that you do not live to regret it," Anne said as she moved to leave the room. "Goodnight, Serena."

The door closed behind her and I was left to the deathly silence of the room broken only by Jaspar's light snoring.

A clock chimed midnight, ushering in the first hours of Christmas.

"Oh, Justin," I moaned aloud, "I do not know whether I can carry on alone."

Jaspar, awakened by my voice, struggled up and lumbered over to me.

I was devastated by Anne's criticism but I was also angered by it. Of anyone I knew, I had expected her to champion my decisions. She was a very independent woman and was not one to side with her husband simply because he was her mate. Certainly she could not believe that I was defiling Justin's memory by allowing Philip to stay at Mayfair. I expected her to understand my determination to bring Justin's dream to fruition.

The door to the library opened suddenly and Philip entered.

# 12

"I thought that I might find you here," he said. "I saw Lady Camberleigh retire but you did not appear to have joined her."

"Jaspar and I were just being contemplative," I replied.

"Do you mind if I join you for a moment, Serena?"

"Of course not, Philip, though I warn you I am hardly scintillating company."

He poured himself a brandy and then poured a second glass, which he offered to me.

I shook my head.

"Take it, Serena. It should do you good and, besides, I would like to toast the Yuletide with you."

I accepted it.

"I should like to propose a toast to you, Serena, to a beautiful woman who has shown great courage over these past months."

"Hardly," I replied, "but it is kind of you to say so."

"Ah, but I have not finished my toast."

"I am sorry," I replied, removing the glass from my lips.

"To us, Serena."

"To us?" I asked cautiously, looking up at him.

"But of course to us. To the success of our venture together."

"Oh," I gasped, embarrassed that I had momentarily misunderstood.

Philip studied me for a moment. "Do I sense that you interpreted something else from that toast?"

My silence was answer enough.

"Forgive me, Serena, if I say to you that I wish that I could have intended that toast to be of a personal nature."

"Please, Philip," I pressed.

"Do not worry," he replied quickly. "I am not so foolish as to presume that I might speak to you of my admiration and intentions at this juncture, Serena. It is, I am certain, of no surprise to you that I find you a devastatingly attractive woman. But I also am aware that you are a woman who is still mourning for a husband that she loved very deeply. I should never intrude on that."

"Thank you, Philip," I replied quietly.

He smiled at me. "There may be a day when I shall not be so cautious, Serena, but for now I am more concerned with what you are going to do about Lord and Lady Camberleigh."

"What do you mean?" I asked.

"I think you know full well what I mean, Serena. They have made it very clear that they resent my presence at Mayfair. Richard has always considered our project foolhardy. I know that he and Justin had almost come to blows over the matter."

"Oh, Philip, no," I argued. "Richard disagreed with Justin's enthusiasm, I know, but they are—were—too close to actually do battle over it."

"I can only tell you what Justin shared with me.

"I could not fathom that what he told me was truthful but then he would have no reason to lie about it."

"It was unfortunate that you needed be a party to that little tête-à-tête earlier, Philip. I must apologize for them both."

"They are entitled to their opinions, Serena."

"Of course they are, Philip, but I am as well. Frankly I was hoping that they would be supportive of my intentions."

"Lady Camberleigh, I presume, continued her damnation of me when you had your little talk after dinner."

"That would be putting it too harshly," I rebuked.

"Would it, Serena? I doubt it."

I did not disagree.

Philip downed the remaining brandy. "I do not think that I should remain here at Mayfair, Serena. And quite frankly I am not certain that you should proceed with the railroad venture. With the Camberleighs so violently opposed to it, all it is bound to create is a schism between you. And I could never forgive myself if that happened.''

"I think you are perhaps making presumptions. Anne is not an irrational woman. I am certain that she will realize in time that I have made the right decision.''

As assuredly as I said the words, I, too, doubted that I would easily gain Anne or my uncle's support in this matter. But I did not want to find myself so intimidated that I would succumb to their wishes.

"Philip, I want you to stay,'' I said resolutely.

He smiled at me broadly. "I said you were a woman of courage and you are, Serena. You know that I did not want to go but I felt that I had to give you the option.''

I sensed tremendous relief in his voice.

"I cannot promise that I shall be able to change their opinion, Philip, but in time perhaps . . .'' I broke off, rising to bid my leave.

I thought I heard Philip murmur something but did not press him to repeat it.

"Serena, before you go there is something that I should like to give you.''

I turned back, surprised at the small black box that he was holding out to me. "What is this?'' I asked.

"Just a small token of the holidays. I thought it best to give it to you now. My instincts tell me that your uncle would not approve.''

"You should not have done this, Philip,'' I insisted. "I must admit that I have nothing for you.''

"Open it,'' he urged.

I opened the box and withdrew a slender gold chain with a single diamond pendant.

"Oh, Philip,'' I objected, "I could not possibly accept this. It is lovely but hardly an insignificant bauble.''

"Well, I would be devastated if you did not accept it, Serena. It can scarcely replace the one you lost but hopefully it will compliment some gown you have.''

"It is lovely, Philip,'' I said, knowing that he would not permit me to return it. "I shall wear it often.''

"Might I put it on you now?'' he asked.

It seemed foolish since I was just about to retire but Philip looked so eager that I did not want to hurt him.

"Of course,'' I said, handing him the necklace.

I turned my back to him and waited while he draped the necklace about the front of my neck. I shivered slightly as he gathered my hair pushing it forward to free the clasp.

"Are you cold?" He asked.

"Perhaps a bit," I lied, embarrassed by the involuntary reaction of my body to the cool of Philip's hand.

He twirled me around to face him.

"Does it meet with your approval, Philip?"

He motioned me to a mirror. "Look for yourself."

In its simplicity it was truly beautiful. "Thank you, Philip," I murmured, my eyes meeting his reflected in the mirror. "And now—if I am to be alert for those children of mine who are bound to be up at the crack of dawn."

I thought he was about to say something more but he simply nodded and turned back towards the fireplace.

"Sleep well, Serena."

"You, too, Philip," I said as I motioned to Jaspar to join me.

I undressed quickly after I had reached my room. Robbie had done as I had bid and taken all the gifts I had wrapped downstairs to await their new owners. The day had proved an exhausting one for me. I had had to struggle with the wrenching emptiness I felt from Justin's absence, not to mention the disagreement with Anne and Richard. I prayed that they would not press the issue again for my nerves were on edge and I did not want to say or do something that I might regret later. I had been very touched by Philip's offer to leave Mayfair. The project meant a great deal to him, I knew, and I appreciated that he was willing to abandon it to protect me. I continued to be embarrassed by my momentary reaction to him when he had clasped the diamond about my neck. It had been so long since I had felt a man's hand touching me. It disturbed me that I should have reacted to one other than Justin. Philip had penetrated a certain numbness that had overtaken me since Justin's death. I once had thought that I should never truly feel anything again. I thought of Monique. She, too, had lost a husband that she had loved dearly when she was still young. She had never remarried, though I was certain that she had had many offers over the years. Instead she had taken a succession of lovers, discreetly, of course, but not with any shame.

Is that how I would wind up? I wondered. Would my needs

turn me to surreptitious liaisons? I could not imagine myself conducting mysterious trysts with men who were now faceless to me. Philip had intimated that at some later date he should like to speak more openly of his intentions. I hoped that it would not be soon, for as he had sensed, my commitment to Justin was as strong in death as it had been in life.

Charlotte awakened me at dawn, knowing that I would want to be up when the children arose. The fire had died down over the night and I dressed quickly to avoid a chill. Cook prepared a large breakfast each year and as I wound down the stairs I could smell that it had already been set up in the dining room.

The children came down only moments later, followed by Amelie, who seemed a bit disgruntled at the earliness of the hour. They were anxious to open their gifts but I insisted that they eat first. I also wanted to wait for Richard and Anne. Robbie arrived with a load of packages and I scolded him for being so extravagant. He insisted that there were only a few items for the children. I hoped that Robbie would meet someday a young woman whom he would marry for I knew that he loved children and would indeed be a wonderful father.

I had almost finished breakfast when Philip, Anne and Richard arrived in tandem. I could tell from my uncle's expression that a night's sleep had not served to pale his anger. Anne was making a concerted effort, I knew, to keep the conversation light for the children's benefit, but I sensed that she, too, was not going to be quick to change her opinion.

It was almost nine when we gathered about the tree and commenced opening the presents. The children doled out the gifts, making certain that each person had received something to open before starting the round again. Anne and Richard had outdone themselves with gifts for both myself and the children. I was slightly embarrassed for although I knew that they expected only a remembrance I had had neither the time nor the inclination to put much thought against my gifts. Fortunately at the last moment I had remembered that Amelie would be with us and had wrapped a small bag that I had purchased some time before for myself but had never had an opportunity to use. Alexander was particularly thrilled, as I hoped he would be, with my bestowal of Justin's crop on him. Robbie promised that he would teach him to use it well, though it would still be some time until his horse, Justin, was mature enough to be ridden. I was very touched that Daphne had embroidered two handkerchiefs with my name on each.

The remainder of the day passed relatively quietly. Everyone was weary from the evening before and the early morning start, and most retired to their rooms to nap. Amelie offered to take the children for a walk. I was surprised when Philip decided to join them but realized that he was most likely avoiding any unnecessary contact with Richard and Anne.

I slept for almost three hours and awakened midafternoon, feeling more refreshed than I had in days. I ambled down to the library but stopped just before entering for I overheard Richard and Philip in raised voices. I did not make it a habit of listening in on others' conversations but I could not help myself and pressed my ear closer to the door.

"I fear that I cannot approve of any of this, Philip," I heard my uncle say. "My niece is particularly vulnerable right now and she scarcely needs the pressures of you and your foolhardy schemes."

"Begging your pardon, Richard, but I should remind you that Serena is a grown woman," Philip countered. "And I resent your implications that I am coercing her somehow."

"You are up to something, Philip. I sense it but I cannot put my finger on it. My wife thinks that you have designs on Serena. Is that true?"

There was a long pause. Philip had lowered his voice and I was only able to pick out certain words: ". . . Care deeply . . . do not know . . . speak . . . sometime soon."

Before I could try and fathom what it all meant, Richard's voice loomed back.

"Damnation, man, have some propriety, please. Justin has only been dead a few months."

I suddenly heard some commotion coming from the direction of the kitchen and quickly opened the door to the library.

"I did not mean to interrupt," I said, averting direct eye contact with both men, "but my ledgers are kept here in the library."

"You certainly do not intend to do any work on Christmas day?" my uncle queried.

I did not know why I had said that for indeed I had no intention of working on this day.

"No, uncle, I suppose not," I mused. "Is Anne up and about?"

He nodded. "She should be down shortly."

I looked about the room. "Where is Jaspar?"

"Amelie put him in the kitchen after we returned from our walk," Philip replied.

"Why would she do that? She knows he has the run of the house."

"I do not think that Amelie is quite the animal lover that you are, Serena."

"Well, that may be, Philip, but I will not have him shut up in the kitchen. Cook must be beside herself by now. I shall have to have a talk with Amelie," I concluded.

"I am certain that she meant no harm, Serena," Philip advised.

"And how did you come to be such a champion of Miss Wythe?" Richard asked suspiciously.

"Richard, you know perfectly well that Miss Wythe was in Philip's sister's employ—that is how I came to have her here."

Just then the doors to the library opened and Jaspar dashed in, bounding directly towards me.

Charlotte, who had given him entry, called out, " 'E was in the kitchen, Miss Serena, an' Cook is fit to be tied, she is."

"I know, thank you, Charlotte."

"Supper should be ready in a bit," she continued. "Can aye be doin' anythin' fer ye?"

I shook my head. "Only to tell Amelie that, of course, I should like the children to dine with us."

When Charlotte left us there was an awkward silence in the room. Richard had risen and withdrawn a book from the shelves. Philip, who seemed particularly agitated, excused himself, promising to return when supper was served.

"I must confess to you, Richard, that before I came in here I was eavesdropping."

He looked up from his book.

"Then you heard more than you should have."

"Frankly I only overheard enough to know that you and Philip were arguing again."

I stopped as Anne entered the room.

"It appears that I have arrived at an inappropriate time," she mused.

Richard closed his book and stood up. "Not at all, my dear. Perhaps you can talk some sense into this sister-in-law of yours. My advice seems to be falling on deaf ears."

When he had left me alone with Anne, I turned to her and said quietly, "Well, I suppose you want to chastise me as well."

Anne sighed. "You paint me such the ogre, Serena, and that is not at all what I—we—intend. You are like a sister to me. We have shared too much to let this pull us apart, particularly now when we need each other most."

"Then you have changed your mind about Philip?"

Her hand poised about her neck as she cleared her throat. "My opinions about him and this railroad project are not as ferocious as Richard's, but I must tell you that I have grave doubts that you are doing the right thing."

I waited a moment trying to formulate my response. "What is about this that concerns you most, Anne? Is it my investment in the railroad project? Because if it is, I am truly only carrying forth what your own brother had planned. So are you saying that Justin was wrong? Or is it the fact that I have invited Philip to live here at Mayfair? I find it hard to believe that you, of all people, have suddenly become so conscious of appearances. Mine is clearly a business relationship. I do not think you could have said the same thing of you and Richard years ago."

As soon as I had said it I regretted it for I saw the hurt reflected in Anne's eyes.

"I am sorry," I continued. "That was uncalled for."

Anne waved me off. "You have a right to speak your mind, Serena, and it is no secret that Richard and I had an affair before we married. But I would say that the circumstances were considerably different. Or have you forgotten?"

I had not and would never forget that Richard had been married at the time of their liaison to a madwoman, the same woman who had ruined my own father.

"I did not have a husband who had just died and I did not move a man who was a relative stranger into my house to share with me and my children."

"Anne," I interrupted "Philip is hardly a stranger."

"What do you really know about him, Serena?"

I paused. "Well, I know that he and Justin developed this venture together. I suppose that they met during one of his trips to London. And I know that Philip obviously has a sister. And most importantly I know that he has been very kind to me and the children since . . ."

"Do you not think it somewhat strange that he has been so attentive?"

"I truly have not thought about it, Anne."

"What I am getting at, Serena, is that I believe that Philip's attentions are for more than friendly, shall we say."

I felt myself flushing.

"Please understand me, Serena. Justin was my brother and I loved him dearly. But I, above all people, know that life must go on. You are still young and clearly beautiful and I do not expect you to live alone for the rest of your life. Nor would I want it for you. But I am not certain that Philip is that person. And even assuming that he is, I think it is far too soon for you to consider a commitment. I know how vulnerable one is after such a loss. I only want to protect you from making a terrible mistake, one that you would regret for the rest of your life."

I found myself laughing. "I am sorry, Anne, but you are talking as if any moment I am about to become Lady Taggart."

"Can you tell me honestly, Serena, that Philip has never made any advances, has never spoken of any affection?"

I averted Anne's regard. "Of course not," I lied.

Her eyebrows raised. "I am surprised. But then perhaps he is being cleverer than I had thought."

"I do not understand."

"He knows that you are not a woman to pressure or one who would be easily wooed by his seductions. No, if what you say is true, then I think he is simply biding his time."

"You make me feel as though I am some bird of prey," I confessed.

"Well, you must realize, Serena, that you are what men refer to as a good catch. Beautiful, wealthy, accomplished—what more would someone like Philip Taggart want?"

"You have left out one important ingredient, Anne. Has it not crossed your mind that Philip might want love? And quite frankly, that is not something that I am prepared to give. I shared all of mine with one man—Justin—and that shall never change."

Anne rose and I came over and we embraced. "Forgive me, Serena, if I have seemed so dour. I really have no right to intrude on you so. I cannot promise you that I will keep my mouth irrevocably shut, but truly I shall try—though I fear

Richard shall not be easily dissuaded."

"Anne, I shall always value your advice," I replied. "I do wish that Richard would come round but he is a man of strong opinions and I suppose I must respect that."

"I think it would be best if we returned to Camberleigh tomorrow, Serena."

"So soon?"

She nodded. "Given the circumstances, I think it would be very awkward for us to be underfoot. The roads should be clear and I truly think it would be best."

"The children will be terribly disappointed," I said, "and you know I love having you about."

"I know, Serena, but discretion is wise to exercise right now. Let us give it some time."

The men rejoined us, as did Charlotte, Amelie and the children, for a dinner of roast squab, fresh beans, yams and a steamed bread pudding. It seemed to me that Alexander was unusually quiet, but as he did not feel feverish, I simply concluded that he had become overtired due to the festivities. We talked briefly of the large ball that Robin and Lilliane were hosting at Kelston Manor to welcome in the New Year. I, too, had received an invitation but had determined that it would be inappropriate for me to attend this year. I did not want to leave the children, and now, having undertaken new responsibilities, I felt that I could scarcely put them aside, even for a few days.

Philip surprised me by announcing that he planned to travel to London for a few days. He would return about the sixth of January. Richard likewise appeared surprised that Philip was venturing if only briefly to London. I was pleased that he had mentioned it, hoping that Richard would perceive that Philip was in fact being attentive to the railroad project and not to me.

His mention of London made me think of Channing Hall. "Richard, you know I have not made any plans about Channing Hall. I left there so quickly, and though I know that it is part of the estate, it seems foolish."

"Certainly you do not intend to sell it," Philip interrupted.

"I scarcely think that is of any concern of yours," Richard grumbled angrily.

Philip looked momentarily ill at ease. "I only meant that it is a beautiful and, of course, valuable property. I would think that Serena would want to keep it, if only for the children."

"Well, on that one count we agree," Richard replied. "I would not act hastily when it comes to your holdings, Serena. In a year or so, if it appears that it would be in your best interests, we can discuss it with Sir Henry but for now I would leave it be."

"You do not need to maintain a large staff there," Anne offered. "Mary, Sidney and perhaps one maid should suffice."

I smiled. "Did you know that they plan to be married?"

"Sidney succumbed after all these years, did he? Well, that makes the arrangement even more perfect."

"It seems such an unnecessary expense," I countered.

"That, fortunately, is not something you have to worry about, my dear," my uncle advised.

"Well, then, I suppose it is settled," I agreed. "Philip, you would do me a great kindness if you would take a letter with you to London that I should like to write to Mary."

"Consider it done," he replied.

After dinner Philip excused himself to the library. Anne and Richard retired immediately, begging that they wanted a good night's rest before their morning journey.

I saw the children to bed and returned to my room. I penned a letter to Mary, advising her that for the moment all should be continued as before at Channing Hall. I had not the heart to ask her to dismiss any of the maids for we were in the throes of the holidays and I was certain that the meager sums they were being paid would scarcely be missed. After I had sealed that letter I commenced another one to Sir Henry, again explaining my decision and requesting that he continue to manage matters of wages and household expenses direct from London.

I was surprised when I heard the clock in the hallway chime eleven times for I had not realized that I had been writing for so long a time. I quickly finished my note to Sir Henry and undressed before the fire.

It felt particularly good to crawl into bed after this day. I had mustered all the energy I could to see that the holiday would pass as smoothly as possible. Keeping busy helped. And for the sake of the children I had to keep up appearances. But it was the nights that left me feeling totally bereft. Any defenses I had fell away from me in the solitary confines of this darkened room. The emptiness, save my dear Jaspar, was frightening. I needed Justin and I grieved for him as passionately at this moment as when I had first learned of my loss. It was again against a tear-moist pillow that I fell asleep.

When I awakened I realized that it was still the middle of the night for the fire's embers were still bright. I heard a motion over by the door and sat up to see what it was. There, by the door, was Jaspar sniffing along the base.

I threw a robe about my shoulders and went over to where he was scratching.

"What is it?" I asked, bending down and stroking him gently. " 'Tis probably only a mouse, nothing to worry about."

When he scratched again at the door, I opened it and peered out, keeping Jaspar at bay with my leg. I saw no one in the hall but then it was dark. Suddenly, I heard what I thought was a rustle at the end of the hall. I stepped forward and called out in a whisper, "Who is there?" For a moment I thought that I saw something move, but when there was no response after I called out again, I determined that it must have been my imagination.

I closed the door, placed another log on the fire and returned to bed. Jaspar had lost interest in whatever the disturbance had been and it was not long before we fell off to sleep again.

When Charlotte arrived the next morning I was still abed.

"An' 'ow ye be this mornin', Miss Serena?" she asked as she stoked the fire.

"Tired," I admitted. "Something disturbed Jaspar in the middle of the night and it awakened me."

"What was it, do ye know?"

I shook my head. "Probably just the wind," I replied. "I looked about in the hall but I did not see anything."

"That is strange," Charlotte said, turning to me. "I found this in the hallway this mornin'."

She withdrew a handkerchief from her pocket and handed it to me.

It was a fine white linen and lace square with a small "A" embroidered in the corner.

"Most likely it is Anne's. She must have dropped it last night."

"Or it could be Miss Wythe's," Charlotte mused.

"Amelie's? I suppose it could be. I shall ask them both."

"Oh, I almost forgot," Charlotte said, withdrawing an en-

velope from her other pocket. "This came early this mornin'.
Delayed it was due to the holiday."

The address was from Cornwall and I guessed quickly that it
was from Master Farraday. I slit the light tissue with a letter
opener and read the neatly scripted words inside.

" 'Tis not bad news, aye hope," Charlotte worried as I put
the letter down.

"No, not really, just a disappointment. Master Farraday's
sister is ill and he has agreed to return but not until she has
regained her strength. I so was hoping that he could commence the children's studies once again."

"A pity that is, but t'wont be long we kin hope."

Charlotte laid a brown velvet dress out for me. I bathed
quickly and stepped into it.

As she brushed my hair I asked, "Charlotte, have you come
to know Miss Wythe at all since she arrived?"

"Kin aye ask why ye be askin'?"

"Only that I wanted to speak to her about a few things and
it might help me to know something about the girl before I
do."

"Ye will not be gettin' a fer stretch, aye kin tell ye if me own
experience be tellin' ye anythin'."

"Are you two not getting along?"

She shrugged. "Has airs, that one does!"

"Perhaps she is just covering a natural shyness."

Charlotte laughed. "Shy? That one hasn't be havin' a shy
bone in 'er body."

"Well, I have not spent the proper time with her, and I
should like you to tell her that I will meet with her after Lord
and Lady Camberleigh leave."

She stopped the brush in midair. "They be leavin' so
soon?"

I nodded. As close as Charlotte was to me, I did not want to
involve her in their dispute with Philip. I trusted her explicitly
but she had endured so much with me of late that I did not feel
that I could burden her further.

When she had finished my hair I asked her to take Jaspar
out to Robbie for the morning. Anne and Richard were
already in the small dining room partaking of breakfast when
I joined them downstairs.

I embraced them both.

"This is delicious," Anne extolled. "I always think our

cook is quite adequate until we come to Mayfair.''

I smiled. "Fortunately her cooking surpasses her temperament."

"Did you sleep well, my dear?" Richard asked.

"It was strange. I was awakened in the middle of the night. Most likely it was only Jaspar thinking that he had spotted some night creature."

"I did not hear anything," Anne noted, "but then I slept as though I had not done so for days."

"That reminds me, Anne, did you perhaps drop a handkerchief in the hall?"

"I do not think so, but one may have fallen inadvertently from my gown."

"Remind me to ask Charlotte to return it to you. 'Tis a very good one with your initial embroidered on it; I should hate to have you lose it."

Anne looked up at me surprised. "Oh, then it could not have been of mine for I have none that are initialed."

"Are you certain?"

"Quite. You know me, Serena. I love to work with yards of fabric but embroidery demands too much patience. Perhaps it belongs to that new governess of yours, Amelie, is that not her name?"

"Yes, of course, that must be it."

"You know, Richard and I were talking after we retired last evening. Why do you not let the children—and yourself, of course—come to visit us at Camberleigh for a spell."

I suspected that it was a subtle ploy on Richard's part to eliminate what he considered a compromising situation as Anne seemed slightly embarrassed.

"It is lovely of you to ask but there is far too much for me to do here at Mayfair and I do not want to be separated from the children now. Master Farraday is also due to return, I hope, in the near future, and since I have specifically sent for him, I fear that he would be terribly upset if the children were not here."

Anne assured me that she understood. They had already bid the children farewell, and after finishing the meal Richard was anxious to commence their journey home. I was almost relieved that Philip was not about when they departed for it would only heighten an awkwardness that lingered amongst us. Anne, I sensed, wanted to say something more to me but

Richard's mood was not one to be pressed and thus she left promising only to keep in touch.

I went to the library, determined that I should commence working on the ledgers now that things had quieted down. My mind was wandering and I was relieved when Miss Wythe arrived, for the ledgers I was exploring were proving tiresome at best.

She entered wearing a slim-fitting deep burgundy suit that served to highlight her trim figure. "Charlotte said you wished to see me, Lady Barkham."

I closed my books and rose, indicating for her to come join me over by the fire.

"Would you care for some tea?" I offered. "It may be tepid but good, nonetheless."

She declined.

"I wanted to see you, Miss Wythe—first, because I have not been able to spend much time with you since your arrival at Mayfair. I hope you have been comfortable here."

"Quite," she replied. "You have been very generous to include me in your festivities these past few days."

"As I am certain that you have observed, we scarcely stand on much ceremony here at Mayfair."

She nodded.

"In that sense you are likely unaccustomed to allowing a dog free run of the house, but I thought you should know that Jaspar is really a part of our family and we never shutter him away. I would appreciate your complying with that as well."

"If I may say so, Lady Camberleigh, I do not think that the dog belongs in the nursery during the day. He appears a distraction for the children and I find it difficult to compete with him whilst trying to discipline the children."

I found myself laughing. "I do apologize, Miss Wythe, but I can scarcely imagine Jaspar being that intimidating."

Her eyes narrowed. "That is not what I said, Lady Barkham. I simply do not appreciate the distraction."

"Well, one thing I am certain that you will be pleased to learn is that I have had word from Master Farraday, the children's tutor, and he shall be returning in the near future. I know that it has been an extra effort on your part to help the children with their studies but I want you to know that it is appreciated on my part."

"Thank you, Lady Barkham," she replied. "And now if

that is all, you will excuse me to return to the nursery."

I was a bit nonplussed for I had hoped that we might spend more time chatting with each other. I knew so little about Miss Wythe, and though it was not my intention to pry, we were close enough in age that an intimate talk might have proven refreshing. I also remembered how lonely it had been for me as a governess at Camberleigh prior to the revealment of my true identity to my grandmother.

"Of course," I replied. "I do hope you shall feel at home here, Miss Wythe."

She turned and studied me for a moment. "Oh, I am certain I shall, Lady Barkham."

I found myself thinking about Miss Wythe after she had departed. There was no doubt that she was an attractive young woman. Not pretty per se, for there was a coolness about her looks, or perhaps it was her character which put a slight distance between herself and another. It was always difficult to know what she was thinking for she—studiously, it seemed—kept her responses terse. I had guessed initially that she might have been covering some shyness or inbred insecurity but I tended now to concur with Charlotte. This woman did not have a shy bone in her body. I was not inherently a critical person, and though I sensed that I did not warm to Amelie I could not fault her openly. She seemed to have established a good relationship with the children and she had done nothing visibly to offend me. And Charlotte, I had to admit, looked more rested since her arrival. Perhaps Philip had been right. I had needed a governess and Miss Wythe temporarily suited all our needs.

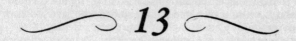

# 13

The next few days I threw myself into my work. Some correspondence that had arrived in the last post was demanding my immediate responses. Robbie kindly gave of his evenings, helping me reconcile the reams of figures tallying the sales of the final harvest. Philip, as intended, left for London two days after Christmas. The weather was inclement and I tried to urge him to delay his journey but he could not be dissuaded. I found to my surprise that I missed his presence at Mayfair. It heightened my awareness that I missed having a man about the house and it served only to remind me that Justin was lost to me forever. Amelie kept the children occupied, and though she did not respond to any overtures of friendliness on my part, she continued to appear quietly efficient.

I tried to take a long walk each day with the children, realizing that since I had undertaken the affairs of the estates I rarely escaped the confines of the house. I was painfully aware that both children had changed greatly since Justin's death. Alexander had always tended to a serious nature, but this quality seemed inordinately heightened now. It was in Daphne, however, that the greatest change seemed to have occurred. Her playful coquettishness seemed to have been replaced with quiet thoughtful moods. Although in the past I had often reprimanded her for teasing Alexander, I now missed the repartee between the two. I tried to encourage each to talk to me, to share their thoughts with me, but I sensed that they had decided to be stalwart on my behalf. I regretted that they did not have friends to play with, but during the winter eves the children of the tenants were forced to remain close to home.

It was likely that on one of these walks I had become over-chilled and found myself on New Year's Eve abed with a high fever and a hacking cough. I had tried to get up but Charlotte would have none of it and put me to bed with large doses of herb tea.

I was rarely ill and I loathed lying about. There was so much work to be done. Robbie insisted that he could take over for a few days but I knew that he was simply trying to ease my concerns. The worst thing about being sick, I decided, was that it gave me too much time to think. In those hours between the times that I slept I was obsessed with thoughts of Justin. It was as though my mind were insisting on reliving the most precious moments that we had spent together. I wondered whether these painful reminders would ever one day become tender memories. I passed the issuing in of the New Year alone, save for Jaspar, who seemed instinctively driven to stay close to me this night.

It had always been a night of significance between Justin and myself. Whether we had been giving a ball or attending one, Justin had always ferreted me off to the bedroom shortly before midnight, insisting that a peck on the cheek was no way to issue in the start of another year. Each year I would protest, insisting that it was embarrassing to sequester ourselves away like that, and each year I succumbed, secretly thrilled at the blatancy of his seduction.

How desperately I longed for the warmth of his strong sinewy body next to mine. There were stirrings in me that I had grown increasingly aware of during this past month. Justin had taught me never to fear our lovemaking; in fact he knew that I exulted in it. He had also taught me not to be afraid to express my needs. I needed him now, I knew, and I was painfully aware that the space next to mine in the bed was cold and empty.

It was not until the sixth of January that Philip returned. I had tried to rouse myself on the second but had only succeeded in heightening my fever and could not fight Charlotte's demands that I return to bed.

When Philip asked to see me I agreed. I had kept the children at bay during my illness, not wanting to transmit any virus to them, but I had missed seeing people and hearing something other than my own thoughts. Charlotte had brought me a fresh robe and gown and had brushed my hair before he arrived. I was weak but I did not want him to think that I was on my deathbed.

"Serena, why did you not permit Charlotte to call for the doctor?" he asked as he pressed his hand against my forehead. The coolness in his fingertips felt good, drawing the heat away from my brow.

" 'Tis nothing that serious, Philip. I simply caught a chill."

He sat down next to me, drawing the chair up to the bed.

"I sense that it is all that work you have taken on. Charlotte told me that you were working night and day after I left."

"Do not scold me, Philip," I urged. "Charlotte has chastised me quite enough. But tell me, how are you? How was your trip, did you see Jonathan?"

"Whoa, not so fast. Of course I saw Jonathan and he specifically asked me send you his regards."

"How nice of him," I replied. "I am quite fond of him, you know."

He studied me for a moment. "Yes, I know you are, though I don't understand why. He is scarcely a man that I would think you would find attractive."

I looked up at him. "Then you do not know me very well, Philip. Jonathan is a gentle, kind soul—those are characteristics that I respect."

Philip was watching me, and when I looked down I was mortified to find that my robe had fallen open, revealing the décolleté neckline of my gown. I hastily pulled the collar back over my breast.

"You need not do that, you know, Serena," he murmured quietly.

"What do you mean by that?" I charged.

"Simply that seeing you—how shall I say—a bit revealed is hardly shocking to me. Indeed it is quite pleasurable."

"Philip, please," I insisted, "you must not speak like this."

"Why, Serena, why must I not? Because you are recently widowed, because you are fearful that you may respond to me?"

I started to protest but he pressed on.

"Serena, I did not mean to broach this now—I wanted to wait, certainly, until you were fully recovered—but I have been wanting to speak to you for weeks now. Please let me finish. Serena, I have watched you. I think you are very courageous to try and take over the running of these estates but I see the toll that it is taking on you."

"I can manage," I argued.

"To the contrary, I do not think you can, at least not without help. Is this the way you intend to spend the rest of your life—slaving over ledgers, working with the tenants, managing the sale of crops?"

"I frankly do not see that I have any choice," I argued.

"But you do and that is what I want to talk to you about. Marry me, Serena."

"Marry you?" I blurted out.

"It cannot come as a complete surprise to you that I adore you, Serena, I think I fell in love with you that first night when you entered my room."

I flushed deeply. "Philip, this is very wrong. If you continue this way you will simply ruin a friendship that I have come to value greatly."

"Is it so wrong of me, Serena? I am not trying to insult the memory of your husband, Lord knows, Justin was a friend of mine as well. But I do not think that even Justin would fault me for my intentions. I am offering you marriage, Serena, and with that some solace in the coming years, I hope. I can help you with the running of Mayfair, not to mention the raising of Daphne and Alexander. And in time I would hope that I could express the love I have for you in more ways than just verbally."

I was truly shocked. Had I been giving any thought to remarriage my astonishment perhaps would not have been as great. It had crossed my mind, of course, but not seriously, for my loss was still too new, the pain of it too fresh in my mind.

"Serena, before you answer, let me tell you that I do not expect a response from you right now, although having now spoken my mind I would look for your response by week's end. Most importantly, I want you to know that you have never said or implied anything that would lead me to believe that you share my affections. You are a woman, I know full well, who loved her husband very deeply. I respect that in you—in truth it may be one of the things that attracted me to you initially. Yours was a very special love and I have not come to you without accepting that that love was for Justin alone. But that is no reason for you not to seek the happiness you still deserve in another union. You are young and very beautiful, Serena. But life passes us by before we know it. Do not be foolish and hide from it. I want you to live it—to live it with me."

He rose and bent over me, kissing my forehead very lightly; then leaving the room without another word, he left me to ponder the delirium into which he had plunged me.

I had now to question the sagacity of having invited Philip to stay here at Mayfair. It had never occurred to me that his intentions had been other than purely business. We had been friends, of course, but he had never intimated a deeper involvement. Or had he? Monique had alluded to it; even Anne had suggested it. And if I were to be honest with myself, I had even pondered certain gestures, certain phrases over the past months. He certainly had intimated things to me over the holidays. Could I have been so naive as to have misunderstood or had my grief been so great that I could not see clearly?

My immediate reaction was that I would have to ask Philip to leave Mayfair. It simply would be too awkward for us both. We could not avoid seeing each other every day and our relationship would be bound to be strained. It would, of course, be difficult for me; having made the commitment to the railroad project, I was loathe not to see it through. Philip would in time find other accommodations, I was certain, but even though we rarely discussed details of the project I felt closer to it with his being ensconced at Mayfair.

Sleep overtook me: When I awakened, I felt puzzled and fretful. I had dreamt. First of Justin. He had been calling out to me but he was so far away that I could not hear what he was saying. I called to him to come to me, but instead of moving closer he seemed to move further away. I waited for him to return, calling to him, begging him to find me. And then I saw his form moving to me. I waved, urging him to run. The form grew larger as his pace quickened. I stretched out my arms and he ran into them. I pushed him back to look at him, to tell him how dearly I loved him. But I gasped when I saw his face—for it was not Justin, but Philip who was standing before me.

What did it mean? I wondered—or did it have any significance at all? I could not possibly consider marrying Philip. It had only been months since Justin's death, but even more importantly I did not love Philip. I was fond of him and I could not deny that he was an attractive man. There would be hundreds of women, no doubt, who would give almost anything to receive a proposal of marriage from Lord Philip Taggart. He had said once that he envied what Justin and I shared. I had encouraged him to find someone with whom he could share his own life, never dreaming that person would come to be myself.

What puzzled me was how Philip could ask me to become his wife when he truly had had no encouragement from myself. I realized that many, perhaps even most, of the marriages I knew were not born of love, but Philip did not strike me as one to enter such an arrangement. Philip, I sensed, was a man of strong desires and I truly doubted he would ever accept a marriage that was in name only.

When Charlotte brought my dinner tray, she sensed that I was preoccupied. I wished that I could share the day's occurrence with her, but this was a matter I knew I would have to resolve for myself.

By the following morning my fever had broken. The cough, though somewhat abated, was still with me and Charlotte insisted that I keep to my bed for at least another day. I asked to see the children, who appeared relieved that I was obviously on my way to recovery. I sensed that since Justin's passing they were both particularly worried about my own state of health. I could understand for I realized how vulnerable they felt. I was their sole sense of security now, and somewhere inside them was a secret terror that I, too, would be wrenched from them.

I shivered at the thought that it could happen. There were no promises in life, but I prayed that I would at least be able to see the children to maturity. I studied the children as they recited a few of the poems that they had recently learned. Was I being fair to them by denying them a father figure? These were their formative years. I could give them love but would it be enough? Alexander, I realized, was particularly vulnerable. He needed male company. Robbie was wonderful with him, but he did not have the background or training to expose him to all that would be expected of him when he inherited the estates—and with it his father's title.

They seemed to like Philip, though he had showered too many little games and trinkets on them that I could hardly think that they would find him an ogre. Not that I thought he had tried to buy the children's affections.

When the children left I realized that I was surprising myself. When I considered how to tell Philip that he must find other quarters before proceeding with his projects, I found myself ruminating about his proposal.

I dearly wished that I could talk to Monique. She was experienced in these matters and would advise me well, I knew, even if her shared liaison with Philip might color her thinking. Anne was my dearest friend but she was not approving of Philip even being at Mayfair. Justin was her brother, and though with the passing of time she would likely encourage me to remarry, she surely would find a marriage to Philip precipitous, to say the least.

That was the one thing that troubled me the most. Philip must have known that, had he waited an appropriate period of time, I might have been not more prepared socially, morally or mentally, but at least I would have been less shocked by his proposal. He had stated that he wanted to help me and, Lord knows, I was terribly close to admitting that I needed help. But why could he not have offered it without any commitment?

I had an opportunity to ask him that very question when he came to visit early that evening. He looked particularly handsome in a dark striped waistcoat.

"You must forgive Charlotte, Serena. I fear that I used my most persuasive manner to convince her that it was important that I see you. May I say that you look much improved."

I pulled the covers up about me. "I feel much better, thank you, Philip. And you, how goes your work?"

He cleared his throat. "I must admit that I have accomplished very little since my return. I have been preoccupied, shall we say. Might I hope that you have given some thought to our conversation yesterday?"

"Philip, I would be lying to you if I said that I have had little else on my mind. You caught me, as you must realize, completely unaware."

He nodded. "I sensed that I had, though I am surprised that you had not suspected how I felt about you, Serena. Frankly, at first I know that I had to fight my feelings—you were, after all, the wife of my friend and partner. When Justin left, I found it ironic that he should have charged me with looking out after you. Had he known how I felt, I doubt that he would have been so magnanimous. But you must give me credit for some self-containment. I was careful to include the children, for I knew that I could not trust myself to be alone with you."

I looked down and found that I was wringing my hands against the sheets.

"How could you have even entertained those thoughts,

Philip, knowing what trust my husband had in you? Have you no sense of decency? And what of myself? Was I being played a fool? Did you finaigle yourself into this house under false pretenses? How do you think I feel having sided with you against my uncle and the woman who is like my own sister?"

He sat forward in his chair. "Good Lord, Serena, need you paint me with so black a brush? I could not help how I felt about you, anymore than you could help feeling the way you did about Justin."

"The way I *still* feel about Justin," I cried out.

He grew silent for a moment. "Serena, I am not asking to replace what you have lost. I know that I could never do that. But what I am offering you is a new life, someone to lean on, someone to help you raise your children. I think I know you well enough, Serena, to know that you do not want to do that alone. I am almost certain that that is not what Justin would have wanted for you. Had it been you who had perished on that ship, would you have wanted Justin to remain celibate for the rest of his life? Would you have wanted the children raised solely by a governess?"

"Of course not," I murmured.

"Then say yes to me, Serena. Tell me you will become my wife."

"How can I become your wife, Philip, when I think of you as a friend? I cannot commit myself to you when I still am in love with my husband."

He eased back in his chair and rubbed his hand about his chin. "Ah, I see," he said quietly.

"What do you see?"

"I see that perhaps what is holding you back is a fear of some intimacy between us. The intimacy of a husband and wife."

I found myself too flustered to respond. Justin and I talked so openly of these matters but the thought of dealing with this with Philip made me less than comfortable.

"Philip, I do not think . . ."

"Hush, Serena. Allow me to continue."

"I cannot deny that I am desirous of you. I would not be a whole man were I not. Nor shall I deny that I would prefer not to have a marriage of convenience. But I am sensitive to your recent loss. I should not press myself on you, Serena. I am confident that in time you would come to me. But until then I would simply have to admire you from afar."

I was terribly confused. Philip was offering me the sanctity of marriage and yet he was willing to wait, to chance that my feelings for him would grow in time. It scarcely seemed a fair match.

"Philip, might I ask you something?"

"Of course."

"What if my sentiments toward you did not change? How long could you wait before I came to you? What if I never could respond the way you want me to? You would be trapped in a loveless marriage. How could I even think of doing that to you, Philip?"

A smile played over his lips. "There is no question that it is not what I want, Serena. But like Justin, I am a gambler. You care for me, you have admitted that. Conceded, 'tis as a friend, but these things can change. Time alone brings change."

"It does not seem fair," I murmured. "I have seen how women respond to you. There are many, I am certain, who would make you an excellent wife—who would be a *complete* wife to you, Philip."

"But it is you whom I have chosen, Serena. That is, if you would have me."

"Philip, this is not a small decision, certainly one that I do not take lightly. I have us all to consider. You, myself, the children—I need time."

"If you remember, Serena, that was the one limitation of my proposal. I asked you for an answer by week's end and I would hope that you would respect that."

"But why, Philip, must I give you my answer so quickly? Is there some reason that I do not know about?"

"No, not really," he said hesitantly. "But you must see, Serena, that now that I have spoken to you, told you of my intentions towards you, it would prove awkward for me to remain here at Mayfair if you should decide not to marry me. I had not intended to speak to you so quickly—I had thought that I could wait until spring—but when I was in London I knew that I could remain silent no longer."

"Philip, you do not have to leave Mayfair," I insisted.

"Is that then your answer, Serena?"

"I have not given you an answer. I simply want you to know that, no matter what I decide, there will be no need for you to leave Mayfair. Your work is here, Philip, and we both have an interest in seeing this project through."

Philip rose. "I can only hope that we should not have to worry about that, Serena. But I doubt that I would change my mind."

"You are leaving then?"

He nodded. "I cannot have Charlotte find me here. I assured her that I would limit the time of my visit."

I smiled. "And she will keep you to it, you know."

"May I see you tomorrow, Serena?"

"I shall be up by then, I am certain."

"Please think well upon what I have said, Serena," Philip asked as he departed.

How could I think of anything else? I wondered.

I found that I was terribly tired after Philip's visit and drifted off to sleep before having any dinner. When I awakened it was the middle of the night. I rose, pulling my robe about me. Jaspar was curled up near the fireplace and his tail beat rhythmically on the floor as I stroked his back. A tray of food had been left, surely hours earlier, for everything now was cold. I took the biscuits and glass of milk and sat down in front of the fire, pulling a lap robe up about my knees.

Jaspar rose and sat down beside me, pressing his muzzle into my lap.

"You are an incorrigible beggar," I said, giving him a small piece of the biscuit which he gently mouthed from my hand.

"What do you think I should do, Jaspar? Would it be wrong of me to marry Lord Taggart?" I whispered aloud.

There. I had actually said it. "Oh, Justin," I moaned, "if only you could send a signal to me. Some word, some message, to tell me what I should do."

But no magical word or message, I knew, would penetrate the stillness of the night. The decision was mine.

I gave Philip that decision the next morning. I had intended to wait. Through the hours until dawn I had deliberated. Philip's determination to leave Mayfair was ironically what brought me to my final resolve. I simply did not want him to leave. I admitted to myself that it was selfish. I felt some sense of security with him about. He had appealed to my vulnerabilities. I was lonely and I was exhausted—exhausted from attempting to handle pressures that had even been awesome for Justin at times. I was also fearful of losing the railroad project. It was foolish because I knew that Philip was committed to it, but I wondered if his fervor would be as great once he was removed from Mayfair and myself.

I took heart at Philip's reaction for he seemed to appreciate how troubled a decision it was for me to make.

Therefore it surprised me when he suggested, "I hope that you will agree, Serena, that it would be best if we were quick to post the bans."

"No, I do not, Philip," I argued. "There are many who are going to question this marriage, as I am certain you are aware. To be precipitous would only serve to wag even more tongues."

"I disagree with you, Serena. The longer we wait, the more gossip there shall be, considering my living with you here alone in this house."

"You amaze me, Philip. It was you who came here asking to stay. We both know that it was a business decision, solely a business decision. And it is scarcely as though I am here alone with you."

"Trust me, Serena, to know what is right."

I took a sip of tea. "You are already sounding a bit like a husband, you know."

"Well, 'tis a new role for me, so allow me to practice a bit. In this case I really do insist that we set a date."

"Philip, really," I begged. "I have only just told you of my decision. There are the children, Anne and Richard, quite a large coterie of people who must be informed."

Philip had risen and moved over to the library fireplace. He commenced stoking the fire. "I do not think that Lord and Lady Camberleigh should be informed until after the ceremony, Serena."

"You what?" I blurted out. "Surely you cannot be serious. Why, it would be an outrage, Philip! Richard—if you have forgotten—is my uncle, Anne is my late husband's sister, not to mention my dearest friend. Your suggestion is unthinkable."

He swirled around. "Is it? I think not and I expect you as my wife to respect my wishes."

I gasped at the ferocity of his tone. "I am not yet your wife, Philip," I murmured in response.

He came quickly to me and took my hands in his.

"Forgive me, Serena, I scarcely meant to be ill-tempered. It is only that now that you have agreed to marry me I am loathe to having anything change your mind."

I withdrew my hands from his clasp, sensitive to his

closeness. "Why would you think my sharing news of our impending marriage would prove threatening? I should think that you would be pleased."

"Serena, you know what Richard thinks of me. He would do anything to dissuade you from this marriage."

"Oh, I think you are overreacting," I assured him. "Richard, it is true, thinks this railroad venture is foolhardy and he was less than enthusiastic about your residing here at Mayfair, but I scarcely think it was a personal judgment. He has never openly been truly critical of your character, at least to me."

"Can you honestly sit there and tell me that you think that they will both embrace the idea of our marriage?"

I could not. "In time, Philip, I am certain, in time."

"Then give it time, Serena. Write them, invite them to Mayfair but do it after the ceremony."

"I trust you think it would be permissible to tell the children before it is a fait accompli?"

"Now it is you who has the edge in her voice," he retorted. "That was unnecessary, Serena. Of course the children should be told. Today, if you like. You simply set the hour and I shall make myself available."

"You think that we should inform them together?" I asked thoughtfully.

"Yes, I do, unless you have some strong objection."

I would have preferred to discuss it with the children privately, but I agreed, sensing that to do so would have created a schism between Philip and myself. Justin would in my mind always be their father, but I knew that I would have to give way to Philip on this if he were indeed to have a hand in raising them.

We decided to talk to the children at dinner that evening. I asked Charlotte to have Cook prepare something special. She was so pleased to see me up and about that it did not occur to her to ask what the occasion was.

Philip assured me that he would take care of all the necessary details for our marriage. Since it was to be a small ceremony there was little planning that I would need do. Charlotte and Robbie, Amelie and, of course, the children would accompany us to the church. I was surprised that Philip had not wanted his sister and her family present but he insisted that the trip would prove too arduous for her at this time of year. His parents were deceased and there was none other that he wished to witness the occasion of his marriage.

As I dressed for dinner that evening I seemed to be all thumbs. I scoffed at myself for being nervous for I was scarcely the blushing bride. In actuality I felt more as though I were about to make a business transaction. I did not know how I had expected Philip to respond to my agreement to marry him, but it was certainly not in the fashion he had done.

For all his talk of his feelings and passions towards me, he had received my acceptance in such a cool, matter-of-fact manner that I wondered whether he had not embellished his feelings for me a bit. And yet, had he taken me in his arms and promised undying love, I should undoubtedly have recoiled from his embrace. Perhaps he had sensed that and preferring not to face rejection had in his own way tried to show me that he would have patience with me. How different this marriage would be than the one to Justin.

When Charlotte arrived I had almost completed dressing, save my hair, which now hung loosely about my shoulders.

"Does me heart good to see ye up an' about again, Miss Serena," she enthused as she began brushing my hair. "But aye not sure ye should be pushin' like ye are. 'Tis only a few days since yer fever broke."

I reached about and patted her hand. "I am fine, Charlotte, truly."

When she had finished with my hair I unfolded the handkerchief on the dressing table which was concealing the necklace Philip had given me. I had remembered it at the last moment and decided that it was appropriate that I should wear it tonight.

I handed it to Charlotte. "Would you help me with the clasp?"

She turned it over in her hand before stretching it about my neck.

"Aye do not be rememberin' this necklace, 'tis a pretty thing, it is."

"I have only had it since Christmas," I replied. "It was a gift from Lord Taggart."

"Oh."

"Is that all you have to say?" I asked, watching her in the mirror.

" 'Tis a grand gift," she mused. "If ye do not mind me sayin' so, aye think Lord Taggart has an eye fer ye."

I turned around to face her. "Charlotte, there is something I must discuss with you."

"Oh, tell me there not be anything else to trouble ye, Miss Serena. There has been enough heartbreak here."

"No, no," I assured her, "'tis nothing as serious as that. But I should want you to hear this directly from me."

She looked at me expectantly.

I took a deep breath. "Philip, Lord Taggart, has asked me to marry him. And I have agreed."

She sank back into the chair behind her. "Ye certainly kin keep a secret, Miss Serena. Why, aye never dreamed."

I nodded. "I know that it shall come as a shock to many people. If truth be known I have scarcely completely accepted the notion myself."

" 'Tis so soon since, aye mean, since we lost the master."

I felt tears well in my eyes. Charlotte, seeing that, leaned forward and handed me a handkerchief.

"Whenever I think that there are no tears left," I whispered, "it commences all over again."

"O' course it does, Serena," Charlotte assured, putting her arms about me. "Ye an' the master, well aye never saw two people who loved each other more than ye did. T'will take time, maybe even years, before the hurt goes away. But ye 'ave te believe that it will."

"My marriage to Lord Taggart, it will not be the same, Charlotte."

"Ye do not love 'im, do ye, Serena?"

I shook my head. "I am fond of him, of course. He has been a good friend over these past months. But no, I do not love him, Charlotte. How could I when I still love Justin?"

"Then why marry him, Serena? 'Tis not my place te be sayin' it, but 'tis not as if ye had no prospects. An' ye havin' no money troubles, are ye?"

"No. Justin left me a very wealthy woman, Charlotte. To be honest, I do not even know what Philip's resources are. I am certain that he must be monied but to what extent I have no idea."

"Ye still 'ave not given me a reason, Serena."

"Would it be so terrible if I told you that I did not want to be alone? Charlotte, I thought that I could handle the running of Mayfair myself, believe me, I have tried. And Robbie has been wonderful. But Philip forced me to admit to myself the toll it is taking on me. I am always tired, I do not spend anywhere near the time with the children that I should. I am not saying that I do not intend to carry on with my responsibilities, but Philip, I am certain, can be supportive not only with overseeing Mayfair but with Daphne and Alexander as well."

"Does Lord Taggart know 'ow ye feel about 'im?"

I nodded. "I could not deceive him. I think that he is hopeful that with time my feelings toward him might grow."

"What 'ave the children said?"

"They do not know. I shall tell them at dinner this evening."

"Hmmm," she mused. "An' what of Lord an' Lady Camberleigh?"

"They do not know. Philip—Lord Taggart felt that it was best not to tell them. Not just now anyway."

"Good gracious why? They be yer family, Serena."

"I know, I know, but there is a strain at present between them. Richard does not approve of Philip's involvement with the railroads. 'Tis all very complicated and not worthy detailing right now. Let it suffice to say that I have tried to accommodate Philip's position and agreed that they should be told after we are husband and wife."

"An' when do ye intend that should be?"

"For myself I should be just as well pleased to wait a while but Philip believes that since we are living under the same roof that there will be far less talk if we marry quickly."

"That will not be stoppin' those that would gossip, Serena. 'Tis not long since the master's passin' an' ye know 'ow word travels."

"You do not think I am doing the right thing, do you, Charlotte?"

I waited for her response to penetrate the silence.

"Serena, 'tis not fer me to say. 'Tis only a decision ye kin make fer yourself. Aye only want ye to find peace in whatever ye decide."

"Ironically I am not making the decision for myself," I replied. "The children need the security, the stability, that I believe my marriage to Philip will provide. If I knew that Oliver would soon return from America and want to assume the responsibilities of the estates, I do not believe that I would proceed with this union. But Oliver left here to pursue his own dreams and fortunes and I cannot expect to rely on him, certainly not in the forseeable future."

" 'E would be on the first ship back if 'e knew of yer trouble, Serena."

I smiled in acknowledgement. "I know he would, Charlotte. Quite honestly I have been fearful that once he learns of the news of Justin that he will arrange passage right out. This is his time and I would always feel guilty if I felt that I in any way had kept him from pursuing his own dreams."

I left Charlotte exacting a promise from her to keep my confidence about my upcoming marriage until it was appropriate to announce it. Philip and the children were already in the dining room. He was trying his best, I could see, to keep them amused but not with great success.

"Mama," Daphne enthused, "you look beautiful."

"It feels wonderful to be up and about again," I acknowledged.

"And you, Alexander, how are you feeling?"

He shrugged. "I am well, Mother."

"Not much enthusiasm there, my boy," Philip said, winking at me.

I cringed at his comment for I knew that Alexander did not like patronizing references.

"Well, Serena, shall we make our announcement now?" Philip queried as the wine was poured.

"Philip, please," I whispered, hoping to silence him.

"What announcement is that, Mama?" Daphne pressed.

"Really, Serena, I do not understand what an hour or so will change. Shall you tell them or shall I?"

I was annoyed. I had hoped that we might finish dinner before broaching the subject.

"Philip, I think, perhaps . . ."

"What your mother is trying to say is that she has agreed to become my wife."

The silence in the room was stony. It was Daphne who spoke first.

"Is it true, Mama?" she asked disbelievingly.

I nodded, fearful that if I spoke it would be to lash out in frustration against Philip.

"But you cannot," she blurted out.

I was shocked by her denial. "Daphne, what would make you say that?"

"Because you are still married to Papa," she cried out, tears spilling down her cheeks.

I rose quickly and went to her. "Darling, of course I am. In certain ways I shall always be married to your father but not in those same ways as when he was alive. You understand that, do you not?''

''No,'' she cried out. ''I want Papa. I want you to be married to Papa.''

My heart was breaking listening to her cries. She broke away from me suddenly and dashed towards the door. Whirling about, she thrashed out at Philip, ''You shall never be my father. Never.''

I started towards her as she brushed past the door, but Philip grabbed me before I could run after her.

''Leave her be, Serena,'' he said firmly.

I shook my head. ''Philip, she needs me. I must go to her.''

''Not now. She needs time by herself, time to sort out her own emotions.''

I tried to wrench away from Philip. ''Good Lord, Philip, she is my daughter. She is hurt and confused by the announcement, which I have to admit you did not exactly deliver tactfully. Justin has not been gone that long. They adored each other. How was I to know that those emotions are still as close to the surface as my own are. Please let me go to her.''

''Let my mother go.''

I turned, forgetting that Alexander was still in the room.

My arm fell free of Philip's.

''I scarcely think that is the way to talk to the man who is to be your new father, Alexander.''

I saw my son's lip quiver, if only slightly.

''Serena, the dinner is growing cold,'' Philip said quietly. ''You and Alexander commence eating and I shall fetch Daphne.''

I started to protest but he insisted that he would be the best to talk to her. I let him go and sat back down at the table, trying desperately to regain my composure. It could not have gone more poorly had I planned it. I picked up my fork, being careful to look down at my plate for I feared that at any moment I should burst into tears. All I managed to do was to push the food aimlessly about on my plate. I was painfully aware that Alexander was watching me but I could not bring myself to say anything to him.

When I finally found my voice I chastised him for speaking to Philip in that manner.

''He was hurting you,'' he replied.

''He did not mean to,'' I assured him. ''He just wanted to

handle your sister in his own way."

The look on Alexander's face frightened me. I could not put my finger on it. Was it distrust or fear? Whatever, his visage was suddenly not one of a small boy. This was an expression which only came with maturity.

I was about to question him when Philip returned with Daphne in tow. I had to admit that I was amazed at how subdued she appeared.

"Well, now that our little crisis has passed perhaps we can resume our dinner," Philip said as he sat down. "And our announcement."

I looked over at him, trying to communicate with my eyes that it was best not to go on at this juncture, but he paid no heed.

"Oh, Serena, I think we have settled our differences, have we not, Daphne?"

Whether she was simply being stalwart or whether he had actually been able to reason with her, I did not know but she murmured a polite yes to his question.

"You see," Philip continued, "now that the novelty has worn off I suspect that Daphne will actually grow to even like the idea of our marrying. And I hope that you shall, too, Alexander. I want you both to know that I shall never try to replace your real father but I do hope that in time you will come to care for me as I have come to care for you both."

There was no response.

"In any case the wedding shall take place within the next few weeks. We have decided to have a small ceremony and of course you both shall be present."

"Will Aunt Anne and Uncle Richard come too?" Daphne asked.

"No," Philip murmured.

"But why would they not?"

"They shall visit in the spring, I am certain," I assured her, hoping that she would not press the issue.

I tried to finish the meal, attempting to lighten the conversation and return things to normal, but I was not making great strides. Philip fortunately did most of the talking and finally, blessedly, the evening came to a close.

I excused the children, kissing them both and assuring them that we would spend more time together that following day.

Philip retired to the library, urging me to join him while he partook of some brandy. He would leave to post the bans the next day and talk to the local parson. We would have a simple ceremony in the church and then return for a quiet dinner at Mayfair. There was no talk of our taking a wedding journey and for that I was thankful—as I would have found it awkward to travel as Lord and Lady Taggart while requesting separate rooms.

Lady Taggart. I said the words over and over to myself in my mind. Would I ever become accustomed to it? In my heart I knew that I should always be Lady Barkham. Could I, feeling as I did, truly take another man's name and share his life?

"Serena. Serena, did you hear me?"

I snapped out of my reverie. "I apologize, Philip. What were you saying?"

He waved me off. "It was not important and I do not seem to have your attention anyway." He drained the glass of its amber liquid. "I believe I shall retire. I shall see you tomorrow evening Serena. Try to have some trust in the future."

His departure was so abrupt that I had no time to respond. I had wanted him to stay and talk to me. The fact that he had not I could not find surprising. It had been a difficult evening and I had done little to be supportive. He had obviously been correct in his approach to Daphne. I realized that as the children would learn to listen to him so must I.

I really did not know what reaction I had expected from the children. They had always seemed to be so fond of Philip that perhaps I had taken for granted that their response would be more enthusiastic. Since my agreement to marry him was in large part for their benefit, I wanted them not only to approve but to be happy at the prospect. I had not counted on the fact that they, like myself, were still mourning Justin.

The fire was dying and a chill had crept into the room. I picked up the brass candlestick resting on the table next to me and left the library for the staircase. As I approached the turn in the hallway which led down to my bedroom I paused, thinking I heard a noise down at the other end where Philip's quarters were. It had been some time since he had retired and I was surprised that he should still be up and about. I decided that like Justin he was undoubtedly a man who turned to work when he could not sleep. I had not ventured down there since he had come to Mayfair, wishing to give him as much privacy as possible. But I was curious about his work. Likely, I would not understand it, but I determined to ask him to show me his designs and plans one day soon.

Jaspar was poised by the door when I entered my room and whimpered at the sight of me. I undressed quickly and, extinguishing the candle, climbed into bed. I had lain there only moments when I heard what sounded like footsteps in the hall. I waited to see which direction they would take, but the patter disappeared as quickly as it had come. That was the second time I had heard someone moving about at this hour. Since the servants were all abed at an early hour I determined that it must be Philip, who grew restless with nightfall.

When Charlotte arrived the next morning I was already up and dressed. As she worked with my hair I recounted the events of the evening before.

"It do not be surprisin' me," she responded. "Ye should not be takin' it too much to heart, Serena. They'll be comin' round, ye'll see."

"I wish I could be as certain as you," I said. "You know, if I had not already given Philip my answer I do not know that I would go through with this marriage. Two days ago it seemed the answer to everything. But today I wonder if I am not creating more hardship by this decision."

"Ye kin always change yer mind, ye know, Serena. What has not been done need not be undone, as me mum used to say."

She was right, of course, and yet somehow I knew that I would go through with my marriage to Philip.

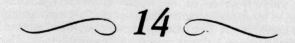

# 14

On the bitterly cold gray morning of February 3, 1823, I became Lady Taggart in the company of my two children, Charlotte, Robbie and Miss Wythe. The parson, who I had long since determined was of service only for weddings and funerals, presided in his usual pompous manner so that what should have been a short, simple ceremony droned on for hours. I had in a way welcomed the length of time we were forced to kneel before the altar of this simple chapel since I had felt quite faint at several times. Due to the chill of the day I had abandoned my original selection of a gown and had chosen a heavy ecru taffeta and velvet, which I supposed had contributed to the dizzy sensations I was experiencing.

I tried desperately to follow the parson's monotone, fighting not to permit my thoughts to be filled with Justin. So strongly did I feel his presence there with me that I felt that if I were to call to him he would answer me. I tried to drive the images of him away from me, reminding myself that I was here in this place of God to take another as my husband. But the more I tried the stronger the sense of him became.

Only when Philip placed the ruby-and-diamond encrusted ring on my hand and we had been pronounced husband and wife did Justin fade from my mind. I flushed as Philip kissed me on the cheek. The parson offered us the traditional celebration wine, which we partook of, and then endeavored to make a polite but hasty exit. He, too, I was certain was anxious to depart for his wife would be waiting, I knew, to hear the details of our nuptials. She would have attended but she was abed with something troubling her lungs. Much to her dismay, I was certain, for she would not have wanted to have missed this wedding.

I was very quiet on the return to Mayfair, opting to study the wintry bleakness out the window of the carriage rather than to try to make conversation. I pressed my hand against the bodice of my dress, feeling for the chain I had secreted under my gown earlier that morning. It was still there. The chain and the ring. The ring that Justin had given me on our wedding day. I had not even realized until the night before that I would have to remove it. And Philip would surely have been insulted had I merely transferred it to my other hand. I simply could not bear to part with it and thus had devised this fashion of keeping it close to me. Some would accuse me, I supposed, of making a mockery of my marriage to Philip. They would be wrong. I was simply not ready to let go of Justin.

The servants had gone to great lengths to make our wedding day feast a memorable one. Philip had been shocked at my insistence that Charlotte, Robbie and the children join us. I quickly found we were of different minds when it came to servants and children—who both, he had decided, were to know their place.

I was surprised at how agreeable Daphne and Alexander were that day. Agreeable perhaps was not the right word. Resigned, I supposed. They knew of my intention to marry Philip, and since I had given them no indication otherwise, I suspected that they had decided that there was little point in being temperamental. I wished that I did not suspect that Daphne was forcing a smile that usually came so naturally to her or that Alexander's silence was harboring secret thoughts. I was, because of my own state, likely being oversensitive.

I noticed during dinner that the antipathy between Charlotte and Amelie had not abated as much as I had thought. Admittedly Amelie's obviously deferential attitude towards Philip annoyed me as well. He had only to open his mouth and she cooed in approval. Granted, Philip could be charming, even amusing, when he wanted to, but I scarcely thought it necessary that she exult at his every word.

Not that he seemed to mind. To the contrary. The more she encouraged the more eloquently ebullient he became. I looked up and caught him studying me as he dabbed the linen napkin about his mouth. He was indeed very handsome—this man who had become my husband only hours before. It was not surprising that Miss Wythe should be taken with him. Yet it troubled me that she was. A fleeting thought crossed my mind and I involuntarily shook my head to be rid of it. And yet there it was. It was nonsense of course, but could I be experiencing a twinge of jealousy?

When at last the meal was completed, Philip asked Amelie to take the children to bed. Charlotte and Robbie, sensing that they too were to be excused, wished us well and made a hasty retreat. I was embarrassed by Philip's curtness with them but remained silent, not wishing to start an argument on this night of all nights.

"I hope that you are not disappointed that we are not to celebrate our nuptials with a brief holiday, my dear," Philip said quietly once we were alone, "but I scarcely thought it appropriate given the circumstances, if you understand what I mean."

I flushed deeply. "That was very considerate of you, Philip. Frankly I supposed that with your work it should be difficult anyway."

He nodded. "Perhaps in the spring."

Did he mean to infer that he expected that by spring the relationship between us would have changed? That was only months away, I reckoned, with some sense of dread.

"Will you join me in the library for some brandy, Serena?"

"Philip, would you mind terribly if I refused? The day, has wearied me more than I had expected and I should simply prefer to retire."

He shrugged. "I am disappointed, of course, but far be it for me to try to dissuade my bride. She is beautiful but headstrong, I suspect."

I pushed myself from the table conscious that he was watching me closely. "Goodnight then, Philip," I murmured awkwardly. "Sleep well."

He made no move towards me but his eyes never left me. "Goodnight, Lady Taggart."

There was only the sound of my shoes against the marble floor as I left the room. I wanted to run from it but I walked slowly until I had crossed the door, then gathering my skirts scurried quickly up the stairs and to my room. When I had closed the door, locking it behind me, I fell against it breathing a deep sigh.

"What have I done?" I choked out to the silence of the room.

I looked down at my hand where the slim jeweled band sparkled against the glow of the firelight. I had married a man I did not love. I had done it for reasons which seemed sound at the time but now as I stood in the confines of my room, alone, with the man I married locked away from me in some other part of the house, it seemed only absurd. I had thrust not only myself into a hopeless marriage but Philip as well. I did not love him but he had been a friend and it was wrong of me to have taken advantage of that. He deserved to expect the love, the trust, the sharing, and, yes, even the children that a marriage could bring. I could not give him that now. Possibly never. Had I thought that he would be content simply giving me his name?

I tore at the buttons on the dress, wanting to shed myself of any reminder of my marital day. I brushed my hair feverishly, venting my frustration against the long locks of hair. It was only when I had donned my nightdress and climbed into bed that I realized that Jaspar was not about. I went to reach for the candlestick next to my bed and saw that a note had been placed by it. It was in Charlotte's almost childlike hand.

"Jaspar be with the children."

I crumpled it and threw it on the table. Charlotte, of course, would have assumed that we would have wanted privacy on our marriage night. I could not blame her, for that would have been normal. Except that this marriage was not normal. Not on this night or on any other to follow would it ever be consummated.

When I awoke the next morning it was to a knocking at the door. I jumped out of bed realizing that I had locked it the night before.

"Aye did not mean to be disturbin' ye, Serena," Charlotte said as she peered around me, "but aye thought ye might be wantin' a fresh hot basin."

"That would be lovely," I replied, reaching for my robe.

"Is Lord Taggart up an' about already?"

"I do not know," I replied quietly.

"Don't go tellin' me ye two 'ave 'ad a spat now."

"Nothing of the sort. Lord Taggart simply will be keeping

his old quarters. And you may as well inform the rest of the household as to the arrangement. It shall serve to quell a lot of unnecessary conjecture.''

Charlotte mercifully did not press the issue further. When she had helped me dress I told her to tell Lord Taggart, should he be looking for me, that I would be with the children for a while.

I made my way over to the nursery where I found everything in a turmoil. It appeared that Daphne had decided not to wear the dress Amelie had laid out for her, opting instead for one of the new gowns which Anne had brought her for Christmas. I had to agree that the dress seemed frivolous for taking lessons in the schoolroom but I had never tried to thwart the children's desire to express themselves.

"Really, Miss Wythe, I scarcely see that this is an issue to become so upset about," I chided. "I quite agree that the dress is inappropriate but it is Daphne's dress and if she so desperately wants to wear it, what is the harm?''

Amelie looked at me angrily. I thought that she was about to say something that we both would have regretted. Whether she thought better of it or whether she suddenly regained her composure I do not know, but her face softened suddenly and she laughed lightly.

"You are right, of course, Lady Barkham, I mean . . .''

I smiled. "That is quite all right, Amelie," I assured her. "I expect it will take some time even for myself to grow accustomed to it.''

Daphne marched off with her dress and I turned to Alexander.

"You have not grown too big to give your mother a hug, have you?''

He came quickly to my arms and I pulled him to me, squeezing him tight.

"You know, Amelie, you have not really had much time to yourself since you came to Mayfair. Why do you not let me take the children today? There certainly must be some letters that you want to write or you might enjoy going down by the stables. Do you ride?''

"I fear not, Lady Taggart, not well at least. But that is most generous of you. I would appreciate the time if you are certain that it would not be a burden.''

"Of course not," I assured her. "Besides, we have not spent

a whole day together for a long time, have we, Alexander?"

He looked particularly pleased at the prospect.

"Well," I said once she had gone, "how shall we spend our day?"

"Might we go and visit Justin?"

The name for the horse had, of course, been the sentimental choice, but every reference to it seemed painful.

"An excellent idea," I agreed. "It shall also give me a chance to talk to Robbie."

Daphne returned in the dress which was fashioned of emerald green velvet with a high bodice and puffed sleeves shirred about the wrists. It made her look so grown-up that I was momentarily speechless.

"You do not like it, Mama?"

"No, no, 'tis not that, darling. You simply look like quite the young lady in that gown."

"Well, I shall be nine next month, you know," she retorted grandly.

"So you shall. And we must plan a party."

"With Aunt Anne and Uncle Richard?"

"If you like," I offered, hoping that by then Philip would have more confidence about their presence at Mayfair. "I think you should wear that dress for the occasion."

She looked at herself in the mirror. "Then I shall take it off now. I want it to be new for my party."

I told them both to dress warmly since it might be bitterly cold down by the stables. I returned to my room and fetched a warm cloak and gloves. As I was leaving the room I almost ran over Charlotte and Jaspar.

"Aye 'ad 'im down with me in the library but 'e was scratchin' at the door te get up 'ere so I figured aye might as well bring 'im up."

I stooped down and scratched his ears as he fell against my legs, his tail wagging incessantly.

"The timing is perfect. I am taking the children down to the stables and this little fellow could do with some exercise. Have you seen Lord Taggart?"

" 'E was in the library fer a while but then 'e left."

"He went out?"

"Aye do not know, te tell ye the truth. Aye t'weren't payin' attention."

"I see. Well, if you see him, would you tell him that I have taken the children to the stables?"

Jaspar trotted obediently after me. The children were already at the staircase landing and when I saw no sign of Philip we started on our way. I would be happy, I decided, to see winter pass. Mayfair was glorious in the spring when the trees turned their strength to putting things into bud. The gardens, many of which Anne had designed, would start to green again and the house would be filled with wondrous bouquets, each more glorious than the last.

Robbie waved, his toothy grin prominent as he saw us approach.

"That horse 'o yours was just askin' after ye this mornin', Alexander," he said, winking at me. "Why don't ye go on in and see the fellow?"

When they had left, Robbie said, "That's going to be one frisky bit 'o horse flesh."

"You do not think he shall be too spirited for Alexander, do you?" I replied, alarmed at the prospect.

"Not if he's his father's son. T'weren't no man who sat a horse better than Lord Barkham."

I flinched at the reminder.

"There I go putting my foot in my mouth again."

"You said nothing wrong, Robbie," I assured him. "I simply must stop reacting this way every time there is some reference made to Justin."

"Aye'll be tellin' you that I miss him, too. Place doesn't seem the same without 'im. Ye know, Miss Serena, I am pleased yer here for I was wantin' to ask ye a favor."

"Of course."

"Mrs. O'Clare—you know her husband's got the farm next to the Roarkes—well, she came down a while back with somethin'. Old Doc Rettiger couldn't figure it. But she's a lot worse. Can't get out 'o bed now. T'would be a big help if we could put some baskets together for the family. There's six 'o them in all. The older girl helps out but there is only so much she kin do."

I agreed readily and also insisted that he contact Dr. Carstairs, who was our physician. Justin had always said he would never let Rettiger treat even his horses, but because he had been treating the tenants for years they invariably went back to him.

"Have Doctor Carstairs send me the bill for his services."

Robbie grinned. "Aye thought that was what ye'd be sayin' but it never hurts to ask."

"You know I meant to tell you that I discovered last week that just before his death Justin had arranged to buy some new machines. There were quite a number of them. I am certain that he would not have ordered them unless he felt we needed them. It is just that I do not recall his mentioning it."

"Those would be the new plows. Ordered them from MacDevitts up here north a ways."

"That is it," I replied, pleased that he recalled. "Then I should arrange for payment to be made?"

He nodded. "Ye could cancel but it wouldn't set too well. An' we need MacDevitt's support."

"I will take care of it immediately."

We went in to find the children, entranced by the colt who was nuzzling each of them against the front of the stall.

"And what does Medallion think of his son?" I asked, stroking the majestic horse which Justin had tamed to his own.

"Proud as punch he is," Robbie replied. "Took him out for a run a few days ago an' he couldn't wait to get back to see him."

"I am grateful that you are exercising him, Robbie," I said appreciatively. "Justin would be, too. He loved that horse and it would be a pity to see him wither here without him."

I saw Alexander shiver a bit and decided that it was time that we returned to the house. When we had returned I told the children to have Cook fix them some warm milk and to serve luncheon in the breakfast room. I shed my cloak and went quickly into the library to warm by the fire.

I was startled to see Philip there with Amelie.

She jumped up at the sight of me.

"Is my husband entertaining you on your day off, Miss Wythe?"

"Serena, please," Philip said harshly, "that was uncalled for. Amelie simply asked if she might borrow some notepaper to send some letters."

"I see. And did you find some for her?"

He shook his head. I went to the desk drawer and opened it. "Will ten sheets be sufficient?"

She nodded.

I withdrew them and handed them to her, while being

angered at myself for the pettiness of my remark.

"Thank you, Lady Taggart," she said, excusing herself.

When she had left, Philip turned to me and asked, "How is my blushing bride this morning?"

"Really, that is quite unnecessary," I replied, rubbing my hands before the fire. "What is all this?" I asked Philip as my eyes took in the piles of ledgers that were strewn about the end of the room.

"If I am to be of help to you, Serena, I need to know something about the running of Mayfair."

"You have only to ask, Philip. I would gladly show you anything. It took me a spell to understand Justin's notations. Actually we can make a fair exchange of it. I shall school you on the running of the Mayfair/Camberleigh estates and you can show me how the designs are coming for the railroad project."

"No," he insisted. "I do not want you prying about my work."

"That is scarcely what I intended, Philip." I replied, shocked at his insinuation. "I only meant that I am interested in what you are doing, and since it is so alien to me I thought you might explain it to me."

"I apologize, Serena. I only meant that my work is very private to me and I do not care to share it with others until it is complete."

"I see. Well, in that case I shall leave you to your own devices."

He winked at me. "Not completely, I should hope."

"Would you care to join us at luncheon or shall I have Cook bring you a tray in here?"

"Might I ask who 'us' is?"

"Just the children and myself."

"I think I can manage that. It is only that Robbie and his mother could drive a man to drink."

"Why on earth would you say something like that, Philip?"

"Because it is the truth. I know they have been in your employ for years and I know that you think Robbie had some magical powers with those tenants of yours, but frankly, Serena, I find them to be bores. It was like some frightful play when they joined us for dinner last evening. Trust me that shall be the last of it."

I was dumbfounded. "Who do you think you are, Philip, to

talk of them that way? You have no understanding of what they endured with Justin and myself over the years. I know that in your eyes they are simply servants, but to me they are much more. And I will not have you talk this way."

"Serena, may I remind you that we are now husband and wife. The life you formed here with Justin meant a great deal to you, I know. But I am not Justin. We are very different men—he and I—and I think that it is naive of you to believe that I should adopt his ways. I should remind you that it is I who am now the master of Mayfair. When you married me you surrendered the rights to all of this, the land, the houses, the furnishings, all of it. I should like to run it from my own shoes. Not a dead man's. You may not always concur with my decisions but I expect you to honor them."

I eased into the chair behind me. I did not really know what I felt. Anger? Yes, that was certainly part of it. Philip talked as if he owned me. How could I have been so foolish not to realize that by marrying Philip I had by the laws of the church and crown given up my rights to the estates? On the other hand, I was not so insensitive as to not recognize some truth in what Philip said. I could not expect him to be Justin or even to live in his shadow. It struck me how little I knew of Philip. He was opinionated and yet I had to respect him for wanting to be his own man. If I allowed it, however, I wondered to what compromise would I be subjected.

When I finally composed myself, I looked up at Philip. "Might I ask you something?"

"Naturally."

"Did you marry me for my money, Philip?"

A smile played about his lips.

"Is that what you think, Serena?"

"I would not ask if I knew what to think."

The smile that had played about Philip's lips disappeared. His eyes narrowed, causing a furrow in his brow.

"If you are looking for me to dignify that with a response, Serena, I fear you shall be disappointed. Even if I were to deny it at this point, would you believe me?"

He was right, of course. The very suggestion of it could not quickly be dispelled.

Philip rose. "For myself I am going to have some luncheon. Are you going to join me?"

I could scarcely refuse since it was I who had suggested it—

not to mention that I had promised the day to the children.

As we approached the small dining room I could hear the children's laughter from within. It had been a long while since I had heard them be so playful with one another and it gave me hope. It was quickly dashed, however, when we entered the dining room for both children quieted instantly at the sight of Philip.

"What were you two laughing about?" I asked, hoping to restore their mood.

"Not anything of importance," Daphne murmured.

"I see."

"Your mother asked you a question and I should think she is owed an answer," Philip interjected.

"It was only something that Cook had said, sir," Alexander offered.

"Ah—and what was that?"

"Only that the last batch of chickens were so thin that they looked as though they had walked here from London."

I smiled at the notion.

"If that is true, then you should have a talk with Charlotte, Serena," Philip said. "There is scarcely a need to be serving sickly fowl these days."

"I am certain she did not mean that they were sickly, Philip," I assured him. "It is not unusual for them to be leaner in the winter."

"In any case it is worth mentioning."

I agreed simply because I found it foolish to sit there debating about what had begun as childlike playfulness.

The levity that Philip had brought to the dining room persisted throughout the meal. Fortunately he seemed anxious to get back to his work so that the children and I were quickly left alone together again.

Against my better judgment they inveigled me to go out for another walk, this time down by a pond which fell beyond the drive to the south of the house. Jaspar joined us, barking at the ducks and geese who, ruffled up against the cold, huddled at the far end of the glassy hollow. They made no move to flee this haven as he announced our arrival, for years before they had come to trust his presence.

As Alexander ran to slide across the pond I put my arm about Daphne and we strolled down to the far end to feed the ducks with some bread she had brought.

"Daphne, I would like to ask you something."

"Yes, Mama."

"You do like Philip, do you not?"

I felt her stiffen.

"You can tell me the truth, darling."

She looked up at me, her violet eyes searching mine. "Do you love him, Mama?"

I sighed deeply. "Philip has been a friend, a good friend, I think. But I could never feel about him the way I did for your father. What we shared was something very special, something that I would hope you will find someday."

"Philip does not kiss you," she observed. "Papa used to kiss you all the time."

The frankness of youth always surprised me.

"That is because the relationship is different," I replied.

I sensed that she wanted a more complete answer from me, but she was still of too tender an age to discuss the intimacies between a man and a woman. Perhaps selfishly I wanted to enjoy the protection of her childhood for as long as possible.

Alexander called to her then and she broke from me, running at full speed to him.

I realized suddenly that Daphne had not answered my question. I would not press her. The important thing was that both children felt that they could talk to me about Philip. I had been relieved that Philip had not, at least for now, asked the children to call him Father. I knew that it would be too painful for them both. One day perhaps, but it was too soon after Justin's passing.

Dark clouds had settled over the frosted lawns and I called to the children to start back to the house. The heavens opened when we were still a fair stretch from protection and I gathered my skirts up, leading the children on a run. We nearly ran over Giles, who was readying to rescue us with a large umbrella.

I sent the children off to the nursery, extracting promises that they would immediately change to dry clothes.

"Have you seen Lord Taggart, Giles?" I asked, shaking out the cloak which was drenched through.

"He is in his quarters. He asked me to tell you that he should like to dine with you alone in the dining room at six," he replied awkwardly.

"Thank you, Giles," I replied, handing him the cloak.

"Would you take this to the kitchens and ask Cook to dry it out for me?"

"Of course, your ladyship."

"Come along, Jaspar," I called. "We both need to dry out, I think."

I returned to my room, toweled Jaspar off and quickly changed my clothes. Taking up a hairbrush, I sat before the fire and let the warmth dry the long dampened strands.

Philip certainly had his nerve telling the servants to give me instructions on what I should do. If he had wanted to dine with me alone, why could he not have told me himself? Besides, I had promised the children to spend the whole day with them. I would dine with Philip, but there would be two extra place settings at the table, I decided.

As it turned out, Philip and I dined alone. The children were tired from the day and asked if they might have trays brought to their rooms. I suspected that there were other underlying reasons but I did not press them.

Philip appeared to be in particularly good humor that evening. The edge that had appeared in his voice earlier in the day seemed to have vanished completely. I was relieved for his cheerfulness but puzzled by this somewhat mercurial behavior of the man who was my husband.

When I told him of my intention to invite Anne and Richard to a small birthday party for Daphne the next month I was surprised that he actually championed the idea. He even suggested that once the weather had improved in the spring we should throw a large ball to officially celebrate our marriage. I was not as eager to flaunt it but then I realized that I could scarcely expect it to be kept a secret for very long.

"You know, Serena," he said, having finished a glass of wine, "perhaps I was a bit harsh earlier about my opinions of Robbie. Not that I particularly wish to dine with the chap but he does know the estates and I certainly have no desires to go off visiting the tenant farms. I think actually he could be quite useful to me."

"I am pleased that you are reconsidering on that score, Philip, though I wish you would not put it quite that way. You will find him not only to be cooperative but quite bright, truly."

"He does seem to have an exceptional grasp for one of his . . ."

"Class?" I interjected. "He was an apt student."

He laughed. "You almost sound as though you taught him yourself."

"I did."

He looked at me unbelievingly.

"It was a trade of sorts. Far too long a story to go into, but suffice it to say that Robbie was very helpful to me years ago when I first came to Camberleigh and I tutored him in return."

Philip shook his head. "You amaze me, Serena."

"Why do you say that?"

"You are a very generous woman."

"Does that surprise you?"

"Let me just say that I find it unusual."

"That sounds vaguely like a statement from a man who is used to a certain harshness in his life."

"And what if it does, my sweet?"

I studied him for a moment. "I would hate to think that of you, Philip."

"Do you mean that, Serena?"

"Of course I do."

"Then you admit you care for me, if only a little."

"Please let us not start that again. Yes, I care for you. You have been a good friend to me, Philip."

"Nothing more?"

I shook my head. "There are times, Philip, when I think this was a great mistake."

He laughed. "That is not very flattering. After all, we have only been married two days."

"You misunderstand me, Philip. What I mean is that I think that it is a mistake for you. You deserve a marriage, not an arrangement."

"I think you should let me be the judge of what I want or need, Serena."

When we got up to retire I was surprised at how late it had become. I expected Philip to go to the library for his usual brandy but found him instead taking my arm at the bottom of the staircase.

"You do not need to do this, Philip," I insisted, withdrawing my arm.

He clasped it again. "I do believe you are nervous, Serena. Is it me or is it yourself that you are afraid of?"

I was angry with myself for showing that I was flustered.

"I am not afraid of anyone," I snapped, allowing him to propel me up the stairs.

"Ah, but perhaps you should be, Serena," he retorted.

We walked in silence down the hallway until we reached the turn which would lead us to our respective rooms.

"You need not be alone this night, you know," Philip whispered.

"Good night, Philip," I replied.

I could feel his eyes on me as I moved down the hall to my room. I did not look back but moved quickly inside. I stood by the door listening until I heard his footsteps disappear.

Jaspar cocked his head as he watched me listening at the door. Satisfied that Philip had gone to his room, I relaxed and began to undress. I chastised myself for my fleeting suspicions; Philip would hardly insist himself on me. He had teased me but it was silly of me to react so to his suggestions.

I climbed into bed, cuddling Jaspar, who had snuggled in beside me. Would I ever stop missing Justin's presence beside me? Would there come a night when the ache in me would subside? I fell asleep, my questions unanswered.

I did not know what time it was when I awakened, suddenly forced out of my sleep by a dream. I had been dancing, twirling about the ballroom at Mayfair in Justin's arms. The music had come to a stop and Justin had kissed the nape of my neck. Then pulling my head back with his hand his lips covered mine. When he released me I gasped—for it had not been Justin that I had been kissing but Philip.

I lay there feeling confused and frightened. It was silly, of course, since it was only a dream but I felt that I had somehow betrayed Justin. Did I secretly want Philip to kiss me or was it that I knew that I had to face reality and accept that Justin was no longer with me. I closed my eyes trying desperately to shut out my thoughts but to no avail. When dawn came and the winter sun began to filter through the windows, I gave up trying to sleep and, lighting the candle by my bed, searched out some notepaper with which to pen a letter to Anne.

"My Dear Friend," I wrote.

*I pray that you have not heard of my news from else-where for I am certain that it will have come as a great shock to you and Richard.*

*Philip and I were married two days ago in a simple ceremony in our local chapel. Quite honestly it still seems rather unreal, even to me. I tell you, in confidence, that on my part this is not a love match. That I lost when I lost Justin. Philip has professed his love for me and hopes that in time I should return his affections. The arrangement seems less than fair for while I am gaining a mate to help me raise the children and oversee the estates he has actually gained little by marrying me.*

*The children have not warmed to the idea as much as I had thought that they would, but then it is not long since losing their father and I trust that in time they shall come to accept Philip.*

*I wanted you both to be present at the ceremony, but the strain between Philip and Richard during the holidays suggested to him that it might be awkward for them both. Philip was anxious for us to marry quickly, feeling that since he was already ensconced here at Mayfair that a hasty ceremony would be socially more acceptable. I am quite certain that both you and Richard would condone his sentiments.*

*I hope, dear Anne, that I should have your support and Richard's, as well, in this decision. I am not one, I saw quickly, to be alone. I wish that I had Monique's ability to have endured on her own lo' these many years. Perhaps if the children had been older, I cannot say. I pray that I have made the wisest decision for us all. At the time it seemed the only one.*

*Philip would like to celebrate our marriage with a ball later this spring. But in the interim I am hopeful that you and Richard might come to visit us next month for Daphne's birthday. She was so excited by the prospect of your visit that I would be loathe to disappoint her.*

*It shall be just a small gathering—hopefully, beyond the celebration, it should have reparative ends as well.*

*I close as Lady Taggart. In my heart I shall always be Lady Barkham.*

> *My Love,*
> *Serena*

The next few weeks passed relatively uneventfully. I threw myself back into working with Robbie and the ledgers. With

Philip secreted off in his quarters most of each day, I saw little of him save during the evening meals. I regretted that, actually, for I felt since we were man and wife it would behoove us to spend more time getting to know each other better. Those few evenings when at his request the children did not dine with us I endeavored to ask him things about himself, his past, his youth. On personal matters, however, Philip did not seem comfortable for he would always deftly change the conversation back to the present.

I was not prying exactly, but I was becoming increasingly aware of how little I knew of this man who was my husband. I was inherently curious by nature and his evasiveness served to pique my curiosity even further. It was during one of these dinners, in response to some query I had made into the profession of his sister's husband, that he had suddenly snapped at me.

"Really, Serena," he exclaimed, throwing down his napkin. "Must you interrogate me nightly? It is scarcely an amusing trait of yours."

"Philip, I am sorry if I have annoyed you," I replied, shocked by his tone, "but interrogation is a bit harsh a word, is it not? I only meant to try to know a little more about you. Do you realize that I am married to you, and other than knowing that you have a sister who resides outside of London, I know little or nothing else about you save your involvement in the railroad project."

The lines which had drawn about his mouth softened. "May I take that as an indication that my wife is expressing an interest in me?"

I flushed, for I knew by the tone of his voice that his question suggested far more than my intentions.

"Philip, I want us to be friends, " I began slowly. "I feel sometimes that we were closer before we were married. A husband and wife should share things. But look at us. You ferret yourself off every day doing heaven knows what. And I am no better. I bury myself in those ledgers. The one time of the day when we are together we talk *at* each other, not *to* each other. You make me feel at times that I am a guest in my own house. Even the children have noticed it. Oh, they have not said anything but I see them watching us. How can they grow close to you when I cannot do that myself?"

Philip, who had been studying me intently as I spoke, suddenly moved his chair back from the table.

"That, Serena," he said flatly, "is a decision that you, not I, have made."

Before waiting for my response he rose and left the room.

I was angered with myself for having spoken so openly. My little attempts before to get him to open up to me had been futile; I had been only foolish to expect he would react any differently when I fully confronted him.

In a sense I felt that he was bargaining with me. Only when I surrendered to intimacy with him physically would he surrender to an emotional intimacy, he seemed to suggest. What he could not know was that I had come to feel my own stirrings within me; I began to suspect that were he to drop his veil of ambiguity first, my own defenses, too, might fall away in time.

There were no other times that I pressed Philip to impart more of himself to me. From that night on, an unspoken truce seemed to have come between us. It left us with little to say to one another. Even the subject of the children's daily activities was taboo since it became readily apparent to me that Philip was neither particularly interested nor concerned with how or why they came or went.

That was perhaps the greatest surprise to me. Philip had seemed so fond of the children in London, even during his first weeks at Mayfair. And he had been good with them as well. I had expected once we were married that he would want to spend more time with them, want to have a hand in their lives. He had made such an effort to assert himself as master of Mayfair that it puzzled me that he did not seem to want to exert some influence over the children. If anything, he appeared to want as little exposure to them as possible.

One afternoon in early March I was working away in the library when there were shouts from the rooms above. At the sound of what appeared to be Daphne crying, I dropped the books I was studying and raced through the hallway up the staircase in time to see Daphne and Alexander fleeing past me with Philip striding after them, shouting at the top of his lungs. It frightened me to see how angry he looked, his eyes glassy with rage, a fist extended. I pushed myself off the balustrade and blocked his passage.

"What is this all about?" I cried, grabbing his arm.

I do not think he would have stopped, save the shock of seeing me there.

"Nothing they could have done could have spawned this much anger, Philip."

"Oh, no? Well, perhaps you do not mind their spying and snooping about, but I shall not have it, do you hear?"

"I can scarcely conjure the image of an eight-year-old and a five-year-old spying, Philip," I replied lightly.

"Well, what exactly were they doing in my quarters then?" he retorted.

I shook my head. "I cannot imagine, though I expect that they were simply curious to see your work. And if that is the reason, then I cannot criticize them too harshly for I, too, have wanted to see what it is that keeps you holed up in your quarters from dawn 'til dusk."

"I see, then, I shall suppose that you, too, have been snooping about my quarters. A normal practice for a wife, I suppose."

I commenced laughing. "Philip, please now you are just being silly. I would resent your accusation except that it is so foolish that I shall disregard it."

He shook free of my grasp. "I do not consider this a laughing matter, Serena. And I suggest that you do not, either. I should not be responsible for my actions if I ever find them near that end of the house again."

"What are you saying, Philip?" I asked cautiously.

"You heard me," he replied and turning on his heel returned to his quarters.

I admonished the children for venturing into his work area uninvited, explaining that Philip needed particular privacy to concentrate. They were so relieved that I had interceded and, I think, in truth so frightened of Philip's wrath that they agreed easily.

It struck me during these days that life at Mayfair had truly changed very little since my marriage to Philip. Our routines were the same, perhaps more regimented due to Philip's presence, but essentially I had become Lady Taggart in name only. I had no real complaints save Philip's unexpected mood swings which always seemed to catch me unawares. Yet as the days passed I could not dispel the terrible ache that loneliness brings. I had married just over a month ago and yet only once before, when I had first come to Camberleigh, had I ever felt so alone.

# 15

It was in the fifth week of our marriage that the first in a series of strange events occurred.

I had risen early one morning, making my way to the library after visiting a spell with the children. It only took me a moment to see that all the ledgers were gone. Giles professed to know nothing about it, and I determined that before I should fly into a panic I would go to the stables and check with Robbie. It seemed strange that he should remove them, but if he had I was certain he had good reason.

I found him in the stables putting hay in the stall for Medallion's colt.

"Aye did not expect to see ye down here, Miss Serena," he greeted, his pleasure made obvious by his smile. " 'Tis a cold mornin' to be walkin' about."

"It is a bit silly of me to come dashing down here, Robbie, but I went to the library this morning to do some work and I found that the ledgers had been removed. Did you transfer them by chance?"

A puzzled look came over his face. "Lord Taggart had me transfer them up to his quarters late last night. But aye just assumed that ye knew."

"He did what?" I burst out before thinking. "Never mind, Robbie. I heard what you said, though I can hardly believe it."

"Serena, aye would never 'ave done it if ay'd a thought that ye did not know. He just said it was time that he took things over, that t'was too much of a burden on ye an' all."

"It is not your fault, Robbie," I assured him, "you were only carrying out his orders. But I can assure you this is not the last of this matter. I have spent months trying to decipher and get those books in order, not to mention placing orders and overseeing the payments. I shall not have undone what it has taken me months to accomplish."

"The master would 'o been proud 'o ye, Serena. Aye do not think he could 'o done it any better."

I knew by his reference to the master that meant Justin, for in Robbie's mind as in mine, there would always only be one true master of Mayfair.

I left Robbie and stormed angrily up to the house. Philip might not like to be disturbed but this was one day that his wishes were not to be honored.

I knocked vigorously at the door to his rooms, thinking as I did that it was absurd that here in my own house I was locked away from my own husband's quarters.

"What is it?" he called out.

"Philip, it is Serena. Please open the door."

I heard him mutter something that I deemed it was best I could not understand.

It was several moments before the door opened and his tall frame enveloped the entrance.

"To what do I owe the pleasure?" he asked, smiling down at me.

"Are you going to invite me in or shall we provide fodder for servants' gossip," I replied momentarily nonplussed by his warm reception.

I do not know what I expected to find but I was amazed by the lack of clutter. This first room Philip was using as his bedroom and I decided that his work was undoubtedly being kept in the anterooms behind.

"You are looking particularly fetching today, Serena. You should wear your hair like that more often."

I flushed, smoothing it back from my face. "I was up before Charlotte had time to arrange it."

"Perhaps sleeping alone does not agree with you."

"What does not agree with me is your removing the ledgers from the library, Philip."

"Ah, so that is it."

"Is that all you have to say?"

"What do you expect me to say, Serena?"

"I expect you to offer an apology, that is what I expect."

"An apology," he exclaimed. "I should think that you would be grateful to me for relieving you of a task that should never have been a woman's in the first place."

"Philip, I do not know your intentions. Nor do I understand why you feel that I am incapable of managing these estates, but I would ask that you arrange to have the ledgers returned to the library in the state that you found them by noon today."

Instead of being remorseful, I was shocked to hear him laughing.

"I would not hold my breath if I were you, Serena."

"Why are you doing this, Philip?" I demanded angrily.

"Now—that is what I like, seeing the fire back in those eyes of yours. I remember it from that first night you burst in on me in this very room. I thought you were the most devastatingly beautiful woman I had ever seen. I still do."

"Philip, you have an infuriating habit of changing the subject, but I will not be swayed from my purpose. I want those ledgers returned."

"That may well be what you want, Serena, but it is not what is going to be done. It is I who am the master of Mayfair now. You seem not to want to recognize that fact, but I impress on you again that when you married me you did forfeit your right to instruct me about this house like some servant. I rather think that Justin would not have fancied your burying yourself each day in these ledgers while he frittered away his time elsewhere."

"Philip, the situation is entirely different and you know it," I argued.

"Only in your mind, Serena. No, the ledgers shall remain here. From now on, you need not trouble yourself with them."

I stood, my eyes transfixed on Philip. Was he taking a sadistic pleasure in this? I wondered. His expression did not belie his thoughts.

"Is that all then, Serena, or would you wish to discuss our sleeping arrangements? I would suggest to you that that is something that needs changing as well.''

He made a step towards me and I stepped back, tripping slightly against a chair.

"Stay where you are, Philip," I warned.

His eyes roved over me. "And if I do not?"

"I shall scream," I threatened.

"What— and bring the servants running? And what would you expect them to do, Serena? Stone me? Cast me out of this house? I think if you employ reason you will see that they will only be amused by a slight squabble between newlyweds."

I knew, of course, that he was right.

I straightened myself to my full height and drew a deep breath. "You may be the victor of this round, Philip, but do not think you have won the game."

"You are mistaken about only one thing, my dear Serena," he replied quietly. "This is not a game."

I was trembling as I returned to my room. I sat down near the fire, clenching at the arms of the chair. I had to get control of myself. I was consumed with anger. And yet I wondered whether I had the right to be. Had I married Philip only because I had needed help in the running of the Mayfair/Camberleigh estates? I did need a man's presence in this house. I wanted the children to have a father image to relate to. And yet instead of welcoming Philip's presence, I found myself resenting it. With Justin we had shared everything. With Philip I felt that I was being manipulated. Justin had always teased me about independence of thought, but he had encouraged it, nonetheless. Philip not only did not ask my opinion, he insisted his own upon me.

I did not broach the subject of the ledgers again with Philip over the next few days. Some part of me secretly hoped that he would recognize the mistake in his decision, but no acknowledgement or apology was forthcoming. We managed to be civil with one another, though I found Philip quieter than usual, almost as though he were preoccupied by something. I found myself somewhat at a loss with the extra time I now had on my hands. Amelie seemed to resent my intrusion in the schoolroom during the day, and although I thought that she overreacted to my presence I did not want to annoy her since I needed her full cooperation until Master Farraday returned. I was annoyed that I had had no further word from him and penned another letter to him, demanding a fixed date of his return.

It had been weeks since I had written to Anne and I was beginning to worry that she had reacted negatively to my announcement. What was even stranger, I realized, was that it had been almost a month since any correspondence had been delivered to Mayfair. Beyond the hordes of papers and business documents that I had come to expect in each post, I missed hearing from my friends. Monique, I knew, had traveled to France, but surely by now I would have had a letter from her. The same with Lilliane Kelston. And it was unlike Oliver not to have written. By now he had certainly heard the news of Justin from Anne and Richard and I longed to hear of his travels in America.

I mentioned the lack of correspondence quite by chance to Charlotte one morning while she was doing my hair.

She looked askance at me. "Aye 'avn't been noticin' that the post 'as been any less. Ye heard from Lady Camberleigh just a week ago. Aye remember seein' the letter myself. Gave it to Lord Taggart, aye did."

"Why would you give it to Lord Taggart?" I puzzled.

"Well, 'es bin gettin' all the post now fer weeks," she replied hesitantly. " 'E said ye t'weren't to be troubled by all those business matters any longer an' 'e would be takin' all the letters."

"And you followed his orders?"

" 'Tis not me place to be arguin' with Lord Taggart. An' aye be thinkin' 'ow kind it was 'o him to be takin' the burden of this place from ye, Serena."

"Why did you not come to me, Charlotte?" I pursued.

She frowned, shaking her head. "Aye did not see the need. Aye mean, aye just figured t'was the way ye was wantin' it. After all, when the master was alive 'e always took the post."

"I see," I murmured.

"Ye do not mean to tell me that ye 'avn't seen the letters, Serena?"

I shook my head.

"But why would Lord Taggart be keepin' them from ye?"

"I do not know," I replied honestly.

"T'was one from Lady Kelston as well, aye know. Aye t'weren't prying, mind ye, but aye remember ye sayin' she was in France an' this was right from Paris, it was."

I was stunned but also thoroughly befuddled. Why would Philip demand that all correspondence come to him? Even if it made some sense—since the majority of it would certainly be documents pertaining to Mayfair—why would Philip not have shared the letters from Anne and Monique with me? Surely they had been addressed to me and me alone. Did he suspect that the letters would reveal some secret information, some personal thoughts, that would be kept from him? Was this but yet another way of his impressing on me that he was the master of Mayfair?

"Serena," Charlotte said, swirling the last tendril down my shoulder, "aye know 'tis not my place but aye am worried about ye. Aye do not want ye to think that aye been talkin' behind yer back, but me Robbie told me what happened with the ledgers. Said ye were right upset. To tell ye the truth, aye was kind of relieved. 'Ere ye've been workin' yerself to the bone lo' these many months an' aye thought t'was time that ye 'ad a man to help ye with it all. Robbie, 'e 'ad a different eye on the matter. An' now with the letters, well, it just makes me be wonderin' about things."

I wanted to confide my thoughts and concerns to Charlotte, but not only did I not want to trouble her but there was no form to them. The fact that I felt that I was married to a man who was taking control of me was truly of no one's concern but my own. I was daily growing to resent his presence and yet there was a large part of me that knew I had no right to.

Philip Taggart was my husband. That I had not thought of the various implications of that before we became husband and wife was, I had to admit, not his fault. I simply had not considered the day-to-day ramifications of my decision. I was, I had to determine, as guilty as Philip. He was trying to fight a ghost, carve a space for himself, and I was desperately trying to hang onto a life as I had known it. Or was I?

Charlotte nudged my shoulder. "Ye kin talk to me, Serena," she urged. "Aye swear to ye aye not be pryin'."

I drew my arm up and patted her hand. "Dear Charlotte," I murmured, "this is simply something I need to resolve for myself."

She squeezed my hand. " 'Tis not the same fer ye these days that aye be seein'."

I buried my head in my hands. "Oh, Charlotte," I pleaded,

"will it ever be the same for me again? Each day I awake hoping that the pain will pass, and each day it is there once again. Will I never let go? Will I never truly be able to bury Justin?"

Charlotte wrapped her short full arms about me, pressing her head to the nape of my neck.

"Ye know, Serena, the one that fathered me Robbie, 'e never even knew that aye was carryin' 'is son in me belly. Oh, we were young an' 'e was only at Camberleigh a bit 'o time. Son of a tenant, 'e was. A looker, a real looker. An' swept me off me feet, 'e did. Aye be fourteen, maybe fifteen 'a the time. But aye loved the bloke, aye did. To this day aye wonder what a become 'o 'im. But by the time aye was with Robbie 'e was gone. Gone to seek his fortunes. 'E never knew 'bout me Robbie. But don't ye see that aye was blessed? Aye got me Robbie. Who knows what 'e 'as today if 'e even be alive? An' ye got Daphne an' Alexander. Aye know 'ow much ye loves those children. An' they loves ye back. Aye also be knowin' 'ow much ye loved the master. But that 'tis over, me girl. An' now ye is married to Lord Taggart. Ye kin make a life fer yerself agin but t'will never be the same. Ye goin' to 'ave to make adjustments, Serena. But not if 'e not be right fer ye. Aye be wantin' ye to be happy. But if ye not, ye should be tellin' yer Charlotte."

I listened well to her. And there was a part of me that wanted to cry out, to shriek of the turmoil that resounded within myself. I knew that I needed to unleash my thoughts to someone and yet something stopped me from doing so. What terrified me the most was the fear underneath it all.

I salved over the situation with Charlotte. This, I determined, was between Philip and myself. And yet when left to my own devices, I wondered whether all I was doing was forcing constant confrontations with my husband.

The repartee between us, as it turned out, came quickly. I left Charlotte that morning and went down to the breakfast room, where to my surprise Philip was lingering over a morning repast.

He looked up as I entered. "And to what do I owe the honor, my dear," he murmured sardonically.

I was surprised by finding him there. "There is nothing unusual about the hour, Philip," I countered, "only that you are still about."

"Are you challenging my right to be?" he cantered.

"Even if I was, were it to matter?" I replied abjectly.

"Serena, I have scarcely known you to sound so down-trodden."

"How else do you expect me to be, Philip?"

"I sense that I am to be lectured again."

"Not lectured," I responded. "Perhaps challenged."

I watched Philip's color rise. He was angry. That I knew. But his kind of anger I did not really understand. With Justin it was a passion that swelled. But it did not peak in fury. He would disagree. He could even be frustrated with me. But that had always ironically been a source of passion between us. What I felt from Philip was not passion. It was strangely and obliquely a real sense of anger.

"I would suggest, Serena, that your selection of words is inappropriate," he replied harshly. "If you have something to say, then say it. But I am scarcely about to be challenged by my own wife."

"I shall not ask you, Philip, what right you have to demand that all correspondence shall come to you and you alone; by now I understand, as you keep reminding me, that as master of Mayfair you have that right. What I do want to ask you is why you feel that you must insult me in this fashion. Do you get some kind of sadistic pleasure from pushing me aside in my own house? Is there some deep-seated need in you to control me? I honestly cannot fathom why you married me for it seems you wanted a prisoner, not a wife."

A smirk played about Philip's mouth. "Really, Serena, your sense of the dramatic overwhelms me at times. I simply left instructions that the post should be delivered to me and you sound as though I have sentenced you to the gallows."

"Why did you not give me the letters from Anne and Monique?" I demanded.

"Did I not?" he replied absently. "Then it was simply an oversight on my part."

"Do you truly expect me to believe that, Philip?"

He threw his napkin to the table. "Yes, in damnation I do, and I shall tell you another thing. I do not like the idea of Lady Camberleigh coming here and snooping about. At least her husband seems to have the good sense not to come where he is not wanted."

"How dare you even imply that Anne would pry into our affairs?" I replied angrily. "I invited them here for Daphne's birthday. I had hoped that now that we were married the differences you had could be put in the past. It was foolish of me, I know."

"Not foolish, Serena" he replied. "A bit naive perhaps. In any event, whatever you intended is not to be. Although Lady Camberleigh feigned illness as the reason Richard shall not be accompanying her, I suspect that he simply has as much distaste for me as I do for him. I, at least, have to respect the fellow's candor."

"So you are not willing to make any effort to try to become friends, if only on my behalf?"

"If you are asking me, Serena, if I can be civil when they are about, then I should answer in the affirmative. But if you are implying that I should in any way compromise myself, then I should suggest to you that you know me not at all."

I rose to leave. "I should like my letters now, Philip. Both of them and any others which had been addressed to me personally."

His eyes widened. "There were only two. I shall see that they are brought to your rooms sometime today."

Philip was true to his word, and later that afternoon one of the maids delivered the two letters to me, which I noted wryly had been addressed to me and me alone.

I opened Anne's letter first.

"Dearest Serena," I read.

> You know I am a woman to speak her mind and I will say to you at the outright that your news came as a great shock to us both. Not that I did not suspect that you would never marry again. It is, I know, what Justin would have wanted. It is only that it seemed to have happened so quickly.

> There was more, I sensed, in your letter that you did not tell me—versus what you did say—but then that makes our seeing each other at the end of this month even more important. Which is my way of saying that, of course, I shall attend Daphne's birthday fete.

> As Richard has been a mite under the weather these past weeks (nothing serious), I suspect that he shall not accompany me but then that shall simply give me more time with you alone—that is, if the new bridegroom should allow it.

*There is so much to say—the days shall not pass
quickly enough. Until the twenty-third I remain your
loving*

*Anne*

I had to admit that I shared Philip's suspicions about
Richard's "illness," but there would have been no sense to air-
ing those truths in a letter.

Monique's letter was longer and full of news of the galas in
Paris. Its lightheartedness was refreshing and I read on, allowing myself momentarily to be transported through a world of
frivolous amusement. Only one thing bothered me about the
letter. It came to a close so abruptly that I had the sense that
something was missing. She had also made no reference to
Daphne or Alexander, which was most peculiar since I knew
she adored them both. I sorted through the tissues again to be
certain that I had not mislaid them. Had someone deliberately
removed them and if so why? I knew that someone would have
to be Philip, but the likelihood made little sense to me for I
could not fathom anything that Monique might say that would
cause Philip to do such a thing. In the end I chastised myself
for my suspicions. There was a small part of me which wondered, however, if I were simply avoiding another confrontation with Philip.

I cannot explain why, but I dressed for dinner that night
with some sense of dread. Philip had taken to making it clear
that most evenings he preferred our dining alone and this was
one of them. I had objected more strenuously at first, but as
the children had seemed relieved I had not pressed it. I had
grown disheartened that Philip appeared to make so little effort with Daphne and Alexander. I could not expect him to
feel as a natural father would, but I had hoped that by now I
would see some signs of a growing interest in and caring for
one another. They did not speak ill of him nor he particularly
of them, but I almost had the sense that they had agreed
amongst each other to keep their distances. After that one day
when Alexander had cried out to defend me against Philip, he
had never done so again. But he was ever watchful and it
pained me to see so much lack of trust in such a young boy's
eyes.

I selected a gown that I had not worn about Philip before.
It was of amber-colored faille with a slightly open neckline

which was framed by ruching of the same fabric and again along the bands of the wrists and hemline. I had excused Charlotte for the evening, and after brushing my hair I simply tied it loosely off my face with a velvet ribbon, conscious as I did that it was the way Philip liked it best. I had left Jaspar with the children since I loathed locking him up in my room, and Philip had made it clear that he did not want him roaming about the house.

I had no more entered the dining room than Philip, who was already seated, called out, "Now what do you think of my bride tonight, Giles? Exquisite, is she not?"

I do not know who looked more embarrassed, Giles or myself, but his composure was better than mine for he answered readily, "Lady Taggart is indeed a woman of great beauty, your lordship."

"And therefore your lordship is a man of great taste, is he not?" Philip pursued.

"You could say that, sir," Giles replied quietly as he assisted me into my chair.

"Philip, please," I rebuked, noticing that he had quickly downed a glass of wine and was pouring himself another.

"Ah, you see Giles, that is the fateful flaw. If only this delicious creature could also be compliant, then our Maker would indeed have achieved perfection. But I sense it is simply knowing how to tame her that is the key."

I felt the color rise to my forehead. Fortunately while the food was being served Philip concentrated on downing another glass of wine.

"Do not tell me that I have embarrassed you, my dear," he slurred. "You should be complimented that I admire you so."

"I would suggest to you that most of that admiration is coming from that wine which you are rapidly depleting."

With that he called out to Giles, "Bring me another bottle, my friend."

When Giles was out of earshot I leaned forward and beseeched, "Philip, at least have the decency not to make a mockery of me in my own house."

I seemed suddenly to have struck a nerve for he quieted suddenly. "Why do you fight me, Serena?" he asked. "It would all be so much simpler for us both if you would only cooperate."

"That is an odd word to use," I mused.

"Not really," he replied, taking a sip from the glass that Giles had refilled.

"And what if I do not, as you are want to refer to it, *cooperate*?"

He frowned. His index finger slowly encircled the rim of the glass. "That would be most unfortunate for us both. You have far more to gain, at least for the moment, by showing some affection towards me. Pretend to like me if it suits you better, but I am tiring of your hostility."

"Hostility," I retorted. "Is that what you think? Good Lord, Philip, you know me not at all if that is what you believe. Do you not think I have been trying? Yes, trying," I pursued, "to make some sense out of this marriage. I cannot blame you entirely for I should have foreseen that this arrangement, if you will, was an almost impossible one. I supposed—I hoped—that it would grow in time. But how can it when I do not even know myself these days? You say that I am hostile. Only you are making me that way. I want a husband, not a keeper, particularly one that I do not even know if I can trust."

Surely I must have misread Philip's expression; in one fleeting moment I thought I caught a look of fear in his eyes. Whatever it was it vanished quickly for he suddenly commenced to laugh.

"May I ask what is so amusing?"

"You refute any hostility, Serena, and yet now you imply you do not trust me. What am I to think?"

I had no answer, only questions, in my own mind. Could Philip be right? I wondered. Were all the things I had been sensing and feeling lately been conjured up by me? But for what reason? Was I afraid not of Philip but of myself? Was I so unwilling to let go of the past that I could not accept the present?

"You have grown very quiet, my love."

"Please do not call me that," I murmured.

"Why? Because that is what your precious Justin called you? Did he murmur it to you tenderly after he had spent himself of his manhood and was lying naked in your arms?"

"I do not have to listen to this," I said, pushing myself away from the table. Philip was even quicker to rise than I. He swaggered over to me, his frame barring my way. I put my arm up to push him aside but he grabbed it instead.

"I want you, Serena," he murmured. "I have wanted you from the day I first saw you. And I give you fair warning. I am a man who gets what he wants."

I felt the blood pounding within me. I was too stunned to reply. For one fraction of a second I thought that he was going to bring me to him. I had seen the force that desire can bring to a man's countenance and there was no mistaking it in Philip.

He unhanded me as quickly as he had grabbed me. I did not wait for him to change his mind but gathered my skirts and fled the room. I was shaking when I reached my quarters and sat down for a moment to steady myself. The flames from the fire danced before me. I wished that Anne was arriving on the morrow. I could not keep to my own thoughts, I needed those of my good friend. My whole being seemed in such turmoil. Were it not for the children I should leave Mayfair, I thought, perhaps go to France and visit with Monique until I could make sense of all of this. But running away was not going to solve the pendulum of emotions that were swinging inside me. Philip had said he always got what he wanted. It was the "always" that frightened me.

I undressed and climbed into bed, wearied not from physical but emotional exhaustion. The room had never seemed emptier than it did that night. My hand stretched out across the pillow where so many nights before I had watched Justin sleeping. I shut my eyes against the tears that insisted my sadness upon me.

I do not know when it was that I awoke, but I knew that I had been startled out of my sleep. I shivered and pulled the blanket up about me. Footsteps moved towards me.

"Who is there?" I called out.

"Were you expecting another, Serena?"

I looked up and in the shadows saw Philip.

"What are you doing here?" I gasped.

"Come, come, Serena, do not be such a prig. You know perfectly well why I am here."

I knew from his speech that he was drunk.

"Philip, I demand that you leave here this instant," I choked out.

Before I could move I felt the full weight of his body on mine.

"Not this time, Serena. This time I shall do what I should have weeks ago."

"Philip, I beg of you," I whispered, feeling as though I was suffocating under his weight.

"You need not be coy with me, Serena. You want me as much as I want you. Though if you want to fight me, go ahead. I rather like a woman who fights in bed."

His hands clawed away at the covers. I threw mine up to try to push him back and realized in horror that he was naked save his shirt, which hung loosely about his chest.

The smell of brandy was so strong that the air about me seemed intoxicating. His lips came down hard on mine. And I gasped as his tongue gorged my throat.

"Take this thing off," he demanded, pulling at the collar of my nightdress.

"Philip, have some compassion. I am beseeching you not to do this," I choked out. "Leave now and we shall forget that it ever happened."

I felt a sharp pain at the back of my neck as Philip ripped the nightdress from my body. I moaned at the sound of the tearing fabric.

"It shall be much easier for you if you cooperate, Serena."

"Never," I spat back. "I shall scream if you do not take your hands off me, Philip."

"No, you won't, Serena. You are not so foolish as to humiliate yourself so. And I doubt very much that you should wish to visit your midnight hysteria on your children."

His mouth found mine again as he pulled that last vestige of my nightdress from my body. I moaned as he forced his knee between my legs prying them apart.

"There, you want this as much as I do," he whispered.

The drink seemed to have not discouraged, but rather heightened his ability, for there was no doubting the hardness that now throbbed against my leg. His hands cupped my breasts, pushing them upward towards his mouth, and he suckled them like a hungry child. I knew at that moment that I could fight him no longer. I was no match for his strength which desire had made almost demonic.

He entered me so quickly that I had not the time to brace myself against him. A searing pain spread through my groin as he swelled within me. His hands pulled my legs up high as he insisted himself deeper and deeper within me. I squeezed my eyes shut at each thrust. Sweat poured from his limbs and I felt as though it were covered in a feverish cloak. When I thought that I could not bear it any longer he brought my buttocks higher to him and began parrying even harder and deeper into me. The smell of brandy and sweat became a stench that overpowered my senses. It seemed an eternity before he was spent, doing so with a fury that seemed more animal than human. I recoiled as the warm liquid of his passion seeped from my body and onto my thighs. I lay very still, my eyes clouded by tears which streamed silently down my face. He murmured something but I could not discern it, then rolled to his side on the bed next to me.

There would be no point, I knew, in trying to get him to leave. To rouse him now would only serve to awaken his desires again, although now that he had done with me perhaps he would be satisfied at least for tonight. I shivered and reached down at the end of the bed where my robe had fallen. I drew it about me and moved carefully over before the fire. I turned and watched Philip's body silhouetted by the firelight as it rose and fell in rhythm to his breath. I had not covered him, and though it was cold in the room I cared not whether he died of exposure this night.

The amount of anger that raged inside me frightened me. I felt nothing but loathing for this man who lay before me. This man who was now my husband. I did not know how I could have been so mistaken about him. Philip had accused me of naiveté and I had to admit he was right. I had honestly believed that he cared for me enough to have patience with me. I had only myself to blame in the end for it was my own lack of belief in myself that had driven me to accept his proposal in the first place. That, and my dread of finding myself and the children alone with no man about to comfort and guide us. I had known it was a ridiculous bargain from the first. That I had truly believed that we could go on this way day-by-day trying to make polite conversation with one another now seemed hopelessly absurd. I could not have foreseen it ending this way—with another man perhaps—but I had never anticipated that Philip would violate me, not in this fashion. He had been provocative, suggestive at times, there was no denying. But not once had I suspected that he would put his words into action. Had I truly believed that this man would be celibate until one magical day, a year, two years hence, when my own needs would undoubtedly have driven me to him? The anger that I felt towards Philip perhaps was in part misdirected, for some shame had to be borne by myself. But he had taken me wantonly, drunkenly, against all my protestations and there would be no forgiveness in me.

I was overwhelmed by a sense of loss. The loss of my beloved Justin, the loss of any hope I had had of building a new existence. There was a hopelessness about it all. And where could I turn? To Anne and Richard? I thought not. I had made my bed and I would lie in it. But I would lie in it alone. I cared not if Philip found release in another but his presence would never darken this room again. He had professed love for me. But this was not love that he expressed here this night. Lust, need perhaps, but not love. I would keep up pretenses but only for the sake of the children. I vowed not to let my own dreadful mistake have a bearing on their lives. And Philip no doubt would soon tire of Mayfair. No matter how hard he tried, he would never understand the land or grow as one with the farmers and the harvests. Once the railroad project was complete, he would, I sensed, return to London. There were women I knew who would thrill to the sight of this man. The skin was taut about his limbs, which were long and sinewy. His maleness, even in passivity, swelled large between his legs. Had the other women he had seduced been left feeling as empty as I? I wondered.

I turned away as he struggled to sit up.

"What are you doing sitting over there, Serena?"

"I am waiting for you to get up and leave me be," I replied.

" 'Tis hardly a way to greet your husband, my dear. You really must learn to be more respectful, Serena."

"The only thing I need to learn, Philip, is how to live with a man whom I find loathsome."

He laughed. "Your choice of words has always amused me."

"Have you no remorse, Philip? Is there no shred of decency in you?"

He rose and began gathering his clothes, which were spread about the room. "Please, Serena, I am in no mood for a lecture. My head feels as though it will split open and the last thing I need is your shrewishness. Now, if you were to suggest that we return to bed, I should be more than pleased to accommodate."

"You disgust me. You enter my bedroom while I am asleep and take me as you would some whore and then you suggest that I should want you to repeat your performance? You have more gall than I assumed."

"Ah, ah, those are harsh words for a woman of such gentility, my dear."

"Philip, I want you to listen to me and listen well, for I shall say this only once."

He appeared to ignore me, continuing to put his clothes on.

"This door shall be locked from now on. You have had your way with me this once but only this once. What might once have been between us is no longer. You proposed to me when I was in a most vulnerable state. I cannot blame you for that. But I trusted you, Philip, and you have destroyed that trust. I will be a wife to you in every way but one. I should expect that you will seek another, perhaps many, for your more prurient needs. I ask only that you do so with some discretion since I will not have my name or those of my children slurred about."

I paused for some reaction. "Have you heard me, Philip?"

"Oh, I have heard you, my dear. A pretty little speech but of no consequence to me. You are my wife, Serena, and I expect you to fullfill your obligations to me in every sense of the word. You are a very beautiful and desirable woman. And although you would seem to deny it, you are a woman of great passion. You will come to want me as much as I do you, so do not test me too far. Last night was a beginning, Serena, not an ending. A locked door is meant to be unlocked. One need only obtain the key. I will add only one thing. Do not get any ideas about discussing this with anyone, particularly Lady Camberleigh. It should prove very embarrassing to us both and I sense that one day you should regret what you might say."

"I shall remain silent only as long as you keep your part of the bargain, Philip. And although it would be a source of some embarrassment for me, I should also remind you that my uncle is a man of considerable power. I should not want to be in your shoes if he in the slightest way thought that you were mistreating me."

Philip looked at me angrily. "Do not threaten me, Serena. I warn you. Do not threaten me."

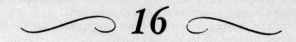

# 16

The next three days I moved about as though I were in a dream. Everything seemed to take on an air of unreality. The only apparent vestiges left from that night were the bruises about my neck, which I realized had come from having the chain bearing Justin's ring torn from me than from the night-dress. Something told me that I should be relieved that Philip had been too intoxicated to have noticed it, for his ardor would certainly have mixed with his anger. Charlotte believed me when I told her that I had decided to wear my hair loose for a while. I hated lying to her but she was too smart not to have suspected that something was awry. I tried desperately not to show my nervousness around Philip or the children, though I could not seem to relax. I jumped at the sound of Philip's voice, and though he made no move towards me I was watchful of him at every turn.

My door was locked nightly, but even that gave me no assurance. I would lie in my bed at night, my eyes transfixed on the handle. Try as I did, I could not sleep. When I would finally drift off, it would only be to awaken suddenly suspicious that something, someone, had brought me out of my reverie.

I rose on the fourth day after the incident determined to snap myself out of this semi-stupor in which I found myself. Anne would be arriving in several days and I wanted everything to go smoothly for Daphne's birthday party, small as it would be. I was about to do down for breakfast when, past the staircase towards the nursery, I heard a commotion. Jaspar who was at my heels barked in response and scurried down the hall. I followed quickly behind, wondering what could have incited such a ruckus. A sense of panic spread over me as I recognized Philip's voice booming in anger. I reached the door and flung it open. Philip was standing over Alexander, who cowed beneath an arm raised as if to strike him.

"What is going on here?" I demanded, running forth to put myself between Philip and the child.

"Amelie—Miss Wythe—has told me that this young wimp here has refused to take his lessons."

"I would doubt that, Philip, but if he did there must be a good reason."

"The only reason is that you have spoiled him to excess. She tells me that he is impudent and that both children have no discipline."

"Is that true, Miss Wythe?" I asked.

"If you will pardon my saying so, Lady Taggart, I have never had charges who were so difficult. I cannot continue to teach children who do not want to be taught. They are unruly and painfully slow, I fear."

"Miss Wythe, I find that amazing since their tutor, Master Farraday, has always commented that he finds both my children to be exceptionally bright. I would scarcely defend them on this score simply because they are my children, but I should suggest to you that perhaps it is your tutelage that they find uninspired. I cannot think what has delayed further word from Master Farraday, but hopefully he shall return soon and you need not trouble yourself any longer with my 'difficult' children. For now may I suggest that you take the rest of the morning off. Perhaps by the afternoon you will feel refreshed and your conclusions shall have changed."

I signaled for the two children to come with me, which they did readily. I said not a word to Philip as we left. I would later, but I did not want the children to hear what I had to say to him. It was hard to know if Philip had only meant to frighten Alexander or whether he actually would have struck the boy if I had not arrived on the scene. The latter thought frightened me more than any sense of what Philip might do to me personally. If for one moment I thought that Philip might be abusive to either child, I should gather them and leave Mayfair this very day.

There are always two sides to a story and the one I extracted from the children was far different than the one presented by Philip and Amelie.

"I must ask you this, Alexander," I said, once breakfast had been served. "Have you been rude or impudent with Miss Wythe?"

A shadow crossed his eyes and he looked down to avoid my gaze.

"By your lack of response, am I then to assume that her accusations are correct?"

When he did not reply, I continued, "Then I am sorely disappointed in you."

He looked up at me, the hurt in his eyes painfully obvious.

"I have no recourse but to punish you, Alexander."

Daphne, who had remained totally silent during this exchange, suddenly blurted out "Mama, you cannot, t'was not Alexander's fault. Truly it was not."

"Then what is the truth?" I posed.

"Amelie is not like she was when she first came here," Daphne pursued. "She was nicer then and she did more with us. Now she just makes us sit in the schoolroom all day. It is too boring for words and Alexander told her so."

"Do you mean to tell me that she is not doing your lessons with you?"

"Not like Master Farraday does," Daphne replied. "She just makes us sit there all day. And then she leaves."

"What do you mean she leaves."

She shrugged. "She just tells us to sit there and then she goes away. She told us that if we told we would be punished."

"Is that true, Alexander?"

He nodded mutely.

I excused myself and told the children to remain downstairs until I had had an opportunity to talk to Amelie.

I found her in her room. If I had expected her to be somewhat wary of me after the row earlier, I was sorely surprised, for there was instead an air of haughty indifference about her.

"Miss Wythe, I have just had a conversation with the children, which proved very distressing to me."

She looked up at me, her dark eyes emotionless.

"I know that you were only hired here as a governess and that you assumed tutoring of the children to assist me while Master Farraday was away. And perhaps I was mistaken for entrusting you with so much responsibility, but our arrangement simply does not seem to be working out. I had thought that you and the children had a rapport, but this morning's unfortunate confrontation leads me to conclude that you might be happier elsewhere."

"Are you telling me that you are dismissing me?" she asked incredulously.

I nodded. "There does not seem any reason to drag this out, Miss Wythe. You made it very clear earlier how you feel about the children and I fear that it would be difficult to change that. I want you to know that I will provide the best of references to you and I will see that you are amply compensated so that you shall not have to worry until you find another position. There has been no unpleasantness between us and I do not want you to suffer from your stay here at Mayfair."

"I have hardly suffered, Lady Taggart," Amelie replied wryly. "Might I ask if you have discussed this decision with your husband?"

"I scarcely think that is any business of yours, Miss Wythe, but no, I have not."

"I would suggest that you do," she replied coolly.

Her impudence shocked me momentarily.

"This is not a matter I need discuss with Lord Taggart, Miss Wythe. I make the decisions when it comes to my children."

"Do you, Lady Taggart? I would remind you that it was your husband who brought me to Mayfair. If I am to be dismissed, I should like it to be from the one who engaged me in the first place."

"I had hoped that we could do this easily, Miss Wythe," I replied curtly, "but I see not. My husband shall be informed of your dismissal this evening. I would not count on his countering my wishes and thus I would suggest that you commence packing today. I shall arrange with our driver to take you to the coach returning to London within the next day or two."

I left the room painfully aware of Amelie's stare following my exit. Her assurance that Philip would take her plight disturbed me, not only because I resented her impudence but because there was an unexplainable fear that Philip would counter my decision. He had indeed brought her to Mayfair and would, I supposed, champion her staying. My task, I determined, would be much easier if Master Farraday had returned to Mayfair. If only he would write, then perhaps I could assure Philip that Miss Wythe was no longer needed.

The afternoon was spent working with Charlotte and Cook in preparation for Daphne's birthday party. I was exhausted from my lack of sleep but I could not rest, for rest today meant thinking and that was the last thing I wanted to do. Charlotte was particularly watchful of me, sensing I knew that there was more than this party on my mind. I did not tell her of my decision about Amelie for I wanted to apprise Philip first. I knew that she would approve, however, since from the first she had not been fond of Amelie. I had thought then that jealousy had been an issue, but today I was more prone to thinking that she simply had known instinctually that Amelie was not right for Mayfair.

As it turned out I did not have to broach the subject of Amelie with Philip that evening since he raised the issue as soon as the meal was served.

"I understand that you have taken it upon yourself to dismiss Amelie," he stated.

"Philip, it simply is not working out. I spoke with the children after the row this morning and learned that she has not even been spending time with them. Until Master Farraday returns I can take over their lessons."

"She is staying," he retorted abruptly. "I am quite convinced that Miss Wythe is handling those children properly. A half year has passed since their father's death and you must stop pampering them. They are overindulged and Amelie at least brings some discipline to this house."

"Philip, this is one instance where I shall not allow you to make the decision," I replied angrily. "You have made it very clear that you can do what you want with me but you cannot with my children. If I am guilty of overcompensating due to Justin's death, then so be it, but they are not going to be governed by someone in whom I have no confidence. Master Farraday is an excellent teacher. Even you, I think, shall find him suitable."

"I do not think that you have heard me, Serena," Philip replied angrily. "I have no intention of allowing you to dismiss Miss Wythe. And as far as your Master Farraday, he shall not be returning to Mayfair."

"What do you mean?"

"I have notified him that his services were no longer needed here. He was compensated nicely, I might add."

I was incredulous. "You mean you took it upon yourself to write to him and tell him not to return without consulting me?"

He shrugged. "I find Amelie more suitable."

"That is all you have to say?"

"Ah, what a clever bride I have," he mocked. "Really, Serena, you are going to get yourself in quite a state if you continue to try and counter my decisions. It shall be much pleasanter as I have told you if you simply do not insist on living in the past. You *were* Lady Barkham. You *are* Lady Taggart and I expect my wife to be grateful that she has a husband who is in charge."

"In charge?" I spat back. "Is your abusing me, manipulating me, dictating to me your idea of something I should appreciate?"

"Do not push me, Serena."

"Do not push you," I scoffed. "Do you not see what you are doing to me, Philip, or do you not care?"

"You know, Serena, you had best get a hold on yourself. That melodious voice of yours is becoming quite shrill and you look very tired. Perhaps you need a rest after all. What would you say if we were to plan a holiday, let us say, next month? Paris might be amusing. A change of scenery might do you good."

"I have no need for a rest, Philip," I assured him. "And as for a holiday I may have to live with you but I do not have to travel with you."

"We shall see about that, my dear."

"We shall see about nothing," I retorted, pushing my chair back from the table. "Good night, Philip."

It was hours before I fell asleep that evening. Philip, I concluded, was right about one thing—I did need a change. I could not continue this way but, try as I did, I saw no escape. I could perhaps take the children and go to London but that was simply not an answer. Philip would follow me—of that I was certain—and it would only prove disruptive to the children. I certainly was not gaining ground by fighting him and yet I could not simply give over to his demands. Talking to Anne, I knew, was the direction I should take, but some small voice inside me advised caution.

When I went to the nursery the next morning I was relieved to find a scene of some tranquillity. Amelie said not a word but I did not mistake the smirk that played about her lips as she wished me good morning. I had not thought this was a contest but it was clear that she thought herself the victor.

"When shall Aunt Anne arrive?" Daphne asked.

"Later today, I suspect."

"Do you think she will bring me some new dresses?"

"Do not be too disappointed if she does not," I cautioned. "She was most generous with you at Christmastime."

"Is Uncle Richard coming?" Alexander asked.

I shook my head.

"Why not?"

"I do not think he has been well these past weeks."

Turning to Amelie, I continued, "Might I see you in the schoolroom for a moment?"

"Of course, Lady Taggart."

When we were out of earshot from the children I turned to her. "I gather that my husband has spoken to you."

"He has."

"I do not like deceptions, Amelie. I am not going to stand here and tell you that I concur with my husband's decision. I am not at all certain that this is good for the children or for you. As he has dismissed their tutor, the responsibility of the children's lessons must fall somewhere. I suggest that henceforth we share it, you and I. Since I understand that you have not been present most afternoons, you will not resent my intrusion. I suspect that you will welcome it. But during those hours that you are with them I expect you to make an effort to relate to them. Do we understand one another?"

The planes of Amelie's face were stony still. "Yes," she complied. From her tone I was doubtful. I sensed that she wanted to say more but she did not. I wished that the relationship had developed differently for we were not so disparate in age that we could not have become friends under different circumstances; now, though, it was unlikely that that would ever happen.

I was in my room writing a letter to Monique when Anne arrived. There was great commotion in the entrance hall and I gathered Jaspar and ran down to greet her.

The sight of her lifted my spirits enormously.

"Dear Serena," she called out as I ran into her arms. "Too thin, my dear, far too thin," she exclaimed as she drew back to study me. "That will never do for I have brought you new gowns based on the old Serena I knew. I expect that husband of yours has been making too many demands of his bride."

"Not at all, Lady Camberleigh."

I looked up to see Philip poised at the base of the stairs.

"Ah, I have been overheard," Anne laughed. "Richard always says that I should cast about for my audience before opening my mouth."

"Not at all," replied Philip, coming forth smiling broadly. "It is lovely to see you again."

I watched him, amazed at the charm that Philip could exude when he wanted to.

"I owe you my congratulations, Philip," she replied. "I need not tell you that I think you are a very lucky man."

"That is right," Philip replied, slipping his arm about my waist. "I have everything a man could ask for."

I had grown rigid under his touch and quickly stepped forward. "Why do we not go into the library?" I suggested, moving Jaspar off my heels with Philip and Anne following.

"Oh, that fire feels good," Anne enthused. "It was dreadfully cold in the carriage."

"Well, then, considering Richard's health it was wise that he did not try to make the journey," Philip mused.

Anne looked embarrassed at Philip's all too pointed comment.

"Serena, I am ashamed of you. You have not said one thing about my new chapeau. What do you think?"

"It is . . ." I paused, searching for the right word.

She laughed. "Richard calls it outrageous," she said, removing the broad-brimmed velvet hat which sported a braid of boa about the crown, "but you wait, it shall be the rage by fall, I predict."

I smiled at her enthusiasm. It seemed months since I had thought about anything so mundane as a hat.

"Now where are those precious children?" she pursued.

"In the schoolroom, I should hope," Philip replied.

"Well, that is scarcely a welcome for their only aunt. Come, Serena, let us go and surprise them."

I was amazed when Philip followed us upstairs. He certainly was not interested in the children. I had a sense that he simply did not want to leave Anne and I alone. Why? Because I would reveal my plight to her, that I would admit this marriage had been an enormous mistake? I wanted to tell him that he need not shadow me for the next few days for I had no intention of speaking the truth to Anne. She was my dearest friend but I would not confide even in her of the cruelties, both mental and physical, that I had suffered at the hands of my husband these last weeks. There was nothing that she could do save sympathize with me and chastise me for marrying him in the first place.

Daphne and Alexander squealed with delight when they saw Anne.

"Goodness, the two of you have grown so that Oliver shall scarcely recognize you when he returns home this summer."

"Then you have heard from him?" I asked eagerly. "I had been hoping for a letter, but I am certain he is busy. There must be so much to see."

"You do not mean to tell me that you have not had a letter from him, Serena."

I shook my head.

"I cannot understand it. This is the second letter we have received and he distinctly said that he had written to you immediately upon learning of Justin."

"Perhaps it was lost," I said, noticing that Philip was watching me warily.

Had a letter indeed been delivered? I wondered. And had he deliberately kept it from me?

"Likely it was lost," Philip said quickly. "You know how the post is."

"Well, that makes me doubly glad then that I brought his latest along with me," she replied, opening her reticule and withdrawing the large envelope. "Come sit by me," she motioned to the children, "while I read it."

" 'Dear Father and Anne,' " she commenced.

> " *'I am still incredulous over the loss of Justin. It pains me to be here when I know how difficult this must be for you all. Particularly Serena.'* "
> She paused for a moment. "Philip, Oliver does not know, I mean about the marriage. I hope . . ."
> "Read on," he said quickly. "It is of no import to me."
> I nodded for her to continue.
> " *'Which is why,'* " she read on, " *'I have decided to return to England in June. She cannot possibly manage*

*the estates on her own, even with Robbie about—though
I know of no woman who would make a better go of it.
Simply it is too much for her to handle with the children
and all. And Father, I know your heart has never been in
it so if you were to step in it would be of no benefit to
anyone.*

'*I know you would say that I seem an unlikely candi-
date, but these many months away from England have
really only served to show me how much I miss it.*

'*Then there is another matter. I have met a girl. A
wonderful girl whom I have asked to marry me. And to
my amazement she has accepted. Her name is Rebecca
Trenton-Worth and she is the daughter of a sea captain.
We met in Boston (a long story which I shall spare you in
this letter). The last thing on my mind when I journeyed
here was marriage but then I had not yet met Rebecca.
You shall adore her, I know, you cannot help but.*

'*I wish that we could be married at Camberleigh, but
her father is not about to allow me to whisk his daughter
off to a foreign land without first making her my bride—
so I shall do just that in a small ceremony here in Boston
on the first of June. I have already booked our passage
back to London and cannot wait to see you all.*

'*I know that Serena will think that my return to help
her manage the estates is because I feel that I must, but
please assure her that my motives are largely selfish. I
would not have traded these past months for anything,
but as it was time for me to set out on my own, it is now
time to return to where I know I belong. So barring any
unexpected turn, I shall see you all again towards the end
of the summer.*

"*I pray that all is well with you. My love to you all and
give Daphne a special hug for me when you see her.*

*Your Son,
Oliver*"

I looked up in time to catch Philip murmur something to
Amelie, who had seated herself beside him.

Catching my gaze, he said quickly, "Well, it looks as
though there is to be another wedding in the family."

"Oh, there is a postscript," Anne continued.

" '*P.S. I inquired after Justin with the captain of the*

*ship on which he had sailed. Oddly, he had no record in his log of Justin being a passenger on the ship. I insisted that he must be mistaken but I did not push it. The poor chap had been ill himself and was not in any condition for my badgering. There is nothing that can be done now, I suppose, save trying to find out any information I can for Serena on the tragedy. In any event Rebecca's father knows the man and he has promised to follow up on it.'*"

I was dumbfounded. "Why would there be no record of Justin being on the ship?" I insisted. "Surely there was a passenger log; it should have been a simple thing to trace it."

"You forget, my dear," Philip said quickly, "Justin was traveling under an assumed name. Oliver could not have known that."

"I had forgotten," I replied.

"What on earth did he do that for?" Anne asked.

"Given who he was, we thought it best," Philip replied.

"It seems senseless to me, but then the whole thing seemed senseless. Anyway," she continued, putting her arms about Daphne, "there is your special hug."

"I don't want it," Daphne said, struggling free.

"Daphne, that isn't nice," I warned.

"I don't care," she pouted.

"She is just mad because she thought Oliver was going to marry her," Alexander offered.

"That is enough," I said, silencing what I knew was pathetically the truth.

"I bet she is big and ugly with pop eyes and crooked teeth," Daphne challenged.

"I scarcely would expect so," I answered, "but even if she is not a beauty on the outside I am certain, since Oliver loves her, that she is beautiful on the inside—which finally is more important."

"By the time you are ready for marriage, Daphne," Anne offered, "you will probably think your cousin Oliver to be old and boring."

"I will not," she insisted.

"That is enough," Philip interjected. "I want you to apologize, Daphne, and then both of you get back to your lessons."

Anne looked up in surprise. "She meant no harm, Philip."

"Daphne has to learn that what she does and what she

means must be one and the same," he said sternly. "Are you coming, ladies?"

I knew better than to argue with Philip. I rose and moved toward the door. "Come, Anne, I'll show you to your room."

She followed Philip and myself out into the hallway. When we reached the room where Anne always stayed I opened the door for her and she went in. I was about to follow when Philip called out.

"Anne, you will not mind if I steal Serena away from you for awhile? There are a few things I must discuss with her."

She stepped back into the doorway. "Of course not, but I do insist that you allow us some time together. We do not get to visit that often and you know women—we are blessed with the gift of gab."

He nodded. "We will see you at dinner then."

When Anne was safely in her room I turned to Philip and whispered. "What was that ruse about? We have nothing to say to one another."

"Ah, but we do, my dear," he replied, pulling on my arm. "I want to talk to you in the library."

"You may say whatever you have to say to me right here, Philip."

He looked at me angrily. "At least come down the hall then."

I could scarcely not follow him for he pulled me bodily in step.

"What is it about, Philip?" I insisted.

"I do not want you gossiping to Anne while she is here."

"If you are warning me not to tell Anne that I find myself trapped in a miserable marriage to a man I have only loathing for—then have no fear."

"You are trapped, Serena, only in that you will not let go of the past. I watched you there in the schoolroom when that letter was read. At the very mention of Justin's name you looked as though you were being transported to some remote space where no one can reach you. It is not healthy, this obsession you have with the past."

"I have no obsession with the past, Philip. And I do not like your inferring that I am mentally unbalanced because a letter from Oliver brings back many memories. If I appear preoccupied or nervous, it is only because you have made me that way.

You are right about one thing, Philip. I am not myself. But you can take the credit for that. And now if you have finished I am going to my room.''

"Just remember what I have said, Serena."

Jaspar, who had stayed close to me during this exchange, barked suddenly and I bent down to quiet him. When I had straightened, Philip had moved off down the hallway towards his quarters. I was almost tempted to return to Anne's room for I longed to visit with her, but I could not chance Philip discovering us; his anger would prove too embarrassing for us all.

I lay down trying to rest before dinner but could not push my thoughts and fears from my mind. Charlotte arrived to help me with my hair, which I allowed since the bruises on my neck had all but disappeared. I selected a silk faille gown, one of Anne's creations, for the evening. I was painfully aware of how pale I had grown over these past months and I hoped its rosy color would serve to heighten my pallor.

When I reached the library I realized that Philip and Anne were already there. I might have imagined it, but both seemed to grow suddenly silent at the sight of me. It was Philip who spoke first.

"You look charming tonight, Serena. Do you not agree, Anne?"

She smiled. "I fear I am prejudiced. I should use that color more often for you."

"I scarcely need more gowns," I assured her. "We are very quiet here these days."

"I have suggested to Serena that we commence giving some parties again, in the late spring," Philip offered.

A shadow crossed Anne's face. "Do you not think that would be a bit premature? It is none of my business, of course, but it is not that long since we lost Justin. I have never been to adhere to appearances only, but I do think it might prove awkward."

She was right, of course, but I said nothing.

"You know I have just the idea," she pursued. "I shall plan a ball at Camberleigh to celebrate Oliver's marriage and we can make it a dual celebration of sorts. How does that sound?"

I knew that Philip was none too thrilled but said quickly,

"That is a most generous thought, Anne, but we should not want to intrude on Oliver's special time."

"The first person who would insist on it would be Oliver."

"Well, we need not worry about this now," Philip said quickly. "I do not know about you two, but I am hungry."

"Are the children not joining us?"

"Philip prefers to dine alone," I replied.

She looked between the two of us. "Of course. One forgets what it is like to be newly married."

I bit my tongue as Philip escorted us to the dining room.

If I did not know better I would have sworn that it was Philip's double who hosted the meal that evening. He was loquacious, even amusing. I could not blame Anne for warming to him, and yet I resented this deception he was forcing me to perpetrate on her.

When we retired that night, I could not fight a feeling of hopelessness which preoccupied me. Anne, bless her, was trying to make an obvious effort to bury past feelings and accept Philip as my husband. And Philip was doing an effective job at convincing her that our marriage was a wise union.

The sun's rays peeked through the draperies early the next morning. I rose and dressed quickly, anxious to gather all Daphne's gifts together and take them downstairs. I had planned a large breakfast with sausages, eggs, smoked ham and her favorite biscuits.

I knocked on Anne's door before descending below. The night prior she had bade me to awaken her early so that she could gather her gifts and get them downstairs before Daphne arose.

I was surprised when she opened the door.

"I know it is a shock to you to see me up and about. I was afraid that you might forget so I had one of the maids waken me an hour ago. Just let me get my packages."

"Good gracious," I gasped, "those cannot possibly all be for Daphne."

She winked. "Of course not. The big ones here are yours."

"Anne, you should not have," I chastised.

"Nonsense, I wanted to do something for you, and frankly I could not come up with a gift that seemed suitable. For your marriage, that is."

"I have everything I need, Anne."

"Well, you seem to have a husband who adores you. Of course, well he should."

I picked absently at the braiding along my skirt.

"If you do not open the packages, I shall do it for you," she said, thrusting the largest onto my lap.

I apologized. "My mind does not seem to have direction these days." I opened the box and gasped as I pulled out a white gown. Fashioned of silk taffeta, it was adorned with what seemed a thousand tiny pearl-drop pendants about the bodice and skirt. The neckline, dropped low in the front, was bordered by a scallop of heavy Alençon lace. There were no sleeves save two large bows of the same lace with a cap of the taffeta which carried the dress at the shoulder.

"Well?" Anne asked.

"It is divine," I murmured.

"You know, when I started it I had no idea about Oliver's marriage, but now it should be perfect for the ball I intend to give. Open the other box."

I did as she bid and pulled out a lacy shawl fashioned of silky white and gold threads with knotted fringes along the circumference. I held the softness of it up to my cheek and was embarrassed as tears escaped suddenly from my eyes. I dabbed them away with a corner of the shawl.

"Goodness, Serena, my designs used to bring radiant smiles to that beautiful face of yours. What are these tears that I see?"

"It is nothing—I am just grateful for your gifts, of course, but also your friendship."

Anne sat down suddenly on the bed beside me.

"Why is it that I hear what you are saying to me but I do not believe it, Serena? I sense that something is wrong, but I cannot put my finger on it."

I shook my head. "I am just being sentimental."

"Perhaps. But that does not explain to me why I feel a certain remoteness, a certain sadness about you. We have known each other too long. Perhaps talking to me would help."

I longed to cry out to her but shook my head instead. "I am just tired," I pleaded.

"Philip told me that you have not been yourself lately. He seems genuinely worried about you, Serena. He even asked my advice about getting the doctor out here to take a look at you.

I must say I championed the idea."

"You have been working so hard of late. It would ease my mind to know that nothing is amiss."

"I am not sick," I insisted.

"Perhaps, but you will have to go far to convince me that something is not wrong. I have to admit to you that Richard was put out when you did not reply to his inquiries. There were some rather important decisions to be made about the estates and I had to agree that I expected you to respond."

I silently gathered that these were letters that Philip had decided should also be kept from me, but I covered my suspicion by saying that we had had trouble with the post.

"You know, Anne," I pursued, "Richard should really be in touch with Philip now about Mayfair. Since we married, he felt that it would be best if he assumed the overseeing of the estates."

"Well, I can understand, I suppose, his wanting to become involved," Anne replied. "I mean, he is your husband now. But certainly you would not blithely turn the guardianship over to him."

"He has been quite insistent," I said quietly.

"Are you telling me that you simply capitulated?" Anne gasped.

I fell silent. I wanted to defend my actions to explain that I had little choice since Philip had been careful to remove even my access to the ledgers but I did not want to trouble Anne even further. She would be incensed, I knew, and challenge his authority, and I was loathe to experience his wrath.

"I assume from your lack of response that the answer is yes," Anne continued. "I must tell you that I am shocked. Richard worried about this very thing. I, of course, came to your defense for I could not believe that you would do anything so foolish. Serena, you had no right to do this. Oh, it is your money. You have rightly inherited it. But your grandfather and my father wanted Mayfair and Camberleigh to be run as the merged estates they are. Before you arbitrarily handed the authority over to Philip, I think you owed it to Richard to discuss it with him first."

I had never seen Anne as angry as she now was. She was right, of course, but she was supposing that I was dealing with a reasonable situation.

"If only you had come to me or to Richard at the first,

Serena. Do you not see that by excluding him you will only serve to anger him further. He is not, as you know, terribly fond of Philip. Frankly, I had hoped with time that the two might resolve their differences. But this is going to drive an even deeper wedge, I fear."

I looked up at Anne. The wedge that she referred to was being driven not only between Philip and Richard but between Anne and myself. She would not forgive me this judgment, I knew. Of course it was a perceived judgment for I could not feel that her decision was just. But I could not do anything to dissuade her without putting too much at risk.

She shook her head suddenly and I called out to her.

"What is it, Anne?"

"I simply cannot believe that you, of all people, would have done this. Believe me, it is not as Justin's sister that I speak to you but as your dear friend. This is not like you, Serena. You are brighter, far more reasoned, than you seem at present. Which is why I have to insist that you are either unwell or that there is something that you are keeping from me."

If I had ever felt myself weakening it was at that moment. I had allowed myself to become so intimidated by Philip over the past months that I realized suddenly that all I need do was to admit my foibles and fears to Anne. The worst that could happen would be that finally my vulnerability would be laid bare.

"Anne," I broached, "I cannot blame you for what appearances seem but it is not . . ."

I had not heard the door open.

"It is not what, Serena dear?"

I turned to see Philip looming in the doorway threshold.

"What has my beautiful bride been telling you, Anne?" he continued. "If it is that I cannot bear to have her out of my sight, then I admit that I am guilty."

"Not at all," Anne replied coolly. "Quite frankly, Serena has just been telling me that you have taken over the management of the estates."

"And that troubles you, I imagine."

"I have never been one to mince words, Philip," Anne replied, "and I do not intend to start now. These estates were started by Barkhams and Camberleighs and that is by whom I think they should be run. I am certain, Philip, that you have great resources when it comes to inventing railroads and things of the like. But I have heard even *you* admit that you could care less about agriculture. These estates do not run themselves, you know. It takes work, hard work."

"Which is precisely why I took over, Anne," Philip insisted. "Serena was working herself into a frenzy over this. Look at her, does she seem well to you? She is exhausted, poor thing. I may not have the interest, as you put it, but at least I have the strength. Or would you propose that Richard carry the burden himself?"

I was captivated by Philip's little speech. Had I not known that every ounce of it was a lie, I would have been quite charmed by it myself.

Anne rose and quickly came over to me, putting her arm about my shoulders. "Then I was right, Serena, you have not been well."

"I am fine, truly," I insisted, daring not to look at Philip.

"She has been very brave for all our sakes," Philip insisted, "but certainly you can see for yourself why I had to wrest the burden from her."

Anne nodded. "Of course. But I must forewarn you that that is not going to ease Richard's mind. Perhaps in time the two of you will see your way clear on each other, but he is a stubborn man, Philip, and one with mighty convictions. In any event Oliver shall be returning this summer and then none of this should concern us any longer. I am certain that I can convince Richard that this is the best solution until then. Now come along both of you; we have a young lady downstairs who, I am certain, is wondering where we have got to on her birthday."

The look on Philip's face told me that he knew that he had been victorious. I doubted very strongly that he would sit still for being moved aside when Oliver returned. But that was months away, and if I knew Philip, I would wager that by then he would have found a way to ingratiate himself with Richard.

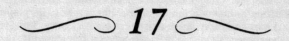

# 17

The day passed pleasantly enough all in all. Daphne was feted from morning till night, when Cook had prepared her favorite supper of curried veal stew and cornmeal cakes. Anne had brought her several dresses suitable for when the weather warmed to spring again as well as a coat fashioned of burgundy velvet with small bands of ermine about the wrists and skirt. I thought it far too extravagant for a girl her age, but then when I was nine I would have simply been delighted by a garment that was meant to fit and not grow into.

Philip stayed with us the whole of the day. At first it surprised me but then I was increasingly aware that he was loathe to leave me alone with Anne. Admittedly, had he not interrupted us earlier in the day, I would likely have succumbed under Anne's pressuring. I was threatened by Philip's warning, but I wondered how long I could sustain this farce. When he wanted to, Philip was able to exude great charm and I could see that his deception was having no small effect on Anne. It was only Alexander who I noticed was not dissuaded by Philip's ebullience, choosing instead to be quietly watchful.

We retired early that evening. I was devastated when Anne insisted that she had to return early the next morning to see to Richard but I suspected that that was only part of the truth. I was not insensitive to the fact that it was difficult to be here at Mayfair, the house where she had spent all save the last ten years of her life. It had many memories for her, many which

included Justin. Although she made no further mention of
Philip having taken over management of the estates, I sensed
that she was disappointed in her assumption of the way that I
had handled it.

It was late when I arose the next morning as I had told
Charlotte to take a few days of rest and Jaspar in his mature
years was no longer prone to awaken me very early. I dressed
quickly, eager to spend as much time as I might with Anne
before she departed. When I heard no movement at the door
to her room, I assumed that she had already descended for
breakfast, but when I reached the dining room I was surprised
to find Philip alone with Amelie. I do not know if it was the
tone of something she had just said which was not completely
audible or the look of consternation on her face that troubled
me.

"Is there anything wrong, Amelie?" I asked quickly.
"Where are the children, are they all right?"

"'Really, Serena,'" Philip replied disdainfully, "you really
are going to have to get a hold on yourself one of these days.
What would make you think that there was something wrong,
and if there were, I am certain that Miss Wythe would have informed you straight away."

"I am sorry," I fumbled awkwardly, "I just thought—well,
Amelie seemed troubled."

"Not at all, Lady Taggart," she insisted quickly.

"Well, then, where *are* the children?" I probed.

"Oh, they have gone to the stables with Robbie. I thought
they might enjoy a bit of an outing this morning."

"I see," I replied. "Well, I quite agree that they have been
cooped up in this house too much of late, but might I ask why
you are not with them?"

"I . . . ah . . . I . . ."

"I insisted that Miss Wythe stay with me," Philip interrupted. "I thought she might inform me of the children's
progress with their studies."

"Since when have you taken an interest in the children,
Philip?" I retorted.

"Do not mind my wife, Amelie," Philip excused. "She has
been a bit on edge of late; have you not, my dear?"

The smirk on his face was unmistakable and, I sensed, in-
tentional.

I crossed the room to leave. That he wished to humiliate me

was apparent but I did not have to remain to listen to it.

"Where are you going, my dear?" Philip called out.

"I shall be with Anne," I replied.

"You shall find that a bit awkward," Philip called out, "since she left over an hour ago."

"Anne is gone?" I cried incredulously.

I could not see Philip's expression since his back was to me, but I sensed that he was very self-satisfied. "She did not want to disturb you, Serena. After all, since you have been ill it was only wise that she leave you to rest."

I said nothing in return to Philip, only took hold of the heavy door and closed it behind me. So he had not trusted me to be with her even this morning. That oddly gave me some sense of satisfaction, for if he did not wholly trust me, then he was not completely sure of me. Perhaps that was to my advantage.

With Anne gone and the children preoccupied I found myself with the very thing I had come to loathe—time. I spent the morning admiring the gowns Anne had brought and sorting out some of the ones that I had not had occasion to wear recently or that I knew I was likely not to wear again. I always passed them on to the younger maids at Mayfair, who were always grateful for any small donation. I had not gone through Justin's things since returning to Mayfair. It was a crime, of course, to let things that someone could be using lie fallow, but I still could not face seeing his clothes, touching those articles that I remembered Justin wearing. I made a mental note to allow Charlotte and Robbie to go through them one day soon. Robbie was considerably smaller in stature than Justin, but Charlotte was clever with a needle and I knew that he would appreciate having clothing that he would likely never purchase for himself.

As the day passed I faced the evening drawing nigh with a sense of dread. I wanted no further interrogation from Philip about what I might or might not have said to Anne. I was therefore astounded as I commenced dressing for the evening when Janine, one of the downstairs maids, arrived with a tray in hand.

"Lord Taggart told Cook, 'e did, that ye were feelin' poorly so 'e asked that she send ye a tray."

I must have shown my surprise, for she added quickly, " 'E also said 'e was goin' to be workin' tonight an' ye is to get some rest. Real thoughtful, yer husband seems, if ye don't mind me sayin'."

Thoughtful? I mused to myself. I would scarcely call Philip that. Conniving, even cruel, but scarcely thoughtful.

"So if ye be needin' anything else, ye jest let me know. Charlotte will be fussin' at me if aye be lettin' ye down."

"Nonsense," I said quickly. "I shan't be needing anything else. If you should see my husband, please assure him that I shall remain in my room and get to bed early as he wishes."

Once alone I went to the dressing table and pulled the hairpins angrily from my hair. While I was relieved that I would not have to face Philip this evening, I resented being relegated to my room. It was one thing to feel that I was a prisoner in my own house, but this had gone too far. Did he really think that he could order me about through the servants? And I resented his perpetual inference that I was ill. I moved forward and looked at myself carefully in the mirror. I was pale, it was true, and my eyes lacked their normal luster, but I knew that the cause was not physical. I was emotionally drained and it was commencing to show in my appearance. I was not sleeping well, but save taking a drought, which I was against, I did not see that I would rest any better as long as Philip lorded over not only Mayfair but myself as well.

I worked a bit at my embroidery after giving most of my dinner over to Jaspar, but I could not seem to concentrate. I knew that I could not continue in this manner, but finding a solution seemed obscure. I went to bed resolved that, unpleasant or not, I had to talk to Philip to see if we might not agree to a truce. There was no hope that the relationship might be reclaimed, but at least perhaps we might stop the destructiveness that pervaded Mayfair these days.

I had no idea what awakened me, for it was deathly dark and silent when I sat up suddenly in bed with beads of perspiration lighting my brow. Jaspar, who had curled up beside me, nuzzled closer to me as if sensing my alertness. Try as I could, I could not dispel a sense that something was terribly wrong or about to be. I climbed out of bed and hurriedly threw my robe about me.

"You stay here," I whispered to Jaspar. "I shan't be long."

The house was very still as I hurriedly made my way towards the nursery. There was no reason to believe that anything was amiss with the children, but I could not dismiss this sense of

dread which pervaded me. I would not sleep until I was satisfied that it was simply the product of my imagination.

I breathed a sigh of relief when I found both children sleeping peacefully. I pulled the covers up about Alexander's neck,
smiling to myself as I noticed that he had obviously inherited
his father's penchant for discarding the blankets in the middle
of the night.

Satisfied that all was well with them, I started back towards
my quarters, careful to be as quiet as possible. When I had
reached the turn in the hall, I paused, disturbed by what
seemed to be voices in the distance. At first I commenced
down towards my room, thinking that it must be again my
overactive imagination this night, but then I turned back,
straining to determine if I had indeed heard someone talking.

There were voices, no doubt, and they were distinctly coming from the direction of Philip's quarters. Who, I wondered,
would he be talking to at this hour of the night?

My curiosity pressed me to move stealthily down the hallway towards his room. My candle was low and I was careful to
shield it from the drafts that pervaded these broad hallways.

As I neared the door to his bedroom I was startled by the
sound of a woman's laughter. I felt no anger, only pity for
whatever young maid he had seduced into believing that he
was anything more than a cad. I knew I should not be listening
to these intimacies, but I stood there as if transfixed by some
outer force.

Philip's voice lowered and I stepped closer to the door,
pressing my ear to it.

"Are you certain she is not suspicious?" the woman's voice
asked. I heard Philip laugh lightly.

"You worry too much, Amelie, my dear. You should know
by now that I have everything under control."

I could not have been more shocked and yet I simultane-
ously wondered how I could have been so blind. Amelie—of
course. Now I understood her superciliousness towards me
and why Philip would always come to her defense. And I had
fired her. No wonder Philip had countered my decision. He
was hardly about to allow me to dismiss his mistress.

Amelie retorted something I could not hear.

"It will do no good for you to become temperamental now,
my dear," Philip replied.

"But what of the letters, Philip?"

"My dear bride never comes down here," he replied. "Besides, those letters are no longer of concern."

"Why?" Amelie asked.

"Because I have destroyed them."

My heart began pounding at the sound of a sudden movement from within. I gathered my skirts and hurried down the hallway towards my room. I did not breathe easily until I had locked the door behind me, listening at it until satisfied I had not been discovered.

My candle was almost extinguished and I quickly covered the remaining flame to light another. Jaspar whimpered about my ankles as I moved forward to stoke the fire.

"Come here, little one," I whispered, motioning him to come and sit beside me before the fire.

I was shaking and it was, I knew, not only from the chill in the room. How could I have been so stupid? I wondered. All the signs had been there. Admittedly, they had been clever. I could not help but wonder how long their little affair had been carried on. Had Philip sought her out when I had rejected him or had their liaison commenced far before he had brought her to Mayfair? Perhaps that was why he had been so quick to propose a marriage without intimacy. He had ensconced someone at Mayfair to satisfy his needs. What puzzled me, though, was why then he had violated me that night. Had he simply been drunk and used whatever his whim fancied? I wondered if Amelie knew of his indiscretion, or was she privy to the terms of our marital arrangement?

What plagued me most was the reference to the letters. What letters and from whom? Obviously they were letters that Philip never intended me to see since he had destroyed them. He obviously felt that they were crucially important. Amelie had sounded worried. No, more than that, frightened that I might indeed discover the contents of those letters.

But how could I find out? I could scarcely confront Philip or even Amelie. They would most assuredly lie or tell me that I was imagining things. And if I did confront them, they would know that I was suspicious. I sensed that I could not afford to play my hand, but what other option did I have? If the letters had been destroyed, it would do no good to somehow ransack Philip's quarters.

I sat there in the dark for another hour with only the fire

lighting my thoughts, trying to puzzle just whom the letters might be from. I remembered how surprised Anne had been that I had not heard from Oliver directly. Could the letters have been from him? I wondered. And if they were, what in the contents would have troubled Philip so? I knew that Philip was far from thrilled at the prospect of Oliver's return to England but surely he would have known that had I not read it for myself, I eventually would have learned the news from Anne or Richard.

Then there was Monique. There had only been that one letter from her and even at the time I had thought that a portion of it had been missing. Had she sent other letters, or had Philip simply, neatly, excerpted a section he had not wanted me to read? Now that Philip took all the business correspondence, I had no way of knowing if there were something that he wanted kept from me in some way. Had Sir Henry communicated news of the estates that Philip deemed would be dangerous in my hands?

None of it made sense. What was increasingly frustrating was that the more I thought about it the further I seemed from reaching a solution.

It was almost dawn when I finally returned to bed and fell into a troubled sleep.

The next morning I awakened to the sound of the door handle rattling. I sat up quickly in bed, calling out, "Who is there?"

" 'Tis only me, Lady Taggart, Janine. Ay've ye basin fer ye."

I dragged myself out of bed and opened the door. "I am sorry, Janine. I must have inadvertently locked the door," I lied. I watched her as she placed the basin down.

"Kin aye be gettin' ye some breakfast?"

I shook my head. "I am really not very hungry. Perhaps I shall take something later. But you could do me a great favor and take Jaspar here down to Robbie at the stables."

Jaspar looked up at me, his soulful eyes exploring mine.

" 'Tis all right, Jaspar," I assured him. "I shall fetch you later."

When they had left I bathed quickly, happy for the soothing heat of the water against my body. The bathing relaxed me and, catching myself yawning, I decided to return to bed for a spell. I had almost drifted off to sleep when the door opened suddenly. I gasped and drew the covers about me as I watched Philip stride towards me.

"What are you doing here?" I cried out.

"Goodness, Serena, is that any way to greet your husband?" he replied, winking at me.

"Philip, I must ask you to leave this room immediately," I said, trying to keep my voice steady. "You know you have no right here."

"Really, Serena, I only came to bring you some warm milk and toasted bread. That little downstairs maid seemed to think you were feeling a bit out of sorts this morning."

"When did you become so solicitous?" I snapped, curious about the real intention of his visit.

"You know, Serena, it would become you much more if you were to show me some gratitude. Like it or not, I *am* making every effort to be a good husband to you."

"Please do not insult me, Philip," I spat in retort. I cringed as his eyebrow raised and he studied me seriously.

"What did you mean by that?" he asked cautiously.

"Nothing," I replied.

He handed me the milk. "Here, drink this."

I shook my head. "I really do not want anything, Philip."

"Don't be stubborn, Serena," he insisted. "What will Cook say if I send it back down?"

"Did she send it up?"

"I am not in the habit of preparing hot milk and toast," he insisted.

I took the milk and drank it down.

"I'll put the toast over here," Philip said, putting it on the table next to me. When I was certain that he had gone, I got up and put the lock on the door. It was clumsy of me to have forgotten it earlier. I returned to bed and drew myself wearily into it. I hated languishing about like this, but an exhaustion pervaded me which I did not think that I could fight. I fell asleep again, wondering what the importance could be of the letters.

In my sleep I kept hearing a knocking. Was someone at the door? I wondered. It suddenly became evident to me that what I was hearing was not through my sleep. I sat up and looked about me. The room was totally dark and very cold since the fire had died obviously some hours before.

The knocking persisted. I remained silent worried that it was Philip.

"Miss Serena, please open the door."

I recognized Charlotte's voice and quickly jumped out of bed and opened the door.

"Oh, thank the Lord," she fussed, "aye thought there was something amiss with ye. Ooh, it's frigid in 'ere. Let me light that fire right away."

"What time is it?" I asked.

"Oh, 'tis goin' on six, it is."

"Six?" I gasped. "But it could not be. How could I have slept the whole of the day?"

"Ye obviously be needin' it," she replied as warmth trickled into the room once again. "An' Lord Taggart left word that ye t'weren't te be disturbed."

I slumped into the chair by the fire. I felt so groggy and the room seemed to be spinning.

Charlotte came to me, placing a lap robe about my shoulders. "Ye aren't feelin' yerself, are ye?"

"I am all right, truly," I insisted. "I just feel a bit foggy. And no wonder, since I have all but slept the day away."

"Aye could be bringin' ye a tray if ye want."

I shook my head. "I shall dine with Lord Taggart."

Charlotte grinned and, tricking her black curls under her cap, said, "Ah, aye guess ye be wantin' te start plannin' the ball."

"What ball are you referring to, Charlotte?"

She looked at me strongly. "Why, the one ye an' Lord Taggart be givin' 'ere next month."

"Who told you that?"

"Why, Lord Taggart did. Told me this mornin' 'e did. Aye told 'im t'was mighty short notice fer a big ball, but if that be what ye want, ye'll 'ave it."

"I assure you, Charlotte, I knew nothing of this."

She frowned. "But aye just assumed, aye mean Lord Taggart talked as if t'was to announce yer marriage an' all."

"He had talked of doing something of the sort, but I thought we had agreed that it would not be until sometime this summer," I mused, annoyed that he had dared to order the household about without consulting me.

"Well, aye've gone ahead an' gotten Cook fired up. An' the girls 'ave started on the silver."

I knew that there would be no dissuading Philip. I suspected that Anne's suggestion that we share the ball for Oliver's return and impending marriage was less than suitable to him. Philip would share the opportunity to be the center of attention with no one, particularly not with one whom, I assumed, he had already designated as foe.

"Would you fetch the blue velvet with the shawl collar for me, Charlotte?" I asked, rising to go to the dressing table.

"Aye think ye should stay put, Serena, but if that 'tis what ye want . . ."

"It is," I said firmly. "Obviously my husband and I have more than I thought to discuss."

I was grateful that Charlotte was there to help me dress for I was not as steady on my feet as I would have liked. I did not feel poorly, certainly I was not feverish, but I could not seem to maintain my balance. I made no further comment on it for Charlotte would certainly insist that I go back to bed and I wanted to confront Philip on his latest scheme tonight.

When Charlotte had finished my hair and left me, I made my way slowly down the hallway, taking care to follow close to the far wall lest I should lose my balance. I held tightly to the balustrade as I maneuvered the broad staircase. Philip was in the library reading. He looked very surprised as I entered.

"Well, my dear, what an unexpected pleasure," he offered as I approached the fireplace.

"Please, Philip, let us do away with the amenities," I replied curtly.

"You seem a bit unsteady, Serena," he noted as my hand slipped from the chair arm as I sank into it.

"Just a bit groggy," I replied.

"You should be in bed," he offered.

"That is precisely why I feel this way now. I cannot think what caused me to sleep the day through. That is unlike me."

"You must admit that you have not been yourself of late, Serena."

"Philip, I am not here to talk about how I feel, though I do not understand why you insist on characterizing me as though I am some invalid. That may be your wish—so that then you could have me closeted away in my quarters—but I assure you that both my mind and body are intact."

Philip was watching me warily and I realized that there had been an aura of challenge in my voice. I would have to be more cautious for I did not want him to suspect that I knew anything about his liaison with Amelie. There was the mystery of the letters for me to solve, and my chances of gaining more information would not be helped were Philip to know that I was fully aware of his indiscretions.

"What I wanted to speak to you about, Philip, was this ball that you have obviously informed the household that we are to be having."

Philip poured himself a drink and rested by the fireplace. "I truly do not think there is anything to discuss, Serena. It is not as though the topic has not arisen between us."

"I simply thought that we would wait until Oliver's return and permit Anne to honor us with a ball this summer. I would advise you that my friends will find it far more suitable that way."

He frowned. "What, my dear, is unsuitable about having a ball to celebrate our marriage?"

I stirred uncomfortably. "It is not yet near a year since Justin's death," I replied quietly. "A sense of decorum alone should tell you that a party now would not be in good taste."

"Damn good taste," Philip replied. "It is time that I am recognized as the master here. I am sick of being holed up in this mausoleum. If your *friends*, as you refer to them, think that they can snub me, they shall have their comeuppance. Two weeks hence, this house shall be filled with every important name from here to London."

"Two weeks is scarcely a great deal of notice," I cautioned. "What makes you think that anyone will attend?"

A wry smile spread across his face. "You, my dear. There are none who would not travel many miles to honor my new bride. Believe me, I have every assurance that they shall attend."

I was about to ask what made him think that I would go blindly along with this plan when Giles announced that dinner was ready.

Philip came forward and reached down, taking my arm in his hands. I tried to shake free of his clasp, but his fingers tightened about my wrist.

"Let me go, Philip," I said, continuing to try to wrench myself free.

"Getting angry will do you no good, Serena," he replied coolly. "You know that your resisting me simply makes you more attractive to me."

I was in no mood to fight with him. I was no match for Philip physically, and I had already seen the lengths that he would go to. He had no scruples where I was concerned and I knew that I would be a fool to test them.

"Philip, I shall strike a bargain with you."

"Pray, what can that be, my sweet?"

"I will not counter you on this ball if you promise that you shall not lay even a finger on me." He laughed, his hand tightening about my wrist.

"You *are* naive my dear. What makes you think that I would even consider such a bargain as you put it?"

I drew a deep breath. "Because you are not stupid, Philip. You may be many things, but you are not stupid."

"I suppose I should be flattered," he interrupted.

"Do not be," I advised. "I only mean to point out that if you are going to have a ball to celebrate our marriage, it would prove very embarrassing to you if your new bride were not to attend."

"What are you saying?"

"I am saying simply that I shall go along with this ball. I shall appear as the blushing, dutiful bride but only if you swear to me that you will stay away from me." I felt his hand loosen about my wrist.

"Do you really think that I would agree to such an arrangement?" he challenged.

"Yes, I do," I retorted, trying to sound confident. "Because I do not think that you would dare suffer the embarrassment of my insult. Imagine how I could set tongues wagging. Somehow I do not think that is what you want, Philip."

There was real hatred in his eyes after several minutes passed and his fingers uncurled from my wrist.

"You think you are very clever, do you not? Well, I shall go along with your little bargain, but if I were you, I would commence thinking about those days and nights after the ball. What are you going to hold over my head then?" I pulled myself forward in the chair but his arm held me back. "Don't push things too far, Serena."

I shuddered at the anger in his voice and dared not reply lest my own would reveal the fear that I felt.

By the time we moved to the dining room the dizziness that I had experienced earlier seemed to have disappeared. The silence between us during dinner was deafening but I saw no reason to try and make conversation. I had won this round but thinly, and I was loathe to say anything that would cause Philip to challenge me. I needed time, and although two weeks was not much, I would have to make it so.

I do not know what I had hoped to happen over the next week, mainly I suppose because I did not know exactly what I was looking for. Mayfair was in a flurry of activity. Invitations had to be delivered, menus planned, floors scrubbed, silver polished—it seemed endless. In some ways I welcomed the turmoil for it left me with less time to dwell on the tragic mistake I had made by marrying Philip.

The children, Daphne in particular, were thrilled at the prospect of a ball, making me painfully aware that life had been dreary for them since Justin had left us. Mayfair had once been such a happy house, so often filled with friends and laughter, and it had seen little or none of that lately.

Philip seemed satisfied with my efforts, or so I had to suspect, since he was true to his word and kept his distance from me. At the same time he was ever watchful of me. Had he been able to have read my mind he would have known that I had resolved to go to Anne and Richard the night of the ball and tell them everything. There were moments when I asked myself what that "everything" was. That Philip had taken me in my own bedroom against my wishes? It was hardly against the law—after all, a man had a right to expect connubial rights from his wife. That he had taken over the running of Mayfair without my sanction? Again, as my husband he had that right unless I had made some other arrangement with Sir Henry. That he was carrying on midnight trysts with the governess? So were half the men in London. Even if they believed me, it would certainly not be regarded as a reason to abandon my husband. How could I prove that I felt that I was being made a prisoner in my own house? Had Philip been effective in convincing Anne that I was not myself these days?

Anne was my dearest friend and I knew I had to count on her helping me. If only I could decipher Philip's words about those letters, I could at lest go to Anne with something that would shake her into trusting me. And yet, without some proof, how could I know or even suppose that there was something sinister there?

I knew that my one hope was to gain more information somehow, but the only way I could do that was surreptitiously. Spying on Philip and Amelie was most distasteful to me but I knew that it was the only way to unravel the intrigue.

A week to the day that I had first discovered Philip and Amelie together, I waited until I was certain that Philip had retired and then made my way down the long hallway to his quarters. The floor was like ice against my bare feet but I knew that I could not chance any sound my shoes might make against the highly polished wood. My heart was pounding so heavily that I could actually feel the blood surging through my veins. If Amelie were indeed in Philip's room, she could leave at any time and there would be nowhere to which I could escape save a thin support column on the far side of the door. Assured that no one was coming from another part of the hallway, I pressed my cheek against the door. No sound came from within. It disgusted me to think that all I might indeed hear would be their lovemaking. I need not have worried, however, for after standing there for a good five minutes I was convinced that either no one was in the room or that Philip was fast asleep. I crept back to my room, disheartened by my excursion. Jaspar snuggled close to me as I climbed into bed, anxious to warm myself. As I knew no pattern to their trysts, I knew that I would have to make this a nightly foray.

It was not until four nights later that my patience was rewarded. I had suspected that it might be so as Philip had excused himself from dinner earlier than usual after seeming preoccupied most of the evening. The last few nights I had taken to leaving my bedroom door ajar a bit so that I could listen for any movement to and from Philip's quarters. On this night I was certain that the rustle I heard in the hallway was Amelie since the servants had bedded down hours before. I waited for ten minutes before starting out, taking care to move close to the wall since there was no light in the hallway. I dared not carry a candle.

When I had gotten within two feet of the door to Philip's room, I paused, for the voices inside were raised and it was clear that the two were in the midst of an argument.

"I am warning you, Philip," I heard Amelie say, "you are taking this far too lightly." 

"You worry too much, dear," he replied. "Now come over here and let us stop this talking. I would much rather caress that lovely body of yours than to squabble over nothing."

"It is not nothing," Amelie argued. "There is too much at risk here. That letter could ruin everything. You can be blasé if you want, but I am frightened. This whole thing is getting out of hand."

"You had better get a grip on yourself, Amelie," Philip cautioned. "We have come this far and I do not need you to fall apart now. Trust me. She knows nothing of any of this."

"But what about the letters?"

There was a pause and I strained closer to the door.

"I have a plan," Philip finally replied. "I don't want to go into it now but I am certain that it will succeed."

I desperately wanted to stay longer but it was clear from the silence that Philip had won his point and that conversation was now a very secondary issue.

I crept back to my room, relieved that once again I had escaped unnoticed but frustrated that I had really learned nothing further about the letters. I was more convinced than ever that these letters were of significance and determined that somehow I had to gain access to Philip's quarters. Creeping around in the middle of the night was serving only to prove what I already knew: that Amelie and Philip were having more than just a casual affair. Gaining entry to his quarters, however, was going to prove difficult since I was not only barred from his rooms but I could scarcely search when he was ensconced there most of the day.

I had to come up with a plan to keep him out of his quarters long enough for me to search them. And I had to do it immediately for I could not chance that he would destroy the letters. There seemed no way but to enlist Charlotte's aid. With the ball only days away she could feign needing his decision on some last-minute arrangement. I hated to involve Charlotte in this deception, but I saw no other way to gain the time I needed to assure an uninterrupted search.

When Charlotte arrived the next morning, I had already risen and dressed.

"Would ye be wantin' me to fix yer hair this mornin'?" she offered.

I shook my head. "Thank you, Charlotte, but actually you can do a favor for me. A rather important one, I might add."

"Ye only have to ask, Serena, ye know that."

"It is going to seem an odd request," I cautioned, "and I fear that for now I really do not want to explain why I am going to ask this of you."

She looked at me expectantly.

"I want you to find a way to get Lord Taggart out of his quarters this morning," I said quietly. "How you do it I shall leave to you, though I might suggest that you ask his advice on china or something having to do with the ball. He will undoubtedly become impatient but it is important that you keep him occupied until I join you."

"Aye think aye kin do that," she replied. "Seein' that 'tis so important to ye aye guess aye'll just have to."

I reached out and grasped her arm. "Believe me, Charlotte, I do not want to be so secretive with you, but it is most advisable, at least for now."

"Aye can't be thinkin' what this is about, but if ye think it is important than aye kin be sure it is."

"Thank you for understanding."

"Ye know, Lord Taggart was in the breakfast room when aye came up 'ere. I could go down now and keep 'im busy for a spell," Charlotte offered.

"That would be perfect," I replied. "But remember, Charlotte, you must not let him out of your sight until I appear downstairs."

She nodded. "If aye 'ave to, aye'll sit on 'im."

I smiled at the thought of petite Charlotte thinking that she could somehow restrain a man who was easily a foot taller than she.

When Charlotte left I waited for several minutes until I was certain that she was downstairs. Jasper was puzzled when I insisted he stay put in the room, but I could scarcely have him trotting after me. I started down the hallway but stopped when I spied several of the upstairs maids heading towards this wing of the house. Fortunately they turned off into one of the bedrooms before seeing me.

When I reached the door to Philip's room I paused and knocked lightly before entering. I had not expected to find anyone there, but if I had I could have explained away my presence far more readily by a certain formality than simply by breaking into the room.

When there was no response I entered quickly, closing the door gently behind me. My eyes scanned the room searching for some logical place to start. I hardly expected that the letters I was seeking would be lying out in the open, but it had never occurred to me that I might have to examine every inch of these rooms.

I started with the desk. It was filled with letters and papers, but everything seemed to pertain to business. From the look of things Philip had quickly tired of overseeing the estates for there were stacks of unpaid bills—many which had never even been opened. The search of his armoire and dresser turned up nothing.

The door to his study was ajar and I moved through to continue my search. I was shocked at how neat everything was. This scarcely was the study of a man who buried himself in these rooms all day long. The desk was free of papers, the ledgers tucked away in the bookcases. There were no drawings here, nothing to even suggest that Philip was working on the railroad project.

I pulled frantically at the drawers looking for anything that would provide some clue as to the letters. Not only was I not finding what I was looking for, but I was befuddled by the lack of anything that even vaguely resembled drawing maps or sketches. What was Philip doing here day after day? I wondered.

I was starting to get nervous. I knew that I had been here far too long already, but I simply was not willing to give up before finding what I was looking for. It was improbable that I should ever have another opportunity.

Satisfied that there was nothing in the study, I moved back to the bedroom, going into the nightstand, even searching under the bed. There were several painted urns on the fireplace mantel and I reached into each, hoping that my fingers would curl about the letters that I sought. It was quickly becoming evident that my search was fruitless and I sat down before the fireplace, trying to think once more where or what Philip might have used to conceal the letters. My eyes suddenly focused on what appeared to be a sheath of paper at the back of the fireplace. I knelt down before it and, aware that the embers were still warm, reached back and snatched the tissue from the fireplace. As I did it seemed to crumble in my hand, leaving only a small corner remaining in my fingers.

There was writing on it, but what the fire had not destroyed it had been nearly obliterated, smearing the ink so that it was all but illegible. I could not decipher anything except for the three words "*returning on the sixteenth.*"

It made no sense to me. Who was returning on the sixteenth? The sixteenth of what? This month? Last? How did I even know that this was a part of the letter or letters that I was looking for? But why else would Philip have burned them unless he was worried that someone might find them?

I was about to use the stoker to see if there might be other fragments not readily visible that might give me some clue as to from when or where the letter had been posted when I heard Philip's voice in the hallway.

Oh, my God, I thought, he cannot find me here like this. I threw the paper quickly back into the fireplace and moved swiftly over to the door, getting there just as he flung it open.

His expression told me instantly that he was both shocked and angered at finding me there. Charlotte was directly behind him, looking at me desolately, shaking her head as if to indicate that she had been helpless to keep him downstairs.

"Well, there you are, Philip," I said, trying to keep my tone light.

"I should think you would be surprised to see me here, my dear," he replied wryly.

"To the contrary," I insisted. "I was looking for you to help me decide which gown I should wear to the ball."

He studied me. "Are you keeping them in the fireplace?"

I looked nervously down and realized that my hands were covered with soot.

"Oh, that," I said slowly. "There was a live ash on the carpet and I foolishly tried to put it out with my hands."

He walked past me and over to the fireplace. "You really should be more careful Serena, you could be seriously injured doing things like that."

Something in his tone told me that he did not believe a word I had said, but I had to keep up the ruse.

"You have not told me, Philip, if you will help me choose the gown?"

He shrugged. "If you wish—but since you have never asked

my counsel before, I scarcely know why you want it now."

Charlotte, who had been lurking by the door, spoke up. "Kin aye be gettin' them fer ye, Miss Serena?"

Philip replied angrily, "Get that woman out of here, Serena. She has been fussing at me all morning with some nonsense about what china service we are to use."

"I am certain that Charlotte was only trying to help," I assured him, embarrassed by his outburst in front of her.

"I won't be needing you, Charlotte," I continued.

"No, you've done your deed," Philip mused. "The ever faithful Charlotte."

With my eyes I silently tried to will her to leave and sensing my plea she silently moved away down the hallway.

"I shall return in just a moment, Philip. That is, if this is a convenient time for you."

I suspected he was looking about the room for evidence that I had indeed been searching his quarters. I had forgotten to partially close the door between the bedroom and study but I hoped that he would not remember how he had left it.

I went quickly back to my room and gathered up several gowns which could have been candidates for the ball. I had not actually given any thought to what I would wear, but Philip need not know that. In the end he selected an emerald green silk taffeta. It would not have been my selection, but what mattered here was only that I had managed to allay some of his suspicions.

I spent part of the afternoon with the children as Amelie had sent word that she was feeling unwell.

It was clear to me that the children were no more enthused about her today than they had been, but for the time I could see no road open to change her role at Mayfair. It was crisp outside when the chidren and Jaspar and I ambled down to the stables. Alexander's colt was growing by leaps and bounds and looking day by day more like Medallion, who had sired him. We missed seeing Robbie, who had ridden out to visit some of the tenants. He came to the house so rarely these days. I sensed that his relationship with Philip was far from amicable and that he resented his having taken over the running of the estates, but I had not seen my way clear to tell him that the decision had been foisted on me.

Dinner that night with Philip was unavoidable. I was very tired and my instinct was to beg off from dinner, to take a tray in my room, but I was curiously aware of our earlier confrontation and sensed that avoiding him now would only arouse suspicions.

"You seem not yourself tonight," he offered as I struggled with the food presented before me.

"I must be tired," I admitted.

"You had a busy morning," he challenged.

There was no question in my mind that Philip knew exactly what I had been doing in his quarters earlier that day, and yet he would not admit or question me about it any more than I would demand to know about the letters. It would serve no purpose for he would not admit anything to me and finally it would only serve to reveal more than I wanted to be revealed at this point.

Try as I did, I could not seem to eat; finally when it became clear that my stomach was to control my mind, I begged Philip to excuse me.

"You should have some milk, some hot milk, Serena," he advised.

"I do not think I could keep it down," I resisted.

"Nonsense, it will calm you. Trust me. I shall have Cook prepare something for you and send it up to you."

I rose, insisting that I would be fine in the morning, but Philip pressed the milk on me. Finally, to avert a confrontation I agreed that it should be sent to my room.

I do not think that I had ever felt such a desolate feeling as when I returned to my room that night. Strangely, I had dreaded the idea of this ball and yet at this hour I was living for it. I could not continue on this way, and however I appeared to Richard and Anne, I knew that I would pour my soul out to them this weekend. It was chancy for I wished that I could have resolved the question of the letters, which I sensed was all important. But I could not continue to live in this fashion and I had not enough to go on to think that a continuum of this life I was living was important.

I returned to my room, cheered only by my precious Jaspar, who greeted me as a long lost friend. He had a constancy that I needed in my life and I was desperate to maintain. His naiveté to my needs was important for it was finally one of the few continuums that I had experienced today. I pulled my clothes off, abjectly longing for the bed that lay before me.

When a knock came at the door, I knew that it was likely to

be Charlotte and called her in instantly.

"Lord Taggart was insistin' that aye give ye this milk, an' te tell ye the truth, aye t'was not about to argue since aye been worried about ye since this mornin'."

I accepted the milk and drank it while she looked on. When I had finished it I replaced it on the tray.

"Serena, 'tis not my place to be sayin' so, but me eyesight may not be what it was, but aye kin still see that ye hasn't been yerself for months now."

I reached out to her and took her hand in mine.

"You have always been such a dear friend to me, Charlotte," I assured her. "And I do not think you could sense me better were you my own mother. I do not mean to keep things from you, but truthfully I am not even certain where my own suspicions are taking me."

" 'Tis about Lord Taggart, isn't it?" she pressed.

I nodded. "But there is no reason to concern yourself," I assured her.

"Ye would tell me, Serena, if there was some way aye could be helpin' ye."

"Of course," I assured her. "You helped me this morning, though I fear that Philip did not believe my ruse."

"Aye did me best to keep him downstairs but aye kept lookin' for ye an' aye think he got suspicious."

I sensed that Charlotte wanted to talk further but I was having trouble keeping my eyelids open. She released my hand and spread hers over my brow. "Ye sleep well, Serena. We'll talk more when yer head is clear."

I whispered a goodnight to her and, pulling Jaspar to me, allowed sleep to come.

When I awakened the next morning I did so feeling that I had not slept at all. I was experiencing the same grogginess I had days before. My eyes seemed sensitive to the light and I could not seem to maintain my balance. When Charlotte appeared with my basin and then my breakfast tray, I tried successively to rise but with such difficulty that I returned to bed on her insistence. Knowing that the guests were to arrive the next morning and how much there was undoubtedly to do in the house, I was loathe to lie abed. But struggle as I did, I could not fight the exhaustion that overtook me.

I had wanted to spend the day with the children, knowing that once the guests arrived I would scarcely have time to speak to them, but I could not fight the waves of dizziness.

When I begged Charlotte to help me get out of bed, she refused, advising that the thing I needed most was bed rest and that all was being taken care of within the household. When she brought my luncheon tray I accepted it for I knew that if I told her that I could not possibly eat anything her frown of concern would turn to outright worry.

Languishing about had never been a want of mine and certainly this day it only served to cause me frustration. That, coupled with the resounding thought that recurred to me, was overwhelming. What did the sixteenth mean? Whom was the letter from? And why did it seem so important that I uncover what it meant?

By nightfall I felt not stronger but weaker. No matter how hard I fought against it I felt powerless against my own body. I was painfully aware that herds of people would be arriving the next day and that Philip would expect me to play the proper hostess. I would do that and do it well for I sensed if I did not that the retribution would be too great for me to deal with.

I had to watch for the right moments. I had to talk to Anne, openly, freely, yet Philip could not be made to suspect that I was violating him. By late afternoon I was not only dizzy but bilious. And yet it was like turning my own stomach upon itself. Though I had not effectively eaten for days my system wanted to regurgitate itself. I tried to rally against the exhaustion I was feeling. I had had periods of illness, particularly after Alexander was born, but nothing like this.

Those moments after I had spewed my guts out into the basin left me feeling terribly vulnerable. If there were ever a time that I needed my mind and body to work as one, it was now—but I felt it all escaping me.

By nighttime I had wrenched whatever was possible from my system, and yet even then I did not feel purified. Charlotte announced that Philip desired my presence for dinner but I begged off, insisting that I was too ill.

If the day had been difficult the night proved only near to impossible. Charlotte brought me another glass of milk, insisting that I drink it down—which I did only to please her. My dear Jaspar stayed close to my side and I admittedly clung to him.

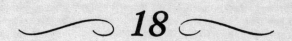

# 18

The morning of the ball I awoke in a weaker condition than I had for months. The exhaustion overwhelmed me. Though I had slept most of yesterday away, I could not seem to fight the tiredness which overtook me. I hoped that Anne and Richard would arrive early so that I might talk to them before the ball commenced.

It was raining very hard when I heard the first of the carriages arrive. I lay in bed listening to the horses' hooves as they pounded upon the cobblestones, trying to will myself to rise to the occasion but desperately aware that I could make no mark against it.

I was also painfully aware that Philip expected me not only to be present but to give him the respect due the master of the household during such festivities.

That I had not been present to greet the guests was obvious. And I knew that it would engender concern on Anne's part. It was midafternoon when she rapped at the door and I ushered her in.

"Good Lord, Serena," she exclaimed as she swept into the room, "you must pardon my saying so but you look ghastly."

I reached out from the bed, stretching for her hand. "Oh, my Lord," she reprised, "what a ghastly thing to say. I only mean that you do not look well. You are not well, are you?"

"Of all the times for me to be ill," I replied.

"Darling. I do not know what this is all about anyway,"

Anne retorted, sitting down beside the bed. "We receive this
invitation, which frankly sounded more like a command performance. Richard is here with me but I can assure you not
without protestation. Really, Serena, I do wish you had followed my suggestion and let me throw a ball for you and Philip
this summer. I thought it was all settled when I was last here."

"Anne," I beseeched, "please do not scold, there are things
that you do not know, you don't understand. The important
thing right now is that you help me get up. I do not think I can
make it on my own."

"Serena, you cannot possibly be planning to attend the
ball," she rebuked. "Have you seen yourself? You need a
doctor, not a ball. Everyone will understand."

"You don't understand, Anne," I pressed. "I must get up.
Philip will expect it."

"You cannot possibly mean that, Serena. Why, I just left
that husband of yours and he is beside himself with worry."

I shook my head, trying desperately to fight the waves of
nausea overtaking me. "Anne, you must listen to me," I
whispered. "We must talk. About Philip."

"Hush, Serena," she insisted. "You know I am ashamed of
the way that I have behaved over the past months. I was simply surprised by your marriage and the changes here. I do not
think you can blame me. After all, Justin was my brother.
You know, I guess I always imagined that he was somehow in-
vincible. Foolish, I suppose, but there it is. What I am trying
to say, Serena, is that I am no longer going to oppose Philip,
your marriage to Philip or his management of the estates.
And unless I have lost my knack with Richard I should shortly
be able to bring him round as well. After all, I have always
regarded you as the most intelligent woman I know. Surely
you have given thought to all this and I can only apologize for
not trusting you earlier."

I rolled over onto my side, trying to get closer to where she
was sitting. It took all my strength to beseech her again to
listen to me. "Please, Anne," I whispered, "you must help
me. Philip . . ."

I broke off as a figure suddenly loomed behind her chair. It
was Philip.

"How is my dear wife doing?" he asked, watching me intently.

Anne turned around quickly, taking a deep breath. "Goodness, you startled me, Philip. I am glad you are here, however, for perhaps you can talk some sense into Serena. She is determined to get up for the ball and you can see for yourself that she is in no condition to go anywhere.

"Of course she is not," he agreed quickly.

I was puzzled by his response for Philip had made it very clear that I was to give the performance of my life this weekend. On the other hand, he was scarcely in a position to counter Anne. I did not know how much he had heard but enough, I suspected, to know that he had won her support. He would do nothing, at least for now, to chance losing what he had charmed himself into.

"You shall be missed, of course, darling," he continued, "but I shall explain to our guests."

"Let me stay with her, Philip," Anne suggested. "I would feel much better about it. At least until the doctor can arrive. You have sent for him, have you not?"

"No doctor," I insisted.

"Frankly, Anne, I think what Serena needs more than anything is rest," Philip offered. "Besides, without her at my side I should be quite at a loss with the hordes of people that are arriving."

Anne turned back to me. "Would you rather I stayed, Serena?"

I shook my head. "You go on along."

She rose to leave. "If you are sure then."

I was not sure—for what I really wanted was that she remain so that I might share with her my fears and discoveries about Philip. But determined as I was that Anne hear me out this weekend, I was in no condition to relay the events and conversations that had brought me to this point. I prayed that I would sleep and that whatever was making me so ill would have dissipated by morning.

"You tell Charlotte, Serena, if you want me to return tonight," she said, patting my arm. "And you, Philip, come with me—like it or not, we are sending for the doctor."

I sensed that Philip wanted to remain behind and was grateful when Anne dragged him out with her.

The next hours were spent feverishly for me. Charlotte took care of seeing that Jaspar went out and was fed, though it was a challenge for he seemed determined not to leave my side. I insisted that the children be kept away from me, loathe as I

was to pass anything on to one of them. When Charlotte
returned Jaspar later that evening, she again brought a glass of
warm milk, which she insisted I drink.

"Kin ye 'ear the music, Serena?" she asked as I struggled to
swallow the warm, white liquid. "Ye should see all the people,
real sad it is ye is feelin' so poorly. Lord Taggart has every
candle lit in the place. 'E's had me 'avin' the poor lasses
cleanin' every crystal till it shone clear. An' the gowns—one's
prettier than the next, though if ye was there there would be
none to compare to my beauty 'ere."

I started to respond and Charlotte quickly silenced me. "Ye
be needin' yer strength. Ye just rest there. Aye'll stay with ye
until the drink be takin' its effect."

Jaspar snuggled closer to me and the warmth of him I found
comforting.

"Aye shouldn't be mentionin' it," Charlotte whispered,
eyeing me to see if I were still awake, "but ye is goin' te hear it
from someone an' it might as well be from me. Who do you
think is down there dancin' about just like she t'were royalty?
Miss Wythe, that's who. T'was shocked aye was, but it t'aint
my place te be counterin' yer husband. But aye'd like to be
knowin' where she got 'er fancy dress. Not from a governess's
wages aye'll tell ye. Aye know what yer thinkin', that aye'm
jealous o' the girl but t'aint the truth. Aye just never took a
likin' to her. If ye ask me, that one is up to no good."

I thought if Charlotte knew the wisdom of her own words
she would be horrified. I had to admit that I was amazed at
Philip's brazenness. Whatever he conducted behind bedroom
doors was one thing, but I did not think that he would be so
brash as to flaunt it.

I had begun to feel immensely drowsy once again and
Charlotte's voice grew weaker and weaker as I slipped off into
sleep.

My condition, if anything, had worsened by morning. The
nausea had disappeared but my sense of exhaustion was even
greater. I pushed against the covers trying to sit up in bed but
everything seemed to spin before my eyes. I dropped back
against the pillows, for the first time truly frightened by what
seemed to be my waning health. I had not before considered
that this illness might be more serious than I had thought. I
had been fortunate in my life that my health problems had

been limited to a few nasty spills from horses. I was not prone to spells or fevers, and although I had not felt myself these past months I had attributed it to the emotional strain I had been under. Philip had kept insisting that I was ill, and although I was loathe to give any credence to him I had commenced to wonder if he were not right.

The thought proved terrifying to me—far less because of my own vulnerability or demise than for thought of the children.

Dear God, if anything happened to me, what would become of the children? Philip would certainly not care for them. It became even more crucial that I speak with Anne.

Charlotte arrived shortly thereafter, troubled that I was no better. She sponged off my face and arms and helped me change into a fresh nightdress. I knew she meant only to help, but it simply served to weary me further.

"Ye need the doctor 'ere, Serena," she insisted. "If yer husband won't be fetchin' 'im, aye'm goin' to get 'im meself."

Dear Charlotte was every my protector. I would argue no longer about the doctor for in truth I welcomed him here to dispel any notions that I might not recover. I wondered if Philip would indeed call for him. If he did, I sensed it would be because Anne had badgered him into it and not because he was concerned for my well-being.

"Kin aye be gettin' anythin' fer ye, Serena?" Charlotte asked as she gently tried to comb the hair back from my face.

I nodded. "It is important that I see Lady Camberleigh," I whispered. "When she rises, would you tell her?"

"Of course aye will," she assured me. "Soon as aye see her. Aye'll be takin' the little fellow down to me Robbie fer the day. If ye be wantin' anything aye'll be close by."

Jaspar did not follow her willingly. Only after I encouraged him did his soulful eyes cease their vigil on me and he left the bed, following in Charlotte's step.

It seemed that I had done nothing but sleep these last days and yet, fight as I tried, I could not seem to keep awake.

I was aware that Charlotte looked in on me from time to time but I grew anxious when Anne had not yet come to my room. When she finally did arrive, my heart sank for Philip was with her. I knew now for certain that he did not trust me. Anne would, I knew, mistake his caution for concern. She could not know that Philip would not chance our being alone.

He had no idea how much I really knew, but he could not risk
my exposing him to Anne or Richard. Not when he had made
such strides to win them over.

"Darling, how are you today?" Anne asked as she pressed
her hand against my forehead and cheeks to check for fever.

"I think she has a little more color today," I heard Philip
say.

"Philip has sent for the doctor, Serena," Anne assured me.
"I knew you were opposed, but truly 'tis the best thing."

"The ball was a great success, my dear, though you were
sorely missed."

Anne took my hand in hers. "That is an understatement,
Philip, but we can talk of all that later. Right now I simply
want to see Serena well again."

I shut my eyes, hoping that if I feigned sleep Philip might
leave us alone long enough for me to talk to Anne, but it was
not to be. As he stood there, calmly convincing Anne that I
was best left to rest, I wanted to scream out that he was cheat
and a liar and I knew not what else. But to do that would be to
play all my cards and then I would never learn the mystery of
the letters. I was chancing a great deal by not challenging him
here and now, but I sensed that I might later regret it. And so
it was with nary a whimper that I listened to their footsteps
leave the room in unison.

In my intermittent waking moments I was vaguely aware of
the sound of carriages on the cobblestones within the front
courtyard. Philip, I realized, had kept to his determination to
have the guests leave directly after the ball. I had thought it
odd when he had advised me of his plan weeks ago since particularly in inclement weather it was considered ungracious to
ask guests to travel long distances without providing more of a
respite, but he had been insistent that he wanted everyone
gone by the afternoon of the following day. I panicked suddenly at the thought that Anne, too, might depart before I had
had an opportunity to talk to her.

Struggle as I did to sit up, I simply could not summon the
strength to endure more than a few moments. I lay back dejectedly, staring at the ceiling. Again, I could not fight the
drowsiness, and sleep enveloped me.

When I next awoke it was to the sense of something cold
against my face. I opened my eyes to see Jaspar nuzzling my

cheek. I reached down and scratched his ear.

Charlotte hovered over me. "Robbie told me to be bringin' the little one back to ye. Was mopin' down in the stables there the whole 'o the day, frettin' 'bout his mistress 'e was."

I smiled as Jaspar licked at my hand.

"Are ye feelin' any better, Serena?"

"It is this weakness, it is so frustrating," I replied "What time is it, Charlotte?"

" 'Tis goin' on six. Aye brought ye some more milk an' toast. Do ye think ye could nibble a bit?"

"Not now, Charlotte. Perhaps later."

I lay quietly as she brushed my hair gently from my forehead.

"Do you know if Philip sent for the doctor?"

"Aye can't be sayin', but Lady Anne made 'im promise that he would before she an' Lord Camberleigh left."

"They have left?" I gasped. "When? Anne would not leave without seeing me."

"She looked in on ye a while back but ye was asleep. Lord Taggart said we was to leave, ye be needin' yer rest an' all."

I reached out and grasped at her arm. "Charlotte, please check and see if they have left. Perhaps they were delayed. I *must* talk to Anne."

Charlotte was obviously frightened by my outburst. "Aye saw 'em leave meself, Miss Serena. Aye wouldn't a let 'em go if aye knew t'was so important but aye didn't know. Aye told Lady Camberleigh this mornin' that ye was wantin' to see her, aye thought she had come."

"She did," I replied dejectedly. "But I was not able to talk to her. Not privately, that is. It's not your fault," I assured her, pulling Jaspar, who had climbed onto the bed, closer to me.

There was a knock at the door and I shuddered involuntarily as Philip entered. "How is my wife feeling, Charlotte?" he asked as he strode towards the bed and stood looming over me.

"A tad stronger, aye think, yer Lordship, but she's far from well. Be needin' a doctor, I think."

"I have sent for him," he replied. "There are a few things I should like to discuss with my wife. In private."

Charlotte looked down at me anxiously. I nodded to her

that it was all right for her to leave. I scarcely wanted to be alone with Philip but I trusted that he would not dare touch me in this state.

Once Charlotte had left he took the chair beside me, his eyes roving my face. "You really do not look well, Serena," he said slowly, "but then I have been telling you that for months."

"What is it that you want, Philip?" I sighed.

"A certain civility," he replied, his annoyance obvious.

"Please, Philip," I beseeched, "I simply do not have the strength."

"Well, then, I shall make it brief. I am leaving for London morning after next."

My eyes flew open. "Is this not a bit sudden?"

"A bit but it cannot be helped. I must meet with Jonathan."

"I see," I replied slowly. "And when shall you return?"

"The eighteenth or thereabouts. It shall depend on how much I—we—can accomplish over the next days."

"Where will you stay?"

He looked surprised. "At Channing Hall, of course. The place is in disarray but then it shall only be a week at the most."

He rose quickly and, motioning to the tray, continued, "You really should eat something, Serena. I scarcely imagined myself marrying someone and burying her the same year."

Once Philip had left I pondered this latest move. Like the ball which seemed to have sprung out of thin air so the spontaneity of this trip to London proved mystifying. He had said he would be back about the eighteenth. I could not think for a moment why that date bothered me but then it came to me suddenly. The letter had said, "Returning the sixteenth." Was he going to London, I wondered, not to meet with Jonathan, as he had purported, but to meet whoever was returning on the sixteenth? It was farfetched but it was the only reason I could give for it.

I knew that Amelie would be with Philip tonight, and I was angry that I did not feel able to fight this lassitude for I sensed that my eavesdropping might have paid off. But even if I could have mustered the energy to make it down to Philip's quarters I could not have chanced collapsing in their path.

Jaspar furrowed under my arm and I stroked his long silken coat. It did not seem possible that my body was again yearning for sleep but this time I did not fight it.

When I awakened I knew that it must have been the middle of the night for the candle on the nightstand had only burned half down. Jaspar whimpered as I struggled to sit up. I was dreadfully weak but for the first time in days that awful dizziness seemed to have abated. The tray that Charlotte had left was still on the nightstand and I leaned over and took a piece of toast. It was cold and dry but my system was so void of food that I welcomed it. Jaspar sat over me, looking longingly at the small morsel in my hand.

"You're hungry, too, aren't you?" I whispered, pulling off a piece and giving it to him.

When I had shared the second piece with him and he was still obviously in want of sustenance, I reached for the milk and poured it into a small saucer on the tray. He lapped at it eagerly. Charlotte would chastise me for not drinking it myself but I was loathe to eat too much in this sudden flush of feeling slightly better. When he had finished I replaced the saucer and blew out the candle, smiling as he licked at my hand.

"I love you, too, sweet fellow," I whispered. "You and I have a lot to accomplish in these next weeks."

The room was very cold when I next awakened. I lay in bed, trying to analyze how I felt. I was weak but there was no dizziness, no further hint of the nausea that had besieged my body these last days. I suddenly realized that Jaspar was not beside me and called out to him. When he did not respond I swung my legs over the side of the bed, straining to see him in the darkened room.

"There you are, you old sleepyhead," I called out, seeing him curled up by the fireplace. "Come over here, it is too cold for you to be lying there."

When he did not come to me, I became slightly alarmed for it was not like him not to respond to my every move or call.

I got up gingerly, careful to hold onto the bedposts as I did. My skin felt hot and prickly, but I knew it was a reaction to my sudden exertion.

"Jaspar," I called out again. "Come here, come to Serena."

When he did not move I forgot all caution and stumbled over, crouching before him.

"Jaspar, what is it?" I cried.

I froze as my hand passed over his coat for his body was icy cold. I leaned forward and cradled his head in my hands. As I did I noticed that blood had seeped from his muzzle. It was now dry and I knew quickly that my dear spaniel had been lost to me hours before.

I moved his body towards my lap, gently placing his head across my knees.

"Oh, Jaspar, no," I cried out. "Not you, please not you."

Tears spilled from my eyes as I held him to me. "Don't leave me now, I could not bear it, not now. What happened, you were fine, what could have happened?"

Jaspar was not a young dog; at fourteen I knew he would be considered elderly by most, but he had always been so healthy. I looked down through my tears at this little bundle of brown and white fur who had been my confidant, my friend, ever my valiant defender. We had shared a bond from that first moment I had found him. My heart ached, not merely for the loss of a dog but for the loss of a part of my life. He had suffered my anguishes with me and had rejoiced in my elations. First Justin, now Jaspar. Was I to lose all that was dear to me?

I do not know how much time had passed when Charlotte found me there, cradling Jaspar's lifeless body in my arms. She seemed to sense immediately what had happened for she rushed over to me, holding me as the pain inside me screamed its way out.

"Hush, Serena," she comforted, "ye must come back to bed."

"I will not leave him," I cried out.

"He'll always be with ye, Serena," she choked, "but he's gone from us now. Come, aye'll fetch me Robbie."

"No," I wailed. "Why did this have to happen, why Charlotte?"

She shook her head. "The Lord be given an' 'e be takin' away, Serena. We 'ave to accept his will. An' our Jaspar, 'e had a long happy life, happier than most folks kin ever dream of."

"But he wasn't ill," I sputtered out. "It isn't fair, it just isn't fair."

Jaspar's fur was sodden with my tears as I continued to stroke the length of his body.

Suddenly the door burst open. I looked up at Charlotte's gasp.

"What in God's name is going on here?" Philip demanded

as he loomed over our crouched figures.

" 'Tis Miss Serena's spaniel, Lord Taggart," Charlotte said quickly, sniffling as she did. "The poor girl is beset with grief."

"Well, don't you have enough sense to get her up from that floor?"

"Get her back into bed right away and see that that mutt is disposed of."

I cringed at his words, pulling Jaspar even tighter to me.

"Well, woman, don't just sit there looking daft, get up, do as I say," Philip demanded. "I expect everything put to rights by the time I return."

The door slammed as he left.

"Not a carin' fiber in that man's body," Charlotte murmured as she struggled to her feet. "Aye'll be fetchin' Robbie, Miss Serena. Here, ye keep this throw 'bout ye."

She draped a woven coverlet about my shoulders, assuring me that Robbie would come soon.

None of this made any sense to me. Charlotte, Robbie, any of them, could tell me that Jaspar was an old dog, that it was his time, but I would listen to none of them. Six hours ago Jaspar had been fine, he had even been hungry, begging me to share the toast with him. I had even given him all my milk.

A jolt suddenly seemed to go through my body. I remembered that I had given all the milk to Jaspar. The milk that had been intended for me. And now, *I* felt much improved but my beloved spaniel was dead. I shuddered at the conclusions I was quickly reaching. Had something been added to that milk? Something that if ingested by a human being would cause them to be violently ill? Something that if accidentally swallowed by a small dog would provoke death? Had Jaspar unwittingly taken some lethal dose that had been intended for me?

I was filled with a sense of dread and fear. Rationally I knew that Charlotte had brought me the milk, which undoubtedly Cook had prepared. That either of them intended me bodily harm I did not even entertain. There was only one person that I feared in this house. Did he despise me so much that he would plot my demise? If I were not around then, he would not need to skulk around the house with his mistress—but that hardly seemed a reason to contrive such a violent act. But then perhaps it would not have appeared violent. Philip had been telling everyone, myself included, that I did not look well. He even had Anne agreeing. The doctor had been sent for and yet he had still not arrived. Had that all been a story simply to placate Anne and Charlotte?

Common sense told me that what I was thinking was madness and yet it would be hard to dissuade my suspicions.

It was only moments later when I felt a hand on my shoulder. I jumped slightly.

" 'Tis only me, Serena," Robbie said as he knelt down beside me.

"Ye must come away now. There's nothin' ye kin be doin' for the little fellow."

I shook my head. "I cannot leave him, Robbie," I cried.

He pried my fingers gently from Jaspar's paw.

"Don't take him from me, Robbie," I pleaded.

"Serena, this is hard for me, too, ye know," he replied, his voice breaking.

I looked up at him, suddenly realizing that Robbie was crying, too.

"Forgive me, Robbie," I whispered. "You loved him as your own, I know."

He nodded. "Was a real friend, 'e was. If ye wouldn't be mindin', Miss Serena, aye'd like to be buryin' 'im down on the hill by the stables. 'E liked it there an' that way aye'll be feelin' 'es still close by."

I leaned down and kissed for the last time the soft furrow between Jaspar's eyes as Robbie moved him gently onto a large horseblanket.

"If it be any comfort to ye, Miss Serena, aye never saw a dog who loved his mistress more. 'E had a happy life, 'e did, an' maybe where 'e is now 'e kin take the memory 'o that with 'im."

I reached forward and kissed Robbie lightly on the cheek.

"You have been ever a loyal friend to this family, Robbie."

" 'Tis like me own, it is," he replied quietly. "The master was the best ever, 'e was."

I knew, of course, that he referred to Justin.

"Robbie," I whispered, "I must ask you to do something for me. I caution it is going to sound like an odd request but I cannot explain for now why I am going to ask this of you. You simply must trust me."

He looked puzzled but replied, "If it be in me power, ye know aye'll be helpin' ye."

I nodded. "I want you to arrange to have a carriage ready to go to London tomorrow morning."

"To London?" he asked. "Aye'm to 'ave one ready fer Lord Taggart, will ye not be travelin' together?"

I shook my head. "No. Lord Taggart, I believe, shall be leaving the first thing in the morning but he is not to know of our plans. It is crucially important that this be kept a secret from everyone, even your own mother. As soon as I am certain that he has left, then I shall join you at the stables. Try to determine what route he shall take for I should not want to encounter him along the way. After Philip has gone I shall tell everyone that I have decided to go to Camberleigh for a week or so. I shall explain that I have asked you to remain with me there to help Richard out with some project."

"Beggin' yer pardon, Miss Serena, but with ye bein' so ill an' all, do ye think 'tis wise that ye be travelin'?"

"Truthfully, no, Robbie," I replied honestly. "But this is not a matter that can wait. I shall have to ask you to help me. I am very weak and it is not an easy journey."

"We'll be makin' it, Miss Serena," he assured me.

I had not let go of the small bundle before me but I knew now that it was time. As if sensing my acceptance, Robbie gently cradled Jaspar in his arms and stood up. Neither of us could speak but I knew that we shared a deep sense of loss.

When Robbie had left me I once again had to face my weakened state. I pulled myself up by a chair before the fireplace. I was chilled, and although I knew that I should be back in bed, I was afraid that I would not be able to cross the room on my own.

The sight of Charlotte, therefore, was a godsend. How she supported my weight against her diminutive frame I shall not know but she quickly had me back in bed and was pressing the hot porridge and tea that she had brought upon me. I made a concerted effort to eat everything, including the slices of bacon and chicken livers, for I would need all the strength that I could muster over these next days.

I wished that I could take her into my confidence, for deceiving her was not my want. I had to do it so that I would be convincing enough for her to believe me.

When she had finished brushing my hair and helping me change into a fresh nightdress, I asked her if she would sit down with me for a moment. As I studied her I realized that her eyes were as red-rimmed as my own. Jaspar's death would have a profound effect on many members of this household. I did not want to think about having to tell the children. They would be devastated, particularly so soon after losing Justin.

"It hurts me to see such a pain in those beautiful eyes, Serena," Charlotte said quietly. "Aye kin remember the days when they fairly be dancin' with joy. 'Tis many a moon since aye've seen that light there."

"Robbie was wonderful," I replied quietly. "I do not know what I would have done without him."

"T'was a cruel thing Lord Taggart be sayin'. Fer ye this is almost like losin' a child. He had no right to speak to ye that way, even if he is yer husband."

"Charlotte, I have made a decision which I want to share with you."

She looked at me expectantly.

"I am going to go to Camberleigh for a while."

She sighed as if relieved. "Aye've been hopin' fer weeks now that ye would take the children an' go there fer a spell. Ye need a change an' ye need rest an' to be takin' care of proper like."

"Well, when I tell you that I plan to leave tomorrow and to go on my own, you may not be as enthusiastic."

"Oh, Serena, ye can't be thinkin' 'o doin' any such thing. Ye've been at nearly death's door fer days now. In a week, when aye kin put some meat back on those bones an' git some bloom in yer cheeks, but not tomorrow."

"I have already talked to Robbie. He is going to help me. And once I am there Anne will watch over me and care for me. You simply must trust me, Charlotte, that it is the right thing to do."

"Aye can't be acountin' fer 'ow the children will react. They've been sort 'o shunted aside these past weeks an' aye fear the news 'o yer leavin' t'will upset them further."

"I am very conscious of that, Charlotte, which is why I particularly ask you to watch over them night and day while I am gone. I do not want to address it now, but let it suffice to say that it has come to my attention that your instincts about Miss Wythe were accurate—to put it mildly."

"Then why not just give 'er the gate? Surely aye kin be handlin' the wee ones fer a week or two."

I shook my head. "For my own reasons it is imperative that

she stay on here at Mayfair, at least while I am away. And when I leave, you are expressly to inform her that I have gone to Camberleigh to rest and recuperate. But no one must be told, not Philip, not Amelie, not even the children until I am gone from here.''

''Aye'll be doin' what ye tell me, Serena, but ye must admit it sounds like a mystery, it does.''

''I wish I could tell you how vitally important it is that you follow my directions to the letter, Charlotte. And one more thing.''

She looked at me expectantly.

''If at any time you sense that you or the children are in any kind of danger, I want you to take them, without a word to anyone else, to Camberleigh.''

''Danger?'' Charlotte gasped. ''Saints preserve us, why would we be in danger?''

''I do not envision that you would be,'' I acknowledged chary of panicking her. ''I only meant that if anything unexpected were to happen, anything that might make you suspicious, if only in the slightest sense, then I would want you to take the children and go straight away to Camberleigh.''

''Ye need 'ave no fear, Serena, aye'll be keepin' a close eye out fer the two. But fer now aye want ye te rest. If ye is determined to be leavin' on the morrow you'll be needin' yer rest.''

I did not argue for I was indeed exhausted. I asked Charlotte to bring the children round in the afternoon. It would break my heart to give them the news of Jaspar, but it was a task that had to be borne by myself.

When Charlotte returned with my luncheon tray at midday I asked her to lock the door and quickly pack a bag for my journey, taking care to keep it as simple as possible. I then instructed her to bury it at the back of the closet and make no mention of it to anyone. I knew that I could not afford to leave much time between Philip's departure and my own and that meant being ready to travel, if need be, at dawn.

She left me, promising to bring the children to me at three and again insisting that I keep to my bed. Sleep did not come to me this time for my mind was too filled with the loss of my dear Jaspar and the events that would present themselves in the days ahead. I was not entering into this journey without some trepidation. Even were I feeling totally fit I was hardly a match for Philip. If I knew what I was looking for, if only pieces of the puzzle could fit together, I might know where and how to start. No matter how I tried to think about it, I was still a relatively young woman who in several days would be sneaking about the streets of London, spying on a husband who would hopefully lead her to some conclusion.

My visit with the children only served to question my decision. They were heartbroken about Jaspar as I knew they would be. I feared that I was not as helpful to them as I would have wanted, but my own pain and anger were so fresh that I could think of little to say to give them solace.

I debated telling them of my impending journey to Camberleigh. I did not want to not chance their saying something to Amelie, but I could not simply leave them without a word. Taking them with me was out of the question for I knew that Philip would likely be ensconced at Channing Hall. As far as I knew, Monique was still in Paris, and though I was loathe to do so I would have to impose on Clarissa's hospitality during my stay. The prospect made me slightly uneasy for I sensed that she had somewhat confused loyalties towards Philip. The express purpose of my visit would have to be veiled in ambiguity.

It had been painful to be around the children these last days. They were not the carefree, happy young people that I had known them to be less than a year ago. I felt that I was to blame. Certainly not intentionally, for in fact a large part of why I had married Philip had been to give them some continued sense of family. They never spoke against him, though I sensed that they had come in their own fashion to fear him as much as I did. There was a wariness about Alexander that spoke of one far beyond his years. Daphne, who had always worn her heart and her thoughts on her sleeve, chose her words carefully these days. My illness had no doubt frightened them; I was certain that they had, like myself, given thought to what might become of them were I to die or be left incapacitated. Had I been able to talk to Anne I could have sent them to Camberleigh, but Philip had made very certain that the guests had left unsuspecting that there was anything amiss here at Mayfair.

When Charlotte returned to fetch the children, I was relieved for I was thoroughly exhausted. She returned with the dinner tray, which did not seem particularly appealing, but I forced myself to eat, conscious that I would need all the sustenance I could get before the next day.

"Aye think ye look a little better, Serena," Charlotte commented as I pushed the tray away. "But aye still be wishin' that ye'd delay yer trip fer a bit, just till ye've got yer strength back."

"I wish I could Charlotte," I replied, "but this is not something that can be delayed."

"Well, then, aye'll be leavin' ye now," she said, removing the tray. "Ye should sleep if ye can."

"It seems that that is all I have done," I murmured.

"Would ye like me to bring ye some hot milk? It might help settle ye."

I shook my head, revulsed at the thought.

"Charlotte, before you go, let me ask you something."

"O'course."

"When you have brought me the milk, last evening for example, have you always fetched it yourself?"

She looked puzzled.

"What I mean is that I know that you have physically brought it to the room, but did you actually prepare it yourself? Or did someone else give it to you, Cook, or perhaps someone else?"

She thought for a moment. " 'Tis Cook or 'tis meself who fixes it."

"I see," I replied, wondering if my theory could have in fact been wrong.

" 'Course, Lord Taggart, 'e was right there makin' sure ye was gettin' yer milk each day. Come te think of it, aye was right surprised that 'e took so much interest. T'was a bit out 'o character, if ye know what aye mean."

"I knew it," I muttered.

Charlotte leaned forward. "Aye didn't be hearin' ye, Serena."

I waved her off. "It is nothing, Charlotte," I lied. "I was just curious."

"Aye'll be leavin' ye then. Ye just ring the bell 'ere if ye want somethin.' "

I settled down under the covers watching the shadows from the candle play about the room. My arm reached out involuntarily and I moaned against the emptiness that was there. First Justin, now Jaspar. My loss this morning brought flooding back the devastation of last fall. Had so many months passed since Justin had left us? If so, then why did the ache within me still feel so real?

"Oh, Justin," I cried to the empty room, "why did you have to leave us? I needed you so and I have not done well without you. I wanted to cope with it all—I wanted you to be so proud of me but I have let you down. I did not mean to—Lord knows, I thought I was doing the right thing. Philip was there and I believed him. I believed he cared about me and the children and it was all a lie. I was so naive, Justin. He said he wanted me. What he wanted, perhaps what he wanted all along, was Mayfair. And now I have come to believe that he will stop at nothing to get it. That is why I have to go to London. I have to have proof, something that will reveal him to be the charlatan he is. And *murderer*."

I spread my hand against the space that Jaspar had made his own each night since Justin's death. Philip could never have foreseen that a small spaniel would foil his scheme. Had I drunk the milk last night, would it have been me who would have been found lifeless in the morning, or was the dosage just enough to simply keep me conveniently ill and out of the way?

I fell asleep resolving to find out the truth, no matter what end.

# 19

When a knock came at the door in the morning I was already awake.

"Come in."

I withdrew against the pillows when I saw that it was Philip.

"What do you want?" I snapped.

"Your tender endearments are not exactly the bon voyage I was hoping for, Serena," he replied, eyeing me closely.

"There is no one here, Philip; we need not keep up this ruse."

He shrugged. "Charlotte tells me you are feeling better."

"That should disappoint you," I murmured.

"*Au contraire,* my sweet. Frankly I only came by to tell you that I shall be departing within the hour. I would hope that when I return that you are up and about again. It does not suit me having an invalid for a wife."

I clenched my teeth to keep from casting out some retort that I would later come to regret.

Philip waited as if he expected me to say something further. "You have nothing more to say, Serena?"

"Not to you, Philip," I replied, "if that is what you are asking."

"Well, then, I shall return within a week or so," he replied, turning on his heel.

I was grateful that he left quickly for I did not know how

long I could maintain my composure. He was, I decided, even more diabolical than I had first thought. He showed no emotion, no fear, before me.

Fortunately I did not have to ponder it further for Charlotte arrived with my basin.

She closed the door behind her and whispered, "aye believe Lord Taggart is leavin' now."

"Where is Miss Wythe?" I asked, pulling my robe about me as I stood up, gingerly aware of my own steadiness.

"In the nursery, aye expect," Charlotte replied.

"After you bring my breakfast tray I should like you to tell the children that I would like to see them. If Miss Wythe says anything, simply indicate that since I was feeling a bit stronger I merely wanted to visit with them this morning. Try to keep an eye on her, however, until the children return to the nursery."

"An' then what would you be wantin' me to do?"

"Ask Robbie to fetch my bag, but only once he is absolutely certain that Philip, Lord Taggart, is long gone from Mayfair."

Charlotte left me to bathe, which I did slowly, taking care not to overtire myself. I selected a green velvet suit for traveling and coiled my hair simply at the nape of my neck. When she returned I was fully dressed, if not suitably turned out for my own taste. I was frighteningly pale and thinner than I had been over the holidays but my appearance was the least of my worries these days. I commenced eating the tray filled with hot porridge and stewed fruits as Charlotte went to fetch the children.

Instinctively I left a bit of the milky cereal substance in the bowl and then turned back to it, sadly realizing that my brown and white friend would nevermore be waiting patiently for me to save him the last bites.

I was startled when the children arrived for they tiptoed into the room, expecting, I suppose, to find me still confined to my bed.

"You are up, Mama," Daphne exclaimed, running towards me. "Are you feeling better?"

"Much," I replied. "I am still weak but I am much improved."

I held her at arm's length. "You are looking very pretty

today. You both seem to be growing before my very eyes."

"Robbie says I grew a whole inch since last year," Alexander interjected.

"I grew even more," Daphne challenged.

"Perhaps," I acknowledged, "but one year soon Alexander, I suspect, will be towering over you."

"Why has Philip gone to London, Mother?" Daphne asked as I braided the long tendrils of golden tresses that cascaded down her back.

"How did you know he had gone?"

"He came to say goodbye to us in the schoolroom."

"He did not come to say goodbye to *us*, stupid" Alexander rebuked.

"Alexander, that is no way to talk to your sister," I commanded.

"He says that Miss Wythe is in love with Philip," Daphne blurted out.

"Miss Wythe worked for Philip's sister, Alexander," I replied carefully. "He has known her for some time and it is only natural that he would want to make sure she is comfortable here."

"Well, I wish she would leave," Daphne pouted. "She is so boring. I do not even think she is pretty."

"Well, I did not ask you here to talk about Miss Wythe," I concluded. "I wanted to tell you both that I shall be going to stay with your Aunt Anne and Uncle Richard for a while."

"By yourself?" Daphne exclaimed. "You are going to leave us here by ourselves?"

I smiled. "You will scarcely be by yourself. There is a whole household here to watch over you, and Charlotte has promised to spend a special amount of time with you while I am gone."

"Why could we not go with you?" Daphne pleaded. "Oh, please, Mama, we would be good. I promise I would not even say one unkind thing to Alexander."

I shook my head. "This journey I must make on my own. I shall just be there for a short spell. Long enough to get some rest, hopefully gain a little weight. I would take you both, but I do not want to place more of a burden than is necessary on your Aunt Anne."

"She likes our visiting," Daphne persisted.

"I agree," I replied. "And in the early summer I promise that we will make plans to go to Camberleigh for a long visit. Remember, Oliver shall be returning and I know that Anne is planning great festivities after the wedding."

She did not seem appeased but I was not about to discuss it further. I embraced both children, holding each as tight to me as I could before releasing them. I prayed that I was doing the right thing by leaving them here at Mayfair. I could not have trusted Charlotte more than if she were my own mother, but the children were my life now that Justin was lost to me and their safe-caring was my first priority.

"Now back to the schoolroom with both of you," I insisted.

Daphne, who was still miffed at not being allowed to come with me, flounced out of the room. I resisted calling to her, knowing that she was partially doing it for effect. I smiled to myself, thinking that if Daphne ever decided to pursue the stage that she would undoubtedly be a great success.

Alexander had made no move to leave and I reached out to him as he scuffed his shoe against the floor.

"Darling, is there something you want to talk about?" I asked.

The next thing I knew he was in my arms, sobbing so passionately that I felt a sense of panic well within me.

"Alex, darling, what is it?" I pleaded. "Is it my going away that is upsetting you so?"

My heart ached at the thought that there could be so much hurt buried within this small boy.

"Whatever it is, you must tell me. Truly, only if you tell me can I help."

"I miss Jaspar," the small voice blurted out. "He was my best friend and now he is gone."

"Oh, darling, I know," I cried out, pulling him closer to me. "I loved him too. And I feel sad and angry that he has been taken from us. But what we must try and do is to think of how much happiness he brought us."

I released him a bit, stroking his head, which was buried into my shoulder. "Remember the time several years ago that you were down by the stables? Your father thought I had brought you back and I thought you were with him. When we realized you were missing we were frantic. Robbie, your father, all of us, were looking frantically for you. But it was

Jaspar who finally found you. You had buried yourself in a mound of hay in one of the stables. Had it not been for that wonderful little nose of his I fear we would not have found you until morning."

"He licked at me and barked until you came," he choked out, wiping the tears from his eyes.

"He was so proud of himself," I replied. "He loved you and Daphne and you must always treasure all the love he gave to each one of us. He enriched our lives and we must be very thankful for that, and because we loved him so much, a part of him shall always be with us."

"Like father?" Alexander murmured.

"Yes, just like your father," I whispered.

We stayed holding each other for some minutes until Alexander finally eased away from me.

"Better now?" I asked.

He nodded.

"Good. Then give me one more kiss and go find Daphne. I think she is hurting a bit as well. Perhaps you can tease a smile out of her."

Alexander had been gone only about fifteen minutes when Robbie appeared at the door to my quarters.

"Lord Taggart will be on his way, Serena. If ye are still fixin' te go we should be startin' soon."

I nodded. "My valise is in the back of the closet. It will only take me a few moments to freshen up and I shall meet you in the front courtyard."

Robbie fetched the valise. "Me mum is puttin' a basket together an' she'll bring it soon as I bring the carriage round."

After I had organized a small travel bag I quickly repinned my hair, gathered my cloak about me and left my room. The hallway was quiet as I made my way down the staircase. I was grateful for that for I did not want to explain my sudden departure to anyone.

Robbie had already brought the carriage round and he was placing the enormous basket Charlotte handed him into the back. When he spotted me on the steps he ran up to take my arm. I did not resist for the effort I had made this morning had wearied me greatly.

"Charlotte, you should be in the house," I chastised. "You shall catch your death out here dressed like that."

"Ye just get in there an' get yourself warm," she replied as she wrapped a heavy wool throw about my legs. "The basket is full an' it's meant to be eaten."

I laughed. "I promise I will do my best."

Robbie had already climbed atop the carriage. Charlotte swung the window door shut and I reached out and clung to her hand. "Remember your promise," I begged. "At the slightest suspicion that something is awry you take the children to Camberleigh."

"Relax, my girl," Charlotte assured. "The children will be fine."

I said a small prayer as the carriage clattered along the drive leading away from Mayfair. I prayed for safety and for answers, answers that would mean that this voyage was not pure folly.

I wished that I could sit atop the carriage with Robbie for companionship would have eased the long trip for us both, but I was too weak to suffer the cold air for any length of time. When several hours had passed I called up to him to ask if he wanted to rest a spell and investigate the basket-lunch that Charlotte had prepared. He agreed and shortly thereafter pulled the carriage off by a roadside stream which, though partially frozen, still provided a liquid refreshment for the horses.

We huddled inside the carriage and munched on chicken, cold meats and crusty breads.

"Do you think we can make Manchester by nightfall?" I asked, commencing to gather up the cloths and napkins and replace them in the hamper.

Robbie shook his head. "We cannot go that way—not unless ye want to chance running into Philip."

"Oh, no," I gasped. "I would not even want to think of the consequences were he to know that we were headed to London."

"That means aye'll be keepin' to me original plan. We'll go overland. 'Tis not an easy trip but t'will be safer."

"Can we keep going until nightfall?" I pursued.

"We kin try, Serena, but Lord Taggart has the strong team. Aye kin only push them so far."

We agreed that we would leave it up to Robbie's discretion.

I tried to sleep as we entered the next part of the journey but the pull and sway of the carriage always lulled me out of my reveries. My obsession with the fragment of that letter "returning the sixteenth" also kept me from enjoying any respite. What about the letters had frightened Amelie so? I determined that one of the first things that I would do when we reached London was to call on Jonathan Leech. He perhaps would have some information, some clue as to what I was searching. I would have to proceed cautiously, however, for although I had no cause to distrust Jonathan I had no proof that he had not been involved in Philip's ruse from the very first.

It was growing dark when Robbie slowed the carriage before what appeared to be a small roadhouse. Only the sign out front told me that we had obviously arrived at our home for this night.

" 'Tis not very grand," Robbie cautioned as he helped me alight from the carriage, "but aye know the owners an' they run a clean place."

"You look tired," I replied, noting the circles under his eyes.

"Now don't ye go botherin' about me, Serena. Ye go on in an' aye'll be along after aye see to these horses. Ye ask for Sire Turpelow. Tell 'im yer with Robbie McKee. He an' the missus, they'll be fixin' us up."

I entered the stone house and was immediately warmed by smells of baking bread emanating from the kitchens. The bell over the door that I had set ringing when I entered was still tinkling when a ruddy-complected man with bushy white sidewhiskers stepped before me.

"An' what can the Yew and the Wren be doin' fer ye, miss?" he enthused.

"I am Lady Barkham, I mean Lady Taggart," I replied, flushing at my faux pas. "Robbie McKee is seeing to our carriage. Would you by any chance be Sire Turpelow?"

"Aye would," he beamed, "an' if yer a friend 'o Robbie's yer most welcome in our wee abode. 'Tis an honor to 'ave ye 'ere, Lady Taggart."

"Actually I am hoping that you have rooms, two exactly, for this evening."

He nodded, looking at me up and down as I removed my cloak. "Aye do but aye 'ave to be warnin' ye that t'wont be nothin' fancy."

"A clean place to lie down and some refreshment is all I ask," I replied.

He beamed. "Then ye've come to the right place."

He twirled around suddenly and boomed out, "Susannah, come 'ere an' see who's come to stay."

A girl around eighteen came forward, drying her hands on a large gingham apron that dwarfed her small frame.

"This is me Susannah," Sire Turpelow beamed, pushing her forward. "Susannah, this is Lady Taggart. Our Robbie McKee tends the stables there at Mayfair up north."

I smiled as the young girl bobbed before me.

"You have a lovely daughter, Sire Turpelow," I praised.

He broke out into gales of laughter. "Susannah is me wife."

"I am sorry," I muttered, flustered at my mistake.

"Needs no apology," he insisted, still laughing, "Aye been accused o' robbin' the cradle many a day. Susannah, why don't ye take Lady Taggart up to her room and be gettin' 'er a basin? Then when you've rested, ye kin come down an ave some o' Susannah's rabbit stew an' scones."

The room, as he had warned, was small but cozy and warm. Susannah saw to it that my valise was brought up to me as well as a large porcelain basin of steaming water. I felt much refreshed after I had bathed and decided to rest for a spell before rejoining Robbie downstairs.

When I awakened I realized that it was to a steady knocking at the door.

"Serena, 'tis me, Robbie, are ye all right?"

I got up slowly, making my way carefully in the darkened room. I found the door and opened it to find Robbie grinning before me.

"Aye thought t'was best te let ye rest but they'll only be servin' supper fer a spell longer."

"Give me just a moment," I begged. "I just want to brush my hair a bit."

Robbie used his candle to light those in my room while I uncoiled my hair and brushed it well. I tied it back loosely with a ribbon, glad to be free of the pins about the nape of my neck.

I followed Robbie down the stairs to the small dining room at the back of the inn. I was surprised to see that there were a number of other guests as my eyes roamed about the room. I had just commenced to follow Robbie to our appointed table when I heard my name exclaimed from the other side of the room.

"Serena," I heard the voice calling, "Serena, darling, over here."

I froze, not wanting to recognize the intrusion.

When the calling persisted I turned to find Lady Jane Bellmore and her daughter flailing their arms wildly at us. I knew that I could not avoid a confrontation and thus moved over to where they sat.

Lady Jane Bellmore was an odious woman whom I had met when I had first come to Camberleigh. She was, I supposed, well into her sixties. After she had emotionally tortured her poor husband to death she then turned her efforts upon her squat plump daughter, who many years before had lost any prospects for escaping her mother's clutches.

"Serena, fancy seeing you here," she fussed as I approached the table. "Isn't that your little stable boy over there?"

"Well, we consider him far more than that, but yes, that is Robbie," I replied politely.

"I have not seen you since the theatre in London. And since you became Lady Taggart," she effused, scrutinizing my appearance carefully.

"Philip, my husband, and I do little entertaining," I replied quietly.

"Now, darling, you know that is not true. Why, I hear that there was just a rather large ball at Mayfair. Though since I did not receive an invitation, I could not know much about it."

"Philip handled most of the invitations," I excused. "I am certain that it was simply an oversight."

"Rumor has it that you have not been well, my dear," she pursued. "I must say you do look a bit peaked to be traveling about. On your way to London, are you?"

I nodded. "Please do not think me rude but I really must rejoin Robbie. This is the last service, I understand."

"Well, perhaps we might travel together. Sara and I are dreadfully bored with each other and we might all go in your carriage or mine."

I smiled, anxious to get away. "Perhaps."

"Well, we shall talk in the morning—it shall be great fun."

When I reached the table Robbie looked up at me. "Ye don't look very happy, Serena."

I unfolded the large linen napkin against my lap. "Of all the people I did not want to encounter. I fear we shall have to get underway very early in the morning for I certainly would not tolerate the thought of she and her daughter riding with us."

The meal was delicious and I was pleased that I was actually starting to relish food once again.

"Serena," Robbie broached as we finished our tea, "aye know that 'tis none o' me business but aye can't help be wonderin' what brings ye to London. Aye know it has to do with Lord Taggart but aye also can't help but noticin' that ye seem outright afraid o' him or o' his findin' out that we'll be in London."

"Robbie, I would tell you if I could, but truthfully some of my concerns are vague even to me. If I were to share my suspicions with you, it would only serve to alarm you—perhaps needlessly. And if there is any danger here, I want you clear of it. When I have some further clue, some information, I swear to you that I shall share it with you."

Robbie looked more distressed than relieved, but I could not do anything at this juncture to ease his mind.

I slept better that night than I had in months and awakened easily when Robbie knocked at my door at dawn. Sire Turpelow was befuddled by our early departure, but we assured him that it was not his hospitality but our schedule that caused us to press on.

There was a fine drizzle in the air as the carriage began the second part of the journey but fortunately it brightened with the full force of the morning. We had decided to stop at a small tavern which Robbie knew of for lunch. The horses were tired and although Robbie said he was willing to drive them on into the night I did not think it advisable. So later that day after we had traveled another four hours, I encouraged him to pull into the Bee and Thistle, a rather stately lodging frequented by Justin and me on our occasional forays to London.

When we entered I immediately questioned the wisdom of our stopping here for I knew anonymity would escape me. Robbie assured me, however, that Philip had taken the more direct route and thus there was no possibility of our encountering him here. The proprietors gave us a warm welcome, and after a hearty meal Robbie and I agreed that sleep would be the best curative for us both. Robbie had been most solicitous during the trip, always checking on me to see if I were weathering the ride well. I did not want to tell him that at times I felt so weary that I did not know if I could endure the next hour. However, whenever I thought I would succumb to my own malaise, some spark of energy, driven no doubt by my own determination, gave me the strength to go on.

I slept well again that night, awakening refreshed and renewed of purpose. It would be about eleven, I estimated, before we would reach the city. The thought of having to deal with Clarissa was less than appealing but there seemed no other option. Robbie was shocked when I directed him to head in that direction but he did not question my motives.

I had a moment's pause when we finally pulled up before the brick house, realizing suddenly that I did not even know if Clarissa and her family were in London.

The house was one of the newer ones in London, having been built but ten years prior. It was larger than most, though I personally felt that Clarissa must have encouraged the architect to sacrifice style for size.

As Robbie helped me alight from the carriage I asked him to get the horses refreshed and then bring my bag round to the front.

The manservant who opened the door was unknown to me but as soon as I identified myself he bade me to enter, leading me to the drawing room to wait until he might inform Clarissa of my arrival.

My cousin's influence was everywhere in this room. It was a mass of frills and bows and ruffles as though one were insisting one's femininity upon the guests. Clarissa was fortunate to have a husband who indulged her so, for the men I knew would not endure this fancifulness in a greeting room.

Almost forty minutes passed before Clarissa entered the room and I suspected that she had changed her gown three times before coming to greet me.

"Serena," she exclaimed, sweeping into the room, "it is you. When Thomas informed me that you were downstairs, well, I must admit that I told him that he must be mistaken. I mean, you are so rarely in London these days."

"I would have written to you, Clarissa," I replied, "but the trip was an impromptu one."

"I see," she answered, scrutinizing me closely. "And is Philip, Lord Taggart, with you?"

I shook my head. "There was really no need for him to make the trip."

"Not spatting so soon, darling?" she purred.

"Of course not," I replied quickly. "It is just that when I left London last I left Channing Hall in disarray and I wanted to put it in some semblance of order, which actually is why I have come here. You see if it would not inconvenience you too greatly I should like to stay here with you for a few days."

"Here?" she exclaimed. "Why would you not want to stay at Channing?"

"As I told you," I continued "the house is in disarray. Not to mention that most of the servants are on holiday. I wouldn't ask if I were not pressed. Monique, as you know, is still in Paris and this seemed the logical place to turn—that is, if you will have us?"

"Us?"

"Yes, myself and Robbie McKee—you know he helped Justin."

She waved me off. "Yes, of course I know. But what is *he* doing here?"

"Our driver was ill and I saw no reason to wait until he had recuperated. He will not be a bother," I insisted, "and I, too, have so many things to tend to that I should be gone most of each day."

"Well, I suppose since you are here, you might as well stay," Clarissa mused. "Actually, with you looking like you do, I could scarcely turn you out. I mean, Serena, you look as though you haven't eaten in weeks."

"I was a bit under the weather recently, nothing serious," I replied carefully. "But enough of me, how are Harold and Constance?"

"I do not know really," she replied. "Harold has taken her down to visit his family in Cornwall. They are such dreadful bores and the weather is so distasteful this time of year that I decided to remain at home. Lucky for you, I should say."

She smoothed the ruffled inset panel on her skirt. "You know, Serena, I must say I was shocked to learn of your marriage to Philip—Lord Taggart. Oh, do not misunderstand me, he is charming and certainly good-looking, but I thought you would wind up with someone, well, someone of more credibility, shall we say."

"Why would you say that?" I replied, curious at her observance.

"Well, he is hardly a man of means. Actually I have heard it said in some circles that he is not even titled. Not that I am implying that he married you for your money, of course."

I brushed the hair back from my forehead. "Clarissa, would you mind horribly if we discussed this at another time? I would very much like to get some rest. As I mentioned, I have not been well of late and the journey has tired me more than I thought."

"Suit yourself," she shrugged. "I shall have the maids prepare your room and the boy, Robbie, can find something in the servants' quarters. I know that you have this ridiculously democratic attitude about his place but I will not have a common driver staying doors away from me."

"I am certain that whatever you can offer he will find suitable," I replied.

Later that evening after I had bathed and picked at the tray which had been brought to my room, I lay in bed wondering what my plan ought to be for the morning. Tomorrow was the sixteenth. If anything were going to happen, if I were to learn anything, I sensed that it would be then.

I purposefully left the draperies open so that the morning light would rouse me. At dawn I dressed quickly and was careful to make as little noise as possible leaving the house. It had been foolhardy of me not to have alerted Robbie that I would need the carriage this morning; Channing Hall was a fair distance from Clarissa's house and I could scarcely make it alone on foot.

I looked about for a public carriage but saw none. My only hope was that Clarissa's driver was in the court and would oblige me by taking me crosstown. It was not her driver but Robbie that I found brushing down the team.

He looked up and called out, "What gets you up at this hour, Serena?"

I smiled. "I could say the same thing of you."

"It was right cold in that back room," he replied. "Aye figured aye better get me blood goin' for aye right froze te death."

"I am afraid hospitality is not my cousin's strong suit," I retorted, "but I shall make certain that you get extra blankets tonight. But right now I need you to take me someplace in the carriage.''

"Ye just name it," he grinned.

"I want you to take me within several hundred paces of Channing Hall in any direction and leave me there."

"An' then what, shall aye be waitin' there fer ye?"

"No. As soon as you drop me I want you to return here. If anyone asks where I am, simply say that I am at Channing Hall."

"But how will ye be gettin' back?" he asked as he helped me into the carriage.

"I shall manage," I assured him.

"Ye'll pardon me fer sayin' so but it sounds a bit odd to me, but if that's what ye want, Serena, then that's what aye'll be doin'.''

Robbie looked troubled when he helped me down from the carriage, but I assured him that I would be perfectly well. As soon as I saw the carriage disappear I pulled my cloak tighter about me and walked briskly, my head lowered toward the house. There was open land immediately opposite Channing Hall with a tall privet bordering it along the lane. It was hardly the most ideal hiding place but I could not risk getting any closer to the house.

I was fortunate for it was milder than usual and I knew that my wait, for whatever I was waiting for, could prove endless. As it turned out it was not, for within minutes I saw the door to the Hall open. Two men stepped out and I separated the verdant bush, peering out to see if I recognized either. The taller of the two had a dark cap pulled low over his forehead and I could barely distinguish his features. The shorter and, I suspected, younger man had red hair and a scraggly red beard. Neither of them looked even vaguely familiar to me and I could tell, simply from their attire, that neither was a gentleman.

I thought that they were leaving alone but suddenly the door reopened and Philip followed them out. I ducked lower behind the privet for he looked straight ahead in my direction, gesturing as he did. Any concern that he had seen me was dispelled when I saw the Mayfair carriage rounding from the back and realized that he was simply urging the men on to meet it.

I looked frantically down the street to see if there were any public carriages in sight. There were none. I swore at myself for having been so foolish as to have not realized that if Philip left the house I would have little chance of following him on foot. As the carriage pulled off I ran out into the street, searching frantically for some vehicle that would allow me to follow the path of the Mayfair carriage.

By the time one passed along I knew that it would be far too late to catch up with Philip, particularly since I knew not their intended destination.

Dejected, I instructed the driver to take me to Clarissa's.

If I had hoped that I could reenter the house quietly I was sadly mistaken for as I crept across the front entrance hall Clarissa called to me from the library.

"Serena, in here," she called out.

I turned and entered the library, where Clarissa was poised on the edge of a chair before the fireplace.

"Darling, forgive me for not moving, but Armande here gets ever so miffed with me if I move."

I turned to see a dark-haired man in his early twenties standing before a large canvas. Large almond eyes looked back at me, studying my face somewhat brazenly, I thought.

"Armande, this is my cousin Lady Barkham, I mean Lady Taggart," Clarissa cooed.

He bowed slightly to me again, his eyes never leaving mine. *"Enchanté, madame."*

"Armande is painting my portrait," Clarissa interjected through her frozen smile. "Harold demanded that I have my portrait done and although I loathed the thought I did think that I should have it done while the face is still holding."

Armande winked at me. "Madame exaggerates, of course. She has never looked more beautiful."

I could not miss the inference that Armande's knowledge of Clarissa had not simply come about through this commission, but I was scarcely about to pursue it.

"Serena, you really should employ Armande to do one of you. I am certain that your new husband would find it amusing, though I would say that you had best wait until you have had some rest. Your cheekbones look as though they are about to pop through your face."

Armande, who had resumed painting, looked up at me.

"I should be honored to paint you anytime, Lady Taggart. Your beauty is legendary and now, meeting you, I can see that it has not been underestimated."

Clarissa, who until now had been frozen in pose, shot a look at me. "Armande is so generous, is he not, Serena?" she purred cattily. "He is such a love and always knows just the right thing to say to bring one's spirits up. Harold did me a positive favor by insisting on this commission, didn't he, Armande darling?"

I was not quite certain exactly what repartee was being exchanged between the two, but I sensed that at least from Clarissa's vantage point I had become an unnecessary voyeur.

"You must excuse me, Clarissa, Armande," I said, "but there are things that I must tend to."

Clarissa was obviously relieved for she said nothing to encourage my remaining.

I left, finding my way to my room, where I sat before the fire trying to think what my next move should be. I could not simply hover behind the bushes in front of Channing Hall all day. I had resolved to see Jonathan Leech while I was here and determined that that would be my next foray into the city.

I requested a small luncheon tray to be brought to my room and told the young maid who served me that she should alert Robbie that I would want the carriage readied within the hour.

# 20

Jonathan lived in a highly populated and certainly modest section of the city. He was not a gentleman born, but I was surprised that he continued to reside in this area, which was known to be a haven for commoners. Certainly with the funding that Justin had provided he could afford a more suitable residence, but then reminding myself that he was a simple, unpretentious man, I realized that perhaps he was more comfortable here.

The flat proved to be a three-floor walk-up. I slightly regretted having been so magnanimous with Robbie, who had tried to insist on accompanying me on my visit. But as I reached the final step and knocked at the door before me I was pleased that I had decided to remain on my own.

The door was answered immediately by Jonathan himself.

He was so nonplussed by seeing me that I worried that I should have sent word ahead of my impending visit.

"Lady Barkham," he spluttered, adjusting his spectacles as if to see me better.

"Serena," I corrected him, noting that his full frame blocked the doorway almost to its entirety.

"Might I come in, Jonathan?" I asked tenuously.

"Come in, oh, yes, of course," he mumbled, stepping back so that I might follow him through.

I was embarrassed for him as he ran suddenly about the

room, picking up parts of clothing and papers that were scattered about.

"You must excuse me, Serena, I rarely have visitors. Had I known . . ."

"Jonathan, please relax," I assured him, "it is simply a friendly visit."

I shuffled a pack of papers together, handing them to him so that I might sit down on the dark couch that was soiled by age.

He sat down opposite me, pulling his vestment to cover an ever protruding stomach.

"Might I offer you a spot of tea?" he asked, peering at me over his spectacles.

I shook my head. "I am fine, thank you. I did not mean to intrude on you, Jonathan, but I thought perhaps unknowingly you might shed some light on some things that have been troubling me of late."

"Whatever I can do, Serena, you know I shall be honored."

"I should like you to tell me, if you would, about your relationship with my husband."

He looked very perplexed.

"Whatever you can tell me," I encouraged.

He took out a handkerchief and mopped at his brow. "Well, I think, perhaps I assumed, that you knew everything there was to tell. Lord Barkham always inferred that you, I mean, well, that you and he . . ."

I shook my head. "No, Jonathan, you do not understand," I said gently. "I am referring to Philip, Lord Taggart, not to Justin."

He wiped his brow again. "You must pardon me but I thought you were asking me about my relationship with your poor late husband."

I paused and studied him carefully. "You do not know, do you?" I broached.

He looked at me expectantly.

"I sense that you do not know that I am now Lady Taggart."

He could not have appeared more shaken had I delivered him a direct physical blow on his person.

"You mean you and Philip—you are married?"

I nodded, outraged to learn that he had not been informed.

"Of course, it is not surprising since I have not seen or heard from Lord Taggart since the unfortunate death of your husband, I mean, Lord Barkham."

"But that is impossible," I exclaimed. "What of the railways? I mean, certainly you are in contact with each other."

He shook his head. "It was unfortunate, of course, but I certainly understood that you would wish to withdraw from the project. Unfortunate, most unfortunate," he spluttered, "but certainly I understood."

I rubbed my forehead, trying to make logic out of what he was saying.

"Jonathan," I began slowly, "are you telling me that you have not been working with Philip all this while?"

He shook his head. " 'Tis the truth, Serena. I have not seen or heard from Philip Taggart since the last time I saw you. T'was that day, that dreadful day," he spluttered, "that we had to tell you about your—about Lord Barkham. After we left, Philip told me right out that you wouldn't be wanting to see the project through."

I must have paled considerably for Jonathan leaned forward and asked if he could not get me some water or tea. I felt as though someone had just slapped me about the head and I did not know if it was to stupefy me or to shock me into a deeper awareness of Philip's treachery.

I accepted the glass of water Jonathan had run to fetch me but could not drink of it for my hand was shaking so badly.

"You're as nervous as a cornered cat, Serena," he worried. "I hope it was not anything I said to upset you so."

I tried to compose myself before replying.

"Jonathan, what I am about to tell you will come as great a shock to you as your news has been to me."

He settled both hands on his spectacles again as if adjusting by sight what he would receive by sound.

"As you are aware, Justin's death was devastating to me. I wish I could tell you that I had met it with more courage but I did not. In retrospect I let everyone down—my family, myself, even you."

"Nonsense my, my dear," he stuttered. "You have nothing to apologize for."

"Ah, but I do," I insisted, taking a sip from the water he had brought.

"When I left London I went to Camberleigh to be with my sister-in-law and my uncle," I continued.

"I had heard."

"Not long after I returned to Mayfair, Philip paid me a visit. It was unexpected but at the time welcome for I was feeling very lonely and very vulnerable. But by then the one thing that I saw clearly was that it was most important that I try, best as I could, to maintain all that Justin had built. He had a vision about the railroads. Many thought that he was a bit mad probably because, as you well know, this was a man whose reputation was built on the land. I cannot say that I was terribly enthusiastic initially, but finally that no longer seemed important. Justin was gone, and it seemed the last way to keep his memory alive was to keep the vision alive."

Jonathan was listening to me patiently but I sensed without much understanding.

"What I am trying to tell you, Jonathan, is that I never withdrew a pound of the funding for the railroads."

"This cannot be true, Serena," Jonathan insisted. "Look about me. Do I look like a man who is deep at work?"

I shook my head. "And for that I am sorry, Jonathan, for I think that you were an integral part of my eagerness to proceed. Had I known that I would have been giving the money to Philip—and Philip alone—I doubt, even then, that I would have proceeded."

"Serena, Philip cannot be doing this on his own. The man knows no more about engines and laying tracks than what I've told him. If it's a railroad he's building he's doing it with someone, but that someone isn't me."

I drew a deep breath. "If the truth finally be known, Jonathan, I do not think my husband has any intention of pursuing the railroad venture. For reasons too complex to go into now I am commencing to wonder if that were ever Philip's interest."

"You are saying then that you think Philip has cheated you?"

"I am saying that I think that my husband is a fraud."

"It's a weighty charge you are making, Serena."

I nodded. "The terrible thing is that I think he may be worse than that, but thus far I have no way of proving it."

Jonathan mopped at his brow. "Lord Barkham was a good

man. Kind to me, he was. And I want you to know that if I can be of help you have only to ask."

"There is one thing, Jonathan, I need to know. How did you meet Philip?"

"Serena, I suppose you would know him better than I," he responded.

"You would think so, Jonathan, but I fear nothing could be further from the truth," I replied sadly.

"Serena, I only met Philip Taggart two weeks, perhaps three, before I met your late husband. He had heard that I had been working on a design for a steam engine and came to me to ask about it. I was reluctant at first but the plight of any inventor is that we have ideas and rarely the money to see them realized. Philip seemed certain that he could raise the funds needed. Perhaps I should not have been so enthusiastic but the prospect of seeing my dreams come to fruition was too exciting. They would no longer be my drawings but would actually take shape and form."

I studied Jonathan carefully. I had thought him to be a sweet, rather absentminded little man, preoccupied by his designs, but I realized that once one got beyond initial impressions there was both logic and sensitivity.

"Then you know very little about Philip," I pursued, "nothing about his past, his family?"

"Nothing, Serena."

"Jonathan, since I have learned that you have not been in contact with Philip, it is doubtful that you would see him, but he is in London, and if by any chance the two of you should meet it is imperative that you make no mention of my visit here. He must not know that I am in London."

"Mums the word, Serena," he assured me, "but with what you have been telling me I am even more certain that t'would be an odd thing were he to show himself about here these days."

I gathered my cloak about me and promised Jonathan that I would be in contact with him. There were certain things that could not be righted but I vowed as I descended the steps to the outside that Jonathan Leech would not be one of them. As soon as I had completed my mission here in London I resolved to write Sir Henry and have him bestow a sizable stipend on our Mister Leech. Philip perhaps had ruined my life but he should not ruin Jonathan's as well. Not while I was alive.

I looked about when I reached the outer steps, relieved that Robbie had obeyed my instructions again and hopefully returned to Clarissa's. A public carriage passed by, the driver looking expectantly at me but I waved him on, preferring to walk a while and give some clarity to my thoughts.

My walk had taken me I knew not where when I paused, realizing that everything about me was blurred. I reached up and wiped the tears from my eyes. I felt as alone and as helpless as I had when I had first learned of Justin's death. But for the first time another emotion stirred within me. Anger. In some strange way I found myself blaming Justin for the state I now found myself in. Why had he been so trusting of Philip? I wondered. Could he have not seen that the whole thing was a ruse? Or had it been? Had Philip plotted and planned this from the very first? It did not make sense, for how could he have foreseen Justin's untimely death? No, it was more likely that his plans had changed after Justin's death. Once I had decided to proceed with the railway project it had all been easy for him. I had even offered him a place to stay. He had not had to do much of anything except play on my own vulnerability. Why had I not seen? As I looked back there had been clues, questions, but in every case I had overlooked them. And now I was left with nothing of any importance save the children. Justin was gone, Jaspar had been taken from me and Mayfair was no longer in my control.

A carriage passed by. The grate of its wheels against the street caused me to look up. When it passed I strained to see down the other side of the road. It was the Mayfair carriage, the one Philip had taken. I looked about quickly, trying to identify where I had come to. This was not a part of London that was well known to me. These were not the slums but it was a seamier side of the city than the one to which I was accustomed. The houses here were in contiguous rows, appearing as though they had been seamed together as in a quilt. Each was uniformly proportioned to the next, making it difficult to distinguish one from another.

I scanned up and down the street, looking for some clue as to where Philip might be, but there was no activity on the street save a peddler restacking his wares in a small cart. Suddenly aware that I was putting myself in a vulnerable position by standing out in the street in full sight, I pulled my cloak tighter about me and looked about for some niche where I might be hidden from view. One of the houses two doors down appeared to be boarded up. A small lane passed at the side and I huddled in a darkened doorway, wondering how long I need wait before seeing Philip.

A light drizzle formed and the once bright sky continued to darken. My feet were growing numb in my light boots and I knew that my resistance was low and could likely develop a fever if I were to continue standing there; still, having happened on the carriage like this, I was not about to let the cold drive me away.

I had been there for at least an hour when I turned suddenly at the sound of footsteps coming up the lane.

He reached me more quickly than I had anticipated. I commenced to move out from the doorway, but before I could his arm thrust out in front of me, barring my way.

"Let me pass," I insisted, recoiling at his foul-smelling breath.

"Now, luv, that's no way to be talkin' to yer elders," he replied, leaning his large frame full against me. "Out a tad early tonight. Lucky ol' Henry 'ere be lookin' fer a little lovin' or ye'd be freezin' out 'ere before long."

"Take your hands off me or I shall scream," I insisted.

"Eh, now, that's no way to be treatin' a customer," he swaggered, "yer bein' pretty grand with ye airs."

"I am not what you think," I snapped back. "I advise that you move on or I should be forced to do something that would embarrass you greatly."

He mumbled something but my attention had suddenly been drawn to some activity at the house across the street. I gasped as I realized that Philip was leaving with one of the men that I had seen him with earlier.

"Oh, c'mon an' give ol' Henry here yer name. We'll go an' get a brew or two an. . . ."

"Hush," I demanded. "I do not want those men over there to know I am here."

He peered across the street, watching intently as Philip and his companion climbed into the carriage.

"Yer goin' te be tellin' me that one o' those gents is yer husband?" he sneered.

I nodded. "The taller of the two," I whispered.

"Ye mean to tell me yer spyin' on yer old man?" he mused.

"If ye were my missus, aye wouldn't be steppin' a foot away from ye."

That he thought I was trying to catch Philip in some tryst could work to my advantage, I realized, for he was obviously pleased to be involved in the intrigue and had relaxed his guard on me.

"It is an outrage," I feigned, keeping my voice at a whisper. "Pray tell, do you know who owns that house he just left?"

"The one over there?" he replied, pointing out into the mist.

"Yes."

"Sure an' aye do. Ain't a chap in London that don't know Moll's place. 'Course, 'tis only the real gents like yer husband there that goes in. She charges a pretty pound, aye 'ear."

"Who is Moll?" I pressed as the carriage started to draw away. "Moll who?"

He shrugged. "Never gave any thought to her family name. She's just Moll."

"Tell me anything you can about her," I pleaded.

He laughed a low guttural laugh. "Seems to me 'tis yer husband ye should be askin' 'bout Moll."

I opened my reticule and searched out several pound notes. I thrust them forward, pressing them into his hand. "Here, perhaps this will help you recall what you know about Moll."

He fingered the bills, shrugging, "T'aint nothin' te me. She runs a clean house, aye hear, if ye know what aye mean. Gets some fancy gents, foreigners, too. Aye've heard told she has some girls from real proper families."

"Do you know the names of any of the girls?"

He shook his head. "Listen, unless ye want te change yer mind an' let ol' Henry 'ere show ye a good time aye'll be movin' on."

"You are very generous," I lied, "but I cannot have my husband be suspicious about my whereabouts." I pulled another note from my bag and placed it into his hand, taking advantage of his preoccupation with the money and moving swiftly out from the doorway. I did not wait for him to reconsider his release of me and moved hurriedly down the street.

I had to go a fair way before I found a public carriage that would return me to Clarissa's. Somehow I had to get into Moll's house, but it was too late to do so this evening and I had to formulate some plan. There was no reason to believe that Moll was part of any scheme, though I scarcely imagined Philip finding amusement in a brothel. Not that he would deny his masculinity, but I simply envisioned that he would explore his more prurient interests in private.

I had hoped that Clarissa would be occupied for the evening for I was in no mood to endure her interrogations, but I found her awaiting me in the drawing room when I returned. She waved me in to join her.

"Serena, you look positively bedraggled," she said as I removed my bonnet. "If I did not know better I would think that you've been hanging the draperies by yourself."

I shook out the folds of my skirt, which were damp from the rain.

"How in heavens name did you get so wet, Serena?" she pursued.

"Oh, I asked the driver to make a few stops," I lied.

"Well, I must say that it is rather silly that you send your own coachman home and are wandering about in one of those open carriages," she continued. "It simply is not something that one does."

Rather than argue with her, I diverted her by complimenting her gown, which was fashioned of a pale yellow brocade shot with gold thread. Fortunately my own gown was clearly damp enough that it needed changing and I excused myself to do so before she could pursue me with any other questions. I only wanted to take a tray in my room and be abed early with time to plot the following day, but it was clear that would only serve to arouse her suspicions. Thus we spent a strained but tolerable dinner together, she rambling on about the perfections of her child and the imperfections of her husband while I forced myself to be polite. My most difficult task was dissuading her from joining me at Channing Hall the next day. I could hardly have her appearing there when I had no intention of being there myself. Nor could I risk her encountering Philip. While she had only inferred by innuendo that her relationship with him had not always been platonic, in truth Clarissa had never held any real care for me so I was careful to keep any mention of Philip to an innocuous vein.

I did not sleep well that night. Precious time was slipping by and I had gained no real clues as to what Philip was about here in London. I was commencing to regret my decision to solve this mystery on my own. Sir Henry would of course be respon-

sive to my plight but his first instinct would undoubtedly be to
involve the chief constable. Assuming that something was
awry, he would more than likely force me to confront Philip. I
had come to know that my husband was a deceptive but also
very clever man. And I suspected that Philip would somehow
appear the epitome of innocence while I would be pitied as
the overwrought wife.

I was pleased when early the next morning a maid brought
me a basin and breakfast tray for I was eager to be underway
before the household was about. I had already decided to take
a public carriage since I knew that Robbie would hardly abide
with my instructions to leave me near Moll's house, convinced, as he would be, that it was hardly an area about which
I should be wandering on my own.

I selected a simple royal blue velvet gown and tucked my
hair loosely under a matching bonnet. The butler seemed surprised when I did not request the carriage to be brought round
but I explained that a brisk constitutional each morning was
my want.

Yesterday's rain had left a heavy mist about the streets of
London and I welcomed the carriage that soon came upon me.
I prayed that when I reached the area of Moll's house I would
find no trace of either the Mayfair carriage or Philip, for that
should delay my findings even longer. The driver, if surprised
at my destination, did not question me about it and it was not
long before we stopped at the commencement of the streets
with their succession of row houses. I hoped that the draperies
would be pulled shut at Moll's again today, for it had been the
one thing to distinguish it from its twin structures the day
before.

As I approached the house I started suddenly for a man was
just departing. I slowed my pace and lowered my head,
hopeful that I would not encounter him. I could not afford to
stare at him but I knew instantly that the gentleman, although
a man of obvious breeding, was not Philip. As he pushed the
low iron gate open he paused, glancing my way for a moment,
then turned to his right, walking at a pace which took him
quickly out of sight.

He had left the gate slightly unlatched and I was surprised as
I pushed it forward to hear a jangling bell set off by my movement. I paused and looked up towards the house, noticing as I
did that one of the draperies on the first floor had parted

slightly. Having been seen, if not acknowledged, I felt that a retreat now would prove foolish, so taking a deep breath, I advanced forward.

My hand closed about the knocker and I was just about to bring it to bear against the door when it opened suddenly, causing me to be thrust slightly off balance. When I recovered my misstep I looked up or rather down into the heart-shaped face of a young girl I imagined to be no more than fourteen. She looked at me expectantly with saucerlike eyes peering out from an incongruous white cap at least two sizes too large.

"Yes, mum?" she said curtsying.

"I would like to see Moll," I obliged.

She paused, looking at me nervously. " 'Tis not real regular, mum, not at this hour. Me mistress bein' hardly up an' all."

"I realize it is early," I acknowledged, "but it is very important that I see her."

As if sensing my urgency she relaxed her hold on the door. "Ye might as well wait in here then 'til aye kin see if she'll see ye."

She ushered me into a small front parlor, telling me that she would return momentarily.

This small room had obviously been designed with the intent of creating opulence, though the furniture facings of gold and bronze mount only appeared ridiculous against the garish wallpaper and drapery hangings. The items in the room were, if gauche, not inexpensive, and I could not but help feel that Moll obviously ran a profitable business.

I had begun to suspect that Moll was indeed not going to welcome any visitors when the door to the parlor opened and a woman whom I knew, even without introductions, to be Moll, entered.

She was a compelling sight, tall with a bone structure and musculature seemingly equal to that of any man. She wore a wrapper of a gossamer-type fabric which accentuated the high fullness of her breasts. As she neared me I was overwhelmed by a strong cloying scent which suggested that she had bathed in one of those bottled scents that some local chemist pawned off on the unsuspecting as French perfume.

I watched her as she sat down opposite me, wondering her age. I guessed her to be in her late thirties but it was hard to speculate whether her own abuses had sped up her time.

"Since yer obviously not one o' me girls, ye've got to be lookin' fer yer husband," she drawled. "Well 'oever 'e is, 'e ain't 'ere. Not at this hour."

I sat there confounded as to what my response should be. I dared not come right out and ask her about Philip for I had no certainty as to what his relationship was with this woman.

"I am not what I appear," I commenced cautiously.

"Few of us are, luv," she replied.

"I was indiscreet," I continued, my mind racing to form some tale that she would believe. "My husband discovered that I had been unfaithful to him. It was only twice, I swear it, but he banished me from the house without anything to my name, only what I had in my reticule at the moment."

She waved her heavily ringed hand at me. "Men," she spat out, "hypocrites all of them. Aye'd venture to be guessin' that yer husband has been to old Moll's a time or two but they think 'tis different fer them."

Her attitude, given who she was, surprised me.

"I have nowhere to turn," I continued, "no relative, at least none close by. I had heard about you, your house from Baron Whittenfeld some years passed. I thought, well, I thought perhaps . . ."

She had grown very silent, studying me intently. I was praying that she would not challenge my story. I had almost choked at the use of Baron Whittenfeld's name for he was certainly the most degenerate individual I had ever met. It was over ten years ago but I still remembered how he had tried to blackmail me in those early months when I had first come to Camberleigh to claim my inheritance.

"Aye must say aye'm right surprised that the likes of ye knows the Baron."

I hoped that she could not hear my sigh of relief.

" 'E's a tough customer, that one is, but aye don't be caterin' to his sort if ye know what aye mean."

I assumed that she meant his proclivity for young men and only nodded in assent.

"So what's 'appened to yer lover, aye mean the one ye were caught with?" Moll continued.

I shook my head. "If you are asking why I have not turned to him, I cannot. He has no prospects and I think my husband would kill him if he thought I was with him."

"That's why ol' Moll only deals with those got prospects,"

she grinned. "There's nary a chance that any o' my girls will be weddin' my customers, but least while they're entertainin' them they're treated real good. Aye had one e'en leave me last week 'cause one o' the gents is settin' 'er up in 'er own place—real proper like."

"So then you are short one girl," I said eagerly.

"Didn't mention that I was," Moll replied, "but now that aye think about it aye am goin' to be short fer awhile. One o' the young ones she didn't listen an' went and got herself with babe. She's good an' aye'll take 'er back, but now that she's showin' aye can't really have 'er struttin' 'er wares afore my customers."

"I could be that new girl," I said, mustering as much assurance as I could.

Moll looked me over once again so penetratingly that I felt she was undressing me.

She shook her head. "This t'aint fer you, luv. Those hands o' yours ain't ever seen dishwater is my guess. I run a clean house mind ye, but even aye'll be tellin' ye this is a rough business. Ye 'avn't told me yer name an' aye 'avn't asked it so if ye decide to leave ye won't ever 'ave te worry that ol' Moll ratted on ye but from yer looks aye kin see fer meself that yer born and bred a lady. An' ladies don't take well te this kind o' work."

"Am I to be penalized then for my breeding?" I asked. "Since your customers, as you say, are gentlemen, they should appreciate someone of, shall we say, of quality."

Her eyebrows raised. "Take that silly bonnet off so aye kin see yer face," she commanded.

I did as I was told, using my hand to shake out my hair as it cascaded to my shoulders.

"Well, look at that," she exclaimed as I turned my face back to her. "Ye might well be me one exception."

"How do you mean?" I puzzled.

"When aye said me girls had no prospects fer marriage with these gents, aye hadn't seen ye before. If yer serious, luv, ye kin make a bundle with Moll 'ere."

"I am serious," I lied. "I need work."

"Why don't ye go an' be a governess fer some fancy family?" she queried suspiciously.

I paused for a moment. "Would *you* want to be a governess?"

She looked at me and suddenly laughed uproariously. "Aye like ye, luv, ye've got spirit. Aye'm not sure this will work, but aye'm willin' to give it a whirl. Ye've got te be bidin' by Moll's rules, though, if yer gonna work 'ere."

"That should not be a problem," I demured.

"First off, me girls only works once a night. Ye'll 'ave yer own room but ye'll ave te keep that clean yerself save the sheets which little Sara tends te. Aye set the rates an' ye'll get one quarter's my take at the first o' each month. 'Course, if a gent gives ye a small bauble, that's yers fer the keepin'. Usually aye tell me girls te act like ladies but in yer case aye think aye'd better be remindin' ye that in this work ye ain't no lady. Ye get one day off every two weeks but yer days are yer own. 'Course aye expect ye te keep te this house. If ye need somethin', aye send Sara te the market and she'll fetch it fer ye."

"Ye got any questions, luv?" she concluded.

"None," I replied, "at least for the present."

"Good," she said, pulling her full weight up from the chair. "Then aye'll be fetchin' Sara an' she kin show ye about."

When she left I realized how considerably flushed I felt and wished that I had a drink of water or something to quiet my nerves. If I were not so frightened I might have quite enjoyed this little farce. I had never been a good liar but once I started to spin my tale I myself found it vaguely believable.

I had had to concoct a way to remain in the house for I knew that any information I could glean would likely come from one of the girls—someone who knew Philip who would know if there were any reason beyond pleasuring himself that he frequented this place. Moll returned almost immediately with young Sara, who had obviously been briefed that I would be joining the establishment, for her earlier reticence with me had all but disappeared.

"Sara," Moll introduced, "this is . . ."

"Samantha," I replied, quickly taking my mother's given name.

"Samantha," she affirmed. "Aye would like ye te take her upstairs and show her where her room will be, Alice's old one. Aye'll be up a little later an' we can get better acquainted."

I followed little Sara, who led me up the narrow wooden staircase to the second landing. By the number of doors on this floor alone I was astounded not only by the expanse of space in the house but also how many girls Moll must have to fill them. It was surprisingly quiet, but then I remembered that most of the girls were likely to be asleep since day was really evening for them. She stopped in front of a door at the far back end of the hall and opened the door.

I could not help but be amused by the appearance of the room for Moll had again spared no expense here in attempting to create an aura of elegance. In its stead she had created an outrageous bedroom scenario with gaudy hangings and overstuffed chaises. True to her word, however, the place was spotless.

"Would ye like a spot o' tea?" little Sara asked as I went to separate the draperies and peer out the window. "Oh, ye mustn't be doin' that," she cautioned. "Moll likes 'em closed."

"Then they shall remain that way," I assured her. "And do not bother yourself with tea, I shall be happy to just rest a bit."

After Sara left I waited until I heard her descend to the floor below before venturing out of my room. There were at least three floors to this house and since I assumed that the girls were kept on the second floor I decided to move up rather than spend whatever time I had below.

There were fewer rooms on the third floor and the doors to each, with the exception of the one at the end, was ajar. Two of the open rooms were empty. One was obviously a bedroom-sitting room combination, which, because it was more luxurious than anything I had yet seen, I assumed was Moll's.

I reached the end room and pressed my ear against the door. Carefully I put my hand on the handle, pulling down as I did. It clearly was locked, though as I let it return I was certain that I heard a noise from inside. I knocked lightly and waited but there was no response. I was just about to knock again when I heard footsteps behind me.

I turned to find myself face to face with a dark-haired, very Irish-looking woman of my own age, her strong jaw accentuated by heavy rouging about her cheekbones.

"Wouldn't be doin' that if aye were you," she cautioned, watching me suspiciously. "Not unless you want ol' Moll down your throat."

"I did not mean any harm," I assured her hurriedly. "I am

new here. I just wanted to look about. My name is Samantha," I concluded, extending my hand.

She took it warily. "I'm Annie."

"Is there some reason this door is locked?" I pursued.

She shrugged. "All aye know is it got locked up yesterday an' Moll told us right off it was off limits. An' if ye know Moll ye know she means business."

"She gave you no explanation?"

Annie shook her head. "Probably somethin' to do with his highness Lord Taggart."

I was so excited at the mention of Philip's name that I almost grabbed her to ask her what she meant. My silence seemed to encourage her to go on.

" 'Course I'm just supposin' since when he was 'ere yesterday he and Moll were hush-hush an' then there was a lot o' ruckus an' she told us all she'd skin us alive if we even went near that door."

"Why do you think that is?" I whispered, trying to encourage her conspiratorial attitude.

Annie stared at the door for a minute. "Likely some gent got himself in a fix an' needs a place te cool his heels fer awhile. Anyway, it's none o' my business an' if yer smart ye'll pretend ye was never up here."

She turned to leave but I put my hand out, touching her shoulder.

"Annie, is Lord Taggart a frequent visitor here?"

"Why, you know him?" she replied suspiciously.

"No, no, of course not," I said hurriedly. "He is a friend of a friend, shall we say."

"Ye wouldn't be knowin' then that Lord Taggart is married to some fancy lady. Now he's not around here much anymore, though before he was right regular."

She had obviously imparted as much information as she was about to and resolutely I followed her back downstairs. Annie explained that she had an early customer and refused my invitation to visit a while in my room. I had no time to ponder on what she had told me for within minutes of returning to my room Moll arrived.

She was carrying several gowns that she laid gently on the bed. "Aye figured ye'd be needin' these," she offered. "Yer so covered up in that gown o' yers that my customers would be thinkin' aye've gone a bit daft. This one should suit ye," she

offered, holding up an emerald green dress with a bodice cut
so low that I gasped.

It had not occurred to me that she would expect anything of
me this evening. I had simply planned to leave as soon as I was
satisfied that Philip did indeed have some involvement with
Moll. My mind was racing as I desperately tried to concoct
some excuse for leaving here that night.

"Moll," I commenced slowly as she held the green gown up
before me, "I cannot stay here tonight."

She dropped the dress to her lap, her eyes scrutinizing me
carefully. "Aye figured it wouldn't work," she said angrily.
"Yer droppin' out on yer first night. It's not a good sign."

I shook my head. "You do not understand. I left my things,
the few meager ones I was able to take, with a friend. He will
be expecting me. I must let him know that I will be all right
now."

"Ye want a roll in the hay once more with yer young man,
eh?" she replied, her eyes gleaming. "Well, aye'll never have
it be said that ol' Moll doesn't 'ave a soft streak. But aye'm
warning ye. If yer not back 'ere by nine on the morrow ye
needn't bother te darken me doorstep again. Aye give one
chance. Only one."

I was amazed that she let me go so easily. Instead of being
grateful it unnerved me, for I wondered if I had given her
reason now to be suspicious of me. But as soon as I was out on
the street again I breathed a sigh of relief. It was getting dark
and I looked nervously about for a carriage. After fifteen
minutes of walking I was chastising my own stubborness for
not allowing Robbie to drive me about town. On the other
hand, I could not risk being seen or indeed having the carriage
recognized, and thus, despite my exhaustion, I pressed on.

Finally a carriage came along that was empty and I fell into
it, wearily putting all thoughts out of my head as it wended its
way to Clarissa's.

I had no more than descended from the carriage and started
up the steps when Robbie appeared from nowhere. It was dark
but the coach lights took his face out of the shadows. I could
see that he was angry even before he spoke.

"Serena, aye'll not stand by any longer an' watch ye
sneakin' 'bout this city. Yer up te somethin', aye know, an' on
Master Justin's grave aye swear aye'll be stoppin' ye. It's
danger yer flirtin' with, aye kin feel it, an' if ye won't give it

up, at least ye kin be tellin' me what yer 'bout.''

I had never, in the eleven years that I had known him, seen him so determined.

I put my hand out and touched his shoulder. "You must trust me, Robbie," I begged. "I simply cannot tell you as yet. I feel soon that I shall have something that I can share with you but not yet."

His eyes bore into mine. "Ye will tell me, Serena, if ye feel that ye are in any danger."

"I swear it," I replied.

The door opened and I realized that the butler had obviously been disturbed by our voices.

"Are you not coming in?" I entreated.

Robbie shook his head. "Clarissa has made it very clear that aye should use the back entrance."

"I'm sorry," I whispered in response. "I fear there is no changing her."

"Give it no mind," he assured me.

I half expected Clarissa to call out to me from the drawing room, but the butler quickly advised me that she had gone to dinner with friends this evening, adding that everything had been arranged for me to dine in the dining room. I assured him that I only wanted a light tray in my room.

I knew that I was taking chances by returning to Moll's the next day but I felt I had no choice. Her house was the only place that I had any information of or connection to Philip. There was the possibility, of course, that Annie's conjecturing was simply that—with one exception. If Philip had been there simply to expel his lust, why would he have been in the company of the other man? I gave thought to Moll. In her tough, street way she seemed almost a decent sort, but what I could not lose sight of was that she was a businesswoman. This was not a woman who cared about principles. What she did care about was money. If indeed she was harboring someone—perhaps even a criminal—I sensed she would do so willingly as long as she was well paid. I puzzled for a moment over the fact that I had seen Philip with two men the day prior, yet the following day he had left with only one. I tried desperately to make some connection, but the more I pondered it the more puzzled I became. And what, I wondered, did it have to do with the charred remainder of the letter I had found at Mayfair with the words "returning the sixteenth"?

Had one of those men been someone that Philip thought important to harbor? By the time I had finished my dinner tray I had exhausted myself with the endless possibilities of what it all meant. The only thing that I was certain of was that I would not stop until I found a clue that would unravel this web in which I was now increasingly entangled.

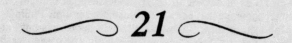

## 21

Unlike the night before, I slept extremely well, awakening stronger and more refreshed than I had for more nights than I wanted to remember.

When I looked at myself in the mirror that morning I recognized myself as I had not done so for months. I was still thin but there was a renewed vibrancy in my skin and color in my cheeks. I could not help but pause and wonder about my health these past months. Had Jaspar not been the unsuspecting victim, would I have ever suspected anything or would I have succumbed before my suspicions were confirmed? There was, of course, no proof, and yet as time passed I became more and more convinced that Philip had concocted some diabolical scheme that somehow included my demise.

But, if that were true, why would he have thought it necessary? He had, by marrying me, gained all he had ever really wanted—money and power. I had railed against him—perhaps that was when he had decided that it was easier to eliminate me than deal with me. How important had Amelie been in all this? Was she pressuring him to legitimatize their relationship? I did not like her but I sensed deep within me that she, too, was somehow a victim. After all, had I died, would Philip have married her? I doubted it.

The house was thankfully quiet as I made my way down the stairs. Robbie would be furious with me when he learned that I had left Clarissa's without requesting his assistance. Moll had warned me to return before nine if I were to expect entrée into the house and I was at best an hour early in my arrival time. There was an awkward exchange between Sara and myself, for several customers were in the midst of departure and I was ushered quickly into the parlor to avoid any embarrassment of which I was also grateful lest I should happenstantially encounter someone that knew me or Justin or certainly Philip.

Moll seemed surprisingly assured about my return, but I attributed that to the earliness of the hour which she clearly resented any intrusion on. I sensed that she was a woman who imbibed spirits heavily, for she repeated the rules of the house again with me as though she had never uttered a word the day before. I listened patiently, not wanting to disturb her by any challenges. Actually this morning I felt real sympathy for this woman sitting before me. She looked very tired, almost beaten, this morning, and I wondered what could have happened to have sapped the vitality she had manifested the day before.

Sara showed me to my room, cautioning me again not to open the draperies.

I was not as confident today about snooping about the house, for walking down the hallway to my room I suspected that not all the customers had departed by the time of my arrival.

But I had no option. I had to get into that locked room. Perhaps it did not hold the key to what I was seeking, but I had come this far and there was no turning back.

I opened the door to my room and turned my ear out to the hallway to determine when might be my best exit. I started at one point but retreated when I spied a man exiting one of the rooms further down the hall. Once convinced that he had descended to the floor below, I exited quickly, winding my way up the staircase to the third floor. I was nervous being up there now for, although not confirmed, I still sensed that Moll's quarters were up here. Not knowing her daily routine, I had to suspect that she, too, used the daylight hours to sleep and luxuriate.

Seeing that the doors to her suite were open, I made the assumption that she had still not returned to bed after our brief meeting a bit earlier. I moved swiftly and as quietly as I could to the room with the locked door. I pulled the handle down only to confirm that it was still barred to my entry. As with the day prior, I was convinced that I heard a movement from within. I wiped my brow, realizing that beads of perspiration had broken about my forehead. They were only the tangible evidence of the fear that dwelled within me. Even if I were to gain entry to this room, there was no guarantee that I would not find an adversary on the other side of the door. Certainly, if it were one of the men whom I had seen with Philip at Channing Hall I could not imagine them to be savory characters or at all sympathetic to my plight. Should I gain entry, I would have to steel myself for a swift escape. Time was still on my side, for most of the household was still abed, but soon that would change and my flight, if necessary, would be hampered.

I raised my hand and rapped gently against the door. Again I was certain that I heard movement. Why, indeed, if someone were inside, would they not open the door? Had some code been established which signaled the occupant inside to open the door, or could it be that whoever inside was a captive—perhaps one of Philip's victims, as I was?

The latter thought seemed to spur me on to gain entry into the room. I tried the handle again, this time putting my own weight against the door in a feeble attempt to sprint it loose. There was no give but I persisted, once again this time pressing harder.

"Can you hear me?" I whispered through the door.

I did not want to abandon my mission but I had to acknowledge that my attempts thus far had proved futile. The only one that I knew who could possibly help me was Robbie, but it would be a month of Sundays before I could leave Moll's again and return expecting any kind of reception. Dejectedly I listened once again at the door, hoping that whoever was inside might have assumed I had passed on and possibly crack open the door.

I decided the best thing to do was to go downstairs. I had chanced it long enough up here and perhaps somewhere I might find a key. Little Sara might have some idea where Moll kept her keys, and if I was clever I might be able to elicit some information from her.

I released the latch but froze on the spot, for there was no doubt that I had heard footsteps at my back. Before I could turn, a hand pressed firmly against my shoulder. I whirled about, wincing as my arm wrenched under the pressure of the intruder's hand. My eyes flew wide as I recognized the full height of Philip before me.

"Really, Serena," he laughed sardonically, "had I known that my bride wished to go slumming I would have brought you to Moll long ago."

I do not know whether it was from shock or fear but I was transfixed before him, unable to move and knowing that escape was impossible.

At last finding my voice I asked, "How did you know I was here?"

"You should not underestimate me so, my dear," he smirked. "When I returned late last evening Moll told me all about her new girl. As she raved about your beauty and your demeanor something started to sound very familiar. Too familiar. I will admit to you that I was puzzled at first. How you had come to London, what has brought you to Moll's house. Fascinating that. You must share it with me sometime. I quite think that I should find your sleuthing most entertaining."

"Philip, you are hurting me," I whispered, trying to remove his hand from my shoulder. "Please, let me go."

"You disappoint me, Serena," he laughed. "Have you come this far only to abandon your search? I could not live with myself, my dear, if I did not reward you for your troubles."

He withdrew a key from his vest pocket and held it up before me. "I should think this is what you wished moments ago had been in your possession. Let me show you how easily it slips into the lock."

He placed the key in the latch, his other hand still in firm grasp of my shoulder. I looked down as I heard it click open. Before I had a chance to respond, he had thrust me through the small opening and I was left only with the sound of the key locking behind me. I reached out, grasping at the space to balance myself against a fall. The room was pitch dark. If there were windows they had undoubtedly been sealed over, for there was not even a shaft of light to guide me. I extended my arm out to the door behind me. I knew that pounding on it would be futile. What fate Philip planned for me I knew not, but I was convinced that my pleas would go unheeded by any who heard them.

I shuddered, feeling suddenly the cold dampness of the room. Had I been mistaken about a presence in this room?

In the deathly silence I pondered whether the sounds I had heard had been my own imagination. Summoning my courage, I called out weakly, "Is anyone there? If you can hear me, please respond," I begged.

My breath halted as I heard a sound at the far end of the room. Pressing my arms out full before me, I stepped forward tenuously. My heart was pounding so fast that it resounded like a wall clock in my ears. There seemed to be nothing before me. I had gone eight, perhaps ten, steps and had yet to encounter anything. Thus far the room seemed amazingly barren. I turned to the left a bit as I thought I heard another movement in that end of the room.

I groped forward again, thinking that if danger lurked before me I was walking towards it, not away from it. My knee suddenly struck hard against a board, pitching me forward. My hands flew out in front of me in an attempt to break my fall. I had doubled over onto what seemed like a bed of some sort. As I tried to right myself my left hand brushed against what I knew immediately to be a man's boot. I recoiled, struggling to right myself.

"Who are you?" I choked out.

I trembled at the deathly silence. I reached down to trace my hand along the bed rail, following it to the head of the bed. My hand grew stiff as it passed suddenly over a man's hand. It was clutching the bed frame, but not from its own volition, I realized quickly, for heavy rope secured the hand in place. Suddenly convinced that this man, whoever he may be, was as great a prisoner as I was, I moved my hand up the shoulder to the head. As my fingers brushed over the mouth, warm breath spilled out against my palm. He was alive but in what condition I dared not guess, for not only had he been shackled to the bed but a gag pulled tight about his face had silenced him.

I tried to turn his head to find where the sheeting had been tied.

"I am a friend," I whispered as my fingers worked feverishly to untie the knotted fabric, a task made even more difficult by the wet cloth soaked in the man's sweat. "If you can just keep your head like that for a few more minutes, I should be able to free you from this gag."

As the knot finally unraveled and I carefully removed the menacing fabric I cautioned him not to speak. If he had been bound in this fashion without food or water for all these hours, I could not imagine what the effect would be on his physical condition.

I started as a sound escaped his lips.

"Hush," I pressed, "you must conserve your strength. Everything will be all right. Just give it time."

He repeated the same sound again and then a third time.

I shook my head in disbelief for I realized that the sound he was forming was that of my own name. Tenuously I reached back down to his head. How did this man know my name? My hand traced the hairline and brow. My fingers were my eyes and it was only seconds before I recoiled in horror, my body plunged into an uncontrollable shudder.

"It cannot be," I murmured. "You are dead. You are dead, I know it," I cried out as my hands flew again against the face that now repeated and repeated my name.

My mind tried to deny the miracle that my hands were insisting upon as now they poured over the face and body of the man beneath me.

I tried to speak but the only word that came from my mouth was his name.

"Justin," I cried out, falling upon him and dissolving into tears of joy, relief, shock, as he continued to murmur my name.

"My God, what have they done to you?" I pleaded. "I thought you were dead. The cholera, they said you died on the ship months ago. I . . ."

"Serena," he whispered.

"What is it, darling?"

"Water. There is a pitcher over behind the bed."

I struggled up in the darkness, groping to where he had indicated I would find the water. My hands closed about a pitcher and I carefully carried it back to the bed. Lifting Justin's head in my hand, I used the other to pour the cold liquid into his mouth. His thirst was great but I was careful to allow him only small gulps, fearful that he would choke in his prone position.

When he spoke again his voice was hoarse but stronger. "You take some, too, Serena."

I complied, taking only a small bit, realizing that Justin would likely need more later and I scarcely thought that Philip would replenish it.

"We have to get out of here," I cried desperately. "If I scream someone will finally have to come."

I jumped up suddenly and stumbled back in the direction of the door. "Help," I called out, "someone has to help us."

"Serena, it is useless," Justin admonished.

"It cannot be," I argued. "Someone will hear us, they have to. Not everyone here can be totally mad."

I pounded furiously against the door. "Damn you, Philip Taggart," I screamed. "I shall see you dead for this."

Against Justin's protestations I continued to slam my fists against the door, not ceasing even when they began burning from the impact. The anger that surged through me frightened me—that I could have so much hatred for one man. That I wished him to endure tenfold the pain that he had made Justin and I endure.

Just when it seemed clear that Justin was right, that we were prisoners with no prayer of escape, I heard the key turn in the lock and the door opened, revealing Philip looming before me. Without a word I flung myself at him, my fists pounding against him as they had against the door. His arm swung towards me, connecting with the side of my head and causing me to fall back into the room. I was dazed, but not enough to block out Philip's laughter rising against Justin's pleas to spare me.

"Well, I see that my wife has been reunited with her long lost husband," he sneered. "This is no way to show your appreciation, my dear."

"Your wife?" Justin gasped. "Serena, what is he talking about?"

"That is right, I forgot, you do not know, do you, Barkham," Philip jeered. "This simpering female at my feet is my wife, Lady Taggart."

I could hear Justin struggle against his restraints. "Is this true, Serena?"

"Yes," I moaned, "but I swear to you he tricked me. It was all very clever, diabolical. I was so lost, I trusted him."

"You swine," Justin blurted out. "I shall make you pay for this if it is the last thing that I do."

"On the contrary," Philip argued, "it is you who have paid, Barkham—and dearly. And Serena here made it all very easy for me. Until now. You really should not have come snooping about, my dear. It has made everything very inconvenient."

"You are mad, Philip," I accused.

"You really do not flatter me," he replied, "though I cannot say that that would do you any good. I, to the contrary, must compliment you on your sleuthing, Serena. I am honestly fascinated how you traced me here. Our wife is really quite clever, Barkham. Tell me, Serena, was it Amelie? I knew my little indulgence might be my undoing. Well, I suppose how you found out is not very significant at this point except that now I shall have to do away with you as well."

"It is what you have been intending all along," I retorted.

"Now that is not entirely true, Serena. You simply were not very cooperative. A little hellion, she was in bed, Barkham, but then I am certain you know that."

"The only way you could have me was to violate me," I screamed at him.

"More's the pity," Philip mused, his face in full shadow. "I quite think your friend Monique was of a different mind. Even that little snit of a cousin of yours found me, shall we say, amusing. It was a pity that Monique became suspicious of me for she is really rather a tantalizing woman. At one point I even thought that I might seduce her into becoming Lady Taggart, but then why should one take the spoils when one can have the riches? She did try to warn you, you know. But it was very naive of her to think that I would let you read those letters. I thought that Lady Camberleigh was going to be my nemesis but she had almost become my champion. You must admit that was clever of me."

I would not honor his statement with a response.

"There are arrangements to be made," Philip continued. "I shall leave the two of you together. I suggest that you make good use of your time since there is not much left of it—for either of you."

I had drawn myself up to a standing position again as Philip talked. He was braced within the doorway but I knew that the only chance we might have was for me to catch him off guard and bolt past him.

It was almost as though he had read my mind for he suddenly narrowed the door opening, slowly saying to me, "I would not try anything if I were you, Serena. I give your spirit credit but you really are not a match for me. And I would not recommend that you persist with your yelling and pounding at the door any longer. Moll has been very well compensated for the use of this room and neither she nor anyone else will be responsive to your cries for help. And if you persist, I should be forced to gag that pretty mouth of yours.''

"I shan't cry out again," I assured him.

"Excellent, then I shall leave you your love nest, such as it is.''

When he had gone I moved swiftly back to where Justin lay.

"I feel so helpless," I moaned.

"Serena, do you think you could release these restraints on my arms?" Justin murmured.

My hands felt about, trying to unravel the intricate roping that bound him solidly against the frame.

"If only I had a knife," I murmured, "something that should allow me to cut this rope. I cannot release these knots; whoever has tied them has done their job well.''

"Some henchman of Taggart's named Haggerty," Justin replied, "not that it matters.''

"I am not making any progress with these knots," I cried.

"Leave it be," Justin murmured. "Come closer to me."

I bent over, my lips finding his.

"Do you know how much I want to take you in my arms, to hold you, to make love to you even here in this hellish pit?" he whispered.

My hands caressed his face, my wonder and astonishment so great that I seemed compelled to continue to reassure myself that it was indeed Justin lying here beneath me.

"Serena, darling, you have to try and talk to me," Justin encouraged. "We may not have much time and I must have some idea of what has transpired these last months. I do not know whether it will be of any help to us but you must try.''

I nodded silently, my hands trying to stem the flow of tears from my eyes.

"First the children," he asked. "Tell me that they are safe and well.''

I assured him that they were. "In many ways," I commenced, "it was for them—or what I thought was for them—that I married Philip. Justin," I beseeched, "I thought you were dead, you must try and realize how devastated I was. For the first few weeks I spoke to no one. I shuttered myself away at Channing Hall, not really caring if I lived or died myself.''

"I do not understand why you thought I was dead, Serena. Did you not receive any of my letters?"

"It was Philip and Jonathan, though I know now that Jonathan was duped in the same way as I. They came to the house, a month, perhaps two, after you had sailed saying that they had had notice that you had perished on board—an outbreak of cholera, they said."

"There is a partial truth there," Justin offered. "There was an outbreak of cholera but I was spared. Surely the ship's log—there would have been ways for you to know."

"Philip told me that you were traveling under an assumed name. He said it was certain that you had perished, that he was to be contacted directly."

"I find it incredible to believe that Taggart had this scheme fully planned before I set sail and yet I can only conclude that this is so."

"Why do you say that?" I queried.

"You recall that I was to meet with a man in America about the railroad project?"

"Yes," I acknowledged.

"Well, I now believe that no such man ever existed. At least not by the name or address Philip provided me."

"You are saying, then, that it was simply a ruse to get you out of the country?" I mused.

"Precisely," Justin confirmed. "I became suspicious only days after arriving but it was not possible for me to book return passage that quickly. I wrote to you several times. First, to assure you that I was well, and then to advise you when I would be returning."

"On the sixteenth?" I said quickly.

"Yes, but how did you know?" he reacted.

" 'Tis a very long story," I replied. "Philip took receipt of all the post. I overheard he and Amelie one night discussing letters. She was worried about them."

"Who in blazes is Amelie?" he asked, straining as he did against the ropes that bound him.

"A girl that Philip ensconced at Mayfair as the governess, though her real position was his mistress. Anyway, I became suspicious because of that and so many other events that are now too tedious to recollect. I gained entrance to Philip's quarters one morning and found the remains of a letter in the fireplace. The only words I could make out were 'returning on the sixteenth'. It never occurred to me that the letter was in your hand for, of course, I had mourned your death some six months before. When Philip said he was going to London suddenly I resolved that I would have to try and follow him. Robbie brought me."

"Robbie?" Justin cried out excitedly. "Then he shall realize that something is amiss and go for help."

"But that it were true," I replied dejectedly. "I have been so conscious of protecting Robbie from all this that he has no idea, not even a clue, I suspect, as to where I am."

"But, Serena, I do not understand. If you found yourself in such dire straits for these many months, why did you not turn to someone—Richard, Anne, Robbie—certainly there must have been someone that you could have turned to?"

"You do not understand," I insisted.

I tried as best I could to reconstruct the events of the past months. My own devastation at the news of Justin's death and the shock which followed it, how hopeless it felt for me to continue. He was deathly silent as I told him of my own determination to run Mayfair and the commitment I had made to Philip for the continuance of the railroad project.

"I am amazed that Sir Henry did not try to intercede," he pondered aloud. "My God, the man should have known that I would never commit such a sum to that project."

"Justin, he did try," I acknowledged. "Even I was shocked at the amount of money involved, but you must understand that I had no reason at that juncture to distrust Philip."

"What was Richard's reaction?" he pursued.

"What would you expect?" I retorted. "But then he had been opposed to the idea from the first. There is no question that it caused a rift between us—even between Anne and myself which played even further into Philip's hands. I was alone, overworked, even with Robbie's help on the estates. I had not been well, though I now have grave suspicions about the nature of my health even then."

"What do you mean?" Justin pursued.

"As I inferred, my emotional state in those weeks following news of your death was not good. I did not eat or sleep and when I did I cannot even recall it. I returned to Mayfair in a weakened condition and then the extra work. . . . Well, at that time I thought it was simply exhaustion."

"You are not being clear, Serena."

I proceeded to tell him of the works leading to my marriage to Philip. Of a persisting malaise which seemed to worsen after it. Of Philip's continued reference to my being over-wrought, of my own fears that I was no longer in control of my own actions or emotions.

"You see, Justin, I now know that for at least the last month Philip has been giving me a drug of some sort. He may very well have been plotting to kill me all along. Had it not been for Jaspar—," I choked.

"What of Jaspar?" Justin replied somberly.

"I gave him the milk," I spluttered through the tears that fell again. "It was meant for me. Oh, Justin, it was awful. I found him lying there in the morning."

"My God," Justin moaned. "What have I done to you, Serena?"

"It was not your fault, darling. I should have been stronger, more resourceful. We've lost everything because of me. There is nothing left."

"We have each other, Serena," Justin replied emphatically. "And the children. You are certain that they are safe?"

"Charlotte knows that if anything seems amiss that she is to take them to Camberleigh. I trust her, and although she has no idea of the extent of my concerns, she is not blind to the relationship between Philip and myself."

"What of this Amelie?" he pursued. "Where is she?"

"At Mayfair," I replied soberly. "But I do not think she would physically harm the children. Unless I am wrong, she has been as much Philip's pawn as I. He will dismiss her as soon as he is done with us."

"Do not talk that way," Justin insisted. "I love you and we have not found each other again only to succumb to some madman's scheme."

"You do not know him, Justin," I insisted, "not as I do."

"Serena, try the ropes again," Justin pleaded. "We have got to get out of here. If I can be freed I can overwhelm him when he returns."

My hands found the knots again but I had no greater success with them this time than the last.

I started to say something but Justin silenced me. "I think I hear someone coming."

I clung to Justin as the footsteps came closer. The key

turned in the lock and the door opened, the light blinding me at first.

"Well, if that is not a scene of domestic tranquillity," he laughed. "Pity, you've found yourself in such a compromising position, Barkham."

"You scum," Justin spat back.

"Philip, I beg you," I pleaded, "please let us go. There can be no gain in harming us now. We will give you anything you want."

"Very touching, my dear, but I should remind you that because of you I already have everything I want," he jeered. "You cannot think that I would be so naive as to think that I could permit you and Barkham there to go free?"

"You cannot possibly get away with it, Taggart," Justin challenged. "For Christ's sake, do what you will with me, but leave Serena be."

"A chivalrous but rather foolish plea, Barkham. No, the two of you will be going on a bit of a journey."

"Where are you sending us?" I asked.

"On an ocean voyage," he replied. "I fear that the accommodations will scarcely be what they were on your last trip, Barkham, but then I will not exactly be paying for your passage. You see, when you are found I suspect you will be well out at sea. With no identification, they will indubitably conclude finally that you were stowaways. And even if they do not, they shall have no choice but to bury you at sea. The captain of the particular vessel I have selected has—shall we say—some rather unsavory things in his past. I should heartily doubt that he would want to report this incident to the authorities. No, I am sure it will in fact go by quite unnoticed."

He started to leave and turned back suddenly. "You shall sail at midnight, which leaves you another two hours or so. Pleasure yourselves as best you can until then."

Justin was so silent after Philip's departure that I panicked that he might indeed be ill.

"Justin, Justin darling, speak to me," I begged. "Are you all right?"

"I was just thinking that I wish I could see that beautiful face of yours and hold you close to me."

"I am not certain that I fully believe that it is really you lying here before me. After I was told that you were dead

you cannot imagine the nights that I lay in our bed, feeling as
though I were drowning in my aloneness. There was, it seemed,
no one to turn to. I know they tried—Anne, Charlotte, even
Richard in his own way—but I could not seem to fight the
desolation that o'ertook me."

"And I had conveniently left Taggart to watch over you,"
Justin replied angrily. "I was so driven by my own obsession
with this damn railroad project that I refused the advisements
of others."

"But you sincerely believed in the future of the railroads," I
insisted.

"I still do," he admitted, "but I took too much on appearance, Serena. If it were something to do with the Mayfair estates, I would never have proceeded with such naive largesse.
My own ego, my own ambition, blinded my reason."

"How could you have known, Justin?" I pursued.

He shook his head from side to side. "I do not know except
to say that I would not have taken so much at face value. I
became so enthusiastic about Jonathan's models and drawings
that I allowed myself to be swept into the project without
proper evaluation. You know, I often discount Richard, but
*he* in fact challenged this whim of mine. It was he who asked
me what I knew about Taggart and Leech."

"It will do no good to chastise yourself this way, Justin," I
admonished. "We were both duped by a man we now know is
a cunning criminal."

"Come closer to me again, Serena," he whispered.

I did as he bid, our lips meeting this time in a hunger and
passion born from our mutual need.

"You had best beware, Serena," Justin chided, nibbling at
my ear, "for my desire for you is such that I might break these
bonds and take you right here."

"If that is true, then you had best kiss me some more," I
urged.

It amazed me that in the midst of our terror my response to
Justin could transport me miles away from this locked darkened room which boded only ill for us.

I lay across him, quieted by the sound of his murmurings,
our hearts beating as one.

"You know, darling," he said suddenly, "we have to conceive of some plan. We will not have many opportunities for
escape, of that I am certain, and we must be prepared to take

advantage of the slightest opening."

I sensed that Justin was being valiant for my benefit and cherished him for it. I did not want to press the issue that I knew Philip far better than he. I had spent these last six months watching him manipulate, denigrate and violate—the extent to which I could never share with Justin. Only I truly knew the levels of debasement to which Philip could sink. I saw no good in visiting this sorry truth on him now.

"When Philip returns, if he indeed plans to remove us, he shall have to untie me from these bonds," Justin speculated.

"You do not think he will act alone, do you?" I queried.

"No. But it seems our only chance for me to make a move once I am freed."

"Justin," I implored, "I cannot let you take that chance. What if they are armed? What is there to stop them from killing us here?"

"I do not think they will," he mused. "Moll may be cooperating but I rather doubt she would relish a double murder to occur in this house."

I thought about it for a moment, then agreed.

"Serena," Justin continued, "you have to be alert when they are untying me. At any time you must be ready to run. And once you are out of here, do not stop."

"I would not leave you here," I replied, amazed that he would think that I should even consider it.

"Do not be foolish, Serena," he argued. "You might be able to get back to Robbie—"

"Not before they would seize you from here, Justin."

"Likely not," he replied. "But you know that their plan is to take us to the docks. It's a starting point. Robbie is resourceful, he'll find me."

"Justin, I cannot—could not—leave you, not now," I cried.

"If you can, you will, Serena," he argued. "There are the children to think of. My safety *must* be placed secondary to theirs."

At least another hour passed before we heard footsteps in the hallway once again.

"Remember what I told you, Serena," Justin whispered hurriedly as the key turned in the lock. "I love you, darling."

"And I you," I murmured, kissing him perhaps for the last time.

There were two men with Philip this time, the one Justin

had referred to as Haggerty and the other one, whom I had seen at Channing Hall. I pressed closer to Justin who encouraged me to stay calm.

"Well, how are the love birds?" Philip asked, crossing the threshold of the door. "Ready for your small journey?"

I wanted to shout at him, but fear seemed to paralyze my voice.

"Stevens," he ordered the shorter man, "you and Haggerty handle Barkham over there. And do not be easy with him, he's stronger than you think."

Before I could protest, Philip strode over to the bed and began pulling at my shoulders. I pressed as hard as I could against Justin, but I was no match for Philip, and against Justin's outcries he wrenched me up to him.

"Oh, now there shall be at least one little kiss," he cajoled, "for your other husband. I rather like the idea of your watching, Barkham. Frankly, if there were more time . . ."

"Shut up, you swine," Justin screamed out.

I saw his leg go up and heard a sound as his boot connected with the man they called Haggerty.

The man reeled back, sprawling before my feet. I, too, kicked at him, connecting hard enough to have him call out in pain.

"Why, you little . . ." he started, grabbing at my leg.

"Let her go," Philip demanded. "You fool, get ahold of Barkham. Silence him if you have to."

The next thing I knew I saw Justin's shadow rising on the bed frame but before he could break fully from his bonds Haggerty struck him full on the jaw. I gasped as I heard a crack as Justin's head came down against the bed frame.

"He's out," Stevens called out.

"It's just as well," Philip replied as he twisted my arm again. "Now listen to me, Serena," he warned, "unless you want to die right here and now, I would suggest that you cooperate. We are going to go down the stairs and into an awaiting carriage. If you make the slightest sound I should only say it will not be very pretty for you or Barkham there."

Philip had brought my cloak, which he draped about me. Pain seared through me as he threw it about my right shoulder.

"I do not know if I can make it, Philip," I murmured honestly.

"You will make it, Serena, because you have to," he replied, thrusting me forward into the hallway.

I had been in the dark so long that the light was dizzying to my eyes. I was able to turn only briefly, long enough to see Justin being dragged between Stevens and Haggerty. I was shocked at how ill he looked and realized that it must have been days since he had been given any food. There was a red spot on his jacket and I knew that it was blood, likely caused when his head struck the bed.

"Keep going, Serena," Philip prodded.

The staircase to this floor was narrow and Philip preceded me, keeping a firm grip on my arm. When we reached the second floor he pulled me to him, his arm about my back. I cried out in pain as my shoulder crushed against his chest. He hustled me along the empty corridor save two men who had obviously just reached the second floor. I looked directly at the second one, hoping that he would read something in my regard which would make him pause or question Philip, but he averted my glance.

In response to one of the stranger's queries I heard Haggerty give some excuse that their friend had overindulged a bit. I was puzzled why we halted on the staircase between the first and second floor but then realized that Philip was waiting for Moll to indicate that it was safe to descend. As we paused on the landing I debated for a second, throwing my weight against Philip, hoping that it would pitch him down the stairs, but I quickly realized that with his hold on me we would likely topple together and it would be me who would not survive it.

A whistle from below put Philip in motion once again. The front doorway lay open and he propelled me forward and through it to the carriage. Justin was still unconscious when they reached us, and Haggerty and Stevens swore as they worked awkardly to maneuver his full weight into the coach.

"Damn you, make haste with this," Philip demanded as he pulled Justin's shoulders up. The other men jumped in and Philip told the driver to get underway. If I had had any hope that he would have used the Mayfair carriage, it would of course been foolish since Philip was not about to risk recognition of the Mayfair crest for this journey.

I longed to reach out to Justin, who was restrained by Haggerty and Stevens opposite me, but Philip's arm kept my hands bound at my sides.

"Can you not see that he is bleeding?" I cried out.

"Do you really expect me to care about that, Serena?" Philip retorted.

I looked up at him, unable to discern his expression in the dark.

"Is there nothing you care about, Philip?"

"I am appalled at your silliness, Serena. I have always credited you with more reason than that. Money, power—now those are things I care about."

I started as a moan escaped Justin's lips. "I am here, darling," I encouraged.

"Very touching, my dear," Philip mocked.

Justin's eyes opened and I knew, even in the darkness, that he was experiencing great pain.

"Serena," he murmured, "are you all right?"

"I am fine," I assured him.

"Tie him up," Philip demanded. "I do not want any mishaps."

"Aye'm not doin' any more o' yer biddin' until we get paid, Taggart," the man called Haggerty demanded.

"You'll get your money, you fool," Philip retorted angrily. "We struck a bargain. You get them on the ship and then you get your money. Now tie him up."

My heart ached for Justin as they bound hands that were already burned raw from the rope restraints. I feared that he would lose consciousness again. If there would be any hope of our escaping, Justin would need all the strength that he could muster.

The dank smell of the sea told me that we had neared the docks.

"Does the driver know which ship our friends shall be journeying on?" Philip asked.

"The *Susannah*—that's what ye told me," Stevens replied.

"Give me some of that rope," Philip demanded, taking my hands in his.

"I regret doing this, my dear, but my friends here do not know what a hellion you can be. I doubt that those delicate fingers could untie your lover's bonds but I shall not leave that to chance."

The carriage came suddenly to a halt.

"I almost forgot something," Philip continued. He lifted my hands again and pulled at the rings which I was still wearing on my index finger. "A pity, my dear, but you shall not be needing these and they are quite valuable, after all. Handsome, are they not, Barkham? Purchased, you should know, with the funds I received from selling Serena's necklace."

"Then it was *you* who stole the necklace?" I amazed. "I should have known."

"I actually regretted having to do that, my dear, but I could conceive of no other way that I should stay solvent during our courtship. Not to mention the purchase of these rings."

"We better git goin', boss," Stevens insisted. "Aye want to git this over with."

"Then 'tis time to say our goodbyes," Philip agreed. "Won't you allow me just one last kiss, my love?" he continued, pulling me to him.

"You disgust me," I spat at him. "There is no hell too great for you."

He flung me back against the seat. "Take Barkham on ahead," he motioned to Haggerty.

"Justin," I screamed, trying to throw my body against the door to prevent his removal.

"Do not worry, Serena," he murmured.

Whether he was too weak to resist or whether he was saving his strength for a more opportune time, I did not know, but he no longer resisted as Haggerty pulled him from the coach.

I whirled about to face Philip. "Do what you will with me but I beseech you do not harm the children. They are not a threat to you. Send them to Camberleigh. Anne and Richard will care for them. They are innocents, Philip. If you have any decency, you will assure me of their safety."

"Unfortunately, my dear, I have no decency" was his icy reply.

"Get her out of here, Stevens."

I bit into my lip in an attempt to endure the pain which flooded through me when Stevens pulled me out by my shoulders.

"Ye'll be right smart te keep yer mouth shut if ye know what's good fer ye," Stevens warned. "Aye t'aint real softhearted when it comes te usin' this."

I jumped slightly at the glint of the knife. "I shall be silent," I agreed.

The ship was alive with activity, which, I realized, made it far less likely that we would be noticed. I fully believed that

Stevens meant what he said about feeling no compunction about using the knife and I complied by allowing him to prod me forward across the gangplank, across the decks and finally into the bowels of the vessel.

There were boxes and ropes cast where we were walking and I tripped suddenly.

"Aye told ye, no fancy business," Stevens warned as he pulled me to my feet.

"I fell," I insisted.

"Well, it's not fer now."

He guided me behind a large beam and suddenly I spied Justin and Haggerty before us.

I called out to him just as I saw Haggerty push him back.

"Don't worry, ye'll be down there with 'im soon enough."

As we approached the gaping pit into which Justin had been thrust I cried out, "You cannot possibly put us down there."

Haggerty laughed. "Don't seem te be likin' their final resting place, do they?"

"Listen to me," I pleaded. "I have money. Do you really think that Philip is going to pay you off? I quite suspect that when you return to the dock you shall find the carriage has suddenly disappeared."

"Eh, what's she sayin' there?" Stevens demanded of Haggerty.

"Whatever he is paying you I shall double it, triple it, if you let us go," I pleaded. "Philip need never know."

"Blimey, she's right, Haggerty. What o' we got te lose?"

"Have ye lost yer mind," Haggerty replied. "All we'd need is te let these two go. Barkham would 'ave the whole o' London down on us in hours an' aye don't fancy myself danglin' from a rope. As fer Taggart, the bloke will be there. E's not about te stiff us. Not unless 'e wants te see his Maker before his time."

I began to protest but Haggerty pulled me over to the hole and without another word had thrust me into it. The impact took my breath away momentarily. I heard Justin calling out to me and I moved toward the sound of his voice. As I did the door to the trap slammed down sealing us in the tomblike structure.

"Serena, are you all right?" Justin murmured.

"'Tis only my shoulder, but I do not think it is broken."

"Lie still for a moment," he replied. "I am going to try and stand. If I can reach the trap I might be able to force it open."

I shuddered as Justin struggled to his feet, conscious for the first time of the dampness and stench about me.

"Can you reach it?" I called out.

"I fear not," he murmured. "If I could get free of these damnable ropes, I might be able to jump up to it, though even if I did I doubt I could open it since I am certain that they threw the latch."

"You mean we are simply to be buried alive in this place?" I cried out. "Perhaps if we scream, someone might hear us."

Justin eased back to where I lay. "Darling, you must try and keep as quiet and calm as possible. The air in here is minimal and it shall lessen with time."

I pressed close to Justin, hopeful that he would not sense my own terror. We talked quietly during those next hours, each of us studiously avoiding mention of Philip. Justin was hungry to know about the children and I tried to bring to life those people who were dear to him. I had lost touch with so many of our friends over these past months and his questions made me painfully aware of how remote Philip had forced me to be.

I knew quickly why Justin had cautioned me about the air, for the longer we remained huddled together there against the cold, slimy walls the more I felt my chest tighten. Justin would jostle me from time to time, more aware even than I that I was beginning to slip into an unconscious state. I marveled at how strong Justin could be, for I knew that he, too, was feeling not only the effects of our entrapment but of those hours which preceded it. As he murmured to me of his love I tasted the salt of my own tears, which fell not so much from despair but from the peace that came from finding him again. I had learned months before that I could not face life without him. I was learning now that I could face death with him.

I realized suddenly that it had been more than a few moments since Justin had spoken and I panicked, pushing against him for some response. He was breathing but it was labored. It was not logical but I was angry at him suddenly. "You cannot leave me again," I wailed, the sound of my cries echoing back to me.

I put my head back against the wall, praying now that the end would come quickly. Whatever bravery I had evidenced I could no longer muster now that Justin could not buoy my spirits.

# 22

At first I thought that the tapping was in my imagination. But as it continued and I knew that it was emanating from above us, I sat upright. Was someone up there or was it merely the rats collecting, sensing that we would soon be prey?

"Help us," I called out shocked at the weakness of my own voice. "Down here."

I waited but the tapping had stopped as soon as it had started. I sank back against the wall again, this time my tears flowing from sheer frustration. Justin moaned suddenly and I tried to support his head against my shoulder.

When the tapping commenced again I did not call out this time and so when there was a sudden rush of air I was too started to call out.

"Serena," a voice called out to me. "Lady Barkham, Serena, oh, God, tell me aye'm not too late."

"Robbie? Robbie?" I whispered.

"Thank the Lord," he cried out.

"Robbie, is that really you?"

"Yes, 'tis me, Serena."

"But how . . ."

"We don't have much time," he pressed. "If aye lean my arms over, can ye grasp hold an' aye'll pull ye out?"

"I cannot, Robbie. My hands are tied. Robbie, Justin, Lord Barkham is here with me."

"Aye know, Serena," he replied. "Look, aye'm goin to be

droppin' a knife down te ye. Ye kin cut yer bonds an' Master Justin's as well.''

"He is very weak, Robbie," I advised, incredulous that he should know that he was alive. "There has scarcely been a sound from him in some time now."

"Stay put now while aye throw the knife, Serena."

I moved towards the spot where the weapon made a dull thud as it came in contact with the ground.

"I've got it," I called back, my fingers gingerly trying to decipher where the blade was.

"Kin ye do it, Serena?"

" 'Tis not easy," I replied, not willing to tell him that I had already cut myself.

The process seemed endless. Just when I thought it was hopeless I felt the rope break and my wrists were mercifully free. I moved quickly to Justin, working at Robbie's insistence as speedily as I could, talking all the time.

"I think he is coming around, Robbie," I called back.

"Kin ye get 'im te stand?"

I put the knife aside and placed my hands under his shoulders, trying to hoist him up. "Darling, you have to help me," I begged. "I cannot do this alone."

"Serena?" he murmured.

"Yes, darling, it's Serena. Robbie is here, he's going to help us. Please try—here, lean on me."

I never knew that I had so much strength. Justin, bless him, was trying to cooperate, but he was too weak to be of much assist.

"He is standing," I called up to Robbie, who was lying over the side of the opening, his arms stretched down.

"Lord Barkham, put yer hands in mine."

"You cannot possibly lift him yourself," I cautioned.

"Aye have to, Serena."

"Is there not someone who could help you?"

"Aye wouldn't be trustin' anyone on this ship. There, aye've got him now. Ye stand clear, Serena, in case 'e falls back."

I watched in amazement as I saw Justin's body move slowly upwards towards the mouth of the opening.

"You did it," I called up excitedly. When Robbie did not respond I called to him. "Robbie, Robbie are you all right?"

"Just a wee out o' breath," he gasped.

"Perhaps we should wait awhile," I opposed as he argued for me to get into position.

"There is not time," he urged. "Grab on to me, Serena."

I did as he bade, struggling to stifle a scream as his hoisting wrenched at my shoulder.

"Just a minute more, Serena," he whispered. "Don't be lettin' go."

We both lay panting on the deck, my hand reaching out to Justin, who lay beside me.

It was Robbie who rose first. "Serena, ye'll 'ave to support 'im with me."

I nodded, struggling to my feet, helping Robbie raise Justin to his.

"If anyone stops ye, don't be answerin', just keep movin'."

We commenced our trek. Thankfully Robbie knew the way, for the ship seemed a maze of twists and turns.

"Aye've the carriage waitin'," he whispered as we neared the gangplank.

"Hey, who goes there?" a strange voice called out suddenly.

I remembered Robbie's insistence that we not stop for anything and kept in step with him as he hurried the pace.

"The carriage, 'tis over there."

We moved swiftly towards it, Robbie doing his best to ease Justin up into it.

I started as whistles blew and I heard shouts back on the deck of the ship.

"Get in, Serena," Robbie commanded, "an' be prepared fer a rough ride."

I threw myself into the carriage and braced myself as Robbie started the team. Justin was murmuring my name over and over and I held him to me, reassuring him that I was with him and that we were safe. He was dreadfully cold and I took the blankets that lay on the seat opposite, tucking them tight around him.

We had traveled about fifteen minutes when the carriage slowed suddenly. Panicking, I looked out the window quickly to see what the problem was. "Robbie? Robbie?" I called out.

" 'Tis all right, Serena," he replied, alighting from the driver's station. "How is the master doin'?"

"He is weak and cold," I replied. "He needs rest and care."

"He'll come 'round, ye'll see," Robbie reassured me. He

grinned at me suddenly. "Aye stopped 'cause, to tell ye the truth, aye don't know where ye want me te be goin'."

I was amazed at the sound of my own laughter. "Robbie, you had me fooled. I thought you knew exactly what you were doing. How in heaven's name did you know where to find us?" I exclaimed.

" 'Tis a long story, Serena, but now 'tis not the time."

"No, you are right," I agreed, sobering suddenly at the position we found ourselves in. "Robbie, we must get back to Mayfair. The children are there and I cannot trust what Philip might do. I hate to test Justin's strength but I fear we cannot risk any delay."

"Then it is to Mayfair that aye'll be headin'," he agreed. Then reaching in back of the seat, he brought out a wooden basket. "There is food and drink in there, even a spot o' brandy. Aye thought ye both might be needin' it."

I accepted it gratefully, amazed at Robbie's ingenuity. "Are you warm enough?" I asked.

He nodded. "Aye've another coat atop the coach. T'will be sufficient."

When we were underway again, I tried to pry some of the brandy into Justin's mouth. He resisted at first, but I persisted, convinced that it would do more than anything to bring him round.

I did my best to clean his head wound, using one of the napkins as a makeshift bandage.

"Serena," he murmured again.

"Yes, darling, I am here," I assured him. "Try to drink a bit more of this. It will help, I am certain."

He accepted it willingly this time.

"Where are we?"

"We are in a coach, on our way to Mayfair," I replied quietly. "It was Robbie who rescued us. Do you remember nothing of the last hours?"

He rubbed his forehead. "Not much. I remember knowing that I was losing consciousness, but I did not seem to be able to fight it off. What has Robbie to do with all this? I was vaguely aware of him but . . ."

"I do not know the whole story," I interrupted. "He must have followed me somehow."

"Thank God for that," Justin murmured. "I do not think we would have survived another hour in that hole."

I encouraged him to eat, partaking myself of the bread and cheese as well. Exhaustion was beginning to take hold of me and soon I found that I could fight it no longer. When I awakened, light was streaming through the window of the carriage. I looked up to see Justin smiling down on me, aware suddenly that my head had fallen during the night onto his lap.

"How long have you been awake?" I yawned.

"Several hours," he replied.

"You should have wakened me."

"Not a chance," he retorted, winking at me. "I have just been sitting here thinking how very beautiful you are and how much I love you."

"Oh, Justin, I love you, too," I cried out as he gathered me in his arms. "I feel as though my very life has been given back to me being here with you like this."

"I should never have left you, Serena. If I had not been so damnably stubborn. Seeing you here now, holding you close, I think I must have been mad to have agreed to have been apart from you."

"Justin," I commenced, "I do not want us to focus on the mistakes of the past. You could not have known the plot against us. I certainly did not. The Mayfair that you love so dearly has been threatened with ruin, thanks to me. The children have been thwarted, ignored—they are starved for the kind of life and love they once knew. As am I. It will not be easy to rebuild it all, Justin. But that is where our energies must be focused—not on those things we cannot change."

The carriage slowed to a stop suddenly.

"Robbie must be exhausted," I said.

"Ye speak the truth, Serena, but 'tis the team aye'm worryin' about," Robbie said as he appeared suddenly at the side of the carriage.

I opened the door and insisted that he climb in. As he did Justin stretched out his arms and the two fell into a long embrace. I was touched to see, when Robbie finally relaxed back into the seat, that there were tears in his eyes.

"There is nothing I can say to you, Robbie, to communicate the depth of my gratitude," Justin murmured.

"Seein' ye 'ere with Serena, alive, 'tis a miracle," Robbie grinned in reply.

"I still want to know how you knew where I was," I exclaimed, "and how you knew that Justin was alive."

"Ye be forgivin' me, Serena, but aye was not about to let ye set out on yer own again so when ye left in the mornin' aye followed ye. When aye saw where ye were headin', aye knew ye was up te no good. An' when ye didn't leave . . . well, in a tizzy aye was. Ye could 'a blown me over with a feather when aye saw Lord Taggart arrive. T'was then aye knew that somethin' t'were amiss."

"Aye'll tell ye the truth, when aye saw those men bringin' ye out with Lord Barkham, aye thought aye must of met my Maker. Aye'm not one te believe in ghosts but te see ye there after we'd gone and buried ye in our minds—well, ye could 'a blown me over with a feather. Aye could a killed Taggart with me bare hands when aye saw him knockin' ye about, Serena, but aye was no match for the likes o' those two with him. One o' them said somethin' about the docks an' when they pulled off aye ran like a horse in gallop back to where aye'd left the carriage. Aye got te the docks in time te see those two leavin' the boat. Aye didn't need a map to tell me ye two were aboard an' not fer a pleasure journey. Aye'll tell ye as the hours passed it looked less an' less likely that aye would find ye."

He reached into his pocket and withdrew a small piece of blue velvet. "If aye hadn't seen this, aye fear ye'd still be shut up there in that hole."

" 'Tis a piece from my dress," I said, amazed as he handed it to me. "It must have torn when I fell."

"Ye know aye knew Taggart was far from a gentleman but aye can't believe all o' this. Aye've been puzzlin' it the whole time aye've been drivin' but it makes no sense te me."

"It is a long and rather complicated story which we will share with you once we return to Mayfair," Justin advised.

"There is a small inn up ahead," Robbie replied. "Ye know the one?"

Justin nodded.

"Aye know how anxious ye are te reach Mayfair but aye can't push those horses any further. We could rest 'ere a spell an' then start out again later this afternoon."

We agreed that that was the best course of action and a half hour later we were ensconced in small but comfortable rooms in the inn. Justin ordered a large breakfast tray and I called for a basin of hot water. I had not realized what a motley sight we were until I looked at Justin partaking hungrily of the plate of eggs and smoked sausages. My dress was mud-stained and torn and my hair fell in tangles about my shoulders. One of the maids found me a brush and while Justin ate I bathed away the tangible vestiges of these past hours.

I had only the dress I was wearing and it seemed a bit foolish to don it again; yet as many times as Justin and I had lain together I found myself experiencing a certain demureness about his seeing me in some stage of undress. The notion made me feel quite a young girl again, and as I wrapped the bath towel about me I wondered if Justin, too, was experiencing any doubts or hesitancy about our being together again.

One dark fear marred the rather giddy anticipation I felt. What if Justin could no longer be stirred by me? What if the thought of Philip having taken me would so disgust him that he could no longer be responsive to me?

My thoughts were intruded upon by Justin calling out to me. "Serena, are you all right?"

I pulled the bathsheet tighter about me and went out to where Justin stood stoking the fire. I approached him tenuously, strongly aware of his eyes roving my body. I stopped about ten paces before him.

"You are thinner," he said slowly.

I smiled. "Do you know that I have never seen you with a beard before?"

"Oh, Serena," he moaned, striding over to me and taking me in his arms. The bathsheet slipped to the floor as he lifted me gently and placed me on the bed, taking a light blanket and drawing it up over me.

I watched silently as he slowly removed each article of clothing.

"I do believe you are blushing," he whispered, coming over to sit beside me.

His hand stroked my brow. I squeezed my eyes shut as I suddenly felt tears clouding them.

"Serena," he said, "I cannot deny that every fiber of me aches for you but I am not so insensitive to realize that you for many reasons may not share my desire. I can be understanding if you need time."

"Oh, Justin," I moaned, "I need you and I need you to need me. Too much time has passed already. I do not want another second to go by without feeling you next to me. I want to be one with you again."

We explored each other slowly, gently at first. I was acutely aware of my own body as his fingers reawakened feelings and sensations that I had thought were lost to me forever. I was moist and ready for him as he penetrated me, his masculinity swelling full within me. We lay still for a moment, savoring our renewed oneness, and then he moved higher above me, thrusting deeper and deeper into me until I joined him in a rhythm that seemed to have a life all its own. His explosion into me was of such a force that I gasped when he seemed to swell almost instantly again, this time driving me higher and higher until I was trembling with the aftermath of my own passion.

When we had spent each other fully, Justin rolled to his back, cradling my hand under his arm.

"Do you know how much I love you, Lady Barkham?"

"Lady Barkham," I repeated slowly. "I may have borne another man's name, Justin, but I was never another man's wife."

It was midafternoon when we awakened. I was concerned that we had slept so long but I knew that neither of us could have gone any further without rest. Justin dressed quickly and went off to find Robbie, returning to tell me that we were set to travel again. Robbie arranged for the food baskets to be replenished, and without much ado we were back on the road to Mayfair again.

We had driven about three hours when Justin insisted on giving Robbie a reprieve from the driving. I argued the thought of it for I did not think that Justin was strong enough, but he would not hear of it, arguing that our lovemaking that morning had revitalized him.

Robbie joined me in the carriage and it gave me an opportunity to explain to him, as best I could, the events that had led to these past days.

"Ye should 'ave come te me, Serena," Robbie admonished.

"I know," I agreed. "But for so long I was confused and then, well, if my suspicions were unfounded, I would only have troubled you."

"Serena, aye was troubled anyway," Robbie argued. "What with Taggart taking over Mayfair. The man had not the vaguest notion of 'ow te run the place."

I was thrown forward suddenly as the carriage jolted and our pace picked up.

"Do you think Justin is all right?" I exclaimed, bracing myself against the seat.

Robbie's face showed alarm. He moved forward to call out to Justin and as he did we heard Justin's voice screaming down for us to hold on.

My blood ran cold as the thundering of the horses' hooves resounded in my ears and the carriage seemed to race through the darkening night.

Robbie grabbed at the door of the carriage, putting his head out the window.

"Can you see anything?" I pleaded.

A sudden jolt forced him back against the seat.

"It's the Mayfair carriage up ahead."

"Oh, my God," I moaned. "Robbie, you must tell Justin to stop. Please, we shall all be killed."

"Serena, for God's sake, hold on," Robbie demanded, pushing me back against the seat.

As he did I saw we had drawn aside the Mayfair carriage.

"It is empty," I exclaimed.

"Taggart is atop with the driver."

I screamed as the two carriages impacted side by side.

"He's trying to force us off the road. Robbie, these horses are no match for the other team."

"I know, Serena," Robbie gasped as the carriages cracked together once again. "But there is no one who can handle them better than Lord Barkham."

I could hear the shouts of Justin and Philip over the incessant pounding of the horses' hooves. Our carriage seemed suddenly to pull ahead and I looked out in time to see Philip wrest the reins from his driver.

"Give me your boot," I screamed at Robbie. "Your boot," I repeated.

He pulled it off and thrust it into my hand. I leaned forward in the seat and aimed the boot out the window at Philip. As I let it fly from my hand, hoping that I might be able to graze him, our carriage lurched forward and the boot flew in front of two of Philip's horses. I watched in horror as one horse shied and reared suddenly. There was an enormous crack as our carriage drew out ahead. I could no longer see anything but the night was a cacophony of whinnying horses and shattering wood.

Our carriage drew abruptly to a halt and Robbie flung open

the door and jumped down. I started to follow but he insisted that I stay inside.

Justin raced by, pausing only to ask me if I were all right. I looked out of the window and even in the shadowy light of dusk I was shocked at what I saw. The Mayfair carriage had overturned but the team was still dragging it, causing whatever parts were still intact to splinter apart.

"Get the lantern," I heard Justin call out to Robbie.

I gathered my cloak about me and climbed down from the coach.

"You should not be out here," Robbie advised.

"Well, I cannot stay in there wondering what has happened."

Robbie took my arm and guided me over to where Justin was working feverishly to unhinge the team.

"Hold this while aye give Justin a hand," Robbie commanded, thrusting the copper lantern into my hand.

"Where is the driver?" I called out.

"He's over there at the side of the road," Justin replied. "He must have been thrown upon impact."

"Shall I fetch a blanket?" I called back.

"Do not bother, Serena," Robbie replied. "He's dead."

"Where is Philip?" I gasped as the team broke free of the shattered bulk of wood.

"He is pinned under the carriage," Justin called back. "Robbie, give me a hand. You shall have to get under the back wheel."

Robbie ran to the other side of the carriage. I followed in pursuit, hoping to provide him better light. As I did my eyes caught sight of Philip, who was pinned under the carriage, with only his head and one arm thrust awkwardly behind it visible.

"Oh, my God," I moaned as Robbie and Justin pressed their full weight against the bulk of the vehicle.

"Aye can't budge it," Robbie called out.

Justin instructed him to move to the other side, which he did. I watched in horror as both men attempted to lift the weight of the frame, to no avail.

"I shall have to go for help," Justin said finally.

I moved tenuously to where Philip lay. I suppose the horror of the accident had placed me in a state of shock for as I looked down on him I felt only hopelessness at the whole scene.

His eyes fluttered and I knelt down beside him, aware that he was trying to talk.

"Hush," I advised, "Justin and Robbie are trying to move the carriage."

"No," he whispered, "it is of no use."

Something in me knew that what he spoke was right. I should have encouraged him, given him some thread of hope to hang onto, but my voice was stilled by the pain that he had put Justin and me through these past months.

Realizing that he was desirous of saying something further, I leaned closer to him.

"Serena, I did not mean . . . at least, not at first . . ." he murmured.

"You did not mean what, Philip?"

"To hurt you. If only you had accepted things as they were."

"Why, Philip? Why," I beseeched, "did you do this?"

He coughed suddenly and I was shocked to see blood trickle from the corner of his mouth.

"You would not understand," he continued when the rasping had eased. "Men like Barkham—he had it all. Money, power, a beautiful wife."

"Then the railroad project was just a scheme to be rid of him?" I surmised.

He shook his head slowly.

"Not in the beginning," he argued. "But then I went to Mayfair. I wanted it all and I had it . . . at least for a while."

I shook my head. "You never had it, Philip. Not really."

I felt Justin's presence standing behind me but I made no move.

"I did not want to hurt you, Serena," Philip repeated again. "But you would not cooperate. It could have been good between us, you would have seen."

"Did you really think by drugging me, trying to convince me that I was unsound in mind as well as body, by rendering me a prisoner in my own house, that you could win me?" I blurted out. "You robbed me of Justin, of Jaspar, of Mayfair, of my own senses, and yet you can believe . . ." I broke off. "You tried to kill me, Philip."

He closed his eyes and I thought for a moment that he was gone.

"There was no other way," he murmured, his voice weaker now. "You were too clever, Serena. I could not chance your exposing me. I could not lose it."

Justin's hand pressed against my shoulder. "I shall have to go for help, Serena," he advised. "Robbie and I cannot budge this coach."

A smile played over Philip's lips. "Tell him not to bother, Serena," he whispered. His eyes raised upwards toward the blackened skies. "You know, it is ironic."

"What is, Philip?" I asked.

"Someday there shall likely be railroad tracks lying right here over my grave."

I watched as his face contorted in pain.

"Can we not do something, Justin?" I murmured.

He shook his head.

Philip uttered no further word. There was one terrible moment when his head seemed to convulse and rise up suddenly, then fell back for its last time, soon to be as cold as the ground beneath.

Justin pulled me up and placed his arms about me, commencing to lead me back to the carriage. Robbie had taken the team from the overturned carriage and hooked it up with our own.

"We cannot just leave them there," I insisted.

"I will send someone back," Justin replied, "as soon as we reach the next town."

Robbie insisted on driving and Justin helped me into the carriage. I fell back against the seat, totally exhausted, and yet my mind raced with the events of these past months. Justin slid in beside me, putting his arm about me, drawing me close to him.

"Are you going to be all right, Serena?" he whispered, noticing that I had shuddered suddenly.

"It all seems like a bad dream," I replied. "I keep thinking that I will wake up and all this will simply disappear."

We both were too stunned, I sensed, to continue any conversation, each keeping to his own thoughts as the carriage continued on towards Mayfair. We reached the first town within less than a half an hour, and Justin, after ensconcing me in a small building that took lodgers, went off with Robbie to arrange for someone to tend to Philip and the driver. The innkeeper offered me some sustenance but I was too devastated to even think of food. Justin had not made it clear whether he intended to drive on that evening but I knew that I could not withstand the journey. I drew back the crocheted coverlet from the bed and, unlacing my boots, collapsed fully onto it, staring blindly up at the eaves.

I had no idea how long Justin had been gone but I awakened to find him gently trying to remove my clothing.

"Were you able to send someone back to the carriage tonight?"

He nodded in assent. "Everything has been taken care of."

I could not fathom where he had gotten the flannel nightdress that he was helping me into, but he quickly explained that he had told the mistress at the lodging that our belongings had been lost in the accident and she obliged by providing a clean gown of her own.

Justin undressed in silence. My heart was already so heavy that I could not bear the slightest reference to Philip or the debacle we had endured only hours before. Justin, I sensed, was of like mind for when he finally climbed into bed, easing my own body against his nakedness, he, too, fell silent, hushed by the darkness of the day.

I awakened only once in the middle of the night feeling terribly cold. The fire was still burning brightly in the fireplace, but I could not dispel the freezing numbness that seemed to spread through my veins. I longed to have Justin's arms about me, caressing me into some space of comfort, but he slept so soundly that I did not want to trouble him with my own inner turmoil.

When he awakened me in the morning his countenance was so stern that I panicked momentarily.

"What is it?" I asked, sitting up quickly and pulling the covers about me.

"Nothing truly, Serena," he assured me. "I just cannot put any of this to the back of my mind. As, I am certain, neither can you, my love."

He came to me and enveloped me in his arms. "Can you ever forgive me for getting us involved in all this?"

"Darling," I whispered, "none of us can bear the brunt of the blame for this. I only wish that Philip had lived so that we might truly understand it all."

"I know," he replied.

"He swore to me there at the last that he had not originally meant to harm me," I offered.

"I do not believe he did," Justin speculated. "It was me that Taggart wanted out of the way. But when he could not conquer you, control you as he wished, he saw no alternative. Ultimately you would have gone to Richard or Anne. He was too deeply ensconced at that point to risk losing it all."

"I still do not understand how he could have schemed the whole thing," I replied. "How could he have known that you would invest in the railroads?"

"I do not think he did," Justin mused. "You know if we had been successful he would have stood to make a great deal of money simply off that venture. He found poor Jonathan, who, I suspect, had no prospects and convinced him that he could find capital for his plans. There are really only a handful of us here in the North who could have afforded the kind of investment he was looking for."

"And he chose you," I concluded.

Justin smiled wryly. "It was a clever selection really. Anyone in the county knows that I have always championed newer and better equipment. And not to be overlooked is that I have a reputation as a gambler. Not at the tables, of course, but a gambler, nonetheless. Philip Taggart gambled on a gambler."

"But why this complicated scenario of sending you to America?" I pursued.

"I cannot be certain," Justin replied, "but I sense that it was after Philip's fateful trip to Mayfair that he began formulating his diabolical scheme."

"You believe that it was a simple case of greed?" I replied.

"Money and power are seductive aphrodisiacs to some, Serena."

"He was mad, Justin," I whispered in reply.

"And quite brilliant at the same time—or perhaps 'clever' is a better term."

"Justin, I want to get to Mayfair," I urged.

"Robbie is readying the team as we speak," he replied. "But now with Philip gone, what harm could come to the children?"

He had read my mind. "With Charlotte there, I do not think any. And Amelie has no news of Philip. She was, in her own way, a pawn as well, but I will not rest until I see both Daphne and Alexander safe."

Justin agreed and we rose, dressed and breakfasted quickly. When I saw Robbie his eyes bleary and red-rimmed I sensed that he had taken a bit of ale the night preceding, but given what he had done for Justin and myself in these past hours I thought it small compensation for the risk he had taken.

It was only when we had ensconced ourselves in the carriage and were on the road again towards Mayfair that I studied Justin, wondering what change had taken place in him.

He smiled at me, obviously amused by my puzzlement.

"I was wondering when you would comment," he grinned.

"It is the beard," I concluded suddenly. "You have shaved the beard."

"And?" he ventured.

"It was simply that I had not seen you for so long. And then these past days seeing you with the beard. Forgive me."

"You approve?"

I shook my head in wonderment. "Justin, you could have grown bald or gained your weight but twice over again—and you would look wonderful to me."

It seemed forever before the landscape changed and began to take on a familiar tranquillity. I watched Justin as he seemed mesmerized by hills and farms that he knew intimately; now, though, each in isolation seemed to take on a new significance for him.

I reached over, my hand taking his. "We're going home, darling."

"You know, Serena, when we arrive I think it would be best that you went in first. This is going to be an enormous shock for the children. Do you think that you can prepare them?"

"I had not even given consideration to that," I replied, brushing my hair back under my cloak.

Justin leaned forward, suddenly pointing out of the window of the carriage.

"Look, Serena," he enthused, "the oaks are in bud."

It was so cold that I marveled that vestiges of spring were evident in this northern clime.

"Perhaps it is an omen," I said quietly.

"An omen?"

"Call it nonsensical, Justin, but we left here in the fall. Understand, I love the season but it does have an aura of ending, of cutting back of all that has flourished these months before. We are returning in the first breath of spring. There is a sense of newness and freshness about it that I find particularly significant.''

"It is our new beginning, Serena."

We drank in the greening landscape as the carriage turned onto the long drive leading to Mayfair. As we rounded the final turn to the house a feeling of panic overtook me, for there, up ahead, stood a green carriage emblazoned with a gold crest that I knew to be the Camberleigh coat of arms.

"Justin, why would the Camberleigh carriage be here?" I fretted.

"I do not see anything so unusual about that," Justin replied.

"You do not understand," I argued. "Anne and Richard have long since stopped journeying to Mayfair unless for a specific reason. Not to mention that when I left Mayfair for London, I told Charlotte that I was going to Camberleigh. She must be frantic."

Robbie pulled the team up aside the other carriage and Justin helped me alight from it. I did not wait but broke into a run the moment the heels of my boots hit the cobblestones. When the front door was flung open as I reached it, I careened awkwardly into the hallway.

"Lady Taggart," Giles exclaimed, running over to steady me. "The household has been frantic for worry of you."

"I know," I said quickly.

"Serena," I heard Anne's voice exclaim from afar.

I whirled about to see her running towards me. We fell into each other's arms.

"Thank God, you are all right," she exclaimed, holding me to her. "We have been out of our minds with worry. Charlotte is unconsolable. She thought you were with us at Camberleigh. Well, the place has been in an uproar. The Constable just left."

"The Constable?" I exclaimed. "What is wrong, where are the children? What of Amelie?"

"They are fine," she assured me, "though we have not been totally successful in keeping our fears from them. Particularly Alexander. That little snit Amelie I took it upon myself to dismiss two days ago when we arrived. She was lucky to get coach fare from me, I shall have you know. Do you know how she had terrified the children? Why, Alexander told me . . . Never mind, we need not go into that now.''

''Where is Richard?'' I replied.''And why was the Constable here?''

''He is in the library,'' she said, leading me there. ''He has been beside himself ever since we received Monique's letter.''

''What does Monique have to do with this?''

I did not think that I had ever seen Richard express so much emotion as when he saw me.

''My God, Serena, where have you been?'' he exclaimed, embracing me.

''In London,'' I answered hurriedly.

''London?'' they exclaimed in unison.

''It is a long story,'' I replied, ''but there is something I must tell you both. It is going to be a . . .''

''Monique's letter had us in a tizzy,'' Anne interrupted. ''I was not easy when we were here last. Philip was too charming, too reassuring. We had no more than returned to Camberleigh than I told Richard I was coming back here. That was before I saw the letter from Monique,'' she rambled. ''I am sorry, Serena, but Philip Taggart is a fraud.''

''Where is that bastard?'' Richard demanded. ''I shall . . .''

''Please, both of you,'' I demanded. ''There is . . .''

My sentence was broken by the sound of a large crash emanating from the hallway, followed by a loud shriek.

''Good Lord, what is that?'' Anne exclaimed.

''Serena,'' I heard Justin exclaim.

I ran past Anne and out into the hallway, where Justin was kneeling over one of the downstairs maids.

''She fainted,'' he said as he rubbed her hands.

I turned just in time to see Anne exit from the library. She looked at the scene of Justin and Molly on the floor and then almost in a trancelike state walked slowly toward us.

''Anne, I tried to tell you,'' I murmured.

Suddenly, as if her mind had just confirmed that what she was seeing was not some figment of her imagination, she screamed Justin's name and came running towards him, embracing him and calling his name again and again.

There were many tears shed and many screams of disbelief that afternoon and evening at Mayfair. I finally realized that no amount of preparation could allay the shock of seeing Justin brought back from the dead. Even the children, whom I had gently tried to guide into their reunion with their father, experienced a certain amount of fear and reticence when they first saw him. I noticed that Daphne kept a continuous hand on him as if to reassure herself that he was truly alive and there before her.

It was almost midnight when we retired. It would take all of us weeks, perhaps even months, to fully sort out the events of the past eight months and to comprehend the impact on each of our lives.

Justin bedded down before me that night, watching me by the light of the fire as I brushed my hair.

"Can you not delay that until morning?" he suggested playfully.

"Just one minute more," I replied, reaching into the drawer where I kept my jewels.

I rose and, going over to where Justin lay, sat down on the bed aside him.

He started to pull the covers back, gesturing for me to climb in.

"Not a chance," I replied.

A frown drew over his brow.

I opened my hand and withdrew from it the ring that, until a week before, I had worn close to my heart.

"If you are to bed me here at Mayfair, then it shall be as your bride, Lord Barkham," I whispered.

"Are you going to insist on a proper ceremony, my love?" he replied, a smile playing about his lips.

I held out my hand and he slipped the ring on my finger.

The only ceremony we needed was the ceremony of love we shared that night.

# Postscript

Over five years have passed since our return to Mayfair. For the most part they have been joyous times save a stroke that left Richard largely paralyzed two years ago.

Those first six months after Philip's death were like a scent which to some can seem sweet and to others only cloying. He had left a legacy of indebtedness which weighed heavily on the Mayfair and Camberleigh estates. The vast sums that he had requisitioned from Sir Henry had been, we discovered, dispersed quickly on the gaming tables.

We were by no means destitute, but it would take years of hard work and prayerful seasons of hearty crops to recoup our losses. That first year Justin, ridden with guilt, would not even mention the railroads, since he believed that so much tragedy would not have befallen us had it not been for his foolhardy dreams.

It was I who finally broached the subject with him. Slowly at first, though persistently, for I was oddly convinced that from all this wrongdoing should come some good. And so it was that Justin contacted Jonathan Leech and set about once again to see his dreams fulfilled.

The summer of that first year was filled with great gaiety in celebration of Oliver's return with his new bride. She is a sweet girl with a loving, supportive nature, and all the family took instantly to her save Daphne, who feigned disapproval, I presume, out of jealousy.

It seems hard to believe that Daphne turned fourteen but a few months back. People say that she is my mirror-image save her large violet eyes, which often hold expressions far beyond her years. Alexander, on the other hand, favors Justin in looks if not in temperament. I think the effects of Philip's involvement in our lives preyed heaviest on him. He had never been one to accept on face value, but it saddens me to think that the experience with Philip might have heightened his already suspicious nature.

That first Christmas back at Mayfair Justin presented me with a wonderful present. He saved it for last, carrying it into the room and placing the box gingerly before me. I untied the ribbons and lifted the lid, only to find soulful eyes peering up at me from a brown and white body that was a replica of Jaspar. I have named him Pluck and, like my beloved Jaspar, he shadows my every move.

Charlotte, though still our official housekeeper, has duties limited by age and an inflammatory condition of her joints. She was so proud, and rightly so, of Robbie's heroics on our part. He has continued to serve us with his same fervor and loyalty and now works full-time with Justin and Oliver on the estates. It has saddened me that he has never seemed to find someone with whom to share a bounty that he never dreamed possible but we are all far from having given up hope.

Clarissa's husband died suddenly last year, and though I had not seen her since, Justin has led me to believe that she is far from well herself. I have suggested that if she does not survive this present illness then we should take her daughter Constance into our home. Monique says that I am mad, for she is a strange and difficult child, but I scarcely could leave her with nowhere to turn.

Anne and I see each other often these days but then we see a good deal of all our dear friends. I was amused to have heard William Cobbett say to Justin just last week that the railroads might have some redeeming qualities after all. I suppose we all have become more accepting with age.

I cannot say that either Justin or myself have ever forgotten those months when Philip threatened our lives. The horror of it has diminished with time, however, and importantly we have been able to go on with our lives.

Sometimes late at night, as Justin is drifting off to sleep after our lovemaking, I look at him and wonder if I shall ever tire of gazing upon his countenance.

Almost invariably he senses this and without opening his eyes whispers only, "Good night, Lady Barkham."

# Bestselling Books from Berkley